PERCEPTIONS

THE SECRET WATCHERS
Book Four

May all your adventures be wonderful!
Lauren Lynne

LAUREN LYNNE

www.thesecretwatchers.com
www.LaurenLynneAuthor.com

Copyright © 2014 Lauren Lynne. All rights reserved,
including the right to reproduce this book or portions thereof in
any form whatsoever without permission.

This is a work of fiction. Names, characters, places, brands, media and incidents are either the product of the author's imagination or are used fictitiously. The author acknowledges the trademarked status and trademark owners of various products referenced in this work of fiction, which have been used without permission. The publication/ use of these trademarks is not authorized, associated with or sponsored by the trademark owners.

Acknowledgements:

To my wonderful friends and family! With special thanks to the following people who helped to make this work of fiction the best it could be: Nathan and Bryan Beals, Marge and Stan Walker, Cipriana and Sharon Mabaet, Marty Herdener, Susan Hamann, Lora Porterfield, Julie Postlewait, Sheila Senger, Angela Theel, Janet and Ernie Barrera, Amanda Wall, Cindi Etten, Sally Paulson, Rachael Fetrow, Christine Birch, Denise Carrier LaMarsh and Christy Slyter. You guys are the best and a simple "thanks" will never be enough! With a special thank you to: Cutsforth Thriftway in Canby, Mail House Plus in Milwaukie and The Latest Trend in Clackamas!

ONE

Thwack... the judge's mallet struck the base, the sound echoing through the courtroom and reverberating off the walls and ceiling, leaving a ringing in my ears. The judge scowled from her seat at the bench. She was one of the few people I had trouble reading. She gave nothing away, not even a hint. I couldn't tell where her sympathies lay and that made me afraid for Lucie.

"Emancipation hearing in the case of Lucie Elizabeth Ness. Theodore Huntley Ness, are you present?"

"Yes," Lucie's dad nearly snarled. He looked both bored and angry. He wanted everyone who looked at him to know that he did not want to be here and that he thought the whole thing was dumb and beneath him. He was wearing an expensive tailored suit of dark gray with black leather oxfords. His light blue shirt had the crisp look of a professionally pressed garment and his dark blue tie looked like it was made of real silk. Maybe he hoped to set off his neatly cut and styled, silvering blond hair and blue eyes. On the surface he was a good looking man, but I could see below that – to his one true love - himself.

Lucie sat rigidly on her side of the courtroom, her back not touching the chair. She looked ready to spring to her feet at any moment. From where I sat, I could see her hands tightly clasped and shaking a little, the knuckles white. She bounced her knee in the nervous tell I recognized. I could see very little of her father in her. Lucie looked like her deceased mother. Her brother Sam, looked more like their father. He sat on his father's side of the courtroom, but as close to Lucie as he could get. It was her, he watched. The look on his face was sad, understanding and resigned. I like Sam. He's practical. After all the emotional abuse I'd witnessed being doled out by both parents, I still couldn't believe that the Nesses had such nice kids, especially considering what screw-ups they were as parents.

I wished I could wrap Lucie in a big hug and hold her close to my heart, to shield and protect her from this, but it was a battle she had to fight more or less on her own. Lucie's attorney sat calmly by her side, offering nothing to ease her anxiety but his calm, confident demeanor. How could he appear so relaxed and unconcerned? I couldn't decide if I wanted to hug him or slap him.

I slid another glance over to Lucie's father. His eyes snapped with icy fire and his body language had altered from merely angry to screaming *pissed off*. I was sure even the judge could see it. His attorney was young, pretty and female. I'd put money down that she wasn't hired for her legal expertise but perhaps I was wrong. I just know Lucie's dad. His attorney frequently had to lay a hand on his arm to stop him from rising out of his chair and yelling. I swung my gaze back to the judge and hid a smile. Her lips were compressed and her eyes were tight. She surprised me with her line of questioning. "What do you want for your daughter, Mr. Ness?"

"For her to come home where she belongs and stop this nonsense!" he sputtered.

"I have gone over all the documents and I'm not sure that your home is the best place for Lucie. What is it that you think she can accomplish in San Francisco that she cannot accomplish here?"

"Excuse me? I am her father. She belongs with me and should do as I say," he thundered back despite his attorney's best efforts to shush him as she yanked desperately at his sleeve. He shrugged her off with a disparaging scowl and turned back to the judge.

"Mr. Ness, what do you see for your daughter's future?" the judge asked, completely unruffled by his outburst.

"She's not going to have much of one if she takes this route," he barked back. Again his attorney put a hand on his arm to quiet him.

"I sense that you are angry," the judge added calmly.

"Absolutely! After all I have done for her – this is the thanks I get?"

"What have you done for her?" the judge asked sweetly. *He's losing and he doesn't even see it. He can't fathom that she would rule against him,* I thought, feeling a little better.

"The minute we saw how talented she was we spent a small fortune on the best gymnastics coaches."

"How did that work out?"

"She fell off the uneven bars and ruined it. She lost her edge. Now my son..."

"I'm not interested in your son at this time," the judge cut in.

I looked over at Sam. He looked wretched. He knew this was not going the way his father had expected and he would be left to clean up the damage. Apparently Lucie's dad did not like to be interrupted. "This whole thing is ridiculous. I say what she does. This is all so she can stay with that underachiever boyfriend of hers who has like a 2.0 GPA or something. She needs to marry the right kind of boy after college, not drop out of school and... We have standards and I have important friends!"

"Is it your understanding that she is living with her boyfriend?"

"No, but she's living on the same street!"

"I see here that she pays rent, maintains her own healthcare, goes to school full time with a minimum of absences and continues her high school GPA of 3.98 in advanced placement classes. She also manages to work at least twenty-five hours a week. How do you suppose she has time for a boyfriend?"

"Boy, has she got you fooled. She works at the same place he does, in a pawnshop no less. It's inappropriate and low class." *Was he ever dumb if he thought he should point out to a judge that she had been fooled, which wasn't the case at all.*

The judge smiled at Mr. Ness and it wasn't the kind that gives you warm fuzzies. "My records indicate that Lucie works at a high end resale shop and is becoming an expert on antiques with a special interest in glass. She helps with acquisitions. Nothing she does for the shop is against the law or puts her in any danger. The shop has been visited several times by the appropriate government agencies both planned and unplanned. Not once have they failed inspection. The home of Sarah Lando has also been visited and has passed inspection every time with exceptional marks."

I figured it was a really good thing that Sarah and White Eagle knew the right kind of people because if the judge had any idea what Lucie and I really did we were sunk.

"But…" Lucie's father tried to break in.

"You on the other hand have been exceedingly difficult to get ahold of and are rarely home. Not once when a surprise visit was set up could you be located. You moved over three months ago, have unpacked the minimum number of boxes and have no food in your refrigerator."

"Lucie did all the shopping after I let the housekeeper go. I don't do that sort of thing. I'm a busy man. I'm important at my work so I'm there most of the time." *Busy with your personal assistant*, I thought snidely.

"I believe I've heard enough from you. I have some questions for Samuel Huntley Ness." Sam gulped and did as he was told. He tried to paint his father in the best light possible but he wouldn't say anything negative about Lucie either. The judge also spoke to the therapist who'd interviewed Lucie and the officials who'd made the visits.

"Lucie, do you wish to say anything?"

"No, ma'am, not unless you have any questions for me," Lucie answered in a soft voice that barely shook.

She didn't even call a recess but got straight to the point. "It seems to me, Mr. Ness, that you want Lucie with you for your own benefit and not for her best interests. She has created a calm, simple life for herself and has appropriate plans for her future, which do include college by the way. I am therefore choosing to grant Lucie Elizabeth Ness her emancipation from you. I want you to put your anger and need to control behind you and think of what is best for your children and not for you."

"If she does this… she is cut off…"

"She has not done this – YOU have!" The judge snarled back. "It was your job to provide for her basic needs which include but are not limited to… adequate shelter, food, clothing, *and* her emotional needs and wellbeing. Since your wife passed away, Lucie has received no financial support from you, no medical care, and *no* emotional support. In addition you did not provide her with a roof over her head nor make sure that she attended school. I have looked at your call records and hers. You didn't even call her once a month. She has been caring for herself and doing a good job of it. Oregon law states that, 'Emancipation gives you certain rights of an adult. You must be at least sixteen years old, able to support yourself, live on your own, and manage your own affairs.' Additionally, 'The judge will decide if it is in your best interest to be emancipated by considering whether you have been living away from your parents and can support and care for yourself without parental assistance and supervision. If the court allows you to be emancipated, your parents will have no duty to support you, you will be treated as an adult under criminal laws, and you will have the right to contract, sue, and be sued. Emancipation does not give you the right to drink alcohol, vote, or marry.' Am I clear?"

Suddenly Lucie's father seemed to realize that things were not going his way. "I would have done those things if she'd have come to San Francisco like I told her to," he whined.

"I said I award Lucie her emancipation."

"But, but, but…"

"She is still your daughter, you just can't tell her what to do anymore," the judge sighed.

Lucie let out a long slow breath and hung her head. Her attorney patted her on the back. She didn't squeal, shout or jump up and down. I wasn't sure what I was expecting but defeated wasn't it. She slowly raised her head and looked at the judge. "Thank you, your Honor," she said so softly I could barely hear it but I knew the judge did because she gave Lucie a small, sad smile.

Lucie's father sent her a scathing look as Sam and his attorney tried to muscle him outside. She looked back at him, expressionless. I would have given anything to keep her from seeing that. I knew it would be burned in her mind's eye forever. Sarah was the first to hug her. She said nothing. Other people began to crowd around Lucie. Didn't they see that congratulations were not what she wanted right now?

Lucie broke away and we met in the middle. I gave her a gentle hug and kissed the top of her head. She pushed away and gave me a watery smile before she exited the courtroom, her spine stiff. I walked out two steps behind.

Her father lunged at her from beside the door and slapped a hand onto her arm. "I can't believe you did this! I can't believe you have embarrassed our family like this and I can't believe you chose him over me!" he sneered.

Lucie rocked back on her heels and pulled at her arm. I knew she could break loose if she really wanted to. I guess she thought she owed him one last small satisfaction.

"I hope he takes really good care of you because I'm done. You are on your own. Completely and utterly... on - your - own!" He yanked his hand back like he couldn't stand to touch her anymore and then he took a step, but turned back. "If this is how you want it, fine. You may consider yourself divorced from me. You always have been a selfish..." The rest was lost as his voice dropped to a mumble as something behind Lucie snagged his attention.

Lucie looked straight at him, grim but determined so he continued on like he hadn't hurt her enough. "You'll get nothing from me... ever. I have no daughter."

I felt rage building within, but I was loathe to make things worse for her. I wanted to scream at him that she'd heard him the first three times, but I saw a bailiff approaching and bit my tongue, tasting the rusty tang of blood. All my muscles bunched as I resisted the urge to slug her father right in his overactive mouth.

Sam put a hand on my arm as he passed to stand between Lucie and his father. "Dad, you're making a scene."

"I'm not, she is. She did this. She has embarrassed our family and ruined our good name. He's nothing. Nothing!" he bellowed like a petulant child.

When did this become about me? I wanted to shout back at him. Mom put a gentle hand on me and scowled at Mr. Ness like she'd happily punch him in the mouth if it wouldn't get her into trouble.

"Is there a problem?" the bailiff asked as he assessed the scene.

"No sir," Sam said, then turned to his father. "Dad, stop. Let Lucie be. Come on. I'll take you back to the hotel."

"I'm billing you for this, Lucie Beth! I'm billing you for the attorney, the flight, and the hotel. Then you'll see how things work in the real world."

"Come *on* Dad!" Sam begged desperately, then turned to Lucie. "I'll call you later." I watched him tug his father out the door and the bailiff sighed and walk away.

Lucie stood rigidly, barely blinking.

"Luce?" I said softly. She blinked once so I pushed her hair gently over her shoulder. She kept her eyes on Sam and her father until they were completely out of sight. Sarah, Mom and White Eagle stood slightly apart from us watching over us like a matched set of guardian angels who were ready for anything. Lucie's attorney stepped up to them and spoke to Sarah who kept a worried eye on Lucie as she listened.

"Luce?" I tried again.

"All I have left is Sam. I'm completely... on my own." Her voice came out hushed, scratchy and incredibly forlorn.

"You will always have us," I said gently.

She said nothing but turned and hugged me, burying her face in my shoulder. I felt hot tears touch my skin through the double layer of shirt and t-shirt. She held me fiercely like she was afraid someone would snatch me away. She hiccupped, clenched her jaw and took a few deep breaths. Finally she sighed, loosened her grip and tucked her head under my chin to cuddle into the curve of my neck. "I don't think I was this scared when we faced Evilia Malvada," she finally mumbled.

"I'm here, Luce. Just breathe, okay?"

People swirled around us, each with their own agenda and none paying any attention to the slender young woman collapsing in on herself. She had used no makeup today and had put her hair up in a simple ponytail. The only jewelry she had worn was the bird necklace I had given her long ago. She wore flat leather sandals and a sundress in blue that exemplified the neat, organized, low-stress life she was trying to portray.

"Come on, Luce. Let's get you home." I kept my arm around her to keep most folks from bumping into her. The bright sun outside the building made me squint. My eyes hadn't even adjusted when I felt the hot wash of unfriendly eyes pass over me. I pushed Lucie to my side and away from danger. I signaled to White Eagle who was just stepping out the door. He touched Sarah's hand and quickly moved away from us and across the street in the direction I had indicated. Sarah and Mom moved closer to us and we hurried up the street. I shifted my eyes, but gave no other indication of a problem. I put most of my energy into pinpointing the location of the bad vibes I was getting.

This was a dark signature I did not recognize. Was it chance or planned? I took hold of the sensations I was getting and really examined them. This person was male, young and had a reckless feel. He had to be new to the *watcher* game.

Lucie sensed the change in my body and opened her *watcher* ability to me, to boost my powers and give me added information courtesy of her gift. Our two way connection snapped into place effortlessly but I could immediately feel how ragged she really was. "It's not the first time he's been here. He's trying to blend," Lucie mumbled for my ears alone. I'm better with objects but she is *killer* when it comes to locations. They literally speak to her. I closed my eyes for a moment and let Lucie guide me. "Gotcha," I whispered.

We turned the corner and moved into the nearest doorway - a deli, good. Mom walked up to the counter and ordered two drinks. Sarah took Lucie by the elbow and guided her to a table away from the window and then sat beside her. I watched all movement happening outside the window from behind a pillar. Mom set the drinks on the table and then followed me out the back door. I have found that when you walk with purpose you can go almost anywhere without being questioned. We had practiced such scenarios all summer. We had mainly practiced protecting my brother, Alex, since he was the youngest and least trained of our group but today Lucie needed defending.

Mom followed me until I signaled a halt. We stepped out of sight into an alcove. "He's watching the deli from across the street. White Eagle will be nearby. Our guy is young and inexperienced. I'll go snap his picture and send it to you both. Are you ready, Mom?"

"Do I have a choice?" she asked in a resigned voice. "You know I'll be fine once the action starts. I don't do well with anticipation."

"Yeah, I know, but you'll be fine," I answered, giving her a hug. I quickly unbuttoned and pulled off my dress shirt, tossed it to Mom and put on my shades. I ruffled up my hair and hunched my shoulders. I made use of my environment as urban camouflage and made my way over to our target using a circuitous route. I did a quick check and it felt like his attention was still on the deli, waiting for us to exit.

I turned my gift back off so our uninvited guest wouldn't feel me coming and edged toward him. I scanned the area and eliminated all three women and an older man. Then I caught movement near a tree. A young guy with a backpack was holding a skateboard. He was slender, creating the illusion of more height than he actually had. His over-large feet were jammed into skate shoes giving him the look of a growing puppy. His dark hair was cut close to his scalp. Heavy brows loomed over his dark, deep-set eyes. His ears were gaged so far out that I couldn't believe the flesh could withstand the strain. He pulled off his ball cap and wiped sweat from his forehead using the edge of his raggedy rock band t-shirt. The hair on the top of his head was so long, it covered his eyes. The jeans he wore had a split at the knee and were shredded at the bottoms where the hems had once been. He wore them low on his hips, showing me a flash of white skin and a tattoo as he swiped at the sweat. The mark was familiar, but I couldn't place it. I snapped several shots and tried to get what I could of his ink. I sent the images to the gang, including Marlo asking him to start the identification process as soon as possible.

I waited and watched from my hiding place behind a planter. The kid was nervous. His body vibrated with barely contained energy as his fingers beat a rhythm against his thigh. As I continued to observe him I realized he really wasn't a kid. He was older than me, maybe nineteen to about twenty-two but he was green. I'd been doing this for three years and I knew that no experienced *watcher* would act like this. We learn to hide and blend or we die.

Mom and White Eagle texted me back almost simultaneously. I edged a little closer to our guy and sensed the area again to see if he had any dark company. I saw him flinch and look around. I knew he felt my gift wash over him – it probably made his skin prickle and the hairs stand up on the back of his neck. He caught sight of me but it was too late. I was on him. He twisted away from me and made to run but he saw Mom coming at him with a determined look. He spun away from her and faced White Eagle. He threw down his board and tried to make a break for it past Mom, but she was ready for him, turning sideways just in time so he couldn't knock her down and delivering a blow between his shoulder blades, sending him sprawling onto the ground. Nice!

He started to scrabble to his feet but I was quicker and tackled him before he even had a chance to fully rise. He struggled until I gave him a jab to the kidney. He cursed and squirmed. I jumped up so that Mom and White Eagle could haul him to his feet, with his arms wrenched behind him. I grabbed his board and we quick-marched him around the nearest corner before we drew any more attention. Mom stepped back as White Eagle thrust him up against the wall for me to pat him down. I tossed his cell to Mom and pulled off his backpack. He tried to fight but White Eagle's forearm pressed against his throat slowed him down. He tried to kick me but I was too fast for him and kicked his feet out from under him so that he was momentarily suspended by White Eagle. Not a place I'd ever want to be.

"Don't make this harder than it has to be," I snarled at him.

"Screw you," was his intelligent reply. I just shook my head.

"Text them, please," I said to Mom. She got busy with her smart phone and then snapped a couple of close-ups for Marlo.

I turned and growled to the newbie *watcher*, "Who are you? And why are you spying on us?"

He gave us a defiant look, twisted and tried to drain White Eagle, who caught his wrist before his hand connected and snapped it back. "Answer him." His voice was filled with menace. White Eagle can be an imposing guy when he wants to be.

The young *dark watcher* raised one side of his upper lip in a snarl making the scar by his mouth pucker.

"Who sent you?" I queried, giving him my best scowl.

"You don't scare me. I'm not telling you anything!" he sneered.

I squinted at him, deep in thought. Did I have the stomach for this? Did I have it in me to be cruel? Could I torture him for information and still live with myself? If I did, I would be no better than they were. Where was the line and should I cross it?

A slow smile spread over his unshaven face where a scraggly beard showed in uneven patches. "You won't do it. You don't have what it takes. You won't do what has to be done to get what you need. You're… moral," he said with disgust like I'd personally offended him. "You're weak. The good guys usually are. They follow the rules. They can't do what needs to be done!"

"Shows what you know!" Lucie came out of nowhere to deliver a perfectly executed upper cut to his jaw. Skater dude sagged in White Eagle's grip, semiconscious as we all turned to stare at Lucie.

"What?" Lucie asked defensively. "We didn't have all day. Somebody go get the van and let's take him somewhere we can really question him."

Mom snapped out of it first, reached into White Eagle's pocket for the keys and sprinted off.

"Lucie dear, if you're feeling upset from the proceedings maybe we should talk and not... um, take out our aggressions on others," Sarah said with quiet dignity.

Lucie smiled at her, a rather sick smile that came nowhere near her eyes. "And *I* don't think we should assume he isn't dangerous. Until we know who he is and what he wants... I consider him a threat." She shook out her hand as she spoke.

"Did you hurt yourself?" I asked with a huge grin.

A real smile broke across Lucie's face. "I failed to make 'good fist'. Sorry, White Eagle."

Sarah rolled her eyes but White Eagle grinned at her and shifted his limp load that was just beginning to moan softly. I brought Lucie's hand to my lips. "You gonna need medical attention?" I asked her, still smiling.

Lucie didn't even get to answer. Mom screeched around the corner, narrowly missed the dumpster, and stopped inches from White Eagle's elbow. To his credit, he neither blanched nor dropped his load. He did slowly raise his eyes to give Mom a dirty look through the windshield and then looked significantly at his elbow and then back to her. She grinned, shrugged and hopped out of the van. "So where do we stow him?" she asked indicating the limp skater.

I popped open the back and rummaged in the compartment where we kept our supply of zip ties, clips and Velcro. We zipped up our guy and tossed him unceremoniously into the back. Sarah pulled a Taser out of a locked compartment and then chose a seat near our now thrashing captive. "You behave or so help me, I'll zap you," Sarah said in one of the meanest voices she employed.

He gave Sarah a long look, then stopped flinging himself around, sensing her seriousness. He subsided into a sullen silence. Mom and White Eagle had a brief, silent argument over the van keys. He finally sighed and relented, making Mom jump up and down in a brief happy dance as she giggled.

"Some things just aren't worth it," he huffed under his breath as he plopped into the seat next to mine.

TWO

Mom did not imitate IndyCar's Will Power on the way home, for which I was thankful. Sometimes it's hard to believe that the mild-mannered kindergarten teacher who taught me to drive could be so... well, vicious – about covers it.

The women in my life had really bonded lately in an almost scary way. Mom, Sarah and Lucie had been making a point of getting together at least once a week to do 'girl' stuff. They would shop, share lunch, cook together or spend other quality, women only time. Personally I think they were trying to make up for Lucie's mom. It's been about four months since she was poisoned by Kraeghton – the man I'd thought of as my arch nemesis. Last May that had... altered. I had learned a powerful lesson – things aren't always what they seem and there are definitely shades of black.

Mom drove us to the pawnshop where we unloaded our cargo of uncooperative skater. Marlo was waiting for us by the back door. He and the skater eyeballed each other in an unfriendly manner until Marlo's eyes shifted to Lucie. His normal sparkle returned and he hugged her tight.

"How'd it go?" he asked warmly.

"I won, I guess." I could hear the sadness in her voice. It was best for her to be away from her father, but not like this. Even I wished there could have been another way.

"Cheer up Luce, you've got us and he'll loosen up in time. It would've killed you, perhaps literally, if you'd been forced to move to San Francisco right now."

"I know, Mars. It's just hard. You got anything on our guy?" she asked. I guess work is better than grief for our kind.

"Come into our lair and I shall regale you with his tale," Marlo quipped back.

We entered the shop to find Sarah ready with her trusty Taser as Mom and White Eagle tied our new acquisition to the weightlifting equipment. I watched him look around our workshop, backroom, and part time dojo. Max, White Eagle's partner in the pawnshop, poked his head through the curtain that separated the shop from the back area. He took one look at our surprise guest and quickly withdrew with a soft, "I don't wanna know."

Max is a great guy and the uncle of one of my best friends, but he does not want anything more to do with what we do than he absolutely has to. I was surprised that Adrian wasn't here today. He often worked with his uncle during the summer. Max was not big on being here alone after some of the badness in the world had found its way into the shop. A deep woof from up front let me know that Max wasn't really alone. His enormous but cowardly pony - I mean dog - Thor was here. He is a really sweet dog who loves Max in an almost needy way, but then he had been abused before we'd rescued both of them from the same lunatic captor.

Marlo cleared his throat to gain my attention. I swung my eyes in his direction to find our *friend's* picture up on his laptop screen in a none too flattering arrest photo. "My friends - meet Devin Dwyer, petty thief, carjacker and juvenile delinquent. Don't you know that crime doesn't pay?" he asked of our grumpy guest.

"Screw you!" Devin blasted back.

"Now, now, language – there are ladies present," Marlo continued unperturbed. Devin scowled from his position on our weight bench and looked for all the world like he'd love to bite Marlo, who smiled back and continued, "May I also suggest a GED? It's hard to get anywhere without a proper education."

"Who are you people?" Devin asked, sounding perplexed and angry as he looked at us like we were crazy.

"Are you saying that you weren't following us?" I asked.

"Just her," he indicated with a jut of his chin.

"Why me?" Lucie asked, stepping close. Devin cringed slightly in response – smart man.

"I just do what I'm told. I follow instructions and she pays me well."

"She? Evilia Malvada?" I asked, feeling like we were starting to get somewhere.

"I don't know," he smiled like he was enjoying the game.

"How does she pay you?"

"Cash in an envelope."

"How do you get your assignments?"

"Heard of a cell phone?" Devin sneered.

"How do you get your 'cash in an envelope'?"

"It's delivered."

"Why are you talking now?" I asked suspiciously.

"Why not? I don't know anything worthwhile," he said with that same infuriating smile.

I glanced over at Mom. She had gloved up and was carefully going through the contents of Devin's backpack. She laid each item out by his skateboard and photographed it. Marlo was already at work on his cell phone.

Mitchell came in from the front of the shop. "Heard we had company," he said with a smile that quickly changed to a frown as his *watcher* gift kicked in. "You shouldn't have brought him here. He's wired or chipped or something. He's sending a signal right now."

"Damn, I was afraid of that. He's too helpful all of a sudden and catching him felt a little too easy. How long do you figure we've got?" I asked, watching Mitchell closely.

He screwed up his face in thought. "Ten minutes tops, seven to be safe."

"Shoot. If we leave, will that help?"

"I would guess so."

Mom was already tossing Devin's belongings into a cardboard box and Marlo was packing his electronic gear. Sarah kept up her Taser vigil as Lucie and White Eagle cut Devin loose and hustled him back to the van.

Mitchell started to follow them out but I put a hand on his arm. "Will Max be safe here?"

He closed his eyes to focus. "Yes, I think so; I don't see anything dark in his near future."

"Sarah, call Rick to come to the shop just in case, please. I really screwed up."

"*You* didn't, Owen, *we* did," Sarah said firmly as she pulled out her cell and dialed.

Lucie sat next to me this time and snuggled close to my side. She closed her eyes and found my hand. "Why?" I heard her voice clearly in my mind. I tucked her hair behind her ear to whisper in it.

"Best guess? You are viewed as weak and vulnerable right now and perhaps easy to take unaware. They know you are important to me and would want to know if you are staying or going. They have to be just as desperate for information about us as we are for info about them." Lucie shivered as my warm breath brushed over her ear. I smiled and nibbled on it. I just couldn't help it. I loved it when I got a reaction out of her. It made me feel like I could control something in our crazy world. It was a wash of power that made me feel good and happy.

Lucie pushed playfully at me and sent another message. "Your timing sucks – maybe later?" I smiled and relented. I should probably be paying attention anyway.

"Got anything yet, Mars?" I asked to change the subject.

"Nope… yes! White Eagle, hit the river at Oregon City, then we'll loop back to the shop after we dump off some equipment." Marlo handed a device to me. "Pass that to Sarah and have her check him. If he's bugged we'll throw him in the river too."

"No! You can't! I'm tied up and I can't swim! In my shoe. My left shoe. Don't drown me. Please!" Devin begged.

An evil smile flitted across Marlo's face for a brief moment and then his normal happy smile returned. "I love research," he mouthed to me. Lucie and I looked at each other. This was a side of our gentle-hearted friend we only saw when he was gaming. He was a negotiator who avoided fights at all costs when possible in real life. I guess he wasn't above a little mental torture.

Sarah and Mitchell quickly removed Devin's shoe and ran the scanner over him. "Shame on you, Devin - you are carrying another bug on you," Sarah said in that calm, scary voice she pulled out when she was extremely disappointed in someone.

"I swear I didn't know!" he cried pitifully.

"Too bad Alex isn't here," I whispered to Lucie.

She whipped out her cell and dialed. "Aid? Lucie. Go pick up Alex and meet us at the shop. Be sure to bring your brass knuckles."

"No way! Brass knuckles? Who's Alex? You can't do that! I'll tell you what I know," Devin squeaked, leading me to believe he was genuinely scared now.

"I thought you didn't know anything," Lucie said expressionlessly which served to freak him out even more.

"I need a hit," he whined mournfully.

"I'm not afraid to hit you," Lucie answered sweetly.

"Jesus!" he exclaimed, looking truly fearful.

White Eagle pulled into the hotel parking lot by the freeway overpass. He pulled to the back away from people and over near a dumpster. Sarah handed me Devin's shoe and belt. Marlo passed over an MP3 player and then shut the GPS off on Devin's cell so he could continue to get other information out of it. I watched him open the back and remove a micro dot from the back cover. "Toss all of that and make sure it sinks. Be fast. I feel… Mitchell, what do you think?"

Mitchell got that look on his face again. "Now, I'd say ten to twelve minutes until they're at this location."

I heard Sarah's voice as Mitchell and I jumped out of the van with our bug infested gear. "It's not too late to dump him too, is it?"

A wailed "Nooooo!" was cut off as the door slammed shut.

"She's just upset because she's afraid he'll lead them to the shop and I'm sure she's right. All we're doing is buying some time," Mitchell said in a serious voice as we headed toward the river with purpose, using all the natural cover we could find.

Down by the river's edge I looked for an appropriate rock to weight the gear. I started to reach for one but Mitchell shook his head. "You want the one to your left."

I had to smile. He was supposed to be watching my six but you gotta love Mitchell's gift. I'd even come to genuinely like the guy himself. He's smart, friendly, flexible and minds his own business which is awesome now that he's my roommate. Lucie had to have a place to stay so he had graciously offered to give up his room at Sarah's house. He was going to live on campus when he went to Portland State University in the fall and offered to start in the summer but White Eagle was adamant that we stay together for now. With Evilia and her gang after us, none of us were safe alone so with three boys at our house already it was a good fit.

I grabbed the rock he indicated, used the belt to secure all the pieces together and lobbed it as far as I could out into the river. We sprinted back toward the van as someone shouted, "Hey!" White Eagle threw the still idling van into gear and we were off before we even had a chance to buckle. I threw one last glance over my shoulder to be sure our package had completely submerged.

It was strange to see sweet Lucie, dressed as she was in that sundress, menacing the tough looking skater. She had his shirt bunched up in one fist to expose the tattoo I'd caught sight of on his lower abdomen near his hip. The image was already up on Marlo's laptop.

"I recognize that symbol. Why?" I asked the group at large.

Marlo looked from his screen to me, his face serious. "It's her mark, her symbol. It means that he's the property of Evilia Malvada, drug lord and master *dark watcher*. The hair stood up on the back of my neck and Lucie let out a low growl.

She tried to sound calm when she spoke. "What do you have on his other ink?"

"He has more?" I asked.

"Yes," she replied tersely. "He has seven that I've uncovered so far. I'll let you look for any more. I don't want to do to him what his buddies did to me." Devin smiled at her like he had won a point.

I put my hand on the back of her neck and squeezed gently. Relax, breathe, be calm and I'm here, my gesture said to her. It was our silent signal to each other. Lucie unbent a little and relaxed into my hand.

Devin's eyes darted from one to the other of us. "I wasn't sure before but now I know! You are Owen. She only gave me a picture and bio of Lucie to memorize. I've heard stories about you two. I can see it now. I've heard that you can communicate without words."

We looked at him still trussed up like a Thanksgiving turkey, though now he was zip-tied to a seat instead of dumped on the floor. I started to speak but Marlo interrupted. "I've got a couple of hits on his other artwork!"

White Eagle drove on, headed back to the shop. Sarah had her tablet out and a Bluetooth stuffed in her ear. I could tell that she was listening to it and also completely aware of what was happening in the van. When she murmured Rick's name I knew she was talking to the team of FBI agents that sometimes worked with us and helped to cover our tracks when necessary.

"What have you got, Mars?" I asked putting my attention back on him.

"Some look like regular tattoos but others indicate that he's a drug runner and dealer for her cartel. They let others know, if they hurt him or get in his way, she will get even."

Devin scowled at Marlo with hate in his eyes. "When I'm loose, I coming for you first, techno boy!"

"I'm sure you'll try," Marlo said bravely but I knew he was shook up.

"You may as well talk," I told him. "As you can see, we can find out stuff regardless. Make it easy on yourself."

"You can't do worse than she would do to me if she found out I said too much." He was right. Lucie and I had seen what she could do in a fit of rage, but I wasn't about to tell him that.

I tried a different tactic. "Oh I see," I said, leaning back in a lazy manner. "You are a mix of truth and lies. Well, don't you worry. We can sift through them. We have more than 'techno boy' to help us."

White Eagle pulled up at the pawnshop's back entrance. The lot out front looked and felt normal so I indicated that we could head on in. White Eagle, Sarah and Mom hustled Devin into the shop while the rest of us took a moment to 'check the force' as Marlo called it. We had been practicing sharing our gifts to try to figure out what Madam Malvada was up to; so far we hadn't had much luck.

It's strange to share. For the average person, the closest comparison I can make is the unveiling of a sense like removing earplugs or a blindfold. I guess it can also be likened to seeing your first-ever 3D movie after only seeing films in black and white. Suddenly everything pops!

As the only one with mentor abilities in the group, I took the lead. I held a hand of both Mitchell and Marlo and they each held a hand of Lucie's. As soon as we were settled I closed my eyes to focus and visualize the connections between us. They appear to me like lines or spider webbing that show all the ways we are connected. I have fewer links to Mitchell than I do to Lucie or Marlo but we are all growing into each other. I still find it ironic that Madame Malvada accidentally showed me how to do it. I realized that she had connected herself to me and I thought to look for it and follow it back to her. She is another rare *watcher* who has more than one gift. Not only can she crush bones with the touch of her hand but manipulate emotions and latch onto people over great distances to read their minds and steal their power. She is… horrific. Thankfully, I have learned to block her… well mostly.

In the beginning White Eagle had believed that by touching an object I could see its story by the images it showed me and I can but it's more than that. He taught me to feel which objects had bad energy associated with them. Soon I could pick those out of a room, but now I could stretch my power to what we estimated was nearly a mile radius. I can't see everything when I *look* that far out, but the dark energy leaps out at me as if I'm standing on a hill overlooking a half mile of forest with a burning tree stuck in it.

I have picked up reading people from my mom and feeling danger in a room from Miles, the previous owner of my watch, whose memories now live within me. It almost seems like my skill is picking up other *watchers* abilities, but as many times as I have linked with Lucie I still have not mastered her gift. I don't get Mitchell's glimpses of the future or Marlo's sense of the balance between good and evil either. Lucie and I tend to see what has happened and not what will happen but mixed together we are a force to be reckoned with. The trouble with looking at the future is that it's ever changing and that is why I believe that Malvada and Kraeghton are so hard to track.

Today we joined our energy to feel who was and would be here. Marlo likens it to the Jedi of Star Wars, but he's a gamer and lover of all things fantasy right down to the hours he's spent playing Dungeons and Dragons with actual character sheets and dice.

Now he feels like we do it for real – well, no dragons, but plenty of demons. Ours just wear a human guise. If underground tunnels count, then we have dungeons covered. Marlo likes to think we feel the force of good and evil, but if no one is actively using their power we can't sense it unless they have done something bad in a location or used an object in an evil way.

Sometimes I think that Lucie is better about sharing my gift than the other way around. She has even hijacked me when I was semi-conscious to use what I knew to help her to fix me. She had believed that she had a lesser *watcher* gift because she only hears the echoes of what has happened in a location but the way she can use my gifts and amplify them is a whole other animal. The fact that she has figured out how to speak right into my mind is downright spectacular.

I wasn't really getting anything so I broke our connection. "I only *feel* Devin nearby." My statement was met by nods. "I still don't understand what his gift is, but I know he's using it."

"Maybe she hasn't taught him to turn it on and off like you and White Eagle taught us." Lucie looked from me to Mitchell and then continued, "And your former mentor Emiline, of course."

"I miss her. I don't know if I'll ever be able to forgive Kraeghton and Carmichael for what they did to her. Why would you torture an elderly lady… I mean really? Who does that?" Mitchell's eyes still held a raw look. I knew his guilt and pain. I'd heard him cry at night a few times when he thought I was asleep across the room. I've never let on that when pain is rolling off of him in waves like that, I can't help but feel it too. I just don't know what to do to help him ease his guilt except to be there for him.

"You don't have to forgive them, but you've got to start forgiving yourself," Lucie said softly. She would know all about that. She really had come a long way. Maybe the fact that we grow up fast and feel deeply makes us *watchers* or maybe it's the other way around. Who knows?

"I think we need to be ready just in case his gift is letting them know where he is," Marlo added in a worried voice. "Or worse, sharing what we're doing and everything we've said."

"They'll find us anyway, I bet. We stopped here for too long to go undetected by them. I'm curious, Mars. Is that the sense you're getting or past experience talking?"

"My gift is swinging wildly right now, but you felt that. Every decision we make and they make, changes the outcome. I don't know what to listen to today. Nothing is clear. Nothing makes sense. It's like it's all a trick."

"I'm having the same problem," Mitchell added. "I keep getting flashes of positive and negative outcomes. It seems like it's better if I don't focus. It's like with the rock at the river. I wasn't thinking about the rock, I just knew all of a sudden that it was the one you should use for the best results because I was focused on what was happening around you so that no one would sneak up on us."

Lucie looked thoughtful. "Do you suppose his ability is to confuse? That would be a handy *dark watcher* gift and also make him the perfect person to follow us. We might not have caught him if he wasn't so inexperienced."

"You could be right. Only someone like Evilia would send someone so green after us. He may not know it, but she doesn't care if he lives or dies. She usually sends them in packs, so I'd bet money, marbles and chalk he was only supposed to spy," I agreed, our eyes meeting in understanding.

"Evilia would be drawn to a gift like that but how do we test it?" Marlo asked.

"We don't even fully understand what all we can do, so how would we begin to measure Devin or even her?" I groaned.

"Well, with all of us together and with your mentor skills, I would think that we could get a grasp on it. I'm sure that you or White Eagle would be best able to figure it out," Marlo replied.

"If we're on the right track she won't be in a big hot hurry to rescue him. She'll want him with us to cover an attack," I said in a resigned voice.

I looked up and met Lucie's eyes. "We need Alex," we said at the same time.

"Won't he be confused too?" Mitchell asked concerned.

"Somehow, I don't think so. His gift is different. If we're right about Devin then Alex could be his polar opposite so wouldn't they… I don't know, cancel each other out or something?" Lucie asked, looking at me. I gave her a nod and a smile. It felt good to be on the same page and even better to have her mind off her own problems. Her cell buzzed just then as we were stepping out of the van.

"Hey, Sam… I'm okay and you?… He is?… I'm sorry to hear that. When does he leave?… So soon? I'd hoped we could… I see. You're sure you're okay?… I wish things were different… Love you too." The dark clouds returned to her face as sadness moved in. Lucie looked at her phone for a minute after she ended the call.

"Go on in guys. Give us a minute." Mitchell and Marlo nodded at me. They each squeezed her shoulder on the way past.

"Do you want to talk about it?" I asked her as I pulled her into a hug.

"What is there to say? My twenty year old brother is down in the hotel bar trying to control our… his forty-eight year old father who ought to know better than to drink himself stupid as he tells anyone who will listen what a horrible person I am."

"Aw, Luce, I wish I could fix it," I said softly. I ran my chin over the top of her head enjoying the silky softness of her hair. My fingers played lazily with a tendril that had come loose. I touched my lips to her ear and nibbled my way around its curve and down the side of her neck. "You smell fantastic," I mumbled against her skin. I felt her smile. She tilted her head back so that I could reach more of her neck.

"You know how to get my mind off my worries," she whispered.

"I'd claim that I'm a professional, but that would sound all wrong. I do know you well."

"That would sound wrong," she giggled. "I'm amazed that you stick around considering the amount of baggage I carry!" Her look had turned sober once more.

"Luce, the only person you can ever really change is you. I know who you are and there is nothing I would change about you."

"You're deluded, but sweet. I think I'll keep you," she said smiling faintly.

"I hope so," I said returning to her neck. I slid the strap of her sundress over to work my way out to her shoulder.

"Owen!" She hissed at me. I smiled into her skin as I moved to her collar bone to work my way back to her throat. Her fingers were no longer digging into my shoulder and upper arm. She had released me to smack me gently. "Owen – Alex!" she said a little more urgently.

I raised my eyes to look first at Lucie, comprehension dawning, and then I looked over my shoulder. Alex had a huge impish grin on his face. "So that's how it's done," he said with a twinkle in his eye.

Adrian grinned at me and tsked. "You know, back in eighth grade, I began to wonder if you even liked girls. I see I was mistaken."

If looks could kill, then Adrian would've been ash. Alex, I have a little more patience for. I should have been paying attention, especially now. I'd heard the car doors slam, I just assumed whoever it was would go in the front and I sure hadn't felt trouble coming.

"I thought you were in urgent need of my services," Alex said, still smiling.

Lucie cleared her throat. "We do. Let me... um... see if they're ready for you." She flew in the back door with barely a sound.

The minute the door was shut I turned the scowl on Adrian he deserved and then I looked to Alex. "Sorry," I said tightly.

"Geez, like I've never seen people kiss before. I've been to middle school you know."

"Thanks, Alex, I didn't know," I said sarcastically as I took him by the arm and led him to the back door. "Be careful of this guy. He's deceptively dangerous and manipulative. I need to know what things he says are the truth and which are lies. All we know for sure is that his name is Devin Dwyer and he works for *her* as a drug runner, dealer and probable spy."

Alex's eyes grew wide but then he nodded. I looked to Adrian who also nodded, letting me know that he was ready. I cracked open the back door and peered inside. Lucie, Mitchell and Mom stood off to the side silently waiting. Devin was once again tied to the weight bench. This time he was blindfolded. He turned his head this way and that trying to sense the room. "Are we done yet?" he hissed.

"So... is he gonna spill his guts now?" Adrian asked sounding more than a little malicious.

"I sure hope so. I'm tired of waiting," I said, moving on into the room. Alex and Adrian followed closely but stayed behind me and off to the side where I could see Alex.

"You know there are others," Devin snarled and Alex gave me a funny squinchy look. I wiggled my hand in a so – so motion and he nodded. Yep, a half-truth. "And she's building an army," he added, sounding pleased. Alex nodded. "Without people like you in the way... she could take over the police and then the military. There'll be no stopping her." Alex used the hand motion this time to show me a half-truth or that Devin believed it but was embellishing.

"I think her plans may be bigger than even she can handle," I said calmly which made Alex smile and Devin tug at his bindings.

"You don't know her," Devin raged. "You don't know her reach, her power." A nod from Alex. Devin believed what he was saying. I also knew he was afraid of her.

"I may know her better than you think."

"She talks about you, you know. She wants you for your gifts." Alex nodded vigorously.

"You really aren't telling us anything we don't already know," I said trying to sound bored and uninterested. "I think you're stalling."

"Why the blindfold? I've already seen you. Who else is here?"

"You won't know how many of us there are or from where we'll strike," I said, trying to sound as vicious as I could.

"You won't touch me. You haven't really hurt me yet, which makes me think you're afraid of her too." I looked over at Alex. He gave me a nod but his jaw was clenched and he looked angry.

I looked right at Alex. "You okay?" I asked without sound. He nodded tersely. Aloud I said, "I need you to do a quick… evaluation and then report to…" I ended by pointing to Lucie. I saw the concentration on both of their faces.

"You want me to evaluate what?" Devin asked, clearly misunderstanding.

I ignored him. Alex signed to me that he needed to see Devin's eyes. I shook my head. "Yes," Alex mouthed at me.

"No," I mouthed back. Alex moved his chin forward and gave me a ferocious scowl. His meaning was plain. If you don't let me do this, then I can't help you like you want. I knew I was hampering his gift but I was afraid for him. I couldn't let him be exposed. He truly was our secret weapon.

"No!" Mom said sharply as I shook my head again. Alex stomped his foot and nodded, *yes*.

"What?" Devin asked in confusion tinged with fear.

Alex threw up his hands and gave me one last look. Then he darted around me and lunged at Devin's throat. Devin opened his mouth in a silent scream as Alex's hands wrapped around his neck. Alex froze in shock, his eyes extra wide. His mouth had gone slack as images and feelings blasted through him with the dark energy he had released. The sickening smell of burnt flesh tinged the air. I jumped to Alex and pried him loose. He stumbled back and looked appalled as his eyes skittered back and forth from the blisters rising from pink handprints on Devin's neck to his own unblemished hands.

THREE

White Eagle burst through the back curtain, picked up Alex and tossed him over his shoulder before anyone could say a word. He sprinted back through the curtain as the rest of us converged on Devin. I froze in front of him not sure who to help first or even knowing if I wanted to help Devin. He hung limply from the bar and I could feel Alex's pain and confusion pounding through me from the other room.

"Go!" Lucie said firmly. "We've got this." Mom and I didn't waste another moment - we rushed through the curtain to the front together to find the shop empty and the closed sign up. Marlo sat on a stool at the cash register. When he saw our frantic look he pointed to the ground near him behind the counter. White Eagle was mumbling to Alex who was rocking and looking at his hands.

I dropped to my knees in front of Alex. "Hey, what happened?"

In a painfully slow motion he turned his haunted green eyes to mine. "I got angry… with you and with him." His voice came out both raw and ashamed.

"We all get angry, Buddy. Tell me what you did to Devin."

"I… I wanted to help you… and you guys wouldn't let me see his eyes. I have to see their eyes... to read them… to know what they're thinking."

"We weren't trying to handicap you, but we couldn't let him see you. We were afraid if he did, he'd be able to report back to Evilia about you and we just couldn't let him do that," I replied in the calmest voice I could muster.

"I wanted to help but I couldn't and then suddenly I knew what to do. I would just take the information from him but now I feel..." Alex turned an unusual shade of green and dove for the garbage can by Marlo's feet to empty his stomach. "I feel terrible," he croaked when he finished heaving.

"I know, Alex. I've been there. I'm sorry but the damage is done and now I need to know what you learned."

"Owen!" Mom hissed.

"He's right, Mom," Alex answered somberly. "She is building an army of *dark watchers* to come for Owen. Today she's not coming herself. She's sending Carmichael and five others. They don't know about me or Sarah. They don't even really know about you, Mom, and are unsure about Sarah's team. They do know about Owen, Lucie, White Eagle, Mitchell and they seem to have a little something on Marlo."

"What about Kraeghton, is he one of them?"

"I didn't see him in what I got from Devin. I don't know what that means. I might have gotten more if you hadn't pulled me off, you know," he said sounding more like his old self.

"Alex, it... it's wrong. You burned him. You were hurting him. It's wrong to take like that."

"They would do it to us. People like them have before. I've seen it. They take our powers and drain our energy," he said defensively.

"Alex, we're *good watchers*. We give; we don't take. How did you even know how to do that? It's not even a skill that all *watchers* have."

"She showed me. She's done it to me in the dreamscape when I'm asleep. I told you. I pay attention. I also told you that I know how to drain her there, but you weren't listening."

"I'm listening now."

"When she's really angry she gets distracted and I can sneak up on her and draw off some of her energy. If I pull it slowly she doesn't notice. I was in a hurry today. It doesn't feel good though. It makes me feel sick."

"Oh, Alex," Mom sighed wearily.

"How does it make you feel?" I asked.

"Besides wanting to throw up? It's kinda..." He scrunched up his face in thought. "You know when you eat way too much candy or drink too much cola? You feel like your mind is racing and you can't hold still? Not that I've ever tried it but it leaves an after-taste that makes me think of burnt motor oil. I just did what I thought needed to be done. Why do I have a *dark* ability?" Now Alex sounded worried and scared.

White Eagle, Mom and I all looked at each other. "She did this to me. Did she make me a *dark watcher*?" Now Alex sounded a whole lot of freaked out.

I took ahold of his chin and raised it so that he would look me in the eye. "Power is power and an ability is just an ability – it's what you do with it that matters."

"But I just did something bad!"

White Eagle tried next. "Alex, none of us are perfect, we are human."

"Don't let a bad choice control who you are or who you will be," Mom added gently.

"She's right Alex," White Eagle said softly. "It's the choices we make every day that build who we are, not a single act."

"We love you Alex," Mom added. "And we believe in you."

"How are you feeling now?" I asked.

"Okay, I guess, I just… I just wanted to help but now I feel guilty. I didn't mean to hurt him. I just wanted to know what he knew. I could tell he was trying to trick you."

"You did help, Buddy, just not like we were expecting," I said as I ruffled his hair.

"Same old, same old for us - we don't do anything quite right. We sure don't follow the one *watcher* to a mentor rule," Alex said, sounding a little lighter.

"It wasn't exactly a rule; it was more of what I knew to be true. My grandmother taught me that a *watcher* and mentor were like a bonded pair. Unless one died or the *watcher* was fully trained you stayed together. Miles was fully trained but we stayed together. Was it because no one else needed me or he still needed me? I sure don't know. Now all these years later I've come to view the *watcher*-mentor bond more like the bond of family and with family there are no rules about numbers, right kid?" White Eagle finished solemnly as he patted Alex's shoulder.

"Now look at you. Owen has Lucie but you have all the rest of us." Alex said.

"Maybe we're different because we are family," Mom suggested.

"I once knew someone who mentored twins. Owen is pretty much trained and Mitchell is nearly there. In fact, Owen is teaching me things now. If we had caught you young, Lila, I think we could have done so much more with you. I'm thankful every day that a *dark watcher* never found you."

"Thanks, Earl," Mom replied sweetly. I could tell she was touched by his words.

Marlo finally threw in his two cents worth. "I'm a different case altogether, Alex. I was never meant to be a *watcher* and I wonder… Don't we all belong to each other now? Aren't you just as much Owen's *watcher* as you are White Eagle's?"

"I suppose that is true in many ways," White Eagle agreed.

"At least Bob has left us alone," Alex said fiercely.

"You, he doesn't know about and I convinced him that we are much more valuable as an intact unit. I did admit that we train together.

He'd pretty much figured it out anyway," I said calmly to let him know it was okay.

"I was afraid you were going to have to fight him!"

"I convinced him it wasn't for the greater good to completely remove me from action, Alex."

Marlo jerked his head up and froze like he could sense something we couldn't and I was pretty sure that was exactly the case. He launched himself off his stool and ran for the back. I jumped to my feet but he was back immediately. "Mitchell says to get ready. I feel it too. We're out of time."

I looked at Alex. "I'm ready," he said bravely.

"We need to keep you hidden. I don't want to show our hand yet," I said firmly.

"Owen, Devin showed me something else – today is... practice for them. They want to see what we've got. He's been following Lucie since shortly after her mother's funeral. He knew where her old house was and he knows where the high school is. He pretended to be a student. He had stayed back, but today he was careless. He needed a hit, but he needed the money from today's job to fund it. They weren't expecting today to be the day. I'm sure she's angry with him. He also knows her personally. I don't care what he told you. She has his mentor under her control and that mentor has others like White Eagle does."

A knock rattled the front door, making us all jump. I snapped my head up expecting the worst but it was Rick, Sarah's team leader. I ran to the door and yanked him inside.

"Sorry we're late. What'd we miss?" Rick asked with a lazy smile that barely covered the eagerness that I could see in his eyes.

I went into commander mode and gave him the fastest recap in all recorded history. He nodded, all business. "We're expecting…" I turned and looked at Alex who held up six fingers. "We're expecting six *dark watchers*. We don't know what abilities they have. I think we should mic up and put you guys on the roof with Mom and Alex. I don't want this to go down in the shop and ruin it. We can only file so many insurance claims." I said with a wink for White Eagle who was nodding and smiling. *The old devil loved a little action now and then.* "We're pretty sure this is a test run for Evilia. Let's try to bag 'em and you can deliver them to your boss. We don't want her to get any intel on us if we can help it. She's compiling info and the more she gets, the weaker our armor."

"Agreed. We have sniper rifles with tranquilizer darts. I liked these guys better when they weren't banding together." I admire Rick; he's a good team leader who isn't afraid to listen. He knows who I am and what I can do, so he rarely disagrees with my plans when it has to do with *dark watchers*.

Marlo handed out the electronics so that we could communicate. Lucie changed into her running tights, a t-shirt and athletic shoes. I missed the sundress but this was a much smarter plan. White Eagle showed Rick's team of Mica and Melody to the roof. Saul made himself at home in the shop so that he would be ready to lend medical aid wherever it was needed. Today Neil had been dispatched to protect my dad and youngest brother Lucas. We never knew when Evilia was fooling us and it was all a feint.

Alex reluctantly went up to the roof with Mom. I could tell that he was excited to see the roof and fascinated by their sniper gear but frustrated to be missing the action so I pulled him aside.

"Alex, you are important. I need for you and Mom to watch and observe. You're going to notice things that normal people can't see. Run everything you get through Marlo so that he can record it and relay what I need to know."

"Mars is gonna be up here?"

"Yeah, Buddy. He keeps track of all we learn and today he's going to take a video, too."

Marlo's head was just clearing the trap door. He was weighted down by his laptop and other electronic gizmos I didn't even recognize.

"Did Owen make you come up here?" Alex asked in hushed awe.

"No my friend, I'm strictly a behind-the-scenes kind of guy. I don't do confrontation – I process the data," Marlo answered completely unflapped by the question.

"You're up here by choice?" Alex pressed out of amazement. *Sometimes I swear he wished Marlo was his big brother instead of me.*

"Absolutely!" Marlo answered with a big smile for him. *Sometimes I think the feeling was mutual.*

"Marlo is up here because we all know that this is where he's the most valuable. He could fight, but then who would watch everything and help us learn what their weaknesses are?" I added.

"Wow, okay, I guess I can stay and help out up here too," Alex relented.

I gave both him and Mom a hug and headed for the retractable stairs. Mitchell poked his head through just as I reached the edge. "I feel them. You know my range isn't good past about ten minutes. I'm really not accurate until closer to five, but at least I'm way past the seconds that I was when you first met me."

"You're doing a fantastic job, Mitchell! Don't beat yourself up. I don't know where we'd be without you. Because of you, we have an estimate of when they're coming and you bought us a bunch of time. Your rock choice at the river must have done the trick and really sunk Devin's gear. That had to confuse them for a bit. We were just here too long so it was the next logical guess. Besides with so many *good watchers* around they can probably feel the energy."

"I guess. I think it's like Marlo said too, as plans change… it affects our perceptions and for all we know… theirs."

We hurried down the stairs and gathered the rest of the parking lot team of White Eagle, Sarah, Lucie and Adrian. We quickly went over the plans one last time and then broke apart to do our various jobs. Lucie grabbed a pad for our hostage so she wouldn't hurt him like she had been. White Eagle brought a bar and zip ties. Sarah manned her Taser and Adrian and I brought out our guest as Mitchell kept his eyes peeled for danger.

Lucie laid out the pad, causing Devin to look distinctly concerned. "What are you gonna do to me now? Haven't I been through enough? She'll get even with you, you know," he huffed. We didn't answer him. We just moved him into position and held him still so that White Eagle could zip tie him to the bar by his ankles. He looked angry and defiant. When he refused to kneel I made his decision for him by knocking him to his knees so that White Eagle could zip tie his wrists to the bar as well. He struggled and began to scream obscenities at us. "You're kidding, right?" he raged. "You're gonna leave me like this? I'll be a sitting duck."

We all ignored him. Sarah moved into position behind him, Taser at ready. The rest of us formed a line in front of him with me in the middle. Mitchell mumbled a soft play by play of the converging dark forces from my right. A part of me craved the information and a part of me wished that he and Devin would just shut up. I could feel the strain and anxiety running up and down our line.

Even Devin fell silent when a black Hummer pulled into the lot, but it didn't last. "Now you'll pay!" he said with a husky laugh. Why hadn't I thought to gag him?

Leave it to Evilia to make a grand entrance, I thought grouchily as I watched the Hummer ease to a stop. Waves of darkness rolled toward me like the ashy plume from a volcano. I took a breath and tried to calm myself even as my eyes rapidly scanned our opposition as they exited the vehicle. They were exactly what I expected. Carmichael was clearly in charge. The others looked like they followed him more out of fear than genuine respect. Their eyes continually darted around to land back on him and judge his mood. Most of the underlings looked like they were ready for a bar brawl, with their visible knives and chains. All wore boots and jeans and nearly all of them wore t-shirts. I could tell that they were your basic bottom feeder, leech-type *dark watcher*. They expected to win and drain our energy for a creepy *dark watcher* high but, they felt unskilled to me. I knew that they were just like the guy who had chased us through the Smithsonian in Washington DC in eighth grade. Back then he had been very scary, but now I wouldn't run from someone like that. I could see that we were beginning to make them nervous. I watched one lick his lips and I knew that they could almost taste our *watcher* gifts, but we were better trained than the people they were used to attacking. Normally they would get a thrill out of hunting us but I think we were a little more than they had been lead to believe. I was thankful for our backup on the roof, even though I thought we could take them.

"So, the boy has led us to you - just as he was paid to." Carmichael rolled his head on his neck and continued. "By the feel of it, you spend a lot of time here. I'm surprised you would have this encounter here when it looks like you knew we were coming. You look ready for us. Why give your hideout away? Whatever, your mistake I'm sure. We are here to take him back," Carmichael finished in a lazy drawl.

"I don't think so," I replied. I was thankful that my voice came out calm and assured because I sure didn't feel it.

"But you have him out here on display. Surely you were planning to give him to us in exchange for your lives?"

"No, we're planning to have you arrested to get you off the streets."

"You should know better than that, Owen. You lock our friends up and we simply let them out again. We are... everywhere. Some people like chaos. In fact you could say some people… support it," he said with a relaxed wave of his hand.

"So, I've seen," I growled softly. I could hear the raspy hiss of Lucie's angry breath to my left as Mitchell shook slightly to my right. He'd practiced plenty, but he hadn't faced many actual *dark watchers*. I could almost smell his fear and I'm sure they could too. I saw one of Carmichael's men take a step. At a look from his leader he froze again and cracked his knuckles.

"I see you've brought the ungifted one again," he sneered.

"Oh, he's plenty gifted, just not in a way you'd recognize," I shot back.

"We shall see, won't we? I've brought a special surprise for you." So have I, I thought. Carmichael snapped his finger and the tallest *dark watcher* opened the back hatch of the Hummer.

A heavy boot, followed by a jean clad leg slid out. Another boot and leg appeared followed by a dark t-shirt. There was something familiar about… and then the dreads appeared… Darren. "I want my dog back and my money and my other stuff. I'll take it out of your hide like I did to Max and Clive… one piece at a time."

This was NOT what I was expecting.

"You see, we're learning quite a bit about you. When one thing doesn't work, we have many new and useful options," Carmichael said with a slick smile.

I felt a tremor run through me, but I put up a brave front and decided to pry for information like we had planned. "You look better today, Carmichael," I said trying to sound calm as I changed the subject.

"How kind of you to notice." Carmichael still looked calm and in control but I could sense the restlessness growing in his men. They were edgy and twitchy in a barely contained way that I could easily read in their body language. They were here to fight and were expecting to drain us for the euphoric high they craved. The talking was getting to them.

"How's our old friend Kraeghton?" I asked more to agitate the men than because I truly cared.

"Being punished, I'm sure," he barked back in a voice that was feathered with a bit of strain. I guess I was getting to more than just his men.

"So you're saying she has him. Interesting."

"Of course she does. He tried to… Enough! That's not your business. Give us Devin."

"I'm touched you care, but no."

"Fine!" Carmichael moved his hand and Mitchell lunged, giving me warning as a flash of silver glinted in the hand of the red-haired *dark watcher*.

"Move!" I bellowed as the blade left his hand. Lucie and I dove to opposite sides. I felt the air whisk past me and the ghastly thunk of it hitting flesh, followed by a cry that echoed across the parking lot. I glanced behind me and to my intense surprise the hilt protruded from Devin's upper chest. Sarah was already on the move to cut him free, Taser dropped to the mat and her knife out.

"Owen!" Lucie screamed. I put my attention back where it belonged. Our adversaries were almost upon us. Each must have been assigned to someone because they all moved with purpose. Adrian was left without an opponent. Too bad for them – they had underestimated him. Then I lost track of what was happening around me to focus on the hulking *watcher* swinging at me. I blocked and then fired a series of rapid hits into his solar plexus. He bent over my assault and then fell onto his backside gasping for breath as his legs gave out. I leapt over him and ran toward Carmichael who was standing by the Hummer observing.

Before I could touch him, the *watcher* I'd knocked down was after me with a piece of chain. He scored a hit across my shoulder blade; sending sharp pains clear through to my chest. I spun as he swung again, but I came under his guard and punched into his armpit. He grunted and tried to backhand me, which I again evaded. He left his center line open so I was quick to use the opportunity to kick him right in the sternum. I heard a crack as my boot toe connected. He bent forward, gasping. I used his momentum to drive his nose into my knee. As he began to collapse, I used his motion to drive him to the ground. I turned back to Carmichael as "Now?" was barked into my earpiece.

"Not yet. We don't know anything," I hissed back.

The sounds of fighting; moans, yelps, groans and the smack of landed blows assaulted me. Carmichael took in all in. It looked like it didn't bother him at all. Then I realized that he had a communications device himself, that he was supplying a running commentary into. No suit for him today. He was dressed in a sport shirt and khakis and looked for all the world as if he were here to watch a sporting event and for him I guess it was.

I closed the distance between us, prepared to strike but Darren lunged at me from the side, intercepting my attack. "You're gonna pay in blood, little man."

He once was terror inducing, but now he was just a guy. I'd faced lots of darkness since we last met and he was no longer the worst of what I'd seen. New scars and tattoos were visible from his time in prison. He pulled a blade, feinted to the right and then lunged to the left. I leaned back and twisted to the side. I whipped out my leg and caught his knee, making him stumble. I used the opening to move closer to Carmichael. He tried to move closer to Darren and stay out of the fighting. Darren was not in the mood to have anyone in his way and shoved Carmichael into the Hummer. Now Carmichael was angry as well and released a blast of raw energy sending both of us into the air. I curved my back to protect my head before it could strike the asphalt. As soon as my shoulders hit, I was flipping back to my feet. Carmichael's eyes widened in surprise – he'd only had time to get his hand on the door handle. I shoved him into the door as he tried to open it and was rewarded by the sound of the air whooshing out of his lungs. I went to elbow him in the throat when I saw his eye flick to the side. I dropped and rolled away, coming back up on my feet, but not fast enough to evade Darren's jab at where I was. His knife caught in the fabric of my shirt and screeched along the Hummer's door.

I lashed out to the side, hitting Darren in the throat with the side of my hand. He stumbled back and I stomped on Carmichael's insole. I saw them both lunge for me at once and slid between them tangling them up. Suddenly Adrian was there and ready to help them the rest of the way down by sweeping Darren's legs out from under him. He then stomped on the hand holding the knife and quickly kicked it away. I did a fast visual of the area. Mitchell was on one knee barely holding off a drain and Lucie had blood running down the side of her face and her shirt was ripped where someone had tried to drain her. White Eagle was trying to free Sarah from another *dark watcher*. "Do it now, Rick!" I yelped into my mic.

The muffley thwump of silenced weapons erupted from the roof, shifting the feel in the air. I heard two distinct thumps as bodies hit the asphalt. A dart protruded from Darren's shoulder. His eyes rolled up in his head and he crumpled in a heap. Carmichael had not yet been hit. Perhaps they didn't have a clean shot. "You'll not take me!" he roared, looking furious as he dove and rolled under the Hummer. I started after him when I heard the clunk of metal on metal and then the resonating hum of something powering up.

"Run!" I screamed for anyone who would listen. I grabbed Adrian by his t-shirt's shoulder, dragging him behind me as I sprinted for cover.

"Get Down!" blasted through my earpiece hurting my ear with an intensity so strong that I couldn't even tell who'd yelled. Adrian and I dove for the dumpster as a click echoed across the lot followed almost immediately by the blast. We were lifted off the ground to be mercilessly slammed back into it. I was thrust from intense noise to muffled thuds as debris began to rain down on us. Adrian blinked at me owlishly.

"You okay?" Was that my voice? Adrian gave me a slow nod and pulled at his ear. I scanned the area. Sarah was being helped to her feet by White Eagle. By the way Devin was starring at the sky he must be gone despite their best efforts. Mitchell stood in the middle of the chaos completely unharmed. Saul was just coming through what was left of our front door. I felt panic begin to surge within me. Where was Lucie? "Rick? Mars? You copy?"

My questions were met with dead air – my com was down. I ripped it from my ear and threw it to the ground in disgust. At least I could hear out of that ear. "Luce!" I screamed with what was left of my voice.

A second minor explosion knocked me back onto my ass, irritating me more. The front shop window gave way in a shower of glass. Apparently it had had enough.

"Luce!" I bellowed again, cupping my hands around my mouth to give it more carrying power. There was no response. Which way to run? Think! *Dark watchers*, sprouting darts littered the ground with the rest of the wreckage. Lucie was nowhere in sight. One, two, three, four, five bodies, but no Lucie and no Carmichael.

I took hold of myself, closed my eyes and felt for her. She was a ways away but felt okay. Rick and Mom came bursting from the front of the shop and sirens began to wail.

"Clear out!" Rick barked harshly at us, "Before they get here. Let us handle it."

I gave him a sharp nod. "Spread the word," I said looking at White Eagle. "My com is down." Mitchell and Adrian began to run toward the back of the shop. White Eagle and Sarah took a more circumspect pace. I noticed that White Eagle had the pipe that Devin had been tied to and he was madly stuffing broken zip ties in his pocket. Sarah and Mom yanked the mat out from under him and hauled it off. I rushed into the shop to collect Alex. He stood in the doorway with Marlo, looking pale, his eyes huge.

"The reality of being a *watcher* is not as awesome as I remembered," he said bitterly, his voice cracking.

"Come on. We need to find Lucie." We ran shoulder to shoulder toward the van and dove in. Mitchell slammed the door and White Eagle was already revving the engine.

I suddenly realized Sarah was with us. "You're not staying?"

"Nope. It's White Eagle's shop. It's a little too close to home if you know what I mean. Rick can handle it."

"Which way?" White Eagle interrupted sounding worried.

"Mitchell?" I begged. "Help us find Lucie!"

"I'll see if her GPS is still activated," Marlo threw in as he fired up the laptop.

Mitchell scowled in thought. I'd asked the wrong question. "What's the quickest way to get to Lucie?" I tried. He frowned briefly and then his face relaxed.

"Left about three blocks? Then go left again by the dense shrubbery."

Well, duh, I thought. You're in Oregon, near Portland. It's all green and lush almost everywhere. I heard a small snort and looked to Alex. He gave me a huge grin and winked at me. Winked! Rascal! "He's from the desert. Give him a break," I said under my breath.

"Oh, okay," Alex drew out sarcastically. "Good thing he's only been here for... months."

I started to reply when I felt the van lean in an unexpected way. White Eagle made a fast right out of the parking lot. I was going to say something, but the fire department pulling in made it plenty clear why he made the choice he did. The police were right behind them. White Eagle made the first right he could and then another. I watched behind us to be sure we weren't followed. I even risked feeling the energies around us but all I got was us and Lucie – a very faint Lucie.

Mitchell reached over and tapped White Eagle's shoulder after a few blocks. "She's near." White Eagle pulled over and stopped. I jumped out of the van and concentrated on Lucie. Movement drew my eye. Lucie stepped out from behind a laurel hedge. The second she caught sight of me, she broke into a sprint. She jumped into my arms hitting me so hard I staggered backwards.

"You're okay," she breathed.

"I'm okay," I said smiling as I turned still holding her. She wrapped her arms and legs tight around me and laid her head on my shoulder to nuzzle my neck. "You're okay," she repeated softly.

I set her in the van and she started to wipe her hand on her pants, but paused to look at it first. She sucked in a breath, "You're not okay. You're bleeding!"

"It happens. You're bleeding too. We'll be fine."

"But Owen…"

"We'll get fixed up at Sarah's. Right now, we have to get out of here. I'm sure Saul will come as soon as he's free. White Eagle can stitch me up if he needs to."

"Oh geez, let me look," she said sharply as White Eagle pulled out and headed home. She tugged at my shirt.

"If you wanted to undress me, I'd rather…"

"Oh stop!" Lucie said with a scowl as she whapped me gently on the shoulder. She hissed in a breath when she saw my latest injury. Now that the adrenaline was wearing off it was starting to burn like the fiery chasms of hell. She had Alex hand her some of the first aid supplies we store in the van and applied pressure the rest of the trip.

"So what happened to you? How did you end up in a hedge?"

"I saw Carmichael roll under the Hummer and out the other side. He took off up the street as the car exploded knocking me down. I was after him as soon as I could stand but he got too far ahead of me. He was picked up by some guy in a black sedan. I wish I'd caught him."

White Eagle pulled the van into Sarah's garage and shut the door. We unloaded and met up to recap around Sarah's kitchen table. As everyone spoke, Marlo recorded all the important data on his laptop. White Eagle and Lucie fussed over my side and back. They rinsed my wound and argued over stitches, finally settling for Steri-strips to hold it closed. Then Lucie fussed over the glass in my knee that I didn't even realize was there. Mom left me alone to take care of Alex's mental health and to deal with the minor cuts and scrapes on Mitchell and Adrian with Sarah's help. I thought Sarah was being overly quiet until I realized that she was listening to her Bluetooth. You gotta love it when the spies spy on the spies.

I slapped my head totally disgusted with myself. "My com, I threw it down. I left it on the ground. Crap!"

Sarah frowned at me. She said nothing, still listening and sent a text. I had to presume to Rick. I hoped I hadn't blown it. Could we claim it had been in the shop and got blown out with the explosion? Could we say I handled it in the shop? But it wouldn't be in our records. I had to be more careful.

When Lucie was good and done with me she finally let me take care of her head wound. I kept an eye on Alex but he seemed fine to me. Perhaps he'd even had a little too much fun. Marlo typed away and the voices around the table were low. The warmth and sense of safety in the kitchen after all the stress had me feeling relaxed and almost sleepy at least until Alex's words soaked in…

"The most important piece of information was that she fully expected to lose people when this confrontation happened. Devin just didn't expect to be one of the casualties. She doesn't care who she hurts. I don't understand how she can't care. The most interesting message I got was that this was all just a test of our defenses. She's gathering data for a larger attack," Alex finished, looking expectant. He also looked small. He was too young and tiny to be a *watcher*. Life wasn't fair.

"That's what you got? I didn't have time earlier to really talk to you. I'm sorry."

"It's okay Owen. I get that you can't do it all. Did you hear me when I said that Carmichael was guessing about Kraeghton? It's true that he's glad he's gone. He respects him but he doesn't like him. Power speaks to power, they say. Right now Evilia is the alpha dog in the *dark watcher* pack but those two are fighting to be second."

I felt Mom looking at me. She was sending me a strong nonverbal message. She did not like having Alex on the scene today when things got ugly. I gave her a single nod and turned back to Alex.

"Most *watcher* stuff isn't like what happened today. When I started out, all I did was stop a couple of school bullies and..."

"I know that you, Mom and the others are worried about me," Alex interrupted. "Taking on that dark energy didn't feel good, but I'm okay. Having me observe from the roof with mom... I was safe. It was worth it - we learned some stuff that will help us. We know things we wouldn't have known if I wasn't there and didn't do what I did. I see that look on your face, Owen. I know this isn't a game. I know people died today... well at least Devin did, but it wasn't our fault and he was a bad person. He hurt people. He would have hurt you. I know it. Devin knew more than what he said. I know what I did helped our side!" he finished defiantly.

Alex seemed fine and felt okay for now, but I would watch and worry. I couldn't seem to help myself. I felt my eyes begin to droop as often happened when all the adrenaline had worn off and I began to crash. When had I last eaten? Breakfast? I'd been so worried about Lucie that all I'd had was a glass of milk.

"Owen? Why am I so tired?" Alex asked in a perplexed voice like he was fading fast as well.

"When we use our *watcher* gifts we expend a lot of energy. I bet you feel like you've run a marathon."

"Yeah, I guess." Alex sighed.

"It will take time for Sarah to collect a full report on what's happening so find something to do to relax. Have a snack if you feel like it or even a nap. You'll feel better in a little while. I promise."

Lucie smiled at Alex as she put her hand over the one he had resting on the table. "You'll get used to the drain. It doesn't go away, but you'll get to know yourself and what you can handle. Your brother, on the other hand, overdoes it regularly and then pays dearly for it." Lucie slid her eyes to mine and gave me a look.

The meeting broke up and we dispersed. Adrian and Marlo headed to his house to game and Alex settled in to do the same on Sarah's PlayStation. Mom went home to check on Lucas and Dad. Lucie had White Eagle lend me sweat pants and a t-shirt and then guilted me into a shower. She checked my wounds and rebandaged me. My little personal nurse and Florence Nightingale even made me eat a sandwich before she would let me nap. Alex was still gaming so we crashed in her room. I wrapped my body around her, holding her close to my chest. I breathed in the scent of her freshly washed hair and drifted.

I swear I had just closed my eyes when I felt a hand on my shoulder. I twisted my neck to look up at Saul, our team medic. "I need to look at your knife wound and I have news," he whispered.

Lucie groaned softly and cracked an eye to look at Saul. She pushed herself out of my arms to sit up on her bed. I winced as I sat up. "How did you get so close without my noticing you?" I asked Saul.

"Perhaps it's my gift, as it were. It pays for someone like me to be quiet and stealthy. Besides you know you're safe here and you know me. You've got three *watchers* in the house for Pete's sake. Well, maybe five *watcherly* types if you count Sarah and White Eagle. I bet your subconscious knew you were fine," Saul smiled.

"Did you check out Alex?"

"He's sound asleep with a controller in his hand. I'm sure he's fine. He looks like a normal kid to me, but I'm not one to diagnose the mental stuff. I do get why you don't want to let Bob have him. On the other hand, he does have access to the best psychiatric help that money can buy - both normal and well, your kind."

"So far he seems okay so I don't feel it's worth the risk," I replied.

"I'm with Owen," Lucie added.

"Of course you are." Saul replied giving Lucie an impressive *duh* look.

"I mean, I don't trust Bob," Lucie said firmly.

"Come on Lucie, you're just mad because Bob wanted to shut Owen down," Saul laughed.

"Yeah, that's it. It's all about Owen and has nothing to do with the ugly vibe I get from the man," Lucie snorted.

Saul's face broke out in a huge grin. "How'd you do on our boy, Beautiful?"

"I gave it heck, but I don't do stitches," she said as she turned a little pale.

"With his luck, maybe you should learn how," Saul replied with a twinkle in his eye.

Lucie's look shifted from pale to slightly green. "I should learn, but I don't know if I can stomach it. I know they can be necessary but it would bug me to hurt him."

"You don't have to, Luce," I said as I ran a hand up and down her arm.

"I know you're teasing me, Saul, but I think you're right. What if you aren't around? Our danger magnet here could use a little more than your basic first aid class level of healing."

"Well, come on then. Let's see how you do, Dr. Ness." Saul led us to the kitchen, where Lucie got out fresh towels and splashed cold water on her face while Saul unloaded his medical bag.

He had me pull up my shirt so he could look at Lucie's handiwork so far. He kept up a running commentary as he worked. I knew he was trying to distract us from the task at hand. He told Lucie that for a normal person, the job she had done would be fine but knowing me, I would reopen the wound. Let the stitching begin. Oh boy. Saul verbalized the thing we all dreaded - I was darned lucky that the knife hadn't been dipped in poison. Rick had recovered it and had been able to keep it away from the police.

He told us that Bob had cut through the local red tape so that all the evidence from the scene, including my earpiece was under his watchful eye. It didn't pay to have local law enforcement know too much about us and finding my blood at the scene would have ranked pretty high on the *not good* scale. We sure didn't want to appear on the local radar. We wanted to help them, but not have them after us. I figured it must be nice to have Bob's connections. I have plenty of awesome ones myself but I sure don't have judges in my pocket.

Bob had managed to wrap up the evidence and had taken all the suspects. A full report would be sent to Marlo through Sarah. The Hummer had been rigged to blow and Carmichael had triggered it. They had found the trigger with his prints on it near the Hummer's remains. Unfortunately, though Caleb Carmichael had escaped, his likeness and vital statistics had been passed on to local law enforcement. Bob's best interrogators were at work on the others but they were getting a whole lot of nothing so far. They needed Alex; however there was no way I was giving him up to Bob. I was sure we would never see Alex again if we did.

Saul told Lucie how to continue the care of my cut and showed her how to remove the stitches. He hugged us and left. Lucie and I moved to the couch. We tried to wrest the controller away from Alex so that we could watch TV but we woke him up. He convinced us to game with him and then we watched a movie together. I had my eye on him but he seemed to have come through our latest adventure completely unscathed. We'd see if he had nightmares.

When Sarah and White Eagle started moving around after their nap we decided on comfort food – breakfast for dinner. Cooking together is one of those happy moments I enjoy and hang onto. After dinner White Eagle walked Alex home and Lucie and I took turns reading aloud from the novel that had been assigned as summer reading for our advanced placement English class. The only good part was spending time with Lucie because summer homework is dumb.

FOUR

Sarah and White Eagle had planned a small wedding that would take place in Sarah's backyard. They picked their date more for Marla Saggio's availability than anything else, which made me smile. Lucie had not wanted to make a big deal out of her emancipation since she viewed it as more of a sadness in her life than something to celebrate, but the wedding, she threw herself into.

She was going to make the most of her new family. Her old family was another story. She talked to her brother once a week but her father pretended she didn't exist. He did not text, call or communicate with her in anyway. I didn't view it as a loss and if that made me a bad person – I could live with it.

The weekend before the ceremony, Lucie dragged me to five different places trying to find the perfect plants to fill in the perceived holes in the flowerbeds. We had already edged and barkdusted the beds, leaving a little extra bark to fill in when we were completely done. I thought that if the house hadn't been painted four years ago we would have had that on our list too. We had scrubbed it inside and out until it shone.

I followed Lucie's bobbing ponytail up and down every row of the five nurseries she had selected. I had no idea there were so many around. When the bed of White Eagle's truck was full, we headed home to begin the next phase of our neverending work. It made me happy to see her happy. She had a glow about her and it was more than the tan she had gotten from time spent outside. She had purpose.

"Why are you smiling," she asked with a grin of her own.

"You make me smile. You're having too much fun. This is work. You should show the appropriate level of monotony and boredom."

"You're so full of crap. You know I love Sarah and White Eagle and I want this to be... perfect. I owe them a lot and this is a way to show them just how much I appreciate them," she said turning serious.

"Uh huh."

"Oh don't be like that. I know you're kinda having fun too."

"Busted," I smiled at her.

I backed the truck into the driveway and Lucie hopped out to retrieve our tools. I was supposed to be unloading the plants but I watched her instead. I admired her shorts and tank top. To be honest I was much more interested in what was in them than the clothes themselves. I even admired her flip flops and toenails that were painted electric blue. She came back wearing gloves with two trowels in one hand and a diagram in the other. She looked at the plants in the truck and then laid out the diagram. Over three hundred little leafy green things with multicolored blooms were waiting to be put into the beds. I did a double take, had we really bought that many?

"You're kidding, right? You want me to dig three hundred holes with a... trowel?"

Lucie put a gloved hand on her hip. "You dig 'em and I'll plant 'em."

"You could have gotten more help. This will take forever."

"I didn't want my diagram to get messed up," she said giving me her best smile.

"And you think I won't mess it up? Wow, you have more faith and confidence than I do in my green thumb."

"Less whining and more digging, Mister. We'll start with the walkway since folks will see that first."

"Tell me again why we're doing all this," I said, trying to look innocent.

"Oh come on, please. I owe them so much. It's their wedding gift." She even looked a little misty.

"Aw, Luce." I pulled her into a hug. "They would love you whether or not I dig three hundred holes in the dirt."

"But it will be pretty and welcoming for the guests," she said softly into my shirt.

I sighed. "You're lucky you're cute. I wouldn't do this for just anybody."

"Don't kid yourself. I can think of a whole bunch of people you would happily work your tail off for."

"Where do I start?" I asked resigned.

"Yay!" Lucie exclaimed and then gave me an exuberant kiss before she set me to work. She had brought out some old towels for us to kneel on. Once she had filled her holes with little plants she would move her towel to the far side of me and take over my old one so that I could move along the row continuously. She set a staggering pace. I was thankful we'd started early because I was sweating by the time I reached the front porch. Almost one eighth of the way done and my lower back was already complaining.

I looked over at Lucie and noticed a smear of dirt on her cheek. Some of her hair had broken free to curl around her face and stick to her neck and temples. She looked fantastic. I reached out a hand to brush off the dirt.

"What?" she asked as she smiled at me.

"You're smudged. I thought I'd help."

"Why do I have the feeling you didn't?" Her tone held a hint of reprimand in with a big helping of humor.

"Did the goofy grin give me away?"

"It's alright, Owen. I don't get mad, I get even," Lucie exclaimed, lunging at me. The impact knocked me over and into the unplanted flower bed. I laughed and held her to me, leaving handprints on her pale aqua tank top. I thought about rolling her over but I figured I'd ruin it. She removed a glove to push at my shoulder. "You're getting me dirty!"

"Maybe I like you that way," I said as I tried to dial down the huge smile that was on my face.

"Huh, and I thought you liked the smell of my shampoo, yet all this time it was dirt," she laughed.

Grubby hands and all, I pulled her toward me for a kiss. "Clean or filthy, you are delicious."

Lucie froze for a moment.

"What?" I asked, worried.

"My past came back to haunt me for a moment. That *dark watcher* who drained me when they held me captive said I was 'delicious.'" A shiver ran through her. "I'm sorry; I thought I was over that."

"Luce, we see and experience plenty of dark stuff. You can't assume it's never going to touch you. You're not made of Teflon. Just don't let it rule you, okay?"

"Yeah, that's true," she said with the ghost of a smile. She took ahold of my t-shirt with her gloved hand to pull me toward her. "Now you have a handprint on your shirt."

"I'm more interested in lip prints." She laughed but complied.

Lucie pulled back and smiled. "Come on, we have work to do."

"I guess," I grumped back at her. I rolled up from the ground with her in my arms.

She giggled and looked at her shorts. "Oh geez, Owen. Now I have handprints on my butt."

"Look at the bright side, that way people will know you're mine." I couldn't help the huge grin that had found a home on my face.

"I think they already know," she accused with a smile.

We continued our planting routine until Lucie dubbed the front yard worthy. We swept and hosed off the walk and watered the new plantings. She moved on to the backyard and I put the remaining barkdust around the new plants. I closed up the front and headed to find my Lucie. I hadn't been back here in weeks and I was truly amazed. I could see how much Lucie and Sarah loved nature and how much attention they had paid to the yard. For me, yard work is about weeding, trimming and cutting the grass. My approach to gardening is simple and utilitarian. Not these gals. I gotta' give it to them. It looked fantastic and we weren't done yet.

I smiled when I caught sight of Lucie's backside where two perfect handprints remained from my grabbing her to roll us to our feet. She had more on her back. Maybe I could leave some on the front? Nope, better focus on the yard. I picked up Lucie's yard choreography sheet from next to her.

"Well, what do you think?" she asked.

"The handprints on your butt are my favorite."

"I mean about the yard, you big dope."

"The yard's pretty nice too but it just doesn't compare."

Lucie rolled her eyes but smiled. "You're such a pain. Cute, but a pain."

Just as we were finishing, Sarah and White Eagle came out back. "Wow, it's beautiful!" Sarah exclaimed. She looked pretty fantastic herself today. She wore jeans and a blouse that made her look closer to my mom's age than her own.

"Amazing," White Eagle added.

"How was your shopping trip?" I could hear the excitement and genuine interest in Lucie's voice.

"I finally found *the* dress," Sarah actually gushed. "And we found the perfect suit for Earl and they can have the alterations done by Friday."

"Can I see the dress?"

"Scrub up first and then I'll show the dresses to you," Sarah laughed.

"Dresses?"

"Yes, sweetie. Dresses - plural. We got one for you too."

The women moved into the house, while we looked on.

"Nice handprints," White Eagle chuckled under his breath.

I smiled and shrugged. "At the time it seemed like a good idea."

"I'm sure it did. Let's finish up back here. You get going on the barkdust and I'll see how the lights are working. Lucie wants the Christmas lights up again. What'd she call 'em? Fairy lights? Good thing I love that girl," he harrumphed but I knew he didn't mean it and if he was scolding me it sure didn't feel like it.

The day of the wedding began cloudy and cool. It had rained overnight giving everything a sparkly, fresh-washed look. I scurried down to Sarah's with my suit in a garment bag so that I could help with this morning's final preparations.

Lucie was in the kitchen helping Marla and Marlo with some of the last minute food prep. No one noticed me yet, so I took a minute to admire the tanned legs that showed below Lucie's shorts. Her feet were bare and I had to resist the urge to make a comment that I knew would make her eyes snap with blue fire. Getting a reaction was more than half the fun.

She must have sensed my presence because she turned around slowly to look at me. Her eyes lit up and she smiled but her voice sounded gruff. "Come on, there's lots to do! How about salad and veggie prep?" I just smiled as she approached me.

She raised her eyebrows at me, waiting for a response. "Okay Boss, whatever you say."

"Is that so?" she asked. This was not the response I was expecting. I couldn't take my eyes off her face. I jumped a bit when I felt her hands connect with my backside to pull me close to her. She rose up on her tiptoes to kiss me. This was my Lucie? In front of Marlo and his mom? She pulled back a little and giggled. "Now, about those veggies?" She swirled away from me. "You know the drill." I smiled at her, shaking my head as I set to work on the pile next to the sink and she returned to the rolls she was forming.

Marlo had a ridiculously huge grin slapped on his face as he worked on a fruit platter complete with edible flowers and other carved garnishes he was creating. I gave him a look but all that did was make him bust out in laughter. Marla smiled at him and Lucie ignored him though her shoulders were shaking. What was going on?

White Eagle walked into the kitchen but stopped mid hum. "Nice handprints."

"Yeah, I know, you said that the other day, but look, different shorts," I said pointing at Lucie.

"Yep, different shorts," he agreed. Marlo and Lucie laughed harder. Marla rolled her eyes and went back to the meatballs she was prepping. Lucie twinkled at me. She gets that sparkly look in her eye when she's up to no good. I thought about her actions earlier and slowly twisted to look at my backside and then right at her. I raised one eyebrow.

"That's grounds for a food fight, but I think Marla would beat me with her meatball scoop."

"You're right, Owen, I would. I do have to add though, that you look fantastic in flour," she ended on a giggle.

I tried to brush off the seat of my dark brown cargo shorts but it was no use. "Gee, Luce, whatever will people think?" I asked sarcastically.

"Gee, Owen, I don't know. What will people think?" Lucie replied with a laugh.

"I think you need to behave!" I said, waving the carrot peeler at her.

"Why start now?" she asked as she grabbed two handfuls of my t-shirt to kiss me again.

I grabbed her wrists playfully and pushed her away. "Too much fun," I warned.

"Aw, and here I thought you said fun was good for me!" Lucie laughed. "Don't you know, forgiveness is heavenly but revenge is divine?"

"Too much fun, I say," I repeated with mock severity brushing at the flour prints on the front of my t-shirt.

"Yeah, yeah, okay."

"Yeah, yeah, get a room is more like it!"

"Marlo!" his mom yelped.

"See what you started?" I said hugging Lucie and we all laughed.

White Eagle picked up a knife and began peeling a tomato in a long strip to form into a rose. I went over to join him at the veggie station.

"I thought you hated garnishing," I said softly to him.

"It's for a good cause," he replied smiling.

"Aren't you nervous?"

"Nah, this is the right thing to do."

"Do you regret all those years alone and not having any kids?" The minute the words were out of my mouth I knew I shouldn't have asked. It wasn't my business. I looked back at the celery not expecting an answer.

"I've had lots of kids over the years. Many of my *watchers* felt like they were my own children. A mentor and *watcher* have a bond like family. Miles was like a brother. I had a special love I shared with Miranda and now I have you. You are like a son to me and I have Sarah. Why not make my family official? When things are right, you know in here," he said, tapping me on the chest over my heart.

I smiled and gave him a one-armed hug. "Where is Sarah?"

"She's off getting her nails and hair done."

"Really? She doesn't seem like one to go for that stuff."

He smiled at me. "Let me tell you about women. No matter how beautiful they are, they always believe that something needs fixing. She is beautiful to me either way, but if this makes her feel more beautiful, then that's worth something."

I smiled back. "Did you pick up your suit?"

"See, now that's another side to Sarah's beauty. She's practical and organized. No wonder she can run such clean operations. Did you see the list on the fridge? It's a timeline. I pick up the suit in an hour. You were early by the way, but I know what draws you here and it sure isn't me." My eyes went straight to Lucie and White Eagle chuckled.

FIVE

The day zoomed by in a blur. Lucie kept smiling and that was about all I cared about. Soon we were cleaning up and changing. I wandered into the hall to wait and to be out of the way now that Adrian, Brenda, Mitchell and Tess were all on hand to help the Saggios.

I heard a door open and turned to see Lucie exiting her room. She shut the door softly behind her. She wore the highest heels I'd ever seen her in. With those she wore a beautifully beaded dress. It skimmed her curves in all the right places. It ended about four inches above her knees and was uniquely asymmetrical with two straps on one side and none on her other shoulder. She had looped her hair up on her head and let a trail of soft curls slide down the back. A few loose tendrils caressed her face.

"You don't like it," she said sounding sad.

"No. The opposite; you look... Lucie, you're beautiful." Now she smiled a little.

"Sarah and White Eagle bought the dress... and the shoes. Sarah thought... maybe... if we went to the prom... I could wear it... again," she finished softly in a shy way. It was strange to hear her sound uncertain.

"Lucie, if you want to go, then I would be honored to take you."

I hadn't moved so she came to me. "You do look fine in a suit," she smiled as she straightened my already perfect tie. She picked up my hand and placed it on her hip. "I won't break."

"I didn't want to damage or wrinkle your amazing dress."

"You think it's amazing? I'd like it if you wrinkled me a little. Otherwise what's the point of getting all dressed up?" she asked as she slipped her hands inside my jacket. It was fun to have her tall. She rarely wore heels over an inch or two. I could kiss her all day like this, but we had jobs to do so I reluctantly let her go.

"Sparkly pink really is your color," she giggled.

"I've been busted for your lip gloss before," I laughed.

"Eighth grade... Katie."

"Yep."

We smiled at each other remembering.

"I'm glad things are like they are now. I'm sorry for Katie but I'm glad I got you," she said with a smile.

"Katie's a nice girl. She just wasn't the girl for me. Come on." I took Lucie's hand and started to lead her off.

"Wait." I stopped and turned. "You look really good except for one thing..." She slowly reached up and ran her thumb over my lower lip. "In fact you look fantastic. That suit, the green shirt with your tan and dark coloring... I could..." she started to swipe at my upper lip but stopped and kissed me again instead. When she reached up to swipe at my mouth again, I kissed her fingers. She closed her eyes for a moment, took my hand and continued on down the hall.

Everything looks beautiful, Luce," I said looking out into the backyard.

Thanks and thank you for all your help and hard work. Love you."

"I love you too, Lucie."

We stood in the kitchen watching through the patio door. The guests were seated around tables in the backyard instead of in the classic wedding rows. They all looked happy and were visiting. Marla and crew were moving around serving sparkling limeade and water when White Eagle tapped me on the shoulder to hand me the rings. Lucie picked up my boutonniere off the counter and pinned it on.

"How'd you learn to do that?"

"My... former parents went to many formal functions. I know all kinds of mostly useless etiquette rules."

"Remember what Mom and White Eagle say, education is never wasted," I added with a wink.

"Speaking of White Eagle... how about pinning me up too, pretty lady," he said to her with a twinkle in his eye. As Lucie was pinning on his boutonniere the music began to play.

I started for the door but Lucie took my arm. "Good luck," she said softly and then pushed me toward the door.

"You too, Sunshine."

White Eagle and I walked to the grape arbor that would serve as the altar. I glanced over at him and he looked calm and at ease. I felt more nervous than he appeared. The music changed and Lucie walked down the aisle. I could not take my eyes off her. The sun caught the crystal beads of her dress and I realized that she had more in her hair. She was radiant and then she smiled at me and I think for a moment my heart stopped.

Then Sarah walked down the aisle with her mom, Bettylou, and everyone stood. I glanced at White Eagle and he seemed to be taken over by the same emotions that had seized me a moment ago. Sarah's dress was similar to Lucie's. It brushed the top of her knees and had a sheer sleeve on one side with a solid sleeve on the other and had the same kind of glistening beads. I had never seen her look more beautiful.

"Friends and family, love is a miraculous gift, and a wedding is a celebration of that magic, and that's what we're here to do today. We are gathered together to be overjoyed for and with Sarah and Earl who are so wonderfully suited to one another that it's a pure delight for the rest of us to see how ebulliently happy two people can be." I let the pastor drone on as I watched Sarah, White Eagle and Lucie.

I blinked when he looked at me as he said, "Since the beginning of time, the ring has been an emblem of the sincerity and permanence of a couple's love for one another and regard for their marriage." *Oh yeah, the rings.* I reached into my pocket and pulled them out as he continued on. "As the circle can begin anew at any point, so a good marriage can pick any point to renew itself. These rings are symbols of your eternal love."

I handed White Eagle the ring for Sarah and readied the ring he would receive from her. I glanced over at Lucie. She was smiling at me as she held both bouquets. It felt strange to be standing here with her. Next thing I knew the pastor was pronouncing them husband and wife and told White Eagle he could kiss his bride. He took ahold of her and tilted her back reminding me of the famous welcome home picture of the sailor returning from World War II, dipping his gal backwards as he kissed her. Sarah came up blushing and giggling.

If I had to go, then maybe they could chaperone the prom. The thought made me smile. They would probably be the best chaperones ever, with their training. Then they were walking down the aisle and it was my turn to bring Lucie. She took my arm with a sweet smile and off we walked as cameras flashed and the guests cheered.

We posed for what felt like hundreds of pictures. The plus side to that was that Lucie and I were excused from serving today. I watched Marla and crew bustle around while the pictures were snapped. It was strange to be on this side of the proceedings. Then we got to sit down and enjoy Marla's fantastic fare. I stripped off my jacket, hung it on the back of my chair and rolled up my sleeves. What I really wished for were flip flops, shorts and a t-shirt. I caught my mom smiling at me.

Soon it was time for me to give my toast to the bride and groom. I clinked a spoon against my glass and rose to my feet. When a hush fell over the gathering, I began. "When White Eagle asked me to be his best man, I was deeply touched and then I was a little scared. As most of you know, I hate public speaking and generally avoid any kind of spotlight. This day is about honoring Sarah and White Eagle so I put my reluctance away to focus on what really matters. When White Eagle asked me to do this, he was letting me know that we are family and mean a lot more to each other than we ever say out loud. Sarah has been a favorite aunt, surrogate grandma and nanny since I was in Kindergarten. I know few people as wonderful as they are. They are the kind who go the extra mile and put others first. They have both been helping to raise me for years it seems, and as wonderful as my own parents are, I appreciate the extra love, support and guidance. They deserve each other in all the best ways because it is rare to find two people who so richly deserve every bit of happiness this world has to offer. May they have... eternity together in happiness. Congratulations. I love you both." I sat with a thump and White Eagle reached over to hug me.

The applause seemed much too loud for the size of the audience. Lucie and Sarah both smiled at me with extra sparkly eyes. When I glanced at Mom she looked the same way. I ducked my head and wished I could disappear.

I caught movement and turned to see Lucie rise to take her turn. "I guess Owen and I should have worked on our speeches together. I'm not sure what more there is to say. We seem to share many of the same feelings toward Sarah and White Eagle. Owen has just had the marvelous opportunity to enjoy and learn from them longer. They have become my family too and have been a wonderful example for what love should be. I will never be able to thank them for what they have done for me and our community. My wish for them is that they enjoy enchantment and jubilation always and know that I will love them and they will love each other - no matter what life brings our way."

Tears slid silently down Lucie's cheeks but she smiled. She quickly hugged them both amid fresh applause and excused herself. I was right behind her. She easily evaded the guests and stepped into a sheltered part of the yard. Even though her back was to me, I could tell that she was trying really hard to pull herself together. She heard my footsteps and turned. She held a stiff posture for a second and then realizing it was me, she began to silently sob. She crashed into me and held me tight as White Eagle began to speak.

"I would like to say thank you to Sarah for agreeing to spend the rest of forever with me. Thank you to everyone here for joining us on our special day. Sarah, my love, the diamond on your finger is radiant and bright, but always remember, that to me, it will never be as beautiful as you are."

Now there were sighs and whooping to go with the clink of dishes and glassware as well as the soft music collection that Marlo had mixed just for them. Lucie still held me tightly as she cried silently into my shirt. "Luce, what is it?"

She sniffled and hiccupped. "I'm so happy for them and thankful for them and for you. I love my dad, but as a parent… he sucks. He always did and my mom wasn't much better. I miss her nonetheless. I just wish… things haven't gone the way I thought they would."

"I know, Sunshine. I'm sorry for your losses. If it was in my power to fix everything for you I would."

"Really you have fixed it. You know that, right? You have fixed me. Can't you feel it? I have a whole new amazing life among people who love me for me and not for what I can give them. I'm… I'm free. I'm free but I feel guilty because… because a part of me is glad this is my new family and I'm scared that makes me a bad person. I feel like I was one of the things you were supposed to fix as a *watcher* but now I'm afraid that I will become a *dark watcher* because of the things I feel."

"Oh Luce, you're not now, nor have you ever been, a bad person. I can't imagine you being a bad person in the future. Forgive yourself and while you're working on that, think about all the good things you've done. I could name at least twenty right now if you need me to!"

"What did I do to deserve you?"

"No, no, what did I do to deserve you? Most people find me moody, introverted and scary, yet here you are."

Lucie laughed. "They don't know you like I do." Just like that she made my heart feel lighter. She took my hand and we snuck around the front of the house to avoid all the guests in the backyard. We went in the front door and Lucie led me to the back of the house past her bathroom and into Sarah and White Eagle's room.

"Why back here?"

"Today, my bathroom is the public one and this will take a few minutes, so have a seat," she said indicating the closed toilet lid.

I paused as I passed the mirror and looked at my shirt. Lucie looked at my reflection and her eyes went wide. "Owen, I'm so sorry! I smeared my mascara on your shirt. I'll fix it, I promise."

"Don't worry about it. Anytime."

Lucie rolled her eyes and then got to work with some makeup remover to fix her damage. She quickly reapplied her eye makeup with an artists' hand. She caught me watching. "Well, modeling was good for something, right?"

"You know, I feel like White Eagle does - no matter what, you're beautiful to me. With or without makeup, in a fancy dress or in cutoffs and a tank top – it's who you are inside and out every day that I find appealing."

Lucie set down her makeup brush, picked up a fresh washcloth and dampened it at the sink. She added some makeup remover and approached me. She started to bend down but then stopped, hiked up her skirt and sat on my knees instead. She focused intently on the stain on my shirt. My focus had nothing to do with the stain and everything to do with her smooth golden skin.

"Owen?"

"Huh?"

"Take off your tie. The mascara isn't coming out. I need to get more aggressive." My mind ground to a halt. *What did she say? My tie?* I reached up and twitched the knot to loosen it. Then I pulled it over my head and laid it on a dry spot on the counter. Lucie set down her cloth to unbutton the top three buttons on my shirt. I swallowed as time stuttered and slowed. She picked the cloth back up and slipped a hand inside me shirt to work against. I was glad she'd gotten her makeup on me so that I could have this moment with her. Maybe she could do it all over again.

I couldn't resist the temptation anymore. I lightly rested my hands on her knees. She paused for a moment and went back to work. I looked intently into her face as I slowly slid my hands up to the edge of her dress. She kept working so I slipped my fingers under the edge of the hem. She finally looked from the stain on my shirt to me with a half smile on her lips.

"You pick now?"

"I'm a guy. Anytime's a good time to kiss you or touch you."

Lucie laughed a breathy laugh. "Bet you only have five minutes until someone comes looking for us."

"Bet I have ten."

"Mmm, we'll see," she said as she slid forward to kiss me. I let my hands glide against her motion and she tossed the cloth toward the sink. Who knows if she made the shot.

"Now your dress is wrinkled," I said softly against her lips.

"Shut up and kiss me." Who could argue with that? All I could think about was her warm skin, her lips on mine and every place our bodies met. I didn't want the moment to end.

Lucie pushed back a little to rest her forehead on mine, her breath moving in quick puffs. Then she looked into my eyes, shook her head, stood up and straightened her dress. She applied some lipstick, but watched me in the mirror, her eyes bright and her cheeks flushed. I stood and moved behind her to better see her reflection.

"You look guilty." I leaned forward to whisper in her ear.

"But we didn't do anything," she said in surprise.

"Then why do you look so guilty?" I asked half seriously and partly just to tease her.

She met my eyes in the mirror, very carefully put her lipstick back in her makeup bag, and turned to take ahold of a belt loop on each side of my slacks. Her eyes burned a trail from the last button she had undone, up my throat and then slammed into mine. "Because I want to and thought seriously about..." She stopped and I could see her swallow. Her words made my stomach clench.

"Lucie," I breathed and she looked away.

"I know how you feel. I shouldn't have said anything."

"It's not what you think, Luce. I want to, but I'm scared. I have all this responsibility and..." I huffed out a breath. "You know that guy in our class that has a baby due in January. I know he's pressing through to graduate early and his girlfriend is a senior... but I don't want that to be me... us. I'm sorry. I... I have to go to college and get a good job before..."

Lucie reached up to put my face in her hands. "I know," she said gently. "I didn't mean to pressure you."

I laughed harshly. "Yeah, that was all about you pressuring me. I didn't do anything. Good thing my hands weren't on your..."

"Oh stop. It's both of us. I'll try to behave, if you will." I just smiled at her and softly snorted. I closed my eyes for a moment and then moved in to kiss her. "We better get back before we're missed," she said softly.

"Yeah, before I do something really stupid," I said shaking my head. Lucie hugged me and moved toward the door. She opened it to find Mom's hand hovering in space ready to knock.

"Are you alright, honey?" she asked Lucie, gentle concern radiating from her.

"Yes, I'm sorry. I just had a weak moment, thinking about my... biological parents and the ones who more or less have adopted me... and I just lost it. Owen was doing what he usually does, picking up the pieces, but I got mascara all over his shirt and..." She flipped a hand in my direction, at a loss for further words.

A strange look passed over Mom's face and for a moment I thought I would get blasted but the look changed to a soft smile. "You both gave beautiful speeches today. I'm so proud of you. It feels like time is going by so fast. It was so strange to watch you walk down that aisle looking so grown up and... it wasn't. I feel like the future is racing toward me. I know we don't know what the future holds and I probably shouldn't have implied anything. I sure don't want to sound pushy or presumptuous."

"It's okay, Lila. I think there's a lot of that going on today. We have a classmate who made a bad decision and now... we just pray everything works out okay. There are some things even we can't fix. He and his girlfriend have a baby due in January. We were just discussing the major responsibility that is going to be for them." I had to give it to her, Lucie was smooth.

Mom hugged her. "I'm happy and sad for him and the baby's mom. It's the best gift you ever get, but you're right, it's a huge responsibility for the rest of your life. At such a young age, it will be a real struggle. Homework and little people don't mix. Who am I kidding? Babies and sleep don't mix, let alone homework," she ended with a sad smile. Arms still linked they moved into Sarah and White Eagle's room and then back toward the party.

I took a moment to look at myself in the mirror. I looked both old and young. My focus drifted to the mascara remnants on my shirt. Lucie had gotten out the majority of the stain. Now it was mostly just damp. I laid the washcloth on the edge of the tub, picked up my tie and took it into Lucie's room. I stopped to look at the piece of stained glass I'd given her and then at all the pictures she had up. Nearly all of them were of us, her new family. A Christmas photo, like you get in cards, of her old family in a formal setting with everyone looking serious was one of the few left from her old life. Another picture caught my attention – Lucie was in her gymnastics garb, a medal around her neck. She was smiling in this one but her parents still looked... strained. In nearly every picture with us, Lucie and the others in the photo looked happy. I could almost feel the joy. This was my Lucie, happy, smiling and knowing who she was and what she was meant for – not the sad, lost little girl of the before pictures.

I tossed my tie on her desk by the digital frame Marlo had given her a couple of years ago with its ever changing photos and wandered back to the party. I saw Sarah and White Eagle hugging Lucie. Marlo moved up next to me to watch. "Rough day for her, huh?

"Happy and sad - I guess you could say she's recovering from her former life," I replied with a half smile.

"Yeah, Bro, I see that. It hurts me to see her hurting so much. I love her too, you know. Not like you do but... If she'd just been born my sister instead of Sam's, it would have saved her a lot of heartache and pain."

"I know, Buddy, but then she wouldn't be our Lucie, would she?"

"I guess not," Marlo breathed on a sigh.

"The best part is we get her now."

"That we do. Come on, they're going to cut the cake and then the final serving and cleaning commences. I know how much you love that, 'cause cleaning is your second favorite thing to do."

"Oh yeah? What's the first?"

"The lip-gloss you're wearing tells me that kissing Lucie is high on your list," he deadpanned.

Lucie came to stand between us, linking an arm with each of us. We watched the care and dedication White Eagle and Sarah showed for each other. I swear, for a moment I could feel their love, soft, warm and enduring, wrap all around us. They delicately fed each other cake and smiled at each other. Their joy filled the whole backyard.

Marla took over the cake cutting so that Sarah and White Eagle could enjoy their guests. Marlo, Adrian, Brenda, Tess and Mitchell quickly scurried about, efficiently serving the pieces as they were ready. Marla brought our pieces to us herself.

"Marla, you really do run a well-oiled machine. I don't think I've ever appreciated it from the other side of your aprons."

"Thanks, Owen, you're pretty wonderful your own self. I've been very lucky to employ such fantastic people over the years, present company included." She threw an arm around each of us. "I'm so very proud of all you kids." She gave us a brief squeeze and then, in true Saggio fashion, rushed off and onto her next project before we could even reply.

It's fortunate that I'm not superstitious or I might have had a heart attack when Lucie caught Sarah's bouquet. She looked at me and quickly passed it to Mica, who gave her a strange look. Lucie turned to speak to her and I was distracted by Adrian who punched me lightly in the ribs on the way past as he wiggled his eyebrows.

Marlo's dad, Lucie and I all donned aprons an hour later to help clean the kitchen and pack up. Marlo's dad was his usual jovial self, laughing and joking with all of us. We let him wrap up all the leftovers. He has quite the knack for getting the perfectly sized container every time. For all I know the man can see geometry. I know where Marlo gets his brains and that is no slam on his mom.

Lucas wandered into the kitchen and looked around. It was clear to me that he was after more cake. I looked out at Mom. She looked up at me, cocked her head to the side and then shrugged at me in an 'oh well' it's a special occasion kind of way. Sometimes our near silent communication was handy. To bad it wasn't more reliable.

"More cake?" I asked on a sigh.

"Well, duh, Mrs. Saggio made it and I didn't try all the kinds yet."

Sensing my reluctance, she hip bumped me out of the way. "You're too stingy," she said with a wink for me. "You let Auntie Marla take care of you, Little Man. What kind would you like?"

Lucas rolled his eyes skyward to ponder. "All of them!" he began with a big impish grin. "But I already had the chocolate with marshmallow icing and the carrot cake with cream cheese. So I guess I'll just have the vanilla champagne with the raspberry preserves and white chocolate icing and the apricot orange with tangerine mango icing."

"Lucas, you're a connoisseur! You even called them by their correct names!" Marla bubbled happily.

"Word to Big Bird! I know good food and I want to cook with you when I grow up. I'm not gonna be just a server!" he ended, giving me a significant look.

"Oh, okay," I replied sarcastically, handing him a fork and napkin. "I'm only good enough to serve and not anything else? Who has made you over a thousand pancakes, my man?"

A shattering crash exploded behind us making Marla jump and nearly drop Lucas' cake. We turned to find Marlo standing motionless, a shattered plate at his feet and a far-off look in his eyes.

"Marlo, honey, what in the world?" his mom yelped in concern as she tossed down Lucas' cake and she and his dad converged on him.

Marlo blinked a few times and then his gaze shot to mine.

"Here, let me help," Lucie said as she grabbed Marlo by the arm and yanked him out of the room as his parents gazed openmouthed. She also sent me a worried glance. To cover their odd behavior, I quickly found the broom and began to clean. Marlo's parents had already picked up the biggest pieces. Mitchell hurried in the back door looking distinctly gray. I signaled with a slight tilt of my head to where Lucie and Marlo had headed. Mitchell bolted for the hall. The back door slammed again and Adrian stood there looking from me to Mitchell's retreating back. I shook my head at him but he just scowled at me and followed them anyway.

"Where did everybody go? We should be cleaning and taking care of the guests," Marla said, sounding bewildered. "How come only Brenda and Tess are working outside?"

"Uhhh," I said. *Come on, think,* I berated myself. *They're the ones working because they don't know what's going on. They can't feel it like we can. I wish I knew what's going on,* I thought, feeling grouchy. I dumped the glass shards in the trash and looked up to see Lucas watching me, his cake forgotten on the counter.

"You should go do your job," he said softly.

"I can't," I whispered sliding a look to Marlo's parents.

Lucas screwed up his face in thought but was saved from action by Mom and Alex coming in the back door. They looked from me and Lucas to the Saggios and back. I gave them a faint shake of my head and went back to work. I struggled to calm myself. I trusted Lucie and Marlo to handle whatever it was but I hated not knowing. Mom and Alex quietly donned aprons and began to help. Marla kept looking toward the hall. I could tell she was torn – to check things out or to let Lucie handle it.

Marlo re-entered the kitchen. To me he looked stressed, but I knew he was trying to hide it. His mom gave him a frustrated look. "What's your deal?" she begged half irritated and half worried.

"Everything's fine, Mom," he answered as he bustled over to the island where some food still waited to be put away.

"Well, I hope so. You've been a little odd lately, you must admit," she continued in the same tone.

"I'm a teenager – I'm still figuring out who I am. I'm supposed to be moody," he replied sounding just as frustrated.

"Mmm," his mom responded with an appraising look. "If you say so."

Uh-oh, not good. I thought. She's going to be grilling him later.

Fortunately, Lucie and the guys rolled back into the kitchen and set to work distracting her. "You all go," Marla said, waving a spoon dripping with suds at me, Lucie, Mom and Alex. Mom and Alex stayed but I took Lucie by the hand. The kitchen was almost too crowded to work in anyway. I looked at Marlo before I rounded the corner, but he nodded at me to go ahead.

Lucie pulled me outside and over to a quiet corner. She twisted her fingers into mine looking worried. "They're planning something. A bigger strike, it feels like. A number of them are joining together. Mars can feel it and so can Mitchell but it's hazy yet. Sometimes I think it's almost worse to know something bad is going to happen and not know what it is, than to either know nothing or know exactly what's headed your way. We feel so helpless. It's like knowing a train is coming and you can't get off the tracks."

"I agree but we have to be thankful that we have some kind of warning. Did you learn anything else?"

"Just the surge of darkness. Even when we tried to work together..." Lucie looked off and I could feel she was reliving what she had experienced with Marlo. "I don't like the unknown."

"I know, Sunshine," I said as I pulled her into a hug. "I know."

SIX

I was back at the White Eagles' bright and early the next morning to finish breaking down the rented tables and chairs. We also planned to restore the house and yard to normalcy.

When we broke for lunch, I hauled out Marla's leftovers while Lucie headed out to get the mail. She was all smiles and happiness today. I heard her walk in the house humming. I looked up to see her sorting the mail. A few envelopes in she froze and her hands began to shake slightly. Soon the other envelopes and mailers were flittering to the floor.

"Luce, what is it?" I begged. She ignored me to stare transfixed at the envelope left in her hands, before sliding a nail under the flap. I moved closer as she slipped out pictures of us working in the yard before the wedding.

She dropped them to the floor and turned to hug me. "Oh, Owen, they're watching us."

"They're trying to scare you, Luce. They didn't do anything yet. They're just watching and intimidating."

"It's working. I *am* completely freaked out. They know where we live. How can I sleep at night... knowing..."

"What's wrong?" White Eagle asked as he came in from the backyard.

Lucie started to reach for the pictures but White Eagle stopped her. "Let Sarah get her kit and process those before we get any more prints on them."

"Yes, of course, you're right," Lucie said, still sounding a little shaky. "White Eagle, they know where we live."

"I'm sure they have for a long time, but we live in a group so it's dangerous for them to attack us here." Lucie still looked fearful and uncertain so he added, "I have a few tricks up my sleeve and Sarah's crew monitors the premises here, Owen's house and the shop twenty-four hours a day. They didn't get in the shop last time and they won't get in here."

"No... That's not right. We had Devin at the shop, Clive got in there and so did Carmichael once," Lucie said, still sounding worried.

"We took Devin into the shop and Clive, dark as he was, was still a normal human. I have done some work since Carmichael snuck up on Marlo."

"Then how are you protecting us?" Lucie begged, interrupting.

"I have used some of my grandmother's old magic. Look around." Lucie's eyes went right to the feather-adorned arrowhead hanging in the kitchen window. "That's right Lucie, now that you know what you're feeling here, you can see it too. This is a talent that I will teach you. You are ready to learn it now."

"Me? Not Owen? He has the Native American heritage."

"Owen does plenty. I believe this is something that would be a better fit for you."

"But what is it? I feel safe and calm here but they... they don't, right? They would feel uncomfortable and agitated."

"See, I was right. This is a good fit with your locational gift. Your abilities are growing but you still have a lot to learn," White Eagle said with a gentle smile. I could feel how proud he was of Lucie and how much he loved her.

"What are you three up to?" Sarah asked as she came in the back door with her hands full of linens from yesterday. None of us spoke right way. She looked at each of us and then at the mail on the floor. "Time to go to work, huh?"

"I'm sorry, my love. This is your territory," White Eagle said gently. Sarah clicked her tongue and tossed her bundle onto the nearest chair. She pulled gloves out of the cabinet by the sink and snapped them on.

"Well, Lucie, I'd say you have an admirer, other than our Owen here. Why don't you call Marlo and Rick and we'll get this off to the folks who can get us answers," she said as she carefully looked at each shot and the envelope they came in.

My cell chirped before Lucie even had her phone activated. "Hey Mars. Were your ears burning?"

"No, why? Hey, I've got some information for you guys."

"Yeah, us too. Can you run on up here?"

"No problem." Marlo was gone without even a goodbye. With the speed in which he burst in the front door, he must have run the whole way. "Guys I got a hit on the girl *watcher* that disappeared from Madame Malvada's house in Happy Valley back in April." Then he stopped and looked at the four of us squatting around the mail. "Uh- oh."

"Yeah, we'll get to this. It's been four months. Geez, I thought finding her was hopeless."

"I deeply regret that it's taken so long. Mitchell and I have done our best," Marlo replied sourly.

"I know you have, Mars. I'm sorry too. You are very dedicated - I didn't mean otherwise. I just feel frustrated when we can't... never mind. I'm thankful that you have a line on her now. I'm proud of you and disappointed that Bob didn't come up with something. He has a whole team and around here *you* are the technology team."

Marlo blushed and waved me off. "She's alive but we need to move on this. How do you feel about San Diego?"

"Are you kidding me?" I asked, half pleased and half worried. This could be good for Lucie. It would get her out of here at least.

White Eagle and Sarah shared a glance. "Honeymoon?" they said simultaneously.

We filled each other in and got Rick called. He arrived with Joy in less than half an hour and our three favorite computer geeks got to work. Sarah, White Eagle, Lucie and I worked out a plan for San Diego with what Marlo had gotten for us so far. As usual the argument ensued – to call Bob or not to call Bob. He could be helpful but it was out of our territory. On the other hand the case had come to us. In the end I left the decision up to Sarah. She decided to call him after we were down there and it was too late for him to refuse. We would drive south so that we could leave more quietly and hopefully sneak up on Evilia's human trafficking network. What can I say? Marlo can find intel like nobody's business.

"Well, look at the bright side Lucie, it's a great opportunity for you to practice your driving," I said with a smile for her, trying to lighten her mood.

"Yay? Someday I want to go somewhere just for fun." I wrapped an arm around her shoulders and pulled her close enough to kiss the top of her head. She sighed and put her arms around me.

"Maybe we'll have time for the beach this time. You could bring your bikini." I laughed, but Lucie just raised an eyebrow at me.

"Always in the gutter."

"What?"

"Your mind is always in the gutter."

"Maybe you just bring out the best in me and it was you who promised to be good – not me."

"Huh," was her only reply.

Mom was fine with the plan but Dad took lots of convincing before he would let me go on a Honeymoon with Sarah, White Eagle and Lucie. He thought it was weird even though I tried to explain that it was really *watcher* business. I'm not sure that he completely bought that it was work and not for fun. It was also looking like I would not make football this year. Adrian would be pissed after all the convincing he'd done and Dad wasn't happy. Maybe... just maybe we would be back in time. Mom had agreed to register me and come up with a worthy excuse for my absence from the first few practices. I guess we'd see. I packed up my gear and headed back to the White Eagles'. We would be getting a super early start at oh dark thirty. *Oh boy. I love getting up at the butt crack of dawn to drive in the dark.*

I called Marlo from Medford for a status update. He had hidden himself away in his man cave that White Eagle had warded before we left. He was also in constant contact with Sarah's team. Together they were watching my house, the White Eagles' and now Marlo's. Adrian's house would also get a little extra attention. I called Mom from Sacramento. She seemed worried even though I knew Marlo was keeping her updated.

"Are you at your destination yet?" she asked.

"Come on Mom, really? We're on a road trip. There are lots of those."

"You know what I mean! Are you done driving for today?"

"Nah, we're pressing on a bit more before we call it a night. We have sixteen total hours of driving time and over a thousand miles on I-5 alone. Be patient."

"You want *me* to be patient. You're a hoot. Who's the one who usually lacks patience in this relationship?"

"You wouldn't be talking about me, would you?" I asked, trying not to laugh. "We're fine Mom, really. We drive for two hours, stop, rotate drivers and go again. Marlo mapped it all out including rest stops and food stops."

"I worry. It's my job. You need to be rested when you get there so that you can... face whatever you find."

"We know, Mom. Trust us."

"I do… I just… I wish I was there. So does Alex. We want to help and we feel like we can't."

"I know. If we need anything, we'll let you know. We just thought we should go in quietly. If we really need the help, I'm sure Bob can fly you in fast. Besides, someone has to take care of things at home. You will need to help Alex and I'm sure Marlo will assist if he can. He is monitoring us and the home front but knowing him he could squeeze in Alex."

"It's hard to let go. I love you."

"I know, Mom. Love you too," I ended, closing out my phone. Lucie smiled at me and then snuggled into my side. She closed her eyes with a sigh.

White Eagle pulled into a small hotel that Sarah had located with her tablet. We stayed in the car while she went in to register under a false name. She had a passport, an Arizona driver's license and credit card, courtesy of some earlier work for Bob. Our favorite spy was back in action. White Eagle and I had changed the plates on Sarah's sedan back in Medford while hiding in an alley. We were doing all we could to avoid Evilia's *dark watchers*. I even limited how often I felt for darkness. If we were being followed they were too good for us to detect.

We quietly snuck into our room and shut the drapes. Sarah put the TV on low and we all took turns getting ready for bed. Sarah was hard at work on her laptop while White Eagle used her tablet. They had gotten on some kind of secure Skype call or meeting with Sarah's team. Lucie was sitting on the bed nearest to me with her knees drawn up and her arms wrapped around them with her chin resting on top. She smiled at me and patted the bed next to her. Her nightwear was pink and orange plaid shorts and a tank top that didn't quite meet the waistband of her shorts. It was like looking at a mash up of her, Mom and Tess. She had twisted her hair up into a knot on her head.

"Rub out my neck, would you? I'm not used to so much driving and when I napped I think I slept weird."

"Sure, Luce." She didn't say anything as I set to work but I could feel her relaxing. She moved her shoulders around and sighed. I ran my thumbs down either side of her spine. She arched her back and I smiled inside. Lucie was like a cat. Sarah cleared her throat and began speaking to us. It was just as well; I was probably having way too much fun anyway.

"We'll be in San Diego by tomorrow afternoon. I just reached Bob and he has arranged a contact for us. We'll meet him at Miguel's on Coronado for lunch. I hope you're hungry for some fantastic Mexican fare."

"Sure, Sarah. Whatever you think," I replied.

When Sarah's attention was back on her laptop, Lucie turned to look at me, "I'm glad you're here."

"Yeah?" I smiled.

"Can't you feel it?"

"What, Luce?"

"Something bad happened here a long time ago. I can hear it like a faint whisper and then there's some other small stuff bugging me, like an itchy label in my clothes."

"Try to tune it out for tonight; we have other work to focus on. Just remember we can't fix everything."

"I know - it's just hard sometimes - like now when I'm tired."

"It's going to be okay. Have faith." I knew when she succeeded. Her muscles loosened and her head lolled. I tucked her in and then sat next to her until she was completely asleep.

Early the next afternoon we finally hit San Diego, headed across the bridge to Coronado and entered the restaurant as arranged. We were seated at a corner table like Sarah requested. It was near the restrooms but away from most other diners. By sitting with my back to the wall behind me, I also had a partial view of the kitchen. We left the seat open across from me and perused our menus.

A woman in her forties approached our table. She walked with purpose. Her dark hair was swept into a knot and held in place by a clip. She wore a filmy, multi-hued blouse over white capris and utilitarian sandals. Her nails were short, neat and unpainted on both her hands and feet. It was her face that was striking. Her eyes were an unbelievable dark brown and her brows dramatic. She had a prominent crease between those brows that I'd bet money came from scowling. She walked right up to our table without even looking around.

"You're the lunch date? I was expecting…" Sarah began.

"I'm your new best friend. Bob sends his regards and wanted you to know that you should take some time to daydream. Working all the time is bad for you." She had supplied the correct password but she looked nothing like the photo we had been sent.

"I'm skeptical," Sarah replied to let her know that the second password would be required.

"Of course you are. You were expecting Sam. He had an accident last night. He would want you to be sure to see the kitties at the zoo while you're here though." Sarah just stared at her, even when her phone vibrated. On the third buzz she snatched it up angrily. She activated it and held it below the edge of the table. I snuck a peek as our waitress arrived to take our drink orders and our guest slid into the open seat. A new photo from Bob was up. This was our new contact. Her partner would likely survive but he had taken a brutal beating last night courtesy of Evilia's monsters and was still in intensive care.

"I'm sorry for your loss," Sarah said with sympathy when the waitress left.

"It happens." I looked at her appalled. How could she be so callous?

Lucie squeezed my hand under the table. I took advantage of the moment and *read* our guest so that she could *see* her too. I felt the wash of White Eagle's power and knew that he was giving her the once over as well.

"I'm Talon."

"Talon?" White Eagle asked, his face set and his eyes shuttered. I couldn't even *read* him right now and I knew him well. I took my cue from him and adjusted myself never letting go of Lucie's hand. I opened my mind to Lucie and put my full attention on Talon.

"Yes, Talon." Her shoulders were back, her hands at her sides, and her chin was thrust slightly forward. She didn't like us nor trust us.

"First or last?" White Eagle asked, with a smile that came nowhere near his eyes.

"Just Talon," she replied with a frown. The rest of the room could only see the back of her head so she didn't have to put on the friendly face that we did. She was making it difficult to act like old friends having lunch but I got the vibe that she didn't care. She didn't want this to work.

"Oh…kay," White Eagle drew it out. "Like Madonna or Prince?" he added making her bristle. Clearly he wasn't happy. "I'm…" he started to add.

"I know who you are," she hissed softly and then loosened up a bit. "Look, I'm not trying to be… difficult." *Sure you are*, I thought sarcastically as she kept talking. "I have a cover to maintain. You may be trying to help these kids but I'm not throwing away years of work on some newbies I just met who think they have a clue. I'm glad they sent me some decent lures for once but you look too young to be seasoned agents. I know the brass is getting desperate but when you get desperate you get careless. I don't want you." Her voice sounded brittle and angry. We were caught in the middle of more than one problem here that was for sure. She started to rise.

"Lures?" Sarah asked.

"That's why you're here. You brought them to catch the traffickers. These two are the bait."

"We are here to rescue a specific girl. We were told you would help us," Sarah snarled.

"No," Talon spit back.

"We're not who you think…" I began as I forced my will upon her to trust us.

Her face softened but her words still held bite, "I don't care who you are. I don't want to know – it's dangerous to know. All I was told was to set you up as bait, but I don't think…"

"Bob told you they were coming in as bait?" Sarah asked, sounding angry and frustrated.

"Yes," Talon all but barked back.

"Give us a chance," I said boldly, still hitting her with all the *trust me* vibes I had. "We will exceed your expectations. We are more than meets the eye." *If we had to pose as bait to save the girl, we would. It wasn't a good trade off but this was our only ticket in.*

She stared at me for a long moment and then turned her brutal gaze on Lucie. "Fine. I'll set you up. You let them take you and we'll come in and clean them out."

"I need more than that," Sarah said with calm authority.

Talon turned to her with a venomous gaze. "I don't have to tell you anything. I only have to use them." Her eyes stayed on Sarah but her hand waved from Lucie to me.

"I'm the senior field agent assigned to this case. You can…"

"Not without prior approval," Talon snapped, interrupting her. "I'm in charge here."

"I see," Sarah replied grimly as she activated her cell and dialed. "Bob, please," she said sweetly into the phone as Talon glowered.

"Thank you... What are you playing at now, dear?" Her tone was friendly but her eyes were frigid and her lips were stiff. "I won't have it... You're wrong... Why do you have to make things difficult? ... I see... Just so you know, I would really like to tell you 'No' but that poor girl's life is in danger. If my children so much as get a hangnail out of this little game of yours, then I swear on my father's grave I will quit... You heard me... That leave of absence was about Owen, not you, you hypocrite... You'd get lots further with honey instead of vinegar, you jackal," she ended on a hiss and hit end with more force than was necessary. Now it was Sarah's turn to smile at Talon like White Eagle had.

I have rarely seen Sarah so angry. Lucie's eyes were wide. White Eagle came around to Sarah and kissed her cheek. Sarah's eyes stayed on Talon, her lips compressed and a frown firmly in place as she waited...

Talon's phone vibrated and White Eagle returned to his seat. Now it was Talon's turn to scowl in our strange battle of power that I suspected almost anyone could sense by now. "Talon," she tersely answered.

Our waitress appeared with our drinks and to take our order. Talon kept her phone clamped to her ear without saying anything to the caller. She put artificial sweetener in her tea as she listened and ordered cheese enchiladas. I hoped she wouldn't throw them at Sarah's pretty light blue top. I could feel the anger building in her. Finally the waitress left.

"What?" Talon barked low and menacing. "No way... Fine... I said, fine... Well screw you... If this gets wrecked there'll be hell to pay. I'm not losing any more agents... They don't have the right kind of experience... No, I don't know them and I don't want to... They look like kids." Her disapproving look now landed on me. "Yeah, that's it. They can fool even me... You're so full of sh..." Talon looked at her phone and then her eyes cut to Sarah as she put it back to her ear and she almost seemed to come to attention. "Yes, sir. I'll cooperate, but I would like it on record that I do not agree or approve of this decision... Yes, sir."

Sarah's cell vibrated and our lunch came. I guess they wanted us out of here. "How do you do?.. Yes, sir. I do, sir… I see… Thank you. You too." Sarah smiled the first real smile I'd seen. "Well it's all settled. Let's enjoy our lunch."

One thing was certain. The food was to die for… I just hoped not literally.

SEVEN

The second we had paid our bill a van pulled up to whisk us away. White Eagle relinquished the keys to Sarah's sedan and an agent from the van got in it and drove it away. We drove around in what felt like circles for almost an hour. No one spoke but the four of us watched constantly to keep sense of where we were.

The van finally pulled into an industrial looking area near the airport and into a huge warehouse. The doors closed behind us and Talon and the driver hopped out and opened the side door for us. She took Lucie by the arm. "Come on. We've got to get you prepped." Talon looked over her shoulder at me. "You coming, handsome? Or did you chicken out?" I jumped down from the van and squared my shoulders. "Looks like I'm stuck with you. My boss will send the file to your boss, Senior Agent Lando." She gave both White Eagle and Sarah another fierce scowl and marched Lucie into the room at the back.

I looked around, amazed. It was bigger than I expected. We had entered what looked like a full service salon, makeup studio and wardrobe worthy of any Hollywood lot.

Talon, still holding Lucie's upper arm, turned her to look her in the eye. Lucie's chin came up and I could feel the renewed tension snap through the air. "I don't know who you are, sweetheart, but whoever that was is gone now. From this moment until I say you're done, you are Salena Edwards, college student." She snatched a file off of the counter and thrust it at Lucie. "Memorize this and leave it here."

She turned to me. "And you are now Joe Phillips." She grabbed up another file and shoved it into my chest. "At least you look more like the guy I was expecting."

I saw Sarah and White Eagle talking to the man who had driven us in. They now had files in their hands as well.

"Candy! Juan! Transform them," Talon barked.

Candy took Lucie by the arm and led her in one direction and Juan came to stand before me. He flicked his dark head to the side and then turned and walked away, clearly expecting me to follow his skinny jean-clad legs and pointy-toed, high fashion shoes. Talon walked behind me grumbling so softly I couldn't hear. Juan handed me a bottle of special soap. I raised an eyebrow at him after doing a quick scan of the label to even determine what it was.

He sighed. "New, huh. Hit the showers and wash with that. Do your hair and body. It removes all the scents from your skin so we can start over. You'll find towels and a robe on a shelf in there. Come back out here as soon as you're done. We have *lots* to do."

I stepped through the door and looked around. It was tiled all in utilitarian beige and *shower room* was right. There was a row of sinks and shelves with towels. There was a hook by each shower. They had no curtains but each was separated by a partial wall. It looked like a sterile locker room without the lockers. I took a towel and a robe and tossed them on the nearest bench and began to undress.

I hadn't heard the feet but the inhalation of breath I did catch. I turned to look and found a startled Lucie. "I'm sorry. I thought… I must not be in the right place."

I heard a gruff chuckle behind her. "Oh no, honey, you're in the right place. Better get used to it. Where you're going, you're going to see men wearing a lot less than gorgeous over there. Now get showered. You've got ten minutes before we get to work on you." Talon turned and exited. She smiled like she was taking pleasure from Lucie's embarrassment.

Lucie and I looked at each other for a long moment. I shook my head, shrugged and stepped behind the partial wall to shed the last of my clothes. I adjusted the water and began to wash with the weird soap as I tried to pretend Lucie wasn't in the room. I couldn't decide what the soap smelled like. It held the aroma of herbs and medicine. It left my skin feeling tight and dry. I toweled off and reached for my clothes only to discover that they were gone. Only the robe remained.

I tied the belt as Lucie stepped from her stall with one towel around her hair and another around her body. She looked small but defiant as she snatched up her own robe, shrugged it on and marched out of the shower room. I saw Candy pull her into a chair and begin to comb out her hair. Juan waved me over to a nearby chair.

I sat as Candy was pulling out scissors. Lucie started to protest but clamped her lips together and looked at me in the mirror, anger shimmering in her eyes. Sarah came and stood off to the side with her arms crossed. Our eyes met briefly. Juan studied me for a moment, referenced some photos and then went to work. Talon came by for an inspection. "Buzz cut the sides but leave the top. He already wears it so short we can't do much. Maybe cut a pattern into one side. Also cut a brow so it gives the illusion of another scar. Any others you find on him see if you can hide with temporary tattoos or something."

I ground my teeth and said nothing. My hair was done before Lucie's. Juan hauled me out of the chair and took me into another room. He handed me a sheet and pointed to a table. Clearly he wasn't one for conversation. I wanted to smack him in the back of head with my robe but I figured it didn't pay to piss off the guy who was 'transforming' you. I lay on the table and covered up with the sheet wondering what this stage held.

Let me say that I greatly admire all the ladies out there for their courage with wax for the sake of beauty. I thought I was getting my temporary tats put on. Wrong. Give me a razor any day. As he yanked the last strip off my chest, Talon walked in. Now here was someone I could hate and I had plenty of resentment built up right about now with my chest and legs stinging.

"He looks different already. Reshape his brows a little more and add some highlights to his hair. I'll get the lenses."

"I don't need contacts," I growled at her. "My vision is fine." That woman was a good outlet for my grumpy attitude over the surprise wax job. When the warm wax goes on, it's not so bad. It's the ripping the hair out with a layer or two of skin that sucks.

"You do need them," Talon replied with a sweet smile that didn't come close to reaching her eyes.

"In case you haven't noticed, my eyes are dark brown and if you try to color them they'll look off. Even I know you can't cover dark brown."

"Is that your expert opinion, Joe? Have you even read your bio? How do *you* know what you know?" She smirked and left.

"I would think that you would appreciate our help," I bit back at her retreating form. Not to mention… when the heck had I been given time to read anything?

She froze for a moment and then turned. "Well, get over it. You are not what I asked for. We don't have time to set you up right. If this crashes down around my ears I'm taking you with me. Now finish up here and read your profile! We have a briefing in less an hour."

I seethed inside but I let her stomp away without saying anything further. Juan dragged me back to a chair and thrust a cap on my head and then used a hook to pull some hair through. While I was processing he applied the tattoos. I don't know about him but I thought I looked stupid when he was done. He took me to wardrobe and started pulling clothes from the racks and tossing them in a pile. He handed me underwear I would never normally wear and went back for pants. When he turned around he gave me a frustrated look. "What are you waiting for? We're almost out of time."

I gave my head a shake and ground my teeth. I dropped the robe and put on the briefs. He handed me skinny jeans in brilliant blue. *Yeah, not my thing – they must be Joe's.* Next he handed me a V-necked stretchy t-shirt in canary yellow. He gave me a thick gold chain to wear around my neck, black socks and uncomfortable looking pointy-toed shoes like his. Finally he handed me a black belt with a multitude of metal studs. It was then he noticed my watch. "That has got to go."

"It's important to me."

"But it doesn't fit the image. Wear this one." He handed me a modern looking digital that probably included GPS. I reluctantly put my watch in my pocket. "No! Get rid of it. You can't have it on you."

"Fine. I'll give it to White Eagle as soon as I see him." I was thankful that all that was Miles was now in my head but I still loved the watch.

When we came out I was seated in the chair again and he demonstrated the colored lenses Talon had left. He even pierced my ears while I was distracted with the lenses, the jackal. "Please tell me you aren't going to gage them!"

"You can take them out after the mission and they'll close. Be sure to keep them clean. You don't want to get an infection."

"Yeah, thanks." *Sarcasm, get me through the day.* Juan led me over to a full length mirror. I didn't look like me - that was for sure.

I followed him to a new door and he handed me my bio. "Good luck, kid."

I opened the door and entered a conference room that was oddly silent but I wasn't alone. A small dark haired woman sat at the end of the table reading. She looked up when I entered. I froze for a moment in stunned surprise. Lucie's blond hair was now nearly black, parted on the other side, layered and she had bangs. It also looked like it had been flat ironed or something. In her ears were large gold hoops and she had on more makeup around her now brown eyes than I had ever seen her wear. Her skin was browned beneath a low-cut top she wouldn't normally be caught dead in. She clasped her hands on the table and I noticed her nails were now long, squared off and painted bright red.

"Hello Joe," she said in a low sad voice I barely recognized.

"Hey, um… Salena. You look a little…"

"Yeah. I hope the color comes out. You on the other hand look hot, but in a weird way. I might grow to like the skinny jeans and fitted t-shirt, though. It's… I'm not used to seeing your body like this. You usually hide it under cargo pants and rock band t-shirts or leather jackets." I walked closer to Lucie and her eyes went wide. "They pierced your ears? Are they still alive?" she asked, nodding toward the other room.

"For now," I grumbled, touching a diamond stud. "I haven't had a chance to read yet. What have you got? How long have we known each other?"

"About six months. We're high school graduates about to start at two different colleges. We're out to have one last fling. According to this we are pretty superficial. You've been seen with other girls and Salena doesn't like it. She's hoping to win you back with sex and partying. Must be a match made in heaven… or hell," she finished under her breath.

I gave her my signature half smile. "So a lot of time spent in our room wouldn't be unexpected."

"Most of our time should be spent at the pool or clubbing. They anticipate we'll be taken from a club or at least near one and we need to be on display so that we can attract the right people." Lucie sounded very businesslike which told me she was panicking on the inside.

I gave her a sad smile and moved toward her to give her hug. "I know it's you under there, but you don't even smell the same."

"It's probably the spray on tan. My skin was the wrong color. You don't smell the same either." I could hear her sadness and worry.

"Keep breathing, little lady. We'll survive this."

"I hope so."

The door banged open and I spun around. "You read your bio yet lover boy?" Talon snapped.

"Yes," Lucie answered as I said "No."

She frowned darkly at me as others filed into the room. White Eagle and Sarah entered last, their worry palpable. We took our seats and Talon spoke. She activated a screen behind her. We all turned to face it as it flickered to life and the lights dimmed. "You are graduates from a high school in New Mexico. The name is in the bios. You met at school this year in physics. You're rich kids here to party and act stupid which shouldn't be hard for you. You will be provided with licenses, cash and cards to fit your image. You will check into a hotel set up by us. You are to spend time poolside and partying but don't get too friendly with others. Do make sure that people notice you. We will rotate agents so that someone is always watching you. You will never know who it is. We don't want you to get made so most agents you will have never seen before so that you don't make a mistake. Lando and White Eagle will remain at the command center with me. The four of you together would be too recognizable. I may let one or the other of them visit you if I deem it necessary and prudent."

She paused for breath so I took my moment and spoke, "Who chooses the hotel, clubs, etcetera? You, I assume and how are we to get there?"

"Yes. I choose based on the research we've spent… years gathering. We will provide the transportation. You will be given information as it is needed. If you are questioned, just stick with the basic story and that you haven't decided what all you will see and do in our fine city yet. The less you have to memorize the better off you'll be. Always mix lies with truth and the less you know - the less you can give away if things go south on us. Play it stupid. That shouldn't be hard for you either."

Talon and I glared at each other until one of her people cleared their throat. Talon resumed speaking, completely unfazed, "We will start at the airport. You will go in as two ordinary strangers and come out as Salena and Joe. You will receive detailed instructions in the car. Now go."

The others remained in the room as Candy and Juan took us back to wardrobe. Lucie put on a longer skirt over her miniskirt and added a jacket and hat. I slid a pair of larger pants over the ones I was wearing and added a hoodie. We were rushed into an older model unmarked sedan and were off. The driver was the same guy from this afternoon.

He met my gaze in the mirror. "There's turkey sandwiches back there for you guys. You aren't gonna get dinner. So take advantage. I put water back there that looks just like what you buy at the airport so you can take it in with you."

"Thanks," I said, meaning it. He was the first nice person I'd met in this department.

Talon hopped in the front passenger seat and we were off. Lucie only ate a few bites but she did drink some water. Any time her hands were free she was holding mine tightly. She said nothing and focused on her bio. I tried to do the same. I skimmed it three times, but it just wasn't sinking in. Talon was right that it was simple and basic. We pulled up at departures before I was ready. We handed our files to Talon and she gave us envelopes with our new IDs. We pocketed what she gave us and waited. She bit her lip for a brief moment. "Here are your new cell phones. Sarah has your old ones. If you dial 911 it comes straight to me. Good luck, you're gonna need it and don't you dare let me down."

"We didn't get to tell Sarah and White Eagle goodbye," Lucie whispered angrily.

"Don't worry princess; they're staying at the same hotel. They're arriving by a different route. Do not speak to them or acknowledge them in anyway in public or so help me I won't let you see either of them again until this is over, one way or another."

"Yes, ma'am," Lucie sneered - netting her another scowl.

We got out and the driver handed us our bags from the trunk and an envelope. He waved and drove off. Talon never looked back. I took Lucie's elbow and led her inside. We entered the airport and I pulled her off to the side. People were moving all around us on their own business and no one seemed overly interested. Other travelers were pulling out documents and arranging their gear so I opened our envelope and read the message, using Lucie as a shield to block it from curious glances. I let her read it and then wadded it up and stuffed it in my pocket. We turned and headed for the bathrooms by the security check point as instructed.

I entered the men's room and looked around. I walked to the last handicapped stall. It opened and a man stepped out giving me the expected two finger salute. I walked in and saw a suitcase of similar size but a different color. I took off my outer clothes and put them in the suitcase I had come with and pulled out the backpack from inside it to sling it on. I added the ball cap I was to wear to the hotel and took a pair of aviators from the side pocket of the backpack. I added my new license, cards and cash to the wallet in the backpack. The last thing I did was flush the note like I'd been asked. As soon as I was sure it was on its way I left the stall. The same guy watched me exit as he dried his hands. As I turned to go, I saw him dart into the stall before anyone else could take it.

I walked out to the hallway to wait for Lucie. She met me in full Salena guise from a crop top paired with a too short miniskirt, to four inch heels that made my feet hurt. The huge hoops were back in her ears and she now sported bright red lipstick to go with the nail polish. Brown lenses covered her beautiful blue eyes. To anyone else she would have been unrecognizable. I took her hand and we headed for the taxis.

"Number 831," she mumbled under her breath for my ears alone. I nodded and kept moving to the stand. As we walked she slipped on a pair of oversized sunglasses. I smiled a bit. They were very unLucie like as was the rest of the get up.

"So Salena, what do you want to do first?"

"Go to the hotel of course," she replied in that low husky voice. "Then we'll see."

I smiled at her. Nicely handled. A cab pulled up but it had the wrong number on it so I waved another group ahead and stopped to kiss Salena as a time filler while I waited for the right cab. "Here we go," I mumbled. I swiped at my mouth but her lips looked unmarked.

"Don't worry, Joe. It's kiss proof."

The driver of 831 hopped out, gave me a two fingered salute and popped his trunk. I helped him put the bags inside as Salena slid into the back seat. I took a quick look around before I climbed in. People had noticed Lucie… er, Salena but nothing felt wrong yet. Once we were on the move the cabbie removed his hat and straightened up. I realized it was the driver from before.

"Welcome back. I'm taking you to a Hyatt. Go to the front desk, you have a reservation. The bellman is not one of ours but your maid is. Regardless, don't trust anyone. The bellman you'll have to tip a couple of bucks per bag you have him carry. You've got cash, right?"

"Yeah, we're good," I replied trying to sound confident.

We pulled up and I lost some of that confidence. This was the nicest place I had ever stayed. Our agent – cabbie turned and shook my hand. "Good luck, kid. You're all set. Don't forget to sign your new name on that company card they gave you and don't flinch at the rate."

"Got it."

Lucie's, I mean Salena's, door was opened by a uniformed employee. I raised my eyebrows at our driver. He shrugged and gave me a slight shake of his head. "One if you want but no big deal," he said cryptically but I knew what he meant. I didn't have to tip this guy. I gave him one last smile and got out on my side.

The expected bellman was waiting by the trunk. "Sir?"

"The two bags," I replied like I did this kind of thing regularly. I slipped my aviators back on so that I could look around without being so obvious. My eyes were staring to burn from the contact lenses and watered from the sun in response.

We followed the bellman with our luggage up to the entry where the man that had opened the car door for Salena waited to open the door to the hotel.

"Thank you," I said quietly as I did a fast scan of the main lobby. Marble, brass, crystal and dark wood were present but nothing evil. By the way Lucie's head was cocked to the side I knew that she was running her own test of the area. She looked at me and removed her shades. It must have sounded okay to her.

"Come on Salena," I said soft and low and took her elbow to lead her to the front desk. I pulled out my loaner wallet and addressed the clerk. "Reservation for Phillips."

"First name, sir?"

"Joe, Joseph."

"Card, sir?"

"Here you go." I handed her the fake credit card I'd been issued and half expected it to blow up or at the very least be declined.

"Will you be parking a car with us?"

"Not this trip."

"Do you have a second piece of ID?" Uh-oh, here we go I thought as I pulled out the fake license and handed it to her. "I have you with us until the 19th, is that correct, sir?"

"That's correct," I answered using every bit of persuasion and charm I had learned from White Eagle as I leaned casually on the counter.

"I have you in a non-smoking room with a king sized bed and Jacuzzi tub. You have a partial bay view on the 22nd floor."

"That's fine," I said and she handed over the key cards to the bellman and we were off to be whisked away to our floor.

The bellman let us into our room and asked if we would like him to show it to us.

My sarcastic mind just thought, *Really? It's a room not an estate.* I told him we were fine. He couldn't take his eyes off Lucie in her Salena guise and it was getting on my nerves.

"May I suggest Acoustic Music San Diego, Club Fusions or Anthology for entertainment this evening?" He tried again in an attempt to spend more time with us.

"We're fine, thanks," I said, handing him ten bucks and looking pointedly at the door. All I could think about at the moment was taking out my stupid lenses to give my eyes a break, but Lucie was staring at the bed. The bellman took the hint and left. I put out the do not disturb sign, brushed past Lucie and fell over backwards onto the bed. I sighed and put my arms behind my head.

"Um… Are we supposed to be doing something?"

"Heck if I know, Luce. Nap maybe, so we're ready to go clubbing tonight."

"I thought we were supposed to get noticed."

I couldn't help but smirk. "The bellman noticed us or more specifically you… looking at the bed. Now he thinks we're up here with our clothes ripped off. The way he was looking at you, I'd say he was wishing he was up here."

"Uh…"

"Relax Luce, I'm not doing anything."

She mumbled something that I swear sounded like, "Maybe you're not the one I worry about."

I cracked an eye open and looked at her. With my eyes closed, listening to her, I visualized my Lucie, but when I opened my eyes a different young woman stood before me… one with a serious and speculative look on her face. "You know, you do look pretty…

fantastic. Just different," she said softly. I was having trouble reading her with the weird lenses in.

"And you aren't my Lucie. You don't look or smell the same but you sound the same and your mannerisms are mostly the same. Do you feel the same?" I asked playing with her a bit.

She approached me warily. I smiled at her. "I promise I'll be good." I closed my eyes and thought about getting up to take out my lenses.

I heard a thunk and looked over to find Lucie removing her other shoe to land with a thud by the first one. She gazed back at me; the look in her strange brown eyes was now making me wary. She bent over and rested her hands on my knees, giving me a clear view of the cleavage she didn't usually have. Obviously they had her in an amazing push-up bra and not what she typically wore. She slid her hands up my electric blue, skinny jean-clad thighs. I rose up on my elbows to meet her. She kissed me, but it was one of her more purposeful ones. She pulled my shirt free of my pants and slid her hands up my torso. She stopped and lifted my shirt to look beneath it.

"What did they do to you?"

I snorted softly. "They waxed just about everything."

"Why?"

"I don't know but it sure does make me look different."

"Well you're not alone. I think they waxed my legs clear up to my armpits and they did those too by the way. Have you ever had your armpits waxed?" She shuddered slightly. "They even reshaped and dyed my eyebrows. At least the dye is only semi-permanent. I would hate to look like this for my student body card photo."

"You're lucky then. My highlights are permanent until I cut them out or dye them. Adrian's going to go ape over them and then there's the pattern they cut into the side. I'm gonna look fantastic for school pictures." *Ah yes, my friend sarcasm again.*

"Let's see what else they did to you," Lucie said as she pulled off my shirt. "Any piercings besides the ears?" She sounded like she was joking but then her eyes widened as she noticed… "My God, they gave you tattoos?"

"Nah, they're only semi-permanent like your hair. They'll wear off. They didn't use any needles."

"Why tattoos?"

"Again, I think they want me to look different. They said something about covering my scars or maybe they just wanted me to look like Justin Bieber. His music sells and I bet young men that look like him are big sellers in the human trafficking market. It's all about creating an image just like when you model. We want them to be so busy looking at the outside that they don't realize who we really are. As costuming goes it's the best I've ever had and agent Ryer was pretty darned amazing."

"I can't believe we fell into this. It's dark all right and paralyzingly scary."

"We'll be okay, Luce. Someone has to save this girl."

"Who's going to save me?" I could hear all the fear, doubt and pain in her voice.

I reached out to run a hand up her arm. "Don't borrow trouble or worry for nothing. I'm sure we'll be given an update soon. Don't stew over the things you can't control."

Lucie still looked like she was tied to the tracks and could hear a train coming. She tossed aside my shirt, pulled out her big hoop earrings and took off her bangle bracelets. She tossed the jewelry at the nightstand carelessly and whipped her shirt over her head.

"Whoa, what are you doing?"

"We're in an impossible situation. I don't want some strange man to be my first. I want it to be you."

I sat up and pulled her down next to me. "Luce, we don't know that's gonna happen. They won't leave us with them longer than they have to. They'll pull us out before things get that far. I understand if you don't trust Talon but trust White Eagle and Sarah. They won't let anything like that happen to you and neither will I."

"You won't let anything happen on purpose but what if…"

I stood and pulled her into a hug. "Luce, it's gonna be okay. Breathe." I could feel the tremor in her body. She didn't have to tell me she was scared – it rolled off of her in waves.

"What if it's not," she persisted. "I want to be prepared."

"I'm not prepared. I have nothing with me and I don't think this is something you do because you feel desperate. Remember what Mom says, 'You can go forward, but you can't go back.'"

"I don't want to go back, Owen. Besides they injected me with all kinds of stuff. I don't know what half of it was but I know Depo-Provera was part of it. They gave it to me right in the butt. Too much other stuff went into my arms I guess."

"They injected me with all kinds of stuff too, in case we're transported out of the country. You can't count on what they gave you to be effective yet. I only got antibiotics, flu, tetanus, HPV, yellow fever and steroids. Yay! And if we're here long enough they'll find a way to get us another series." I couldn't keep the sarcasm out of my voice.

"How can you be so… clinical?"

"Lucie, I love you. I don't want to hurt you. When we do this we'll both be ready, not rushed and we won't be doing it for anyone but us. We especially won't do it because we are pressured from the outside…"

"But what if…"

"Shh," I interrupted. "Don't say it. It's going to be okay."

A sharp staccato knock vibrated the door. "Just a minute," I replied to the intruder. Lucie gave me a sad look, picked up her suitcase and top and headed into the bathroom. I went to the door and paused for a moment to sense the other side before I opened it.

"We interrupted something," Talon stated with a smirk. She shoved her way in with White Eagle behind her.

I gave her my best stink eye as she passed and left the door to White Eagle. "You wanted us to get noticed, right? We thought we'd hit the pool," I said just loud enough for Lucie to hear through the closed door.

"Good boy," Talon replied like I was a dog.

I heard a squeak from the bathroom and flipped my head in that direction as the door banged open and Lucie stormed out. Talon smiled but White Eagle's eyes only landed on the hand towel held over Lucie's front for an instant before he turned his head away. She completely ignored him and spat her wrath at Talon, "What is this?"

"I thought that was obvious."

"Where's the rest of it. This barely qualifies as an eye patch!" Lucie held up the smallest swimsuit I'd ever seen outside of an issue of Sports Illustrated. In fact it looked alarmingly like the one the cover model wore on the Sports Illustrated Swimsuit calendar Adrian had gotten me on my last birthday.

"That's it, sweetheart. Like I said, we need you to get noticed and we need it to happen quickly. We're on a timeline here. If we're lucky they'll take you in the next couple of days. I brought the next phase of your itinerary and don't think that because you don't see me, I'm not watching and aware of your every move."

Lucie and Talon eyeballed each other. "I won't wear it," Lucie said through gritted teeth.

"You didn't think we did all that waxing for his benefit did you?" Lucie's jaw dropped at her words. "You will wear that suit and you will get noticed. Be Salena, you don't have to be… you." Talon threw the envelope at me that I caught by reflex. She didn't even wait to see if I'd made the catch before she was headed out the door.

The silence stretched as the seconds ticked by. It was White Eagle who finally broke it, "You don't have to do this. Bob will just have to send someone else. If we lose Julie, then… blame me." I watched him swallow hard and felt his despair. I reached out and touched his arm.

"Yes, we do, White Eagle." It was Lucie who spoke the words that were on my tongue. "We don't have to like it, but we have to try. And just so you know - no one can make me like that woman. Why is she so mean?"

"We're on her turf. We're breaking into her case. She can't let herself get close to you. In her mind, she has to prepare to lose you so it won't hurt so much if she does."

"Well she'd find me a lot more cooperative if she was nice," Lucie growled.

White Eagle looked at Lucie like his heart was breaking. "Sarah and I will be watching for the other side. Don't be afraid to play your parts. We know who you are on the inside. We don't think Evilia is down here right now but this is definitely her show. It has her mark all over it. I don't know if any of her people down here are *dark watchers*. Marlo has determined, and sources here agree, that kids are taken, run down to Mexico and some on into South America, right back to her roots. It was a little careless of her really, but then Marlo is getting to know her well and can find her even when she's hidden from the professionals. I promise you, we will do everything we can to prevent them from taking you across the border. The shots were precautionary. We just need you to get inside so we can get to Julie."

"Julie? Is that the name of the missing *watcher*?" I asked.

"Yes. It is unclear how she got mixed up with Evilia. Was she drawn to the darkness or were they drawn to her light? She's from Salem.

Her day job was as an ER nurse, which I bet put her in contact with plenty of *watcher* business."

"Why do you suppose they kept her stateside so long?"

"We're not sure. She may be bait for us or she may have been difficult as *watchers* can be. It's possible she was used to feed *dark watchers* and this is a way of disposing of her or she may have some medical training and was forced to help them." As White Eagle talked about the *dark watchers* draining her, Lucie's hand went automatically to her chest where the faint scars from her near fatal draining remained.

"Don't be scared, Luce," I said quietly.

"He's right. You're not alone. You even have Marlo. He's really good, you know. He knew there was a missing person's report on Julie and he's somehow tagged that so his computer will alert him if any information pops up in the internet traffic. When certain criteria are met, he's alerted. Part of the reason that Talon's so bent out of shape is that we know so much about what was going on here. She's pissed that we have Marlo feeding us intel even before she gets it. What can we say? We've got the better guy. Julie is our priority. Talon's job is to bring the whole thing down. You two got stuck in the middle by Bob and Julie is just one of their many priorities. Talon cares, she's just built up a thick skin to protect herself and our team, including Marlo, is getting under it."

"I wish we had everyone here. I feel naked without our team… That was an unfortunate choice of words," Lucie ended blushing a bit.

"I agree, we could use Mitchel and Alex, but it just isn't practical," I added to cover for Lucie.

"Granted they aren't as good remotely but they are somewhat aware of what is going on here and they could get a message to us through Marlo," White Eagle said.

"I'm just glad my mom's not here to see this. She would flip a biscuit for sure."

"You two just remember that the outside is an act. On the inside is who you really are. Make them want you as a salable item and then we'll clean them out starting on the inside." Now there was the old familiar glint in his eye. "Oh, and don't forget to read your instructions. Then give them to me because we don't want them found in the room."

I slid a finger under the flap and read the brief message. Pool for 30 to 45 minutes. Nap until 8 pm. Get ready for clubbing. Tomorrow was wash, rinse and repeat except that we would add a visit to the zoo to look touristy. More instructions would follow. A special cab would be waiting for us each time we left the hotel as if we'd called the company ourselves to provide contact. An agent would always be about - we just wouldn't know who or where and they would not contact us. *Well, I might know who they were but I wasn't going to tell Talon that.*

EIGHT

White Eagle hugged us and left. We could both see the regret in his eyes for what we would have to do.

As soon as he left. Lucie tossed the towel onto the bed, looked at the suit still clutched in her hand, gave me a dark look and headed for the bathroom to change. I rummaged through my own bag while she was occupied. Periodically I could hear her mutter through the door. I found my own suit which was marginally better than hers but way lower cut than I was comfortable with. At least they were more of a board short style. I was grateful it wasn't a speedo.

After I changed I sorted and evaluated my gear. I wasn't happy. The clothes were fashionable but not fight worthy for the most part. The clubbing shoes alone were going to be slippery and make my feet hurt. James Bond I'm not. I don't fight in a suit. At least the skinny jeans had some stretch to them. There were no weapons but they had provided condoms. *How thoughtful.* I buried them back under the clothes. What did I want? What should I do? I looked at myself in the mirror. Who was this guy in the red, orange and blue Hawaiian print, super low-cut swimsuit? I pulled on the short-sleeved button up shirt and slid my feet into flip flops. I was just securing the room key in my pocket when Lucie finally opened the door.

She stood behind the door and looked at me around the edge. I watched her shoulder move up and down for a deep breath and then she yanked open the door before she could change her mind.

"I feel… naked." Her tone was a mix of disgust, irritation and something I was afraid to analyze too closely.

I tried to break the tension, "You look naked." Oops, bad choice of words. Her eyes had narrowed and then bugged out. One hand fisted and came to rest on her hip. "Okay, I'm sorry. Truly. It was a bad choice of words. I just wanted to make you smile, not make you mad. What there is of that suit is an amazing shade of raspberry that looks really good on you and you look like you belong on the calendar that Adrian gave me."

"I don't feel like me."

"You aren't you. You are Salena and she belongs in that suit. Remember we want to catch the eye of the traffickers and if I'm not mistaken you will catch the eye of every guy here from ten to one hundred."

"That's what I'm afraid of. I've gotten so used to blending in that… It just feels weird. The bottoms are too low in front and too narrow in back and the top… I don't have that much but what I do is showing on both sides. I guess I'll pretend that my spray on tan is a suit of armor."

"Breathe, Sunshine. It'll be fine. The good guys will be watching Evilia's minions watching us. If the armor idea doesn't work, pretend you're on the runway. Today you look like a celebrity."

Lucie twisted her hair into a messy bun and secured it with a clip. Then she put on her cover-up and I use the term loosely. It was a knit lace affair that you could see right through. She slid her feet into high heeled sandals, grabbed her tote and we were off. Everywhere along the journey people of both sexes stopped to stare. Lucie held her head high and looked as if the attention didn't faze her a bit but I knew it was killing her on the inside.

The pool was one of the nicest I've ever seen for its simple design. Plenty of lounges were occupied by sunbathers. Palm trees rustled in the breeze and flowers bloomed in profusion around the edges of the area. Lucie and I found a spot away from other people and settled in.

"I have to start out on my belly and work up the courage for exposing my front side. A bare back scares me less. Would you put some sunscreen on me?"

"Uh, yeah, sure, okay," I stuttered, entranced by all that bare skin. As I rubbed the lotion into her back she closed her eyes and tried to ignore the voyeurs staring at her.

"When I'm done, I think I'll swim a couple of laps, but I swear I'll keep my eyes open and on you... I mean the area... watching for people, watching you."

"They won't steal me off the lounge, silly. It will be in a quieter place like in a hall or an alley somewhere. It will be a place off camera. I think we're relatively safe here in the crowd and I don't hear any bad whispers either."

"You're right. At the moment... it *feels*... normal." At least around the pool was normal... what was going on inside of me was... well normal but now was not the time. I couldn't even form a coherent thought. Clearly I needed to swim because Lucie was filling my head and everything else was disappearing.

I dove into the cool water and felt myself begin to relax. Each time I took a breath in Lucie's direction, I watched her. People seemed to leave her alone. One brave man approached and spoke to her. She said a few words to him and pointed in my direction. He shrugged and moved on. I exited the pool, picked up a towel from the hotel stack and dried off as I approached her.

The sun kissed her skin, turning it the golden brown of lightly done toast. Her eyes were closed as she appreciated the warmth. Anyone else would think she was dozing but I knew she was fully awake and aware. "You should roll over or you're going to burn." I advised.

"Mmmm." She peeked at me through one slitted eye, the corner of her mouth turning up. She slowly turned onto her back. It was probably to make sure her micro bikini stayed in place but I couldn't stop my eyes from travelling over her and a zing from zipping through my nerves.

"Your suit is killing me. Everyone is watching you. I hate it."

Lucie closed her eyes and giggled softly. "Jealous?"

"More like nervous."

"I thought you said it was a good idea for the bait to look appetizing."

"You are that alright," I grumbled.

Lucie smiled at me, sat up and reached into her bag for her sunscreen. I was transfixed watching her as she rubbed it into her face and legs. Then she began on her arms. "You want help?" I asked wiggling my eyebrows at her.

"That's probably not a good idea," she answered turning her head away from me so that she could look at me out of the side of her eye. I watched her scan the pool area and then turn to face me. "The back I couldn't reach, but the front I can. I'm supposed to be bait, remember?"

"Maybe I'll make them a little crazy," I grinned.

"Them… me… or you? Fine. Here." She handed me the sunscreen. "This is a terrible idea."

"From my end, it's looking fantastic." I couldn't stop smiling as I started with her shoulders. I worked my way down her arms to be sure she hadn't missed any spots. She swung her legs back up onto the lounge and laid back and then I started on her chest, running my fingers under the edge of her suit top. None of her skin would burn on my shift, especially the parts that had never seen the light of day before. I looked at Lucie's face. Her eyes were closed and her jaw clenched as she tried to ignore me. I smiled, knowing it wasn't working.

I put more sunscreen in my hand and moved on to her ribs and down her waist. I hit her belly button and she twitched. I worked my way down to her hipbones and the space between. When my fingers brushed the edge of her suit bottoms I felt her muscles quiver and she growled at me, "Stop."

"Yep, I think you're right. I feel like we got someone's attention. At least one person is wishing they were me." I leaned forward to drop a kiss on her nose and then rolled onto my belly. I needed to reign in my hormones and sense the area anyway. I scanned it in quick bursts so that I would be more difficult to pinpoint. I couldn't find the source but I felt it. At least the wash of dark intent got my mind off Lucie for the moment. What I wanted was one thing, but what this guy wanted was… wrong. Now my jaw was clenched.

"I don't feel comfortable. I want to go back up."

"Give it ten minutes, Salena. Please," I said as I opened one eye to look at her.

She frowned at me but relented. "Fine, tell me when you're ready to go."

I checked the time on my cell and waited for something to happen. Other than feeling malicious eyes on us, it was quiet at the pool. I still couldn't figure out which of the many pool guests held dark ideas, but it was someone towards the building. I checked my phone again. It had only been seven minutes but I couldn't stand it anymore either.

"I give up. Let's go back up to the room." I sat up and slipped my shirt back on as I slid my feet into my flip flops. Lucie sat up and reached for her cover-up. I watched every motion she made, my eyes Velcroed to the fabric of the cover-up as it slid over each bit of exposed skin.

Lucie reached out and swiped at the corner of my mouth playfully. "I do believe you were drooling, Joe."

I smiled and took her hand. She gathered her tote and I picked up the hotel towels to dump in the used towel bin on the way to the exit. We walked to the elevator like we didn't have a care in the world. We were lucky enough to get a car to ourselves so I pushed her into the corner away from the camera. I put my hands on her waist and pretended to nibble her ear. "So tell me, Salena," I whispered. "What took so long in the bathroom earlier?"

"I... uh... was going through my stuff and... I... the clothes make me uncomfortable. I was hoping for another swimsuit to surface and then I tried to stretch this one and squeeze as much of me into it as I could. I know what they're trying to do. I'll do this for Julie but I miss... my life. This isn't who I am."

The bell dinged to announce our floor. I once again took Lucie by the hand and we walked down the hall to our room. An older gentleman stared open-mouthed at Lucie until his wife hit him. All I could think was, *yeah, fella, I know how you feel.*

Lucie watched me pull the key card from my inside suit pocket. I guess it was only fair after the attention I had given her. I put it in the lock and turned the handle as she reached out to touch me. At the moment her fingers connected with my skin I felt something else... a presence in our room. I pushed her behind me and put my full attention on my other sense. I knew that presence.

Sarah sat in a chair by the window. Her body language screamed upset but she was trying to hide it. I heard the door click shut behind me. Her eyes looked hard and determined. Her voice was grim when she spoke, "Lucie, go take a shower. I want to speak with Owen."

"No." Sarah snapped her attention over to Lucie, looking completely taken aback. "I know why you're here. You've been sitting here worrying and trying to decide how to say what you think must be said. Don't look so surprised. It's a strong unhappy emotion you're exuding. But, Sarah, you've got the wrong guy, so to speak."

Sarah continued to stare at Lucie. I looked back and forth between them, light beginning to dawn. I started to speak but Lucie shook her head at me and continued, "Sarah, this is my fault. I tried to... seduce him."

"That's not what I saw at the pool. This is going too far. You used to be sweet and innocent. I have allowed you to be put in this position. I saw the form you signed, Lucie... White Eagle signed Owen's and we got a signature from his mom but..."

"Sarah, it's okay. What Owen did at the pool worked."

"For who?" she asked sadly. "For him? For you? What were you going to do when you got back up here? You may not look like you on the outside but don't forget who you are on the inside." For a moment I thought she would cry but she turned to me and went on, "Owen, what would your mother say? And Lucie, Depo-Provera is only immediately effective if you have it injected during your period. They just wanted to protect you from as much as they could in case things went terribly wrong. Why do you think Talon's the way she is? She's never used anyone under twenty-one for something like this before."

"And here I thought she was just naturally bitchy," Lucie bit back.

"Ladies, this is getting out of hand. Relax Sarah, nothing happened except we got someone to notice us. I couldn't spot them but I felt them. Someone in the pool area had some very dark thoughts."

"I feel like I need to pull the plug on this. I'm sorry for Julie but I can't… I won't… ruin you both to save a stranger."

"Sarah, no!" Lucie and I spoke as one.

"We can do this," Lucie added.

"That's what I'm afraid of," Sarah answered softly.

Lucie gave her a firm look. "Don't blow our cover. Please. Give us a chance."

"I…"

"Sarah, please," Lucie begged. "Trust us."

"I want to… On all counts… but I know what can happen…" she sighed. "Fine, I won't stop the use of you as bait but I'm sleeping in here tonight and Owen can bunk with Earl."

"That alone could blow our cover," I said trying to sound both soothing and calm.

"Take it or leave it, young man. I saw you at the pool and could feel the flood of hormones from here. No one's that good of an actor.

It's only a matter of time and bad choices will not happen on my shift. Of course I blame that thoroughly inappropriate swimsuit they never should have given you to… almost wear."

Lucie again took the bull by the horns, "A part of me wishes you could have heard what he said to me earlier. You wouldn't doubt him so much. I don't know why you think it's all him anyway. You really are old fashioned if you think I couldn't want… things…" Lucie trailed off and went to stand looking out the window.

I looked at Sarah and then walked over and put a hand on Lucie's neck. I loved Sarah but it was clear where my allegiance lay. She was stepping over the line as to what was her business in my humble opinion.

Sarah sighed again. She didn't say another word but turned and walked to the door. With her hand on the knob she finally spoke. "I do know," she said so softly I could barely hear her. Before I could reply she left the room and closed the door behind her.

Lucie tilted her head so that she could capture my hand between her shoulder and cheek to squeeze it gently. "I've disappointed her."

"She'll forgive us. She thinks she needs to be our mom and she's taking her job very seriously."

Lucie turned into my arms and held me tight. Before I could fully formulate even one bad idea, one of the new cell phones rang in her tote. She looked at me and scowled before she turned to answer it. "Hello?… yes… okay." She hit end and turned to me. "We have forty-five minutes to change and be downstairs to get picked up. Yay? I'll take the first shower and then do my hair and make-up out here while you have your turn."

I nodded at her, feeling tired and sad. I'd rather stay in and watch a movie but we had work to do so I turned to my suitcase of costumes to figure out what to wear clubbing. Maybe if I'd ever been to one, I'd have a better idea about what was in style. Most of the choices were about the same but a black pair of pants, shinier than the rest was probably meant for tonight. I found a shirt in a weird black fabric that I could almost see through and found a lightweight, short, fitted jacket. This was just all so… strange. I'm no fashion expert. I'd rather be comfortable and able to move.

I turned the TV on and had just sat on the edge of a chair when the bathroom door opened. Lucie stood framed in the doorway in a beautiful, but scary dress. Her hair was wet and combed back, her skin bare. It gave her the illusion of a mermaid. The top of the lavender dress had lace cups with a sheer fabric twisted at her ribs to curve around the cups and then went over her shoulders to attach at the back above her waist. The rest of the lacy bodice was fitted down to her hips where more of the sheer fabric swirled to make a skirt that ended several inches above her knees.

"Lucie, you're lovely but where's the rest of it? Did you leave off a skirt or something?"

"Funny."

"No really, how will it stay up when you try to dance?"

"It's fine. The bodice is held in place with boning."

"With what?"

"Stiff plastic strips that are sewn into the fabric and I used some special tape like models use. Now go shower and get dressed. I need to do Salena's hair and makeup."

I finally noticed the shoes in her hands along with all the other stuff she was holding. "You're gonna wear those shoes? They may be beautiful, sparkly sandals but they look painful."

"I see that look in your eye. I'll fight barefooted if I have to but I have to look the part. Besides I'm counting on you."

"One thing is for sure, you will get noticed in that dress. You look… you look like you belong in an advertisement or on the red carpet or something."

"You did notice the hair, right?" She shook her head and smiled. "Try that line again after your shower, when I have my hair and makeup done."

I gave her a grin and headed into the bathroom. I had lots to think about. I needed to figure out where I stood and sort out all the conflicting voices in my head.

Lucie was just finishing her mascara when I stepped out of the bathroom. Her eyes looked huge with the added makeup. She blew on her nails with lips painted a dark sparkly cherry color and then her eyes met mine in the mirror. Seconds passed before she broke contact to pick up her cell and check the time.

"We should go."

She was not in the mood to talk, that much was clear. I pulled on my jacket and pocketed my loaner cell phone and wallet. Lucie stood and straightened my collar. Maybe she wasn't mad at me after all.

"You should lose the tie and unbutton the top three buttons." With her hands on my lapels she fixed her gaze on my tie, deep in thought.

"Luce, we should… talk."

"Not now. Later. We'll talk later. I promise. I need to focus on the job now and not… get into anything else."

My cell vibrated. I checked the read-out. The text read, "Cab #628 ETA 2 min. Be there."

"We gotta go. Cab number 628 this time."

Lucie took my hand and we left the room. White Eagle was sitting in the lobby sipping coffee and reading the paper. I glanced at him and then away. I knew he saw us but he gave nothing away either. A surprisingly cool breeze blew in the front doors. The strange malevolence from the pool whispered past my senses and Lucie gave a slight shiver. I was afraid to look at White Eagle. I tried again to send out a quick shot of power to get a sense of direction from our adversary. Whoever it was, they were near. This felt different. This was not a *dark watcher* but it was definitely someone with evil intent.

Lucie almost stumbled when we hit the threshold. I was glad I had her hand to keep her from falling in her crazy shoes.

"May I call a cab for you sir?" The doorman asked.

"Already covered, thanks."

"Have a good evening, sir."

"Thanks, you too."

The sky had grown hazy and dim. Colors glowed in the west throwing the palm trees into black relief against the glowing sky. Headlights flashed in the drive and the cab pulled into the portico. I checked the number - 628.

I opened the back door to find Juan in the driver's seat. "Evening, sir. Club Fusion?" he said loud enough for the doorman to hear.

"That's right," I replied as if I knew.

Once we were on the road I had to ask, "So… multipurpose today, are you?"

He chuckled, "Yeah, I'm actually here to check your wardrobe. You guys did fine by the look of you. I hear you got some attention at the pool. Good work."

"Thanks?" Lucie replied with a sidelong glance at me.

"You'll visit two or three clubs tonight but you won't see me again. The next cab will be 330 and you will catch it at 10:30 pm on your left as you exit. Wipe your text and call records before we get to the club. Good luck."

Juan dropped us at the first club. I sighed inside and thought, *here we go*. I looked at the line and it wasn't as bad as I'd expected. As we walked to the end, Lucie got all kinds of glances both admiring and jealous. I could feel my hackles go up but tried to look superior.

Inside, the club was darkened with only touches of sparkly lights. I realized that the lace portion of Lucie's dress had crystals in it to catch the light. Just one more way to get noticed I guess. We checked my jacket. Lucie would not let them check her small beaded bag but instead drew out a strap and slung it from shoulder to opposite hip.

We headed to the dance floor joining the crowd that was enthusiastically gyrating around. The crush of people, noise and flashing lights pounded at my senses. Even my *watcher* skills were feeling a little… maxed out. Back in eighth grade I would have shut them off but the stakes were too high tonight. As much as she faked that she was having the best time ever, my purple princess was giving me the vibe that this was a bit much for her too.

I scanned around the room and found a clock near the bar that I could use to track time instead of constantly pulling out my cell phone. One hour. I can do this for one hour and then I'd set a plan for the next phase of our adventure.

By the time 10:25 rolled around I was ready to call it quits. I had been groped, fondled and rubbed on by people I didn't even know and I was pretty sure they weren't all women. Lucie had gotten pretty skillful with her elbows and heels. My mistake – those high heels were a smarter choice than I'd realized as more than one would-be admirer walked away limping and cussing. I'm pretty sure a pickpocket left with a broken finger. That's my girl.

The cab was right where Juan said it would be just after we walked out the door so someone was obviously watching us. A new driver gave me the two fingered salute as we sat and he pulled away from the curb. A screen activated in the back of the driver's seat. Talon appeared looking angry which I was beginning to believe was her normal look.

"Try harder," she barked. "You aren't going to pull this off if you break any more toes or fingers. It's not very Salena-like of you and I know *you* at least read the bio. Think of yourself as a model not a martial arts champ!" Lucie scowled at Talon's image on the screen as she delicately snorted and crossed her arms over her chest defiantly.

"I didn't get much negativity from that spot. Are you sure it's active?" I asked to get the spotlight off the steaming Lucie.

"We know what we're doing. The next one is more likely but it would be too obvious if you went there first, now wouldn't it! Driver, are you being followed?" Talon spat.

"No ma'am," the driver replied in a calm serious tone.

"Damn. Have some water, you two, but leave the bottles in the cab."

"Talon, I need to pee. Can we stop?" Lucie asked as she reached for the water.

"Go at the club. That could be a place you are taken from. Have handsome wait outside the door for you and I'll place a female agent to spot any activity."

"Why place an agent? Don't you want someone to try to take me tonight?"

"I would like nothing better. Trust me, but that is not where they usually take victims from. The hall near there yes, the bathroom itself, no. We don't know why. They also seem to follow people for a few days before they make their move. This would be too quick. Just so you know, when they make their move it will come fast and hard. I just want eyes everywhere."

"Ma'am! We are being followed. Dark blue sedan."

"Fantastic. You're better than I thought. I was afraid they'd lost interest."

I looked over and squeezed Lucie's hand as the screen went blank.

"Hey kid," the driver called. I swung my eyes to meet his in the rear view mirror. "Last cab tonight will be five blocks north of the club. Leave the club at 11:48. You'll be watched and followed by an agent. Hail the cab that comes by. It will flip on its duty sign half a block from you. Got it?"

"Yes."

The cab pulled to a stop. Lucie sighed, gave me a tired half smile and we were off again. This line was shorter than the last one but the patrons were no less aggressive. I guess they thought in the close press and low lighting, they could get away with stuff they wouldn't normally think was acceptable. The last club had pounded at my senses but now I was figuring out what to pay attention to. In some ways it wasn't so different from school where a barrage of teenage angst buffeted me daily.

I could feel how tired Lucie was when a slow song finally played. She held me close, letting me take some of her weight. I ran my fingers over her back and nibbled her neck. A wave of aggression and lust rolled into me like thick fog coming off the ocean. This was not the person from the pool area. This... scout was doing more than just watching; they were formulating a plan. I had a direction pinpointed by the way feelings pushed into me. I looked around and felt their gaze shift from us so I tried another idea. I whispered in Lucie's ear and connected with her. I processed the sounds she was picking up. Three people had been taken from this club. Lucie could distinguish their frantic, frightened voices. I tried to take my mind off that and put it on our current perp. I turned us a little more. With Lucie's arms around my neck it would give them a great view of her semi-exposed side. That ought to up the stakes a little.

"Hang on," I whispered. "I'm going to draw the *wrong* kind of attention." She gave me a slight nod. I drew my hand from her back to her side and then slowly ran my fingers over her skin, placing my palm almost on her crystal covered cup. As my hand moved I could feel a burst of attention that steadily grew more intense. It almost felt like I was in a movie and we had been targeted by missile lock. Someone hated me intensely. Jealousy and lust pounded at me with an almost physical affect.

"You're going to earn us more Sarah time," Lucie warned.

"It may be worth it. Feel that?"

"Your fingertips under the fabric of my dress or the sense that we're being observed by a hungry lion?"

"The lion thing. With the tape, I couldn't get anywhere even if I wanted to."

"Whoever's watching doesn't know that and at least the dress stayed in place. I sure hope we don't get snatched tonight; the dress and shoes are pinching me. I'd rather be you."

"You think my shoes aren't pinching my toes? Did you look at these things?"

"Owen?"

"Yeah?"

"It's not a man. It's a woman that's watching us and she's headed this way."

We rotated again and I caught sight of someone who looked slightly out of place. She was older than the average patron and looked… harder somehow. She didn't look directly at us but eased her partner near. Her red dress pulled at my attention, but I knew that was the part that could change. She wanted people to remember the dress because she wouldn't use it again. I tried to focus on her height, weight and build. She was tallish, maybe five foot eight inches and wiry. She knew how to handle herself. She had confidence. Today she was a brunette but that didn't feel right.

I moved us closer as if by accident and we rotated again. The tempo of the music increased and I changed my position to pull out some *Dirty Dancing* moves, thank you Miles and Patrick Swayze. The woman's eyes locked on us for a brief moment that seemed to warp time and slow it. I watched in slow motion as her eyes slitted, her jaw locked and her face turned feral. Her nostrils flared and I knew I would never forget her face or the look on it. This is how the zebra feels when he knows he's been singled out by the lioness.

I turned again to pretend that she was one of many in a sea of people I was ignoring but it didn't keep the chill from racing along my spine, my mind from screaming or the powerful urge to run. I took hold of my fear with both hands and forced myself nearer. "So Salena, what do you want to do tomorrow?"

"I want to sleep in," she giggled convincingly. "And then I want to go to the zoo. You owe me a real dinner and then maybe we could try this club again? I brought another dress."

"Whatever you want, Princess," I replied just loud enough for our stalker to hear.

"Let's go back to the hotel, Joe. My feet are tired. Be good and I'll let you rub them," Lucie whined in an unLucie-like voice.

I checked the clock I had located in this establishment. She was good. We'd made it to 11:40 and had just enough time to make it back to the entrance. We eased away from the woman in red and off the dance floor. I retrieved my jacket from the coat check and ran my hands over it to see if there were any obvious bugs.

We stepped out into the cool night and I put the jacket around Lucie's shoulders. She pulled it close and took my hand. As we strolled to the pickup point I watched the window glass of the surrounding businesses. Sure enough, I caught a flash of red. I pulled Luce closer by her neck and whispered, "Be ready to run."

We hit block number three. I didn't want her to catch onto our cab ruse. Did I dare ditch it? It would be hard for us to run in these ridiculous shoes. At block four I saw her reflection again in the glass of a closed shop. She was closer and she wasn't alone. We stopped at the corner for traffic to pass.

The light changed and we crossed the street. The woman in red and her partner were almost upon us. Lucie and I continued on, I heard a vehicle and turned – not our cab. It was too soon anyway. The sound of another engine approached so I looked again. A cab was coming. It flipped on its light to *on duty* so I made a snap decision and hailed it.

The woman and her partner walked on past us without a glance and I sighed in relief. Lucie and I crawled in. "To the Hyatt, please," I said as I shut the door. The screen behind the driver activated. Lucie quickly flung my jacket from her shoulders and over the screen as she leaned forward as if talking to the cabbie.

"What are you doing? Talon growled.

"If you're smart, you'll shut up for a moment," Lucie barked right back. To my amazement she did. Two blocks and a corner later, Lucie took the jacket off the screen.

"What was that about?" Talon inquired more calmly than I expected.

"We were followed out of the club. I didn't want them to see you on the screen," Lucie said sounding exasperated.

"You're mistaken. It was just another patron."

"You're wrong," I replied firmly.

Talon snorted. "And that's your expert opinion?"

"I think you should have a little more faith in us. We aren't as green as you seem to think we are."

"Whatever. My agent didn't see anything unusual in the behavior of the couple who walked out of the club behind you and happened to go in the same direction."

"Did you run a profile on them?"

"It takes time and money to do that stuff, kid. You've been watching too much TV."

"I'm telling you – the woman in red is the one you want."

"Alright, I'll bite. What makes you think so?"

"She was out of plac…"

"Did you snap a picture?" Have I mentioned how much I hate it when people ask you a question and then interrupt you before you can even answer?

"Of course not! That would have been…"

"How do you expect me to process…"

"I've worked with sketch artists before."

"Fine!"

"Fine!" My reply had come too late. The screen was already black. I resisted the urge to punch it. Lucie took my hand, brought my knuckles to her lips for a kiss and then she shook her head at me. *Let it go*, her eyes said.

We pulled up in front of the hotel and our cabbie turned. "Be down here ready for the zoo at 10:00. Cab 144 will take you there and give you further instructions."

"Got it," I said tiredly as we got out and headed for the door. This time the lobby was empty except for the doorman and one clerk. Lucie pulled off her shoes and I wished I could do the same. We moved off to the elevators and rode to our floor. I fully expected Sarah to be in the room but it was empty. I fell into a chair and pulled off my shoes and socks. "You can have the bathroom first." It came out sounding as weary and tired as I felt.

"No, you go first. It's going to take me forever to get out of this makeup and tape."

"No, really. You first. I'm expecting Sarah. Take your time." Lucie gave me one sharp nod, spun, stepped into the bathroom and closed the door behind her with a soft click.

The minutes ticked past. I found something to sleep in and clothes for tomorrow's adventures. I could hear water running in the bathroom and still no Sarah. It was almost 1:00 in the morning and I began to wonder if she forgot, which I found nearly impossible to believe, or if she had fallen asleep, which was also extremely unlikely.

Just as Lucie was opening the bathroom door a knock sounded but not from where I expected. This came from the connecting door. Lucie and I looked at each other for a beat. Then I turned my attention to the other side of the door. I moved forward to answer it.

"What took you so long?" Sarah asked with a frown.

"I'm being cautious." My response was a little abrupt but I was beginning to fight a headache. I could feel my neck and back tighten with tension.

"Are you alright?" Her tone had changed to one of worry.

"Yes – no – I'll be okay."

"Go get ready for bed next door. Maybe Earl can fix you." I realized Sarah was wearing a robe.

"I didn't know you guys were next door."

"We weren't. We were on nineteen but Marlo hacked into the hotel's guest registry and initiated a chain reaction that put us here."

I was too tired to argue much. "You don't think this will blow our cover?" The frown reappeared on Sarah's face. "Just asking," I added snappishly.

"We have a team meeting at eight. To get there, you will go for a jog and Lucie will go for a nail appointment. The nail studio's back room is where we're meeting. Lucie will be picked up by a Pampered Princess Limo at 7:40. Owen, you have a route map to memorize." *So NOT awesome.*

I picked up my stuff, sent Lucie a half smile and slunk into my new quarters. At least this room had two queen sized beds. I washed off the sweat and stink from the clubs. Nothing against the clubs; they're just not my thing and all those people packed together… I crashed on the nearest unoccupied bed and was out.

NINE

Moments later White Eagle was shaking my shoulder. I was amazed to see that it was 7:00. I stumbled into the bathroom and then dressed in running garb. My left ear was grumpy from the piercing. It was red and warm to the touch. I swabbed both ears with cleaner, took the protein shake White Eagle offered and studied my route map. He was shooing me out the door before I even had it all locked in my head. I recited the street names all the way down in the elevator and out the door. I started at a brisk walk, but the minute I was out of sight of the hotel I whipped out the GPS app on the phone and checked the route as I stretched. I put in my ear buds as if I was listening to music, but I was really listening to the automated GPS voice instead. *Do I know how to have fun or what?*

I felt my surroundings. No one was on to me yet. Maybe it was too early even for bad guys. I began to jog, making sure to run through the places where cars could not go. Right now was not a good time to pick up a tail. I turned a few more corners and cut through a business where I paused to detect dark energy one more time. Then I took a moment to wipe everything I could from my phone before heading out the rear exit and over to the back of the shop across the alley and next door to the Pampered Princess. The owner of the boutique let me in after only one knock. She looked at her smart phone and then back to me before she moved aside to let me in. As she was locking the door I realized she had a gun in the hand that had been out of sight.

She pulled me into a storage area and moved a stack of boxes to uncover a small door. It was a dumbwaiter. I hoped it would support my weight. She had me climb in and reached for the button but paused. "Thank you for what you're doing. They took my granddaughter." She clanged the door shut and hit the button before I could come up with an appropriate reply. Over the sounds of my elevator I could hear her moving the boxes back into place.

Talon's drawn weapon met me at the other end of the ride. "It's nice to see you again too," I quipped sarcastically.

We were behind an oriental folding screen set up in a yoga studio. There were pictures of poses all over the walls in the open, well-lit room. Skylights let in natural light and lent a warm glow to the old but highly polished wood floor. Tables had been set up in the middle of the room. I was happy to see food in the center of them.

I stretched again as I waited for the others to show. When everyone was gathered, Talon invited us to food and her lecture. She looked a little pained as she began. "We did more digging and one of the people who chooses the victims could be a woman. We had been led to believe they were all men. I brought the artist for you to work with. Sarah told us about your having a feeling at the pool and in the lobby that someone was watching you. Part of the reason we picked that location was because we suspect a link there. It's not the hotel but an employee. You are more intuitive than I gave you credit for. The traffickers have a vast network and I'm afraid that if we take out only one or two they will quickly be replaced. That is why we must go for the heart."

"You're assuming that when they take us, they will take us to the heart, but what if they don't. If they were smart they wouldn't," Lucie sounded so calm, but I knew she was shaking on the inside.

Talon looked at her with the first spark of kindness I'd seen. "We don't have to get them all. I can live with losing a few of the little fish in the pond but I need to at least get to middle management. The goal is to take down the whole thing. The lowest level traffickers will go to work for someone else but we'll catch them eventually.

We've been working on this for months as you know. We tried hiding trackers on a few minor players we suspected… They all lead to one place. We got undercover agents in there twice as one of them. The first one made it all the way to South America before he had to escape and return home because his cover was blown. The next attempt was made by my partner and we know how that turned out. Neither one of them gave up a woman as part of the pick-up team but both admitted last night that… that they didn't see everything and that they may have made a mistake."

I watched Talon. Her admissions had cost her. She liked being the crusty commander, but she was hurting. She'd put years of her life into this and she was feeling like they were wasted years. Into the silence following her speech I reminded her, "We can do this. Give us a chance."

She sent me an incredibly sad look. "We will set a routine. You will do a tourist visit during the day and a club or two at night. Each taxi driver will tell you when and where to get the next one." Lucie and I nodded.

"I have an odd question," Lucie threw out. "There are only two clubbing dresses. I hung up the one I already wore but it really should be…"

"It's handled. Your maid will pick up your dirty clothes each day as if you've sent them to the hotel laundry. They will be replaced by Juan and Candy as appropriate and returned to your room."

"Fine. How long do we stay at the zoo and is there anything particular we are to do there?" Lucie asked almost sounding bored.

"Just be tourists. Have lunch, but be out front to catch your cab at 3:00. Then it's more pool time. You'll have a late dinner at 7:00 in the Gas Lamp Quarter where a reservation will have been made for you. You'll get that cab at 6:40. A new cab will take you to tonight's clubs."

I could say one positive thing about Talon. She made me feel much less grouchy when she provided food. As I listened to her drone on about the op, I watched one of her techies come in and take our phones and make some adjustments. Even though I'm not Marlo, I knew that they would be squeaky clean now with no trails to give us away and probably some false leads just in case.

I turned my attention back to Talon. Maybe it was the way she did things that got to me. She expected us to be perfect but she didn't give us all the information we really should have to do a good job. She was high-handed and rude. I bit my tongue or pressed my lips together most of the time she talked so that I wouldn't say anything to irritate her further. She ran through the rest of the information she had for us, including the photos and sketches of the traffickers they knew about. The promised artist arrived and we added the drawing of the female and male that Lucie and I had noticed at the club.

I was released to work with White Eagle for a short time while Lucie was led downstairs so they could check her tan, redo her brown Salena locks and repaint her nails. Talon watched us spar and whispered to her techie and soon I was presented with a phony guest pass from a nearby gym and told to run back to the hotel. Not fun, but better than getting my nails done.

I hurried through a shower and dressed for the zoo. I heard it was warmer there than down here by the water. I was relieved to see that, true to her word, Talon had replaced some of my clothes. Today I would be dressed much more practically if not like I normally would. They had provided me with Nike Free 5.0+ running shoes in bright orange that perfectly matched the orange in the plaid of the Peter Millar Queens Park shorts, whoever he was. She had also sent over a frosty aqua Etro polo. Who did she think I was? Oh yeah, not me, Joe.

On closer inspection I could see that all of my used clothes were gone and replaced by different ones. It was weird, like having Dobby the house elf around to do everything for you. The room was spotless and the bed perfectly made. Even the connecting door was resecured but that was probably White Eagle's doing. I jumped on the bed, leapt into the air and landed flat on my back. Then I turned on the TV while I waited for Lucie.

A soft knock sounded against the connecting door. I felt the other side and sensed good energy. I opened it quickly to find White Eagle waiting. I about slammed the door in his face when I heard the other door's lock disengage. As soon as Lucie had shut it behind her I reopened the door for White Eagle.

"Geez, you're quick. Maybe you should apply to the secret service," White Eagle said, sounding serious. *Me in the secret service... that'd be like jumping right under a microscope.*

"Thanks, White Eagle, I'll keep that in mind," I laughed.

Lucie whizzed past, mumbling as she snatched up today's zoo outfit. She was about out of time.

"I just wanted to wish you luck. I have a..." He lowered his voice and continued on, "I have a bad feeling about today, but I want you to know that... I will do anything to get you both back if this goes wrong. Anything, do you understand?"

"White Eagle, it's going to be okay. I'll take care of us and I trust you. Talon won't leave us hanging. As much as she seems to hate us, I feel that she'd never waste a good opportunity. She'd follow us all the way to hell if it got her, her pile of traffickers."

"I'm concerned that she will put the mission first, but we won't. Sarah and I... you're our family. We take care of our own – no matter what."

I didn't know what to say. My throat felt tight so I just hugged him. I hoped he knew that I would do the same for him.

Lucie stepped from the bathroom in low cut white capris and a bright halter top to wear with yet another pair of strappy high heeled sandals. This time they were platforms, which made her almost as tall as me. I couldn't help myself, "Aren't your feet about dead yet?"

She rolled her eyes which was extra impressive with the false eyelashes they had her in now. "My feet will survive, my nerves may not. We have never done anything quite like this and never for so long at this level of intensity. When we rescued your dad and grandpa we were... *doing* something and not... I don't know how long I can hang around waiting for something to happen. I miss

Marlo. I miss my life. I miss the old Sarah, White Eagle and I especially miss my Owen, not the strange mock-up they've given me. In Florida we were still… us. I feel so disconnected."

"I know, Luce. I feel it too. I wish things were different."

She stepped into my arms and gave me a hug. "Come on," she sighed. "We're gonna be late for the zoo."

We walked hand in hand to the lobby. This time I caught sight of our driver from yesterday. He was dressed like a tourist and leaning against a pillar. He even had a camera around his neck and a false mustache. I saw him glance our way and then begin to text. We really were being watched all the time and now I knew how the cabs arrived at the prefect time.

Just as my feet crossed the threshold I hit a wall of malice. I turned my head slightly and caught sight of yesterday's bellman talking to the valet. I sent out a pulse of energy to see what I could read. One of those two was definitely part of our problem. Our cab pulled up and I said loud enough for them to hear, "Zoo, please." I agreed with Lucie. It was time to move this thing along.

I glanced down at her feet. "Driver, would you please stop at a department store or somewhere that carries sporting goods?"

"That's not authorized."

"Please! Have you looked at her feet? You can see rub marks and blisters from yesterday and they put her in similar shoes today," I begged.

"It's not authorized. We're to go straight to the zoo," he replied back stiffly.

"Ow… Joe, it's fine."

"It isn't. I've been to this zoo before. It's amazing, but it's also hilly and there's stairs. You will be miserable in those things for the next five hours and then you'll never make it clubbing tonight."

The driver sighed. "This is on you, not me. Just so we're clear."

"We're clear," I replied tersely. "Also tell Talon to watch the bellman and valet. Tell her they give me bad vibes."

"Okay, kid, but she won't like you telling *her* what to do."

"Yeah, but that hasn't stopped me before." I couldn't help but smile a little.

Lucie crossed her arms over her chest and tried to give me a dirty look but failed and broke into a grin. "Thank you," she mouthed at me and then leaned in to kiss me.

"Really?" the driver whined. "Do you have to do that in my cab?" But he did take us to a store that carried suitable shoes. We found Lucie some Keen sandals that would work for hiking and still look somewhat fashionable. I knew they would be a whole lot more comfortable for her.

As the cab pulled up at the zoo I sensed for dark energy, but nothing pulled at my attention just yet. Most people here were happy. I bought our tickets and we entered. Lucie picked up a map, but we decided to take the bus tour first so that we could study the lay of the land and make a plan as we got an overview and scoped everything out. The wait wasn't bad but I made good use of the time by holding onto Lucie and stealing a few kisses.

We chose to sit on the top tier so that we would have the best view. We kept our conversation cryptic and to a minimum because it was crowded.

"Thank you for the hiking sandals."

"You're welcome, Salena."

"What do you think of the bus?" she asked innocently, but I knew what she meant.

I closed my eyes for a moment and did what she was really asking. Then I expanded my reach beyond the bus to cover more and more of the zoo in an outward wave like ripples from a stone tossed in a lake. When I touched the freeway I snapped my senses back into place. Nausea swamped me for a moment and then settled back but sweat still lingered on my brow. Lucie put her arm around me and rubbed my neck and shoulders.

"The bus is okay," I muttered.

"How do you feel about the zoo?"

"Most of it's great."

Lucie squeezed me in a one-armed hug and laid her head on my shoulder. "What did you find?" she asked in her special wordless way. I opened our connection and let her feel what I had. Something terror-inducing was coming for us and it was coming soon. I suppose this is how a mouse feels just as it notices a cat about to pounce. I could feel someone watching us now and my heart rate increased. The wave passed. I wasn't wrong, the bus was clean. We had passed someone who knew we were on the bus and wanted to harm us.

"Are they going to take us from the zoo in broad daylight?" Lucie asked, again without words, her anxiety clear as clean glass.

I nodded my head glumly and tried to show her that although I'm not Mitchell or even Marlo, the skills I'd learned from Miles made me think so, but I didn't want to be taken from here with such a big time window to have us go missing. It would make us harder to find even though our clothing was tagged with some kind of fancy GPS. If they found that… we were dead.

I couldn't relax and enjoy the tour. I knew what was waiting when we left the bus. If we snuck off would it give us away? Thoughts zipped around in my head twisting and tangling. I looked at Lucie. She was already nervous and I wasn't helping. I took a breath and reminded myself I'd be fine once the action started. I could hardly wait for the bus tour to end.

I was amazed when I saw the woman from the club trying to act like a tourist among the other people milling around near the exit. Was she dumb? No, I'd put money on her believing that we were the ones who were dumb and naive. Different clothes and hair can't hide who you really are underneath for someone who knows what to look for.

Neither of us made eye contact but I knew Lucie was on to her too even though she didn't react in any way. We turned back toward the entrance and hit fern trail so that Lucie could see the waterfalls and lush vegetation. She and I are both big cat fans and I knew she'd want to see the Amur leopard brothers play if they were in the mood to chase and frolic like they were known to in the mornings. Orson, the rare black cheetah, is another big draw on the Big Cat Trail. Whoever our admirer was, she kept following but at a distance. If I didn't know the things Miles had to share I wouldn't have caught her at it. She was good. I had to admire her talent even if I didn't appreciate her or what she was doing.

She stayed with us as we moved from Orson's cage past Africa Rocks and to Elephant Odyssey. Wherever we went we were sure to keep people around us and we stayed away from any service areas and gates. We kept up with our cryptic dialog and acted cutesy. We stopped for lunch at the Sabertooth Grill. Lucie picked up a yogurt and fruit but I went for the nachos with turkey chili and the works.

"How can you eat that? My stomach is in knots," Lucie commented, sounding half disgusted and half jealous.

"I'm cast iron, baby!" I replied with a laugh.

"Sure you are… and don't come crying to me if you need antacids later."

I slurped up the last of my coke and took care of our trash. "Come on; let's go see the hippos and polar bears."

We walked on but bursts of malice were pounding over me. I felt like I was trapped in ocean waves, tumbling and twisting, and couldn't come up for air. Just before the polar bears I pulled Lucie quickly in the direction of the sky tram, hoping to lose our tail.

She got on behind us but was a ways back. I caught a glimpse of her on her cell phone. She definitely had at least one partner here.

It was a bit of a relief to sit for a moment in our own car away from other people so we could talk freely.

"Did she get on behind us?" Lucie asked without turning to look. I could tell that she was strongly resisting the urge to do so.

"Yeah, I saw her. She's about five cars back."

"Do you think we can break away? I'm not ready to be taken. I'm scared, Owen." She didn't need to tell me. I could see that this was getting to her.

"From here I'd say our chances are decent, but I bet you dollars to doughnuts she has a partner. I saw her use her cell. By the time we arrive at the other end they'll be there. Let's ride it back to the polar bears and try to lose them on Monkey Trail. It has lots of twists, turns, and forks in the road. Also, our pick-up isn't until 3:00 so we have over an hour to burn."

"Well then, let's do the primates and cut through the gift shop and head on out."

We left our car, dodged around a bunch of people, vaulted a stroller and got back in line. I caught sight of her talking to a man in Bermuda shorts and a safari hat as we lifted off again. Unfortunately she caught sight of me too. Lucie and I scanned the crowd as we came in to unload and hurried as fast as we dared over to the primates.

Winding through the Monkey Trail was a mistake. It was too crowded, so instead of giving us cover, it provided the opportunity to get separated. I hadn't felt any *dark watchers* but I didn't want to draw too much attention to us either. We had enough problems and I'd released plenty of good energy already. *Dark watchers* were sure to feel it and if Kraeghton, Carmichael or Madame Malvada were here they'd know it was me.

I began to worry and feel trapped. If I sensed the zoo again I'd be about drained – if I didn't, how would I know where the attack was coming from? There were so many people concentrated here that I would be swamped with feelings if I tried to pinpoint it too closely. There would be so much raw data to process that I doubted whether or not I could even do it, but I had to try, right?

I began to sweat with the strain of watching, listening and using my other sight all at once. A couple of the more sensitive people around me turned to look at me with concern. Lucie noticed and put a hand on my arm to try to lessen the drain on me and give the people around us the feeling that she had me under control. A blast of hatred and lust hit me and I knew one of them was close.

It was the guy with the safari hat but not her partner from the club. I felt his essence change as he came to a decision about what he was going to do – he darkened. Lucie still had a hand on my arm and must have felt it too. As he went to step right behind her, she let go of me and nimbly leapt over the front of another stroller. She did a half jog, half fast walk as she darted past several people in an attempt to elude him. She was using all the skills she had learned to hide in plain sight by using her surroundings. I kept an eye on her and dropped back behind the man. His focus was on Lucie, he'd lost interest in me. That would be his mistake.

He glanced over his shoulder to locate me but I'd already moved behind a plant at a bend in the trail. He looked back to Lucie in time to see her disappear behind some foliage after making a sharp right at the next exhibit. He froze for a beat, undecided, knowing he was between us now. He spun in place and headed back toward me. I made note of my surroundings and let him get close. At the last second I reached out and pulled him toward me, delivered a quick sharp jab to his solar plexus and then another to his jaw. I kept ahold of him and slid him onto the bench right behind him. Lucie reappeared just in time to help me prop him up. We crossed his arms over his belly and pulled his hat over his eyes. Then we walked away casually. No screams followed us. No one had processed what they'd just seen and newcomers would think he was napping.

"Where is she?" Lucie mumbled soft and low.

I took her by the elbow and quickly led her past the service entrance to the back area. I knew the woman would see us but we'd slowed her down just a bit while she tried to figure out what was going on with her partner. I checked my watch. 2:30. We dodged, wove and took a circuitous route up to the gift shop with my sensors on high. To heck with the *dark watchers* - maybe I'd just tangle them up with the equally evil traffickers.

Lucie darted into the zoo shop and behind the nearest display. I did the same and then moved up the steps into the main section. Then I walked over to a location where I could watch both doors, yet look like a shopper until it was time to hit the exit – the only exit as far as I knew. Lucie pretended she didn't know me but stayed within my sight.

The woman entered at the lower door. I signaled to Lucie and we melted out of sight. She did a fast walk-through and stood outside. She grabbed a map and looked around like she was trying to decide which way to go. I knew she was waiting for us as she analyzed every person that went past.

The minute the clock hit 2:55, we darted from the shop while she was turned but she caught sight of us and made to pursue us. At the last second we abruptly halted in front of someone looking for solicitations. I tossed her a donation and then zipped around the far side of the big flowerbed with the advertising posters in it, throwing the woman's rhythm off. She made a grab for Lucie but she wasn't there. She didn't seem to realize we'd made her. She spun in place like she'd just realized she'd lost something, to fool the tourists, and then moved away again to prepare another strike.

Our cab pulled up at 3:00 on the dot and we slid inside. I didn't even say a word this time.

A low voice rumbled as we pulled from the curb, "Close shave?" I looked into the rearview mirror and met the gaze of the agent from the first day. "You do know the idea is to get caught, right? Talon is pissed."

"How do you…"

"We're following you too, remember? Nice move in the zoo though, I couldn't have done better myself. His partner, Zelinda, left him on the bench. Doesn't look like she has any idea what happened to him. As far as we can tell it was just the two of them. Guess if you're a bad guy and go down, too bad for you, but lucky for us. While you had Zelinda occupied we snatched him off the bench and took him in for questioning... when he wakes up is he ever going to be in for a big surprise."

"You know her name now?"

"We've identified both people at the zoo and we're pretty sure we know who the guy is who was with her at the club from your description. The men are local part-time troublemakers probably looking for a fast buck, but she's another story. She *is* the same one from the club, right?"

"Yes."

"I'd put money on her being out again tonight. She won't lay low after nearly getting you at the zoo. Why didn't you let them take you?"

"It was the wrong place. There was too much lag. I was afraid you guys could lose us," I answered.

"Have a little faith. We won't."

"We know you wouldn't on purpose," Lucie cut in. "But if something went wrong that was a huge window to go missing in. We could've been across the border before you even knew we'd been taken."

"You should be glad this cab doesn't have the screen in it. Talon is... well, let's hope she has a glass of wine before she sees you, but don't be surprised if she gets even. She can be a bit... vindictive. Don't tell her I said so. I'll deny it," he ended, giving us a hard look in the mirror.

"Fantastic," was my sarcastic reply.

The agent let us off and we walked into the lobby like we'd had a wonderful day at the zoo and nothing was wrong. Lucie bumped me to let me know our favorite bellboy was watching. He was also texting. I'd bet my first car that it was Zelinda he was contacting and I'm pretty sure he snapped our picture on his phone.

We took the elevator to our room. The connecting door was closed and our room looked just like we'd left it except for the new swimwear laid out on the bed. I would get to wear the same kind of board shorts and Lucie had another skimpy bikini, not that I minded. Sarah and Talon must have gone to war because Lucie's suit had a little more coverage. Our evening clothes were also laid out. This time they were putting Lucie in a peacock colored halter dress with a swirly skirt. The heels were a tad lower as well. Had my defiance paid off or was Sarah on the job?

Nobody had done me any favors. My pants would be even tighter, but at least they seemed stretchy. My shoes were still the pointy-toed variety. The shirt was a weird see-through short-sleeved freak of nature. Oh well.

Lucie took the bathroom again and I took the main room. At least I planned to, but I was interrupted by the connecting door easing open. I yanked on my board shorts without even tying them, ready to attack a flabbergasted Sarah.

"I'm so sorry… I thought… I apologize," she stammered.

"Heard of knocking?" I groused.

"Why are you changing out here?"

"Because Lucie's in the bathroom and we're on a tight schedule," I sighed.

"I see. Well, I'll just… let you get on with it then."

"I guess we'll see you at the pool," I replied as she backed out of the room and closed the door. I shook my head.

"Welcome to my world," Lucie said with a smile. "She means well."

"I know she does but I'm afraid she just caught a glimpse of something even you haven't seen yet."

"Not for lack of trying," Lucie quipped back. "Let's get going."

I decided that it was better to leave it alone so I said nothing. I'd try to put Sarah out of my mind too. If I thought about it too much I'd probably die of embarrassment.

White Eagle and Sarah weren't the only ones at the pool wearing disguises. The guy from the dance club was sunbathing and reading the paper. What luck, I thought sarcastically, both the good guys and bad are rotating around. White Eagle and Sarah were watching him and playing cards under the shade of a huge patio umbrella. I was beginning to feel like one of the animals from the zoo we'd just visited. When this was over, I'd need a real vacation for sure. I sighed inside again. No vacation. I was going home to football and the start of our junior year.

Other than being watched, our pool time was quiet. Too bad it wasn't restful. This time Lucie had spray-on sunscreen. No one watched her as closely as they had before because of that or the better coverage suit. I was pretty sure Sarah had a hand in the change in sunscreen too.

At the designated time, we headed back up to our room for our next adventure. I changed and waited for Lucie. This time I made sure the connecting door was locked. I suddenly realized that it was quiet… too quiet.

I knocked softly on the bathroom door. "Luce, what's wrong?" It was silent so long I raised my hand to knock again and placed my other hand on the knob.

"It's the dress," she said in a beaten voice.

"What about it? Do you need help? Do you want me to get Sarah?"

"No… I…" Lucie cracked the door open. She was holding the part that would connect behind her neck in her hand and had her shoulders rolled forward as if the fabric hurt her.

"What's the problem? You look fantastic." Her eyes were the same shade as the dress without the lenses in. Her hair was clipped up with rhinestones and her ears glittered with more gems. She looked at me and bit her lip. Then she moved her free hand up to hold it and released the top of the dress. My eyes zeroed in on her pale flesh marred by ugly red marks. She looked like she had a horrible sunburn but in stripes. One stripe even went through the pearlized remains of her drain scars. "Oh! What happened? You looked fine at the pool."

"It was kind of bugging me then. I used some makeup to cover it but now I need to use that darned tape again and when I went to reposition it… I swear I took some skin off and I have to use it or when I move I'll be showing off more than my bare shoulders."

"How can I help? Hydrocortisone? Band-Aids? What?"

"A night off?" Lucie quipped.

"I'd do that for you if I could. Tell me how I can help."

"I guess I could use some hydrocortisone. The cold compress helped, but I can't do that all night."

Talon had not provided us with any but I knew who would have some. I kissed Lucie on the top of her head and then went over to rap gently on the connecting door. White Eagle opened it, his eyebrows raised in query.

"Lucie needs hydrocortisone."

He waved me in. Sarah was already rummaging in her bag. "What's wrong?" she asked, her concern palpable.

"Lucie's skin and the dress tape aren't getting along."

"Ah," she said sounding relieved.

"I'm beat," I blurted. They both looked at me in surprise. "I'm sorry. I'm sure you are too. I just realized that I like it better when we're in control. This is exhausting."

Sarah gave me a hug. "Hang in there. We're close. I can feel it."

White Eagle squeezed my shoulder. I looked at him over Sarah's shoulder. At least I wasn't alone. I could tell that he felt like I did.

I returned to our room to help Lucie. She tried the tape in a new location and smeared some cream on the red spots. We returned the tube to Sarah on our way to dinner. Talon ranted at me on the Skype call during the whole ride over to the restaurant. At least she'd followed through with the reservation so we didn't have to wait to be seated. I caught sight of Sarah and White Eagle entering as we were led to our table.

I was glad that they had given Lucie a short-sleeved sweater tonight as the breeze off the water was really chilly and I was pretty sick of people looking at her like she was either a celebrity or a pastry in the baker's case.

Pleased as I was on those two counts, I still couldn't enjoy my meal. Someone new was watching us. I could feel it but at least this time it just felt like simple watching and not the creepy hunger, lust and rage that I had come to expect.

When Lucie rose to visit the ladies' room, I saw Sarah also rise to join her. She had put on a blond wig and wore glasses. I saw that White Eagle wore a small Blue Tooth that could have passed for a hearing aid. I skimmed my eyes over all the other people in the restaurant pretending that I was bored and waiting.

Lucie returned with Sarah a short distance behind her. I had to tear my eyes away from White Eagle's table as they began to sign to each other. I had no idea they could do that. We'd signaled to each other, sure, but we'd never really used actual sign language before.

We finished our meal, paid our bill and left. We hopped in the next designated cab in the specified location and were off to get captured. Maybe I should have hit the head as the women had. Nerves were making my whole system go crazy.

I wanted us taken together so I would have to play this delicately. I squeezed Lucie's hand. "I won't leave you behind, I swear. If we get separated, I'll come for you. I won't stop until I have you safely back."

She smiled at me, but it came nowhere near her eyes. She couldn't fool me, I felt her fear but then she probably was just as tuned into mine. "And I'll come for you," she whispered raggedly. There was determination behind her words.

The cab pulled up at tonight's club and we got out. I took her hand and we walked over to get in the queue like everyone else. Would anyone notice that we lined up like we were headed for death row? It's hard to fake happiness when you feel like you've been handed a death sentence. It just doesn't matter that you're surrounded by happy revelers.

The club was dim and crowded. I felt for evil intent. Darkness was coming for us and soon. I saw the woman. She had on a different dress and wore a wig but she couldn't fool me. She continued in that particular way she had of watching us without looking right at us. She was good. I had to respect her for that. I tried to get a sense of how this was going to go down, but I couldn't tell.

"Come on. Let's go check in your sweater. It's warm in here."

"Okay," she replied sounding a little reluctant. I figured she must be able to sense the impending doom rocketing toward us.

The hall was unusually dark. It was also mostly deserted. Dark carpet quieted our feet. The only other occupants ignored us. They were just past the coat check making use of the dark and quiet. Lucie averted her eyes and focused on the coat check girl. I was getting a weird vibe off of her that I was just starting to process when a powerful, rushing avalanche of malice crashed over me. A startled breath was sucked in next to me. I turned just enough to see Lucie overpowered by the two people who'd been making out a moment before. A rag was held over her mouth and nose but exposed her frantic eyes.

I spun to fight, but was tazed by the coat check girl who let out a little squeal. She'd set it too low, but I crumpled anyway. This I could fake. I'd been zapped by more experienced wielders than her. A panel slid open next to the coat check. Two men stepped out as the woman from the zoo, Zelinda, turned the corner to enter the hall. We were hauled through the panel. I kept my eyes slitted but I could make out enough of the room to tell that it was an overflow area for the coat check. The panel was slammed shut and secured as dark sacks were yanked over our heads and we were tumbled into a laundry cart and covered with linens. At least they smelled clean.

The cart was put into motion so I pushed up my hood to find Lucie motionless. I wiggled carefully until I could get my fingers on her neck to feel for a pulse. It pounded away under my fingers. That's my girl! She must have held her breath and faked it like me. I pushed up her hood causing her eyes to fly open even if they were a bit out of focus. I could feel her fear so I held her as best I could in the confined space, knowing that she probably wanted to scream like I did.

I began counting off the seconds and noting each change in the vibration of the cart as it was run across different surfaces. When I felt it stop, I mouthed to Lucie, "I love you." I pulled our hoods back down. I felt her breathing accelerate and then we were tumbled from the cart and onto a new surface, linens and all. A heavy door slammed, an engine roared to life and we lurched into motion. My counting resumed.

I tried to see through the hood but it was nearly impossible due to the dark fabric and tightness of the weave. I kept counting and making note of the turns but I was getting confused. Pushing down the terror was becoming more and more difficult as my mind spun out frightening scenarios that I fought desperately to ignore so I could focus. I had to keep track of where we were in case we needed to save ourselves.

TEN

Fifteen minutes and some odd seconds after we were dumped in the van, it came to a sudden stop and the engine was shut off. A door opened and shut and then the side door rolled opened and we were roughly dragged out, smacking the ground hard enough to leave bruises. I tried to roll to my knees but was kicked for the effort. I held still and waited. A foot was pressed into my spine holding me down.

I heard Lucie groan softly as her shadowy form was yanked to her feet. I continued to wait and see what would happen. I tried to sense how many were here but all I could tell was that we were outnumbered by a large margin. I heard the unmistakable sound of duct tape ripping and Lucie hiss as she was bound and then the thump of her shoes hitting the concrete as they were removed and tossed aside. I heard the sound of more tape and my hands were roughly yanked behind me to be secured together. My own shoes were yanked from my feet. I fought my urge to strike back. I was supposed to be normal.

"What do you want?" Lucie asked with just the right amount of terror.

Her question was met by silence except for the clatter of her purse contents hitting the concrete floor. Another pair of hands began to pat me down, removing my wallet and cell phone. Finally a voice spoke. "What I want is my money… for you… um, Salena."

So far so good. They didn't know who we were.

"Money?" She asked sounding surprised. "Are you hoping for a ransom?"

The man just laughed and began talking to someone else. "Here, take this stuff. Strip the cells and clean them up. Destroy anything that's not useable."

The click of heels announced a new arrival. "Let's see what we've got." The voice had to be Zelinda. I could feel her malice so I schooled my face before the hood was ripped free. After the darkness of the hood the light was nearly blinding, making my eyes water. I blinked, conscious of my colored contact lenses and prayed I wouldn't lose one. "Nice," she continued in a silky voice that made my skin crawl. She appraised us like cattle at an auction as she continued to comment, "Slender, in shape and nice featured. They'll bring a good price."

She sliced her look from us to her crew. There were five people in this room. With free hands we could take them. Taped up I had my doubts about our success. Her eyes narrowed and her anger flashed over my skin. "What are you doing with their cells still here? Are you trying to get caught? Idiot! Now we have to move by dawn for sure! Go! Now!" she screamed. The man holding our cell phones slunk away in fear.

"You," she snapped at the other female. "Stand guard at the door and tell Mike to listen to the scanners."

"Hal, prep the room and find the examiner."

I looked around the extensive warehouse, making note of the huge industrial lights that were suspended by chains, the lights themselves covered by cages that must have been a couple of feet across. Three or more stories up, large skylights were a deadened black but probably provided all necessary light during the day. I could see a counter and a windowed office space overhung by what was likely more offices above it but my angle was bad so I couldn't be sure. The large open space was cut into portions. Enormous double doors that looked like they could accommodate an RV or at least a small jet plane were slid closed at the rear of the space.

"What do you want?" Lucie demanded again.

"Who knew you would be the brave one, little lady? After the zoo, I have to admit that I'm surprised." Zelinda even had her head cocked to the side, showing her curiosity.

Lucie continued on, her tone turning cold. "If it's ransom you want…"

Zelinda laughed. "It's not. We're looking to sell you to the highest bidder!"

Lucie and I both gave her a stunned look. We knew it was the truth but to hear her actually say it was… terrorizing.

Without breaking character Lucie squeaked, "Sell us?"

I took the moment to sense the room. To them I probably looked defeated. Dark energy crushed in on me from all sides. Objects throughout the building screamed at me but the van itself was virtually silent.

"Take them to be processed, strip the van, wipe it clean and abandon it by the airport."

Well that explained its silence; they used a new rig for each abduction. One man gave her a sharp nod and headed to the van. The others gripped us firmly.

"You know, you have me curious. You were pretty proactive at the zoo. I thought you were onto us and now…"

I shifted my gaze from my feet to her face. "Ah, now I see the fire that drew my attention. Feisty is good. Feisty brings in more money. Our buyers find humor in it and it gives some a great excuse to beat you. Works for me either way," she smiled but Lucie had turned chalky white under her fake tan.

I continued to stare her down, saying nothing. "Oh, I see. You're waiting for your moment. We'll just have to find a way to expend all that pent up energy then." I cringed inside, but held firm to my cold exterior. We couldn't fight… yet. We had to be led deeper into the organization and catch as many of these… people as we could. It went against every instinct burning through me, but I held my body still as my mind raged and adrenaline made my chest ache – fight or flight… fight or flight.

I balked when we reached a stainless steel room that looked like it had been set up for modern torture. My hair stood on end and every sphincter clenched. Sweat broke out on my brow as dark visions from the room attacked me. So many young people treated so brutally. My breath froze in my lungs, tears burned at the back of my eyes, and my throat tightened like water solidifying to ice. I could feel myself shaking as my chest seized up and my heart beat erratically.

I could barely bring myself to look at Lucie. When I did, her eyes said things that her lips could not. Even if she wanted to speak, I was pretty sure she couldn't. I watched her throat work and a flush bloom on her chest, neck and cheeks. I couldn't decide if she was trying to hold in a sob or vomit. I could see the vibration in her limbs, yet there was nothing I could do for her since I barely had control of myself. The light caught the sheen of tears in her eyes. I might be seeing the horrors of this room but my Lucie could hear the anguished screams and cries of young people begging for mercy.

I struggled as Lucie was backed up to a metal table that was tilted to hold her in a standing position. One of my captors punched me in the face for my trouble.

"Not the face!" Zelinda screamed. I could tell they didn't feel a bit guilty.

Lucie's ankles were shackled to either side despite her efforts to fight them off. Once her arms were secured to the sides of the table she went still, except for the shivering she couldn't control. Her eyes were extra wide and her jaw was clenched. When had I ever felt this helpless? Thoughts of what they would do to us and what had happened to others in this room were tearing me up. I fought to even breathe. The men holding me wrestled me into submission, took my shirt, pants and socks and then slammed me into the wall and chained me to it. I was expecting the worst but they surprised me by filing out of the room. I barely caught one man mumble something about us filling their quota for this shipment.

I looked at Lucie. She met my eyes for a moment and then looked away. Neither of us said anything. We knew we were being watched if not listened to. A malevolent red light blinked on a small camera installed in the corner of the room, near the door. I felt dread wrap around me like a hungry python. She might have looked away but I couldn't seem to take my eyes off her. I wanted to brand every bit of her into my brain, just in case. *No! Don't think like that.*

I kept expecting them to come back in. I figured they must be celebrating or something. Time passed; the minutes crawled by at their very slowest pace. The adrenaline was wearing off and exhaustion crept in to fill the space. I slid down the wall and sat on the cold floor, my arms held up awkwardly. Only fear kept me awake.

I pushed myself part way up so I could touch my bruised cheek. I froze as I heard a small sound over the clink of my chains. The door opened slowly and someone shuffled in. Her head was bowed as if she was watching her feet or possibly she was looking at the tub in her hands. A few dark strands had escaped her sloppy braid. I could tell very little about her but her aura screamed – abuse.

My gaze traveled down her body. She was smallish but I had the impression she'd lost a lot of weight recently. She looked too young for saggy skin though most of it was hidden under baggy scrubs. When my eyes reached her feet I realized the shuffling was due to hobbling devices they had attached to her shoes. She couldn't move her ankles… she couldn't run and those weren't just any shoes. They looked like they had stiff soles.

Her head turned slightly in my direction and I met her eyes. Scars crisscrossed over the left side of her face affecting her eye and mouth. She froze for a moment but managed to keep hold of her tub – Julie. I was afraid she'd give us away. She looked incredibly sad and almost broken. She had circles and bags under her eyes. She also had the look of someone who wasn't well. Her skin was slightly yellowed. We had to get her out of here soon.

She set her tub down on the small table by Lucie. No one else came in, which confirmed, in my mind, that we were observed.

Lucie struggled a bit and moved as far away as her shackles allowed. "Let me go," she whispered pitifully.

Julie just shook her head with remorse. "I can't," she mumbled softly in a voice I had to strain to make out.

"Can't or won't," Lucie asked with a little more courage.

"What's the difference?" Julie asked with a sigh that showed she'd about given up all hope. She recorded Lucie's height and weight. A thermometer was stuck in Lucie's mouth and then she listened to her heart. While she used the stethoscope I saw Lucie take hold of her wrist. A look passed between them.

"What's going on?" Zelinda growled over the intercom. "Get on with it!"

Well, now we knew for sure we were being watched and they didn't care that we knew it. It was probably part of the routine they used to break people.

"Nothing," Julie answered meekly. "I'm doing what you asked."

She added some notes to her clipboard and then she began to look Lucie over. I could tell that she was blocking as much of her body as she could from the camera. I pulled at my chains as I watched Lucie tense. Julie tilted the table so that Lucie was now lying flat on her back.

"What are you doing? Why am I here?" Lucie tried again, keeping up the charade of victim.

"I'm not allowed to answer your questions," Julie answered softly. I noticed that Lucie had her hand on Julie's arm again. I could only guess at what they were sharing.

She made another note on her clipboard and then moved her body so that it blocked the camera's view again before she mouthed "sorry" to Lucie. I averted my own gaze as she looked at all the places covered by Lucie's dress and then made more notes.

"Why are you doing this? Why are we here?" Lucie's voice sounded plaintive.

"I'm doing my job," Julie said gruffly but her eyes told a different story. She was trapped, scared and helpless.

Before Julie had even pulled Lucie's skirt back down, three men entered the room. A tear escaped Lucie's eye and she shook with fear. I rose to my feet. One of the men tilted the table back upright quickly making Lucie whimper when her ankles and wrists hit the metal of the shackles. I lost sight of her for a moment as my view was blocked by the other men. I lurched in her direction but got tripped up by my chains that only allowed me to move a little over a foot from the wall.

Lucie screamed as the model's tape was ripped free. Julie shoved a hospital gown over her as fast as she could. Lucie struggled but it was not berserk or crazed. It was the struggling of one who is giving up.

Two of the men broke away to come and unchain me but they had to have help to muscle me over to the now empty table. I heard the frightening clink of the shackles being latched and the clunk of Lucie's chains. I glanced at her to find her huddled on the floor, her side pressed into the wall as if she could blend her molecules with it and pass on through. I was fully expecting a beating. My only satisfaction came from the fact that took all three of the men to secure me to the table.

I shivered on the cold surface. One of the men laughed softly, probably thinking it was fear. I wished I could project all the terror in this room into his brain. The room continued to bombard me with images. I was getting some of the most horrible ones I had yet to witness. I could see what had happened here and I could feel the fear and horror. Julie's job was to make sure we were healthy so that we would fetch the highest possible price but not everyone here was as business-like and ethical as she was. We were lucky she was the new examiner.

Julie frowned as she came across my old scars. I noticed that she only documented some of them. Clearly it wouldn't pay to be too detailed and make me identifiable or give me away. My attention was diverted when one of the men took an intense interest in Lucie. He'd been watching her closely but he hadn't touched her yet because he was afraid of who would notice. I saw from the images the exam table provided that he had to know he wasn't allowed to sample the merchandise but he wanted to. I could feel just how much as his dark desires oozed in my direction. Lucie had become a craving. I could taste the conflict within him. What was he willing to sacrifice for a few moments with her? He noticed my attention, smiled a sick smile and moved behind another man. He could hide but I could still feel his intent.

Julie gave me an odd look and I realized I was holding my breath and had gone rigid, my body straining against the bonds. He was plotting Lucie's rape and I was secured to an exam table. The images in the room began to intensify, alter and change as the memories of Lucie's would-be attacker wove together with what the room alone had to share. A glimpse of another dark-haired girl rolled out. I helplessly watched her ghostly image, the memory of what had happened, being replayed. Lucie shuddered and curled into herself; she was probably hearing it. Tears leaked from my eyes and I began to ache all over as my muscles strained.

What I saw next was even more frightening and repulsive. Evilia Malvada entered this room where the perpetrator was now strapped to this very table. I recognized several people from the present time file in as she spoke to them and taught them how to behave. She castrated him herself in front of everyone and left him to bleed on the table. I gagged and snapped back to the present. Julie rested her hand on my forehead as she looked deep into my eyes to communicate without words.

The extent of Evilia's malice and cruelty made my very soul shrink in fear. A cold sweat beaded on my skin. I was so freaked out that

I barely noticed as Julie finished her inspection by looking at the parts of me that were still covered.

The door opened and the men moved back for their leader, Zelinda. "Well? How do they look? Are they clean?"

Julie looked at her clipboard as she answered. "There are no obvious abnormalities in either one, no sign of sickness or disease. There are no needle marks or tissue damage from drug use. He has a couple of identifying tattoos and some scars. She has a scar and…"

"Fine," Zelinda barked. "It's cheaper to change the tats. Hal, call our guy and make an appointment for tomorrow at the conditioning center. I want these two out of here and sold with the next batch. Their reservation is good until the 19th. No one will worry until then. People will think our little friends are partying and being stupid. Lock them up with the others. Nelson, call and confirm our arrival."

Zelinda walked over to me and ran her fingertips over my torso. "You are quite the prize. We'll get you fixed up and make a small fortune on you. Julie, fix his cheek as best you can. We wouldn't want that pretty face marred for his premier on the auction block."

Julie cringed. Her eyes held terror and remembered pain.

Lucie and I were injected with something. Nearly instantly I began to feel dizzy, weak and disoriented. The lights grew strange halos and things fuzzed out of focus. I couldn't make my limbs cooperate as they chained us together and dragged us down a darkened hallway that smelled of sweat and fear. Lucie was thrown into a cage with another girl and I was locked up with a boy, still in my underwear. Super. Our cage contained a chemical toilet and pump sink as well as one raggedy blanket and thin mattress on the floor for me and a set for him. Even in San Diego it can get cool at night. The coolness was a blessing because it helped me to stay somewhat focused.

As soon as they left, I tried to question my cellmate. "Can you drink the water?" Ugh, this must be what it feels like to be drunk.

He nodded, I think… I crawled to the sink. I felt the water, smelled it and finally took a small taste. I drank a bit and waited.

I had pretty much lost track of time but it was extremely dark judging by the skylights. It had to be between dusk and dawn. I thought back to White Eagle's teachings; it had to be between 6:30 in the morning and 7:30 last night. We'd had dinner at seven and then headed to the club but we were taken right away. We must have been at the warehouse by 9:30 so it must be what now? Midnight?

I tried to close my eyes and relax so that I would have energy in the morning but the uncertainty and fear ate at me. Well, that and the weeping of the other occupants. I dozed but I was so cold. I huddled up in a tight ball. The warehouse had cooled rapidly, the air moved with industrial fans set high in the walls. I prayed for rescue or at least for the night to end. Strange and unfamiliar sounds woke me repeatedly. I tried to talk to the young man penned up with me, but he wouldn't even meet my gaze. He turned his back on me and faced the corner. The unmistakable smell of alcohol wafted off of him. I guess he got way more than he was expecting from underage drinking. He also smelled like his deodorant had given out. By the look of him he hadn't slept in the time he'd been here and I wasn't sure they'd fed him. Who knows what else they'd done.

Whatever they'd drugged me with helped me to doze again but the murmur of voices woke me and then the rush of evil jolted me completely awake. A hushed argument was commencing. I could make out the words as they passed my enclosure.

"Don't do it," the shorter, rounder man said. Nelson… that was his name.

"You tell and I'll kill you. Help me and I won't tell about your little habit," the man named Hal snarled back in a low menacing voice.

"You give me up and I give up the dirt I have on you," Nelson growled back.

"Look, let's play nice. I'll share the girl but I get her first."

The argument continued but my attention went to my surroundings. I frantically searched it again. We were trapped within four walls made of chain-link. Each cubicle was secured to the others in the row and was capped off with more chain-link fencing. The corners were set into the concrete of the floor. I couldn't lift it but maybe I could damage it enough to break free. There was a pump sink with limited tubing, a chemical toilet, two thin mattresses and two raggedy blankets. No tools, no weapons, no clothes and no shoes. Think!

I could feel my heart rate accelerating. They were already down to Lucie's enclosure but I could tell she was awake. I heard the jangle of keys and tensed up. Would the chemicals damage the metal? Probably not. I began to work at the nuts and bolts that secured the sections of fencing to each pole. They had been sloppy. I got one nut loose and went to work on the next. They were rough and cut into the pads of my fingers. I dropped the second nut and froze.

They didn't even look around as they opened the gate to Lucie's cage. Think… think! Save Lucie, save Julie, next bolt, focus. My mind ran in circles. My cellmate was no help. He looked at me with huge, frightened eyes. Others up and down the row were waking up. My body nearly vibrated with adrenaline, fear, and rage. I would punish this man for his thoughts alone. Please be able to hold him off. Please!

This nut and bolt were more difficult. It was slippery and stubborn. I wiped at it with the blanket but it was instantly sticky again. I was bleeding. I tried twisting the nut with the blanket, but it was no use. This one was solid. I moved on to another one. *I'm sorry, Lucie. It looks like I was wrong. I should have listened. This is not what your first time should be. What more can I do? I've failed you. Please God, help me to save her.* My eyes burned from unshed tears, my throat felt hot and dry.

I heard a clang and looked up. Lucie's door had banged open. I looked on in horror for a stunned moment and then frantically went back to work but I couldn't tear my eyes away. Lucie rolled to her feet. Her cellmate cowered uselessly in the corner. The men smiled as they entered and relocked the gate behind them, the click of the latch sounding extra loud in the near silence. It felt like every prisoner's attention was drawn to the spot where Lucie flowed into her fighter's stance. They should have been scared but they just laughed. As my third nut began to loosen I watched Lucie's cellmate try to vanish into the corner. She averted her gaze and covered her head with arms that shook with fear.

Hal moved toward Lucie as he loosened his belt. "You think you can hold me off, little girl? I don't think so. I want to show you what the rest of your miserable little life will be like. Things will go better for you, if you're cooperative." His voice was a harsh whisper.

Lucie waited until he was ready to grab her to explode outward with a strike. She had gone right for his throat.

He coughed but chuckled. "You'll have to do better than that," he rasped as he struck back at her.

She threw up an arm and the blow headed for her cheek glanced off her forearm instead. She came right back with a kick but they'd taken her shoes and she was hampered by the hospital gown. Pain shot through my hands as they convulsed on the fencing and I realized that I'd stopped working.

I forced my attention back to escaping my enclosure but I felt helpless. She wasn't going easy. Lucie fought hard in the small space as I fought my cage for escape. Lucie's cellmate was becoming more of a hindrance than anything as Lucie was forced backwards and tripped over her. Hal laughed again. Nelson stood by the door, looking around with a worried expression on his face. His eyes connected with mine for a brief moment and a slow, knowing smile spread over his lips. Rage beat within my chest with each squeeze of my heart.

My gaze snapped back to Lucie when she let out a small sound of frustration and fear. The tears that had threatened began to slide from my eyes as Hal got in more hits than Lucie could return. His boots and the sheer size of him were taking a toll that her bare feet and small form could not match. She was fast but she was slowing. Blood dripped from the side of her head onto her shoulder leaving strange patterns. Blood ran down my arms as I tried to rip the unforgiving fencing away with my bare hands.

Two cells away Lucie was shoved into the side of her cage. She hissed in a breath as it cut into her arm. Hal tried to kiss her but she turned her head away and kneed him. He avoided the worst of it and shoved the side of her face into the fencing. Some of her hair caught in the links. He changed his grip on her and pressed into her neck with his forearm. He used his shoulder to pin the left side of her body. Lucie did all she could but he soon had hold of her wrist. She tried desperately to knee him again but her angle made the shots next to useless.

Lucie dropped low enough so that she could twist to the side and drive her left arm up past his guard. The heel of her palm snapped his head back and he lost his grip long enough for her to break away, panting. A chunk of her hair dangled from the links. She hadn't taken but two steps when he tripped her. She went down hard on her knees and tried to roll away but he was too fast and dove on top of her. I could feel the breath leave my own lungs at impact. Lucie's cellmate began to cry but Lucie didn't make a sound.

"Nelson, help me! Tie her up, damn you. Feisty is fun but I'm tired of this."

Nelson moved slowly, looking for an opening as Hal pressed Lucie into the floor. From his pocket, Nelson drew out a pair of handcuffs which he clamped on her wrist and then dragged her by the cuffs as Hal rolled free. The moment he was close enough to lock the other half of the cuffs around the support post he clicked them into place. Lucie became crazed. She lashed out with both feet and her free hand as she tried to drag herself to her feet. How could the others not hear this? Why would no one help? I tore apart our sink looking for another way to escape our cage. I had to do something! I tried to lift the cage, knowing it was hopeless. Fear gripped my gut and rage possessed me as I watched the men wrestle her into the fencing to shackle her right ankle. She twisted and bucked. She tried to scratch, hit, kick and bite. Hal tried to push the hospital gown aside but Lucie got in one more good knee to his kidney. In a fit he ripped the gown causing Lucie to cry out. I gritted my teeth, feeling her pain. She spit in his face, so he slapped her and grabbed her roughly. I knew she'd bruise but all I could see was the skin of her shoulders and back conforming to the fencing as she tried to back up with nowhere to go. Nelson lost his grip on Lucie's left leg. She got in another knee to Hal's groin, dropping him to his side. He grabbed his crotch as she tried to kick him again and again until Nelson got a firmer grip on her flailing form.

"You got her?" Hal wheezed.

"Yes," he grated back.

"You're sure?" Hal growled as he struggled to his feet. His tone was so condescending. I was gripping the enclosure at the loose corner. I must have rattled the fencing because Hal's eyes snapped to mine and a smile slithered over his face. It wasn't a nice smile. It was the kind that makes your skin crawl and your stomach do a flip. He kept his eyes on me as he slowly pushed up Lucie's gown. Blood seeped from her shoulder where she'd been scraped. I ripped at the fencing as Hal found his zipper and slid it down. Lucie choked and turned her head to the side. She continued to struggle. The agony, fear and hatred racing through me coalesced into something tangible.

"I saw you at the pool. I'll give you what you really want – what you were asking for – what he couldn't give you," he said, reaching a hand around Lucie's butt to grab a handful of underwear.

And I have something for you. I thought as I took all the emotion I had bundled within me and threw it at him. For a moment time stood still and then I was collapsing onto the floor, my head pounding and my body shaking from the power blast. I became aware of blood oozing from my nose. I tried to swipe at it with my bloodied, shaking hands. All I could hear was the pounding of my too loud heart.

ELEVEN

Nelson and Hal were on the floor and Lucie hung limply from one wrist... I tried to think... but my mind just wouldn't work... the lights snapped on, nearly blinding me. Sound surged back. I could hear sobbing – was it me? Lucie?

"What is this? What's going on?" I knew that voice. I tried to pull myself together. I rolled my head to a better angle and was rewarded with an upside down view of Julie hovering behind Zelinda. "You come out of that enclosure this instant!" She raged at the two men as Julie cowered. "What is wrong with you? That one is damaged now. We'll have to hold her back and take less money. And it's coming out of your share. Do you hear me?! Stupid, lecherous, mongrels!"

Neither man replied, both were on their hands and knees, looking like they were recovering from a near drowning, as if they'd been flattened by a huge wave and perhaps they had. I must have done it but now I was beyond exhausted and wasn't sure.

I lay panting on the floor. From my point of view I could see Lucie in about the same shape. They had released her and now she lay in a heap with her back to me. Julie knelt by her. I watched her ease Lucie's hospital gown back into place. She twisted to open a messenger bag and from it she unloaded first aid supplies. I dimly sensed Julie's good energy wash over Lucie. It had to be a healing gift. No one else seemed to notice so I remained still.

I watched Lucie twitch and then become completely motionless as Julie touched her face gently. Then she relaxed and her body became almost boneless. I wondered if Julie's gift wasn't a healing one but perhaps something else. Had she put Lucie to sleep? If she had, why did she do it? How would Lucie defend herself? How would I? How many attackers did we still have to survive?

Zelinda was ranting again. I put my attention back on her and the two men who were still on their knees. "Get up! Get out! What's wrong with you? What if *she* caught you? You know what happened to the last idiot! Did you think it was a joke?"

The men struggled to their feet looking confused. Hal's pants fell to his ankles when he tried to stand. Zelinda huffed at him in disgust and for a happy moment I thought she'd hit him.

"What happened?" Nelson begged.

"You tell me," she snarled back. "You done?" she snapped turning her angry gaze to Julie.

Julie nodded once and edged out of the enclosure behind the men as if she was afraid to get too close to any of them. Zelinda relocked Lucie's cage with a furious snap. She shoved at both men, making them move faster back up the aisle. Julie lagged behind, her head down and her eyes on the floor. When she reached me, she slid a glance in my direction but made no outward sign to our captors. A wad of gauze and a small packet of antibiotic ointment fell to the floor within my reach – I snagged them and held them out of sight.

She moved on and out the main door which Zelinda clanged shut behind her. As the night noises gradually resumed I couldn't help but think that help could not come soon enough. I watched Lucie, who lay virtually motionless except for the rise and fall of her chest. I kept my vigil until I saw her roll onto her side and draw her knees to her chest. Then I cleaned my hands as best I could.

I finally closed my eyes to rest and just listen, but I heard a small sound and snapped them back open. My roommate was watching me from his corner of our cell. "What did you do to those men?" he asked softly when he realized I was looking at him.

"What do you mean?" I asked, playing dumb.

"I know you did something... I felt..." he drifted into silence probably realizing how crazy he sounded. "We're gonna die and it's going to be slow and horrible, isn't it?"

"We are not going to die," I grated.

"They'll addict us to drugs, degrade, dehumanize, beat and rape us. If we survive that we'll either wish we were dead or they'll do it for us the minute we aren't pretty anymore," he moaned softly as he began to rock back and forth and shiver with fear.

"Wipe those thoughts from your mind. Don't let them control you or your fear will win."

"Who are you?"

"I'm just a guy named Joe. Go to sleep, cellmate."

The rocking continued but at least he quit talking. All I needed was for him to suck everyone else deep into his world of fear and anxiety. I could feel the tension in the warehouse continue to spin up even though our current reality wasn't as abhorrent as his words indicated. The girls penned between Lucie's cell and mine began to cry softly. Others up and down the row murmured. I waited for the dawn knowing for me, sleep would never come.

I had barely closed my eyes when the sound of a lock turning touched my ears. I opened my eyes to slits. The skylights were barely pinkened by dawn. I watched as pen by pen the prisoners were systematically released and chained together. Nelson and Hal still looked pretty awful, though not as bad as I bet we looked. They smelled of coffee and we'd had nothing.

It felt like the whole town was asleep when we reached the loading dock. No one made a sound. The gags would have made it difficult but the weapons trained on us reinforced their commands. There were fourteen of us in all, Lucie was in no shape to help and the other kids would be nothing but a hindrance. I would have to wait. Where was our help? Why weren't they coming? When was enough, enough or had they... lost us? *Please. Just save Lucie. I can live this life until I can escape; if you just save Lucie.*

A hand firmly shoved me between my shoulder blades and I stumbled into the back of a panel truck where we were secured inside in two rows with seven on a side. The door slammed shut and we were surrounded by nothing but darkness, vibrations and terror as we lost our balance and all sense of direction. I tried to sense the truck but it was like trying to listen to every conversation in a crowded room at once. One thing was for sure – this was not the first of these trips this truck had made.

The ride went on and on. Soon the chilly interior became too hot and someone became ill. The sounds of choking and gaging were almost more than I could stand but the smell was worse and soon more of us were gagging. Hopeless, helpless, hobbled and chained together, we were a mass of human suffering. I couldn't be the only one who was praying. I missed having Lucie in my mind but I figured she was too weak to communicate. Whatever drug or gift of her power Julie had given her had left her glassy-eyed and weak but at least she was still alive!

The truck finally came to a stop. Sunlight blinded us as they threw open the back doors of the truck. Dry heat burned my nose. Rough hands yanked us out, making us stumble in the hot dust. The intensity of the heat was crippling. I felt instantly light-headed and nauseous. All I could see was dirt, waves of heat and misery. I couldn't smell any water, so we must have headed south and east. As my eyes adjusted I saw that we were being led into another facility - a low rectangular bunker of cinder block with few openings and no real windows. As far as I could see in any direction past the razor wire, there was a whole lot of nothing - unless you wanted to count the sagebrush and scrubby plants - I didn't.

The guards began pushing the girls in ahead of us. The weapons trained on us kept us quiet and docile. We were prodded into a shower area where we were instructed to strip. Bye, bye GPS. Maybe if the signal ended they'd finally come save us. Please let that be the case. I'd had enough.

After the heat and stink of the truck, the lukewarm water wasn't awful – just embarrassing in front of the other guys and clothed, armed guards. I didn't know where the girls were but for now I was glad they weren't here. We were given soap that smelled like medicine and made my skin feel tight. The towels they gave us were so rough they almost hurt. Finally they handed us flip-flops and what looked like pajama bottoms or scrub pants – nothing else. Let the degrading begin. I tried to let nothing show on the outside but inside, anger was building. Some of the guys looked ill and some scared but only one other looked defiant. I knew what happened here but I didn't want to look too closely at the images and emotions that beat at me. I was afraid they would suck me under.

We were led into another room where we were each handed a bottle of water and told to be silent. A guy older than me tried to speak and was slapped so hard he fell to his knees. His cheek turned bright red and began to swell. He spit out some blood before he was yanked back to his feet. His defiance was broken just like that and it served to keep the others in line.

A panel of three sat before us. I felt the tingling creep of *dark watcher* energy flit across my skin and tried to clamp down on my own desire to answer back. Most of us looked at the floor but a few looked at the panel of... monsters.

I ran my eyes over the three. This one I knew... but from where? Then it hit me. She was the woman we'd come across when Lucie and I had taken Sarah's file and found out who her birth mother was. She watched me with intelligent reptilian eyes. She was dangerous and she knew what I was. I had to have given something away.

We were individually examined while the rest stood silently waiting. I could see a copy of our medical reports from Julie sitting in front of each panel member. They took notes I couldn't read on the papers or in *her* case on a laptop. They did not speak or confer with each other in any way that I could see. The routine was always the same, name, age, skills, physical description and then a photo was snapped and uploaded.

When it was my cellmate's turn he began to shake violently. His mind must have been running away with him again. Another guard bearing a tray with syringes on it entered through a side door and he lost it. He peed his pants, his eyes rolled up in his head and he fell to the floor, screaming and crying. They finally had to tranquilize him. He was removed from the room but the syringes remained on the table as a warning to the rest of us.

When it was my turn, I was eyed critically by the woman and a man who also had to be a *dark watcher*. The third member of the panel looked more bored than anything. He was definitely not a good person but he was no *watcher*. Fans stirred the rapidly warming air sluggishly as our staring contest continued.

The door opposite of where we'd entered opened and Zelinda appeared leading the group of female prisoners. All had wet uncombed hair and wore hospital gowns or something much like them. Most of them watched their feet but Lucie stared straight ahead, making eye contact with no one, but I knew she was taking it all in.

Zelinda spoke to the male *dark watcher*. His eyes flitted over all the young women except Lucie. On her, he left his eyes the longest. She gave a slight shiver and blinked more than normal but gave nothing else away… until she turned her head slightly… Crap! She had one brown eye and one blue eye. IF we were lucky they wouldn't notice with her black eye from last night but I was afraid it would only highlight it.

Time stuttered to a halt and then flashed forward. The male *dark watcher* came out of his chair, vaulted the table and took Lucie by the throat. She tried to resist as I sprang in her direction but the unmistakable sound of guns being cocked froze us both in place.

"Who are you?" he snarled, giving Lucie a shake.

"Sa… Salena," Lucie gasped.

"No, you aren't," he growled back placing a hand over her heart. She gritted her teeth and tears streamed from her eyes, her jaw flexed and her face squinched up but she refused to utter a sound other than a soft guttural moan as he drained her.

Six handguns of various makes and models and seven traffickers... I would be impeded by five male and seven female victims. Whoever said I was smart... didn't know me. I did the only thing I could do and still live with myself. I dropped and leg swept the nearest trafficker who fell over backwards and smacked his head on the floor. The next two closest ones turned and fired hitting each other instead of me since I was no longer where they expected. I rolled under the evaluators' table, flipping it over, startling the non-*watcher*. I grabbed him in a headlock, jerking him to his feet.

"Let us go," I bellowed into the chaos.

Zelinda and the *dark watchers* laughed. Everyone froze. The trafficker I held hostage whimpered. He had to be brains 'cause he sure wasn't brawn. I tightened my grip and he clawed uselessly at my arms, his face reddening.

The male *dark watcher* held a now limp Lucie up by her neck but addressed me. "Not even a green *watcher* would allow herself to be placed into this situation alone. Now I know what you are - partners. I couldn't figure it out at first. I wasn't sure what I was sensing – you are something different - so young but yet so old. My mistress will be very interested in you."

We were at a standstill. The victims were of no help and the traffickers were regaining their composure. I'd lost the element of surprise and the upper hand. The male *dark watcher* looked from his female counterpart to Zelinda and then back at me. "Go ahead. Kill him."

"What?!" the trafficker I held squealed.

"You heard me. Go ahead. We could have ten different replacements for him by tomorrow. Her money can buy anything. You can't win here, cowboy." He let go of Lucie and she fell toward the floor barely catching herself before she hit face first. I slowly released the trafficker I held.

"See there, Zelinda, you can always count on them to do the right thing." A small sound behind me was my only warning but it was too late. Pain exploded across the back of my head, pitching me forward. The side of my face slapped the concrete and the last thing

I saw before my vision deserted me, was Lucie with the *dark watcher's* foot pressing between her shoulder blades.

TWELVE

Something disturbed my sleep. I blinked, feeling disoriented. I wasn't at home or even in a bed. I was lying on concrete. My vision swam as I tried to get up, my head pounded and a wave of nausea tore through me. I held myself still as I listened to my surroundings and evaluated my injuries.

My chest hurt over my heart and my head continued to pound, one eye was swollen mostly shut and my cheek seemed to be spilt. It didn't hurt much but it was wet with blood and stuck to the floor. I could hear a fan running but its uneven thrumming sound made me think it was out of balance. I could also hear the chitter and buzz of insects but nothing more.

I blinked my eyes and my vision was clearer. I closed them and tried to heal myself but I had too little energy to work with. I'd been drained almost completely of what little had regenerated after last night. Maybe I wasn't as physically abused as I first thought. Draining can give you a headache and make you feel… well, drained. Now I knew exactly how Lucie felt when I'd saved her from the warehouse almost a year ago. Now I understood why she thought her gift was gone. When you feel this awful it's easy to feel helpless. But what had wakened me? I listened some more and tried to rise. I heard the creak of a wooden chair and the rustle of clothes. "There you are. I wondered when you'd come back to us. You know, it's interesting what you can learn when someone isn't guarding their thoughts. We've had some trouble with Salena. She hasn't been very cooperative. I wonder if your name is really Joe but it doesn't matter because Madame Malvada will be here soon to take charge of you. I'm so pleased to be able to deliver you. This will raise me in her eyes and the reward will be… extravagant, I'm sure. She pays well for trafficking but she pays more for *watchers*."

"You know what happens to those who get too close to her, don't you?" my voice came out raspy and weak. I shifted myself until I could look him in the eye.

"Funny, you don't look so tough now, wonder boy."

"It's amazing what a good draining will do for you, isn't it?"

"Still a smart mouth, I see. Shall I drain you again? Or maybe I'll make you watch while I hurt the girl. That seems to bother you more than anything we do to you."

"You've never met Madame Malvada."

"Why do you say that?"

"Because you don't show the appropriate level of fear. I've experienced her… gifts first hand. I've seen what she does to those she's not pleased with. She will crush you under her fancy high heel like a bug."

"You know nothing. If you'd really met her, you wouldn't be here to talk about it."

"We'll see…" An explosion interrupted my speech. The building shook and bits of debris rained down on us. I saw fear and confusion in my captor's eyes. Help must be on the way. He lunged for the door and I made to escape behind him but struggled to my hands and knees. He beat me to the door easily and locked it behind him, leaving me to scrabble helplessly over the surface trying to open it.

Well damn. I looked around. I was in a concrete cube of about nine feet per side. The metal door was three inches off the ground and had a one foot square window covered by thick wire mesh. Light entered the cell from outside through a six inch by six foot opening six feet off the ground broken by bits of rebar. I saw no way to escape through that.

I took a deep breath, grasped the rebar and pulled myself up to get a better look out the opening. I knew those black cars and an evil so strong even my weakened gift could discern it. Evilia. Another blast shook the building and dust obscured my vision. When it cleared the *dark watcher* from interrogation lay on the ground, the last of his life force and gift hovering around a kneeling Evilia like a black cloud and then it was gone. The female *dark watcher* and Zelinda stood behind her, eyes glazed and dazed looking. Evilia raised dead, dark eyes toward the building. Instinctively I dropped out of sight. I was so drained I'd bet she couldn't feel me. And then I thought of Lucie…

The building shook a third time. I huddled in a corner and prayed it would afford me a little protection. Huge cracks fissured up the outer wall and a piece of the roof fell in. Before the dust even settled I was back at the window for another cautious peek. Evilia had her hand on the female *dark watcher's* throat. Blackness crawled up her arm like a vine. Evilia let go and the woman fell to the ground. She took hold of Zelinda the same way. Male voices near the outside wall distracted me and I glanced in their direction. I could see them setting another charge part way down the side of the building. I froze. If I felt for Lucie, they'd find me. If she was hurt I couldn't get to her at the moment anyway. Please, let her be okay, please. Please let me survive this blast. Before I could move, I was thrown from the window. The whole upper corner of my cell gave way and part of the roof tipped dangerously low.

When the dust settled this time, all I could see was the black cars pulling away with their own cloud of dust. Zelinda and the other female were gone. As the vehicles withdrew, the feel of oppressive evil went with them so I risked searching for Lucie. I couldn't sense beyond my own cell so I'd have to try the old-fashioned way. I figured I could just make it through the shattered corner.

As soon as I pulled myself up, I realized I'd have to hurry. Not much of the building was left and part was smoldering. Rubble, dust and ash billowed in the soft warm breeze. It brushed over my skin gently in sharp contrast to the brutal landscape and destroyed building.

"Lucie?" I called. My worry was as thick as the dust but I wasn't completely freaked out yet. I could panic later – right now I was at least doing something. I felt the concrete scraping my bare chest and stomach as I struggled through the opening. Drops of blood pushed to the surface from places scraped too deeply but the sting was bearable and kept me focused.

I stood for a moment on the ruined wall to scope out my options. I could see a whole lot of nothing except for a tiny dust cloud that was likely Evilia's caravan moving steadily west. The building itself was a large concrete rectangle reminding me of a lone Lego dropped from a child's careless hand.

I would have to systematically search what was left. Priorities... find water, find people and get them to a safe place. Finally I needed to get some help. I hung by my hands and dropped the few remaining inches onto the ground outside the building. I cautiously approached the *dark watcher*. He had been killed just like Claudia but no message had been left for me this time. I didn't understand Evilia and I hoped I never would. I checked for a pulse just in case but it was too late. I felt every pocket hoping for a phone or even a knife. No luck but he wasn't much bigger than me so I took his clothes and shoes. I started back to the building and saw two more charges. Panic seized hold of me. I shook, my chest hurt and I broke out in a sweat. It took all I had to approach the first one. I knew next to nothing about bombs. The blinking lights told me there was a good chance it was doing something. Was it remote controlled or on a timer? If I touched it, would it go off? Did I have a choice? I took a breath, picked it up, approached the fence and threw it over on the demolished side of the building. I ran away before it even hit the ground and repeated my actions for the second one.

Now, I needed to find water and survivors. The smoke and dust was making my eyes water and throat burn. I could see now that we had been brought in a side door. This must be the front office where the customers entered and transacted business because bits of burnt paper, destroyed filing cabinets and smashed computer components were hopelessly jumbled with chunks of the building. A shoe off to the side seemed out of place. I moved closer and found it attached to a no longer living body. He was not alone. The man I'd tried to hold hostage and another one were dead. None were *watchers* and each one had been shot in the head. I'm no forensics expert but from the powder burns I'd say it had been at fairly close range.

I hadn't heard the shots which I found interesting. Could they have done it before I woke up? Since there was nothing I could do for them I moved on. So far it looked like Madame Malvada had left no one behind to question.

There was nothing left of the interrogation room except for the female *watcher's* broken laptop that I had sent to the floor when I tipped over the now smoldering table. Straight across the hall had to have been the buying room. Now it was all but destroyed yet I could see remains of grandeur: A broken champagne bottle, shattered flutes, a warped silver tray, expensive shredded fabric and burning pieces of mahogany chairs. A raised stage still stood off to the side. Behind what was left of the door in the north wall I found what used to be a marble and gold-plated bathroom. Water spurted from a broken pipe near the sink. I had no way to test it, but it smelled fresh and it sprayed with the intensity of incoming water, so I paused for a much needed drink. I hadn't had all those shots for nothing, right?

Now that the dust was less intense and I'd rinsed my throat I yelled again. "Lucie!" I heard a small scraping sound and my heart leapt. I went back toward interrogation to try to get through to the cell block since there was no way I could break down the steel door without a tank. I would have to waste time looking for a key in the ruined office or see if another damaged cell on my side of the building would let me through.

I crawled over what was left of interrogation's outer wall to the shower room where water still sprayed. My side of the building was in horrible shape but at the far end where I'd been in solitary the walls were extra thick. Looking at the outside I realized it was a miracle that I'd survived. All the cells on this side appeared to be crushed and empty. The cell closest to the showers was the most ruined so I tried that way first.

Something didn't feel right as I stepped down into the cell. It was then I saw it… an arm. My stomach rolled… I'd stepped on someone. I found his wrist and felt for a pulse. I cleared the debris off as much of his body as I could. When I reached his head I felt again for a heartbeat at his neck. It was my roommate from yesterday. I swallowed hard. I barely knew him but it still hurt. His eyes stared up at nothing and were covered by a layer of dirt and ash. Blood had run from both his ears and his nose but it was already drying. I closed his eyes and moved on.

How many others had I missed in my cursory inspection going the other way? I heard a faint scraping sound again. It was a little louder. Somewhere in the gloom of the shattered building someone was still alive. Please, God, let it be Lucie. I studied the cell and then threw my shoulder into the cell door. I was right, this part of the building was so ruined that the door broke free from the hinge side. I suppose I was lucky it wasn't jammed shut from the weight of the building above it.

I took a breath of dusty, smoky air before I entered the listing hallway where the lights hung at odd angles and spit sparks. The building gave a warning moan and water ran across the floor in muddy rivulets. Death by electrocution was not high on my list of fun activities. I had to watch in every direction all the time. My eyes zipped left, right, up and down, taking in the destruction. Chunks of concrete littered the floor, broken by a splotch of sunlight from the hole in the roof. Two more bodies lay just ahead, making my heart try to beat its way out of my chest. I moved closer. Both were dead and neither was Lucie. I couldn't help but feel relieved.

In solitary, I had been separated from the rest of the prisoners but here the cells were mostly exposed to each other through rods of rebar sticking up from the poured concrete floor and secured above by thick strips of welded metal. There would have been little privacy here under normal conditions but my view was obscured by the dying building. "Lucie?" I croaked again, feeling desperate.

It was difficult to hurry yet find a safe path. The building gave a shudder and another piece of wall fell away taking a huge chunk of ceiling and most of the first cell with it. I lunged out of the way but I wasn't fast enough to avoid the falling light fixture that smashed into my shoulder. That was gonna leave a mark.

I dragged myself back to my feet to the faint sounds of weak coughing, crying and ragged pleas for help. Whoever was back here had been quiet but with the cellblock giving way they were likely now more afraid of death by crushing than abuse from our captors. Movement near the end of the row caught my eye so I moved faster despite my aching shoulder and the numbness in my arm.

Any cell that appeared to be occupied I forced open with whatever I could find to pick the locks or pry at the doors. I had any who were able, help others back out the way I'd come in. I told them to drink some water and asked them to try to find something to hold water in case we needed to walk out. The building heaved another sigh and more of it crashed down around us. I still had not located Lucie. I could feel sweat beading up and my hands begin to shake.

I reached the last cell, my last hope. There was Lucie holding pressure on a pretty nasty looking head gash on another girl. She was covered in blood and grime. I couldn't tell how much was hers but I could finally feel her. Relief and joy surged through me. Our eyes met and I knew she felt the same.

The sound of vehicles snapped me back to the task at hand. I worked frantically to break Lucie from incarceration. Her door was double locked. I could barely hold myself together I was so shaken and spent. I couldn't get my quaking fingers to pick the lock.

As the vehicles drew nearer the pressure and vibration caused more of the building to crumble away and one of the bombs I'd thrown to go off with a cacophony of sound. The latest shift of the building jammed Lucie's cell door, warping the second lock. Car doors slammed and my heart rate accelerated, slamming against my ribs and pounding in my ears, obscuring what was left of my hearing.

"Owen." Lucie spoke softly.

I didn't so much hear it as feel it. I looked to her. She had propped up her patient and had her holding a strip of Lucie's hospital gown to her head. I hadn't noticed before but now it was clear as she walked toward me. Her arms and legs were scrapped and her nails were broken. There was even a smear of blood on her face but she looked abused, not broken. Time stood still and then her hand closed over the fingers that gripped the bars of her cage so tightly the knuckles were white. Electricity traveled up my arm and not the downed wire kind. How could she look so calm?

"It's okay Owen. Leave me. Come back with help. I can hold on…"

"No!"

"Owen, I love you. I believe in you. Now, go… quickly, before it's too late."

My throat got tight, making me feel like I'd swallowed a golf ball. "I love you too, Luce. I'll be back. I swear!"

I kissed her once quickly though the bars and then melted into the shadows. I watched her move back to the other girl who shared her cell and murmur softly. I took a deep breath and found my resolve.

I could hear voices but I couldn't make out the words. I edged over to a broken section for a closer peek, but I was at the wrong angle. I looked for a weapon and a means of escape. I snatched up a piece of broken rebar on my way to the next opening. More voices had me skittering deeper into the shadows. The scrape of a foot over the loose debris on the floor startled me, it was so close. I turned, power washed over me, I raised my weapon but froze. Wait, I knew the familiar feel of that gift…

"I see you've survived to fight another day."

I relaxed my stance but didn't drop the rebar. "Bob," I replied, my voice on the shy side of friendly. "I'm surprised to see you here. I thought you were above this sort of thing."

"Madame Malvada was here and I want her."

"She's gone, so how about helping some of her victims, including Julie, before Evilia gets back there and destroys that part of her operation."

"We've already been there but we missed you. Marlo called Sarah. Seems your buddy Mitchell has been having nightmares and seeing flashes of your untimely demise. How'd *she* miss you? I was expecting a body." Was it me or did he sound almost sad about that.

"Help me free Lucie and I'll share my theories on Ms. Malvada."

"Is every dealing with you going to be a negotiation?"

"Yes sir, it is," I ground out, not liking him very much even though he was here for us at long last.

Bob gave me an assessing look as he let his power wash over me again. I couldn't tell what his gift was but I sure could feel the prickly brush of it over my senses. The building shuddered and groaned as more chunks of debris broke free. Bob didn't even flinch. It was as if he thought it wouldn't dare fall on him or perhaps he thought he had the power to hold physical objects at bay.

I broke eye contact first and made my way back to Lucie. I looked back at Bob. I could see him measuring the situation and then he began barking into his communications device. Soon a cement cutter was buzzing away at Lucie's prison from the outside. She tried to cover her patient. I pushed past Bob so that I could meet her on the other side.

Bob followed me out and around the building but he seemed uncaring and unfeeling. He was here to help yet I wondered what the cost would be. He must have felt me looking at him. "It's your job. Someone has to do it, so quit looking at me like I'm the cause of your predicament, young man."

I gave him my best scowl. I know in my heart that it isn't just *dark watchers* who have evil in their hearts and it's not only *watchers* who do good things every day, but if Bob continued to use us like this, how could he remain good?

One of Bob's peons pulled Lucie's patient from the new opening and I helped Lucie through. We walked around to where Bob's cars were parked. Sarah and White Eagle jumped from the nearest vehicle. They ran at us and knocked us to our knees in an enormous hug. Both had tears in their eyes and I knew they had been through their own kind of hell the last few days.

Of the fourteen of us captured only eight would return home. Was death better than a life of slavery and prostitution? The few staff members who remained at the facility could give us no answers but I knew Talon would give it hell. I watched her barking her own orders as her team sifted through the ruble.

"Why does Evilia Malvada kill off her henchmen?" I wondered aloud. "I understand that we can't question them this way but…"

I was surprised that Bob answered. "She works using fear. Killing off underlings forces loyalty from the others. The threat of death for subpar performance would be a strong motivator – don't you think?"

"I see your point but I think it's foolish to get rid of your allies."

"Is that so? Then we're on better standing than I thought."

I gave him a hard look. "Earlier I was under the impression that you were almost disappointed that I wasn't among the dead."

"I don't want you dead." I could still feel something hanging in the air.

"I think our relationship has suffered a backslide this mission but at least we haven't tried to kill each other yet."

Bob actually laughed. "No. Not yet. Lucie is out of her cell so I believe you owe me a theory."

"They didn't ID us and they'd drained us so low that I don't think *she* could sense us. She did get some information out of the *dark watcher* she killed and some out of Zelinda and a female *dark watcher* but I don't know what. She took the women with her."

I slid my gaze to Lucie and she broke away from Sarah, White Eagle and the medic trying to help her. She took my hand and gave Bob a stern look. "Look at you, being all friendly and stuff. Is this our reward for a job well done? Do we get one more notch of respect?"

"I think 'well done' may be going a bit far, Miss Ness. You did not capture Malvada and the evidence here is mostly destroyed. It will take us months to piece what little there is back together."

"She lost her house in Florida and another in Oregon. We have shut off her human trafficking operation down here. What more could you possibly…"

"You are so naive. Do you really believe this is even the tip of the iceberg? Do you think this is a tiny fraction of what she has in assets, trafficking operations, drug operations or reach?" Bob laughed again and it didn't sound happy, kind or understanding.

I felt angry. Lucie's grip tightened on my hand and a flush crept up her neck.

Bob looked at us steadily. "I do have a small reward for you though." He whistled through his teeth. A beefy agent I'd never seen before wearing a flack vest and shades hopped out of the lone dark pickup standing between the SUVs and slammed down the tailgate. I could see jean covered legs and scruffy running shoes. The agent's muscles bulged as he gripped an ankle and yanked. A body fell from the truck bed to the dirt.

Lucie sucked in a breath. It was her *friend*, Hal. The agent gripped the next leg that the owner was trying to draw away. He didn't have a chance of escape though. With a thud Nelson landed on his partner. Lucie made a strange sound in her throat.

"Yes, I know about what happened to you before they brought you here," Bob stated without any feeling. "They don't want to tell us what they know about Madame Malvada. I thought you could help."

"What about Julie?" I interrupted.

"She's alive, but barely. We got there just in time to stop these fellows at the gate and then to pull Julie from the burning building. They did admit that they were instructed to get rid of her and burn down the facilities by Ms. Malvada herself. It seems she caught us spying on that part of the operation. Your GPS stayed there long enough for us to know that was a place to watch. We rounded up several small players before she caught on. We also salvaged some video surveillance from the facility."

Lucie broke away from me and yanked Hal to his knees. "What'd you do to Julie, Scum?"

"What she deserved," he laughed. The laugh was quickly cut off by a blow to the throat. He grabbed his neck, choking and gagging. Lucie elbowed him in the side of the head and he fell over only to have her yank him once again to his knees.

"Where's Malvada," Lucie screamed. When he didn't answer she delivered a nice front kick right to his sternum. Her hospital gown flapped with her movements and she didn't even seem to notice or care. Hal was not doing a good job defending himself this time. One on one, Lucie was the much better fighter.

"Make her stop! What's wrong with you? You can't just stand there and watch her beat him like that!" Sarah yelled, sprinting forward.

"Sure I can," I replied, still smiling.

"What?" she yelped.

"Think of it as therapy and it won't bother you so much, Sarah."

"That is utter asininity! Letting her do that is NOT therapy!"

"Maybe not for you, Sarah, but for her, it is."

"Well, I'm thoroughly disappointed in both of you."

"I'm sorry you feel that way. I guess we're both having a weak moment, but you don't know what it was like. I don't want you to even imagine it. Nelson and his buddy attacked her in a cell, cuffed her to a post and tried to rape her. I want Lucie to know she is in charge and not a victim." I glanced over at Sarah and noting her clenched jaw added, "I'll stop her now."

The guy was sitting on his heels trying to hold Lucie off with an arm held up in a weak block. An agent was recording his every word as he alternately begged for Lucie to stop and spewed what little he knew about Madame Malvada.

"Luce," I said calmly. "Luce," I repeated, raising my voice slightly. "Lucie," I shouted, but still she ignored me so I decided on a new approach. "Luce, I can see your... ah..."

"My what? My Spanx?" she replied with a wink. Yeah, she was okay and it looked like her therapy session was about over.

"I thought if I referenced your underwear I might actually get your attention since calling your name wasn't doing it."

"My hearing is fine. My attitude wasn't done being adjusted," she replied with a final kick. "I should make him write, 'I will never hurt another woman ever' with his own bodily fluids."

"Call her off, will ya?" Hal begged pitifully.

Bob and his crew took over for Lucie. Hal and Nelson were both talking, but I had the sense that Bob had lied about needing Lucie to convince them as they didn't have much to add. As low on the totem pole as they were, Evilia would have told them next to nothing. I believed they had only met her once before today. They followed Zelinda's orders. Bob was after something and I hoped it wasn't dirt on us.

I wrapped Lucie in a hug and Sarah scrounged up a blanket for her. "You stink," Lucie mumbled softly to me.

"I know. I'm sorry."

"You stink like a *dark watcher* and what are you wearing?"

"What? Oh, the guy from interrogation, ah, loaned me his clothes."

Lucie sighed. "I just want to go home. I'd rather be there getting threatening mail than be here."

"I wish things were different, Luce."

"We are who we are. We can't change that."

Bob bundled us all up in the rigs and drove us to the San Diego office. Julie had been transported to the hospital under guard. Now it was up to the cyber geniuses like Marlo to track Evilia for Bob and we had a debriefing to look forward to.

Lucie and I were allowed to shower and then dress in some of our own clothes. We were led to a windowless room and told to sit at a large conference table where several agents, Sarah and White Eagle were already sitting. Bob walked in last. I snagged a water from the center of the table and drank deeply. I wondered when I'd stop feeling thirsty and exhausted.

I tried to listen and respond but like Lucie, I just wanted to go home. I found it difficult to keep my scowl under control. I even found myself snapping and growling my answers. A part of me felt like I was being unfair but mostly I was pissed. I didn't need a critique of my job performance right now.

Once the attention was off me, Sarah leaned in. "What is wrong with you? You're not acting right. I mean not like yourself. It's not like you to blow things so out of proportion," she remarked as she laid a hand on my knee. Her eyes were full of sadness but held a hint of forgiveness too.

I closed my eyes for a moment and dug deep before I took advantage of a break in the conversation. "I apologize, Bob. I'm very tired and I guess I'm feeling used right now. Maybe we could do this tomorrow."

"We will do this now. I'm flying you home tonight. Then you can have a day off," he snapped.

"How about some food and a nap? We haven't slept in over forty hours," I snarled back, returning immediately to my previous attitude.

"Look kid, it's your life – you make the choices but then you have to live with the ones you make. I'm telling you I need answers while they're fresh in your mind. Don't underestimate the allure of darkness. It's strong. Now talk to me and then I'll let you go." Bob turned to the nearest agent. Pull up the photos and video.

"Stop it! You're making my butt tingle," Lucie begged when they brought up all the shots of where we'd been and the bodies Evilia had left behind.

Bob was relentless. He made us talk about the examination room. He finally stopped when Lucie began to heave. Nothing but water hit the garbage can that was quickly shoved in her direction by a worried agent.

"Fine," he snarled. "Bring in some food and we'll take a short break."

Sarah tried to talk to him but he shrugged her off and left to deal with other matters. Most of his agents left with him. *Ran behind him like loyal dogs was more like it.* I was touched that we were so important to him. NOT! I had to remind myself that to him we were nothing but tools and not to take it personally.

Not two minutes later one of the agents returned with a tray of breads, fruits and cheeses. Maybe I should have been nicer and not quite so free with the sarcasm. Then I looked over the tray skeptically and changed my mind. The level of sarcasm had been just right. I was hungry but this didn't look good. Cardboard would be more appealing.

"What is this? I can't eat this," I said looking at what was in my hand.

"It's bread, you dope," Lucie replied with an eye roll before she devoured her slice.

"It can't be bread. I don't believe that bread should have *stuff* in it. I declare this to be unbread and unedible."

"You're so weird! Just eat it."

"But I am entertaining," I exclaimed as I slid my slice over to her.

"Put a little something on it and it's not so bad."

"Yeah, sure," I said and bit into an apple instead.

Bob was back shortly, though no less grumpy and finished quickly with us. We were then rushed from the building, shoved into a company SUV and then into a plane in quick succession. Two and a half hours later we were in another SUV headed home. After our misadventures in California, school would feel so… boring.

THIRTEEN

A day later I would have believed it had all been a nightmare except that I still had my fake tattoos and Lucie's hair was still nearly black. Sarah vowed she would have it all undone before school started. I would have to keep my battered body hidden at practice today that was for sure.

I had decided that I would go ahead and lay off of football but my father felt that I needed to be normal. We made it back just in time – if I'd missed any more practice I would've been cut. It seemed like all we did was argue from the moment I walked in the door and I was *so* not in the mood. He didn't even ask how our trip had gone. He just looked at me and shook his head. I couldn't bring myself to tell my mom what had happened but she knew that not only was I not quite right mentally at the moment but that I was definitely keeping something from her.

Daily doubles were not fun and about killed me. Adrian looked at me skeptically. He knew I usually kept in pretty good shape but today I was a mess. I only spoke when spoken to and even then my answers were abrupt. When I pulled it again the next day, he got in my face.

"What's wrong with you? You were fine and then I don't see you for two weeks and now you're all weird and stuff."

"Sorry."

"I don't want to hear that you're sorry, Owen. I want to know what's wrong?"

I looked around to be sure no one was listening and then whispered, "We had work in California."

"I figured," he interrupted.

"Let's just say it didn't go well."

"Can I help?"

"Please don't. It's almost more than I…"

"Then let me help."

"No."

"Fine!" He turned and walked away, his shoulders hunched and his back stiff.

I closed my eyes for a moment. I didn't belong here – not anymore. My dad could make me play football but I would never fit in the normal world again.

I hadn't seen Lucie since we came home and that worried me and now Adrian wasn't speaking to me. My head was not in the game and I was growing to hate football. It bit into my *watcher* time… and whatever happened to a break? Right now all there was time for was eating, sleeping and football. More than ever I was unable to help my friends and even had to push some minor visions I collected off onto them that I didn't have time to pursue. I could feel the balance shifting and I didn't need Marlo to tell me. Something was brewing and it wasn't a good pot of Joe. Between daily doubles I went to the shop so that I wasn't too far out of the loop of what was going on but I felt a gulf widening between me and the rest of the team.

Bob and the San Diego team were cleaning out the rest of the traffickers but we were still on the lookout for Madame Malvada. I guess we just didn't trust Bob to find her or to tell us when he did. I knew from personal experience that he'd rather use us as bait anyway so he was probably just fine with sitting back and letting her come to us. Once her numbers were down, Bob could sweep in and finish her. I got to where I was angry all the time and having Lucie act weird wasn't helping. She said she was too busy for me. I tried to be patient because I knew that our trip down south had screwed her up too. When her hair returned to an almost normal color her attitude improved but she was still not my Lucie.

We'd been home for almost three weeks and I felt like a stranger in my own life. At least school began and with it came our new routine. Boy was I looking forward to graduation. The only good part about football was spending some guy time hanging with Adrian, Jesse, Josh and Joel but it took me away from Lucie, Marlo and the training of Alex. Adrian warmed up a little but I knew he was still kinda mad at me for not sharing more *watcher* stuff with him. Mitchell, Lucie and Marlo had really stepped up to the plate where Alex was concerned. If nothing else he would be well rounded with all the attention he got. Everyone worked with him on the things they were good at. When Neil had time off he also came in to teach his skills to everyone and to learn from us. White Eagle oversaw all of it and Marlo did the scheduling. I knew it was strange for White Eagle but he'd adapted well from working with just one or maybe two *watchers* at a time to the herd he now had. Using the talent Evilia had taught me I could see their bonds growing and strengthening.

Too bad I couldn't find those same bonds on the football field. After another frustrating practice the coach yanked me aside. "I'd kick you off this team faster than you can say 'touchdown' except you're my only backup."

"I'll try to do better," I replied, not feeling it.

"Ryer, you're killing me. What is it with you? It's only the third week of school. You're grades are almost down to the cutoff line and you show no interest here or in class. Are you depressed or something?"

"I've just got a lot on my mind."

"You wanna talk?"

"No thanks, I'll try harder," I sighed.

He let me go but he didn't look happy. I knew that unfortunately I was back on his radar. I thought about it all the way to the shop. I was going for my usual quick check-in and to help close but things didn't get any better there. Lucie sat with her chin propped on a hand staring blindly at a book on Depression era glass, a piece sitting in front of her. Marlo had two laptops running but his eyes were on her. Neither one had noticed me yet.

"Are you okay?" Marlo asked her in a worried voice.

"Sure Mars, I'm fine."

"No you're not. Ever since you came back from California you're not the same. You try to pretend you are but I can see that you've changed." *At least I wasn't alone in that thought.*

"It's the hair color. All the brunette dye didn't wash out and they cut it in a new style. I tried to have a stylist here put in some highlights to cover it up but I look different."

"Lucie, you don't have to talk to me about it but at least be honest with yourself – it's not your hair that's the problem."

She sighed, "You're right, Mars. The things I heard will haunt me forever, as will the things I experienced. Perhaps worst of all, Bob showed me the darkness I carry inside. I know I'm not a good person…" her voice trailed off. I wanted to burst through the curtain and tell her she was wrong but I hesitated. She had already said more to Marlo than she had to me. Maybe I'd been wrong to let her fester. I just thought she'd work it out on her own.

"Lucie, we all make mistakes and we all have regrets. Do NOT let them own you. You're a good person and I'm proud to call you friend."

"Oh, Mars."

"Listen to me…"

"You don't know," she interrupted, her voice thin and raw. "You weren't there… I… I beat someone who was defenseless and… laughed. It was… wrong."

"You were in a bad place. Horrible things had happened to you and you hadn't slept in at least three days. Don't be so hard on yourself. Think of it as going through a crucible and living to tell the tale. "

"I'm a better person than that. I should never have let Bob manipulate me and I shouldn't have been so easily encouraged to do something I knew was wrong. I came out of your crucible… dark."

"He should never have manipulated you! He was wrong. You need to forgive yourself and move on. Remember what Lila says, 'You only need to be the best you, you can be. No other expectations are necessary.'"

I heard Lucie sigh again and then mumble, "I guess."

I pushed through the curtain. Lucie scowled at me. "You were listening," she accused.

"Yes."

Her scowl deepened.

"Luce, I love you. It hurts me to see you in pain. I want to help but you won't talk to me."

"What's there to talk about? You were there."

"I saw it from my perspective, not yours."

She hesitated, rounded her shoulders and hung her head. "You're right. I feel like a rotten human being. You're Teflon, nothing bothers you. I felt dumb talking to you about anything that happened down there because... well, it had to be just as bad for you and talking about it is like reliving it."

"You're wrong. Stuff does bother me. I try to use it all as learning for the next time. I ask myself, what would White Eagle do? I also think about how I can be the best example I can and I try not to repeat my mistakes. That doesn't mean I don't make plenty."

"Wow. Channeling Miles much? Now you really sound old."

"He's part of me, Luce. I can't help but be influenced by that."

"Fine, you asked for it. I feel like a bad person because it felt good to get even with Hal and Nelson. What they tried to do to me… that helpless, hopeless feeling… I guess something broke within me and then the slightest nudge from Bob and I was doing things I knew were wrong and I was so out of it that I didn't even care that I was on display, half naked, with my hospital gown flapping in the breeze and showing off my underwear. At least my bare bum wasn't hanging out and Talon's stylists hadn't put me in a thong."

I touched my forehead to hers. "You are the bravest person I know."

Lucie laughed a little. "Yeah, I'm ferocious."

Marlo was right, she was different. I just hadn't wanted to really admit it to myself. I was different too. Not all *watcher* scars are on the outside. We tried to act normal but most kids avoided us like we carried around an invisible bubble of free space wherever we went. It showed in the classroom where the seats by us were often the last filled and at lunch where few were brave enough to sit by us. Our motto had always been heads down and don't draw attention - now we were paying for it.

"I'm sorry, Luce. I wish I could make all the bad feelings go away and block out the ugliness that you and I experienced but I can't. It will take time."

"At least we've gotten very little hate mail since we've been back. She must be busy somewhere else. She must not realize it was us in San Diego or I feel like the hate mail and threats would have escalated. I kind of wish she'd just get it over with."

Marlo interjected. "She is busy elsewhere. As best I can tell she has returned to South America to regroup and retrain her team and you know no one will let us go down there. We'll have to wait for her to come back here."

"We have a lot of work to do to get ready then," I sighed.

Marlo and Lucie looked at each other and then at me. I knew that look – how do you prepare for the unknown?

Even though it was just after my birthday, our mob went to Rhinelander for some good German food and to celebrate my birthday. I really wasn't in much of a celebratory mood but I tried to fake it. Lucie got another picture for her wall when they sang to me and a waitress put whipped cream on my nose. At least I looked happy. I'd asked Adrian along as a peace offering and to his credit he accepted. I tried to tell him about what was going on with me but I wouldn't tell him everything. I just wished he could see that I was trying to protect him.

I felt helpless to fix Lucie or even myself so I put lots of my energy into Alex. He was good at *watcher* business. Somehow he was managing the middle school alone. They were mostly small problems like I had when I was there but he handled them deftly, without drawing attention to himself which helped him to be better accepted than we were right now. He had always been more outgoing. It made me feel proud of the work I had done with him and like a failure because no matter how I tried, I would never fit in like he did.

It felt strange to be wearing a sweatshirt again. I couldn't believe that just a few weeks ago we were wearing shorts and t-shirts while we worked up a sweat just sitting in class. It made it hard to think and made most everyone grouchy.

"Ryer!" Oh crap. I'd zoned out like in middle school.

Marlo kicked my foot with his. My eyes snapped to his paper where his pen rested and back to our teacher.

"$C_6H_{12}O_6$ is the formula for glucose or fructose," I answered, trying to sound like I'd been paying attention.

His eyes squinched up a bit letting me know I'd irritated him but then he moved on to someone else. I heaved a silent sigh of relief. A few questions later and he turned us loose to work on worksheets in partnerships. Once the room was at a low murmur he called me to the front.

"What's with you?" he asked in a low, soft voice so other students wouldn't overhear.

I looked him in the eye trying to formulate an adequate answer.

"I've talked to your football coach. You're not performing out there either. The only thing keeping you from flunking this class is that you've done okay on classwork and the homework you've managed to turn in. I've seen the strange stuff you've taken to doodling on the edges of your papers. Talk to me."

"I'm fine," I managed to force out through stiff lips.

"If you won't talk to me, then at least talk to someone. Talk to your counselor or go to the clinic. You're a good kid. Don't… blow it. You flunk another quiz; I'll have to email your mom."

"I hear you."

I slunk back to my seat and tried to focus but it was hopeless. I was a wreck and people were noticing. Crap. Maybe I should fake a nervous breakdown. I was about there anyway. Maybe Evilia would just come kill me and then I wouldn't have to worry about it anymore.

School and football were suffering. Heck my life was suffering. What was wrong with me? I couldn't bring myself to care about anything except revenge. I began to dream of our final confrontation. Fear and anger ruled my soul. Sometimes I dreamed that I won and sometimes I lost in a nightmare. Either way I was not sleeping well. During the day it was becoming an effort to pretend that everything was okay. I was not immune to the worried glances I got from the people who loved me but I was scared for them too.

Anger on the football field was useful, if I could channel it, but the depression was almost incapacitating. My mind wandered and I was tackled again. The coach yanked me up by my pads and screamed at me like I deserved. "Run two laps and then come talk to me. I need to cool off."

"Yes, coach." I took off. This sucked. Maybe I should just quit. I saw Adrian watching me. Maybe I should keep my head down and keep moving. When I finished the second lap I returned to the coach. I wasn't sure he'd cooled off any though.

"Ryer, I'm disappointed in you. You showed such promise, but this year – your mommy signed you up and you missed all the practice you could miss at the beginning. You didn't even attend one camp. You've gone from super star to mediocrity. AND when I actually get you here you are either distracted or slow. I've seen you be amazing. What happened to that guy?"

"I'll try to do better."

"We've had this problem before – you and I." I looked at him and I looked at Adrian. "What are you looking at him for?"

"Maybe I'm not here for me anymore. Maybe I'm here for my friend and maybe that's the wrong reason. Look, I know my mom told you… I missed practice because of work. I may miss more. I guess you'll have to choose if it's worth it. I'm wondering if it is anymore."

"What are you, sixteen? You should be a kid, Ryer."

"I'm seventeen and I haven't been a kid for a time."

"Is something going on at home?"

"No sir. There is life after high school and I have to pay for that."

"You could've had a football scholarship. You still could if you focus. Our last game is next week and there'll be a scout."

"That's the trick isn't it? Do what I know pays or gamble on a scout giving me a scholarship."

"Bring me your work schedule and I will try to be a little more understanding."

Awesome, I thought sarcastically. I'd have to have Marlo make one up. I had no set hours. *Watcher* stuff… happened - there was very little planning. On the other hand, Madame Malvada, Kraeghton or Carmichael could kill me tomorrow and then I wouldn't have to worry about school or football.

It took everything I had to keep focused the rest of practice. I wasn't even sure I wanted to go to the shop afterwards but I drove my Kawasaki there anyway.

I could hear the rhythmic thump of a martial arts practice session commencing in the back. Max smiled and waved as I passed through the front of the shop but he was busy with a customer so he otherwise ignored me. It was past the time he usually went home anyway so this must be a good customer.

I paused at the curtain. Alex moved fluidly across the floor. He was scary good. He was accelerating in rank at about the fastest pace allowable in karate. I watched him spin completely around and strike at Neil, the heal of his palm to the side of Neil's face and then lightning-quick flip away before Neil could block, let alone retaliate. I knew Neil was good, but Alex was better. I had watched him work with all of us including Adrian and the triplets - no matter what we threw at him he adapted and improved on it. Each of us had a different style and it... didn't matter. White Eagle came and stood next to me. "I know... he's very dedicated and focused. He will attract the wrong kind attention if he isn't careful."

"I feel sorry for him. What else does he have? He'll be able to participate in so little at school because someone will have to be with him all the time... watching. He's become withdrawn from most of his friends for the same reason. If one of us can't go where he is or at least be nearby then he can't go. It's not so bad for Lucas but for a seventh grader... We're making him weird."

"He is powerful. He may become more dangerous than even you. Who knows? I see him changing before my eyes. His body is changing as you would expect for his age but his personality is too. He is like you, taller and skinnier by the day. Marlo's going to have to put him on an eating plan as well."

We continued to watch until Neil called a halt. Alex smiled at him and thanked him before bouncing over to us. "See? I need this too. You can't just train my mind and abilities, Owen. I want to be at least a fourth degree black belt of karate one day but I won't neglect my other styles of fighting. I plan to be a force to be reckoned with."

"I'd say you're there," I replied a little gruffly. "I know Neil has been teaching you Krav Maga, Lucie has taught you gymnastics, Mitchell to throw knives and shoot and Marlo has tutored you on the computer. What is left for us?" I finished as I flicked a hand between myself and White Eagle?

"Are you jealous?" Alex asked as he tilted his head to the side like Mom often did when asking a question.

"No! Maybe. I didn't get my gift until after my fourteenth birthday and here you are almost two years early. Now I'm busy and you are starting to get your own messages. The middle school will be lucky to have another *watcher* but..."

"I know, you worry like Mom does, but you have to let me do this. It's part of who I am."

"You're too driven," I snapped.

"Did you say that to him, back in the day?" Alex asked White Eagle.

White Eagle slid me a glance. I knew how he felt. There was no right answer here. He could not win this one. He finally settled for, "Mmmm, let's get back to work on your other talents, shall we?"

I laughed. I couldn't help it. Alex was right, he was turning into a mini me and White Eagle was still White Eagle. It was good to know that some things remained the same when it felt like my world was fracturing around me.

When I opened up enough to vent to White Eagle about being gone so much during football season he reminded me that we had to live. We could not be just *watchers* twenty-four hours a day. I knew that, but it made me cranky so I reminded him that he hadn't had a honeymoon. He just smiled and told me things were different for them. He wasn't – they weren't twenty anymore. They had a longer view of life and I should relax and learn to enjoy the small moments.

I did appreciate Marlo once again for making sure that he, Lucie and I had all our classes together. Adrian had dropped out of the college credit classes but had all the other ones with us. He had even arranged for Adrian to have all his other classes with his buddies. Having a friend like Marlo is truly priceless. *There, White Eagle, I appreciated a 'small moment'.*

Weeks later, White Eagle and Sarah still had not taken a real honeymoon or even a mini vacation. They were afraid to be caught off guard, just the two of them or to not be here when the time came. Much as they trusted us and our growing abilities they didn't feel comfortable leaving us completely alone. I felt bad about it but I didn't know how to fix that either. I did finally convince him to at least take Sarah to the beach for a few days. I just wished it was Lucie and me who were there as I tried to listen to my teacher ramble on about our latest novel in English. I just wasn't into it. I mean really, with all the problems I was facing right now, who cared about what people were doing in Greece several hundred years ago? Besides, right now all I could think about was our latest upcoming virtual meeting with Bob.

One of the few things that made me marginally happy was when Marlo would find electronic clues to Madame Malvada's activities. Just as Marlo had predicted Bob would not authorize us to go to Colombia. He wanted the intel, nothing more. "Be a kid, junior, and do your schoolwork," he said in a condescending tone as he ended our latest Skype.

"I just want to be done with her," I replied in disgust. "And I hate it when he calls me 'junior' like I'm a child."

"Sometimes hurrying just means that you stumble into disaster faster," Marlo said looking completely serious.

I wanted to say more but Sarah agreed, "Don't rush it. We will learn more as time goes by."

"Ugh –fine," I grumbled.

I changed into practice gear and took it out in sweat. I pulled out my old broom and swung it around like a staff. I might not know when she was coming at me or how, but I would be ready!

Lucie joined me. No one else had experienced what we had in San Diego. No one else had seen or felt what we had first-hand so how could they understand?

I was a little surprised when Adrian bounced in. "I thought I'd work out with you guys today and I brought treats."

"Mt. Dew, ugh, I just smell it and I get a caffeine headache. It's like a bad drug," she whined as she grabbed her head for emphasis.

"You're nuts, Lucie! I love Dew! It's the bomb and the rush of caffeine is pure power, baby!" Adrian snapped back at her.

We all laughed – it felt good to break the tension. I just worried that Adrian had an ulterior motive for being here. I didn't want him getting hurt by Evilia.

"I'll take one," Neil enthused, grabbing a can. "These guys are too healthy, like Mica. I need a little junk food." Adrian's grin widened.

Neil was not getting many *watcher* hits so he focused on his FBI job which was now mainly to watch over us. It didn't seem to bother him at all but it would have made me crazy. He and Marlo helped Alex with the small problems that I was too busy for and together they worked on the bigger ones with Lucie. We tried to foresee what was coming with no luck so we all taught any skill we had to the others in a never-ending cycle of 'always be prepared'.

"Remember, the more you sweat in practice, the less you will bleed when the enemy comes for you," White Eagle said, repeating what he'd been saying almost daily.

Practice and preparation became our main objectives but when the attack finally came it did so without warning and from a completely unexpected direction.

FOURTEEN

I looked at the sky as I dragged myself down our street to the bus stop. It was black and gray with glints of the deepest blue seeping past the clouds. Dark as it was you could tell it was morning from the glow of the many house lights. All over the neighborhood porch lights glimmered and kitchen lights were on, warm and friendly. It was a sharp contrast to the petulant clouds. Rain was coming; it wasn't a question of if, but when. Who goes to school in the dark anyway? Me, apparently.

I was so tired this morning that it was hard to work up the energy to care about anything. I just wanted sleep. I seriously considered skipping. It's a good thing I was older and wiser now because back in eighth grade, I would have done it in a heartbeat.

I looked over to Marlo and Lucie where they stood waiting for me by the street sign. They too showed all the signs of exhaustion. All of us dozed on the bus. We didn't say a word as we walked slowly to our first class. Adrian held a cup of coffee and wore a big grin. It was almost more than I could stand this morning.

Why wouldn't he be full of energy? I thought uncharitably. He'd had a good night's sleep and he could look forward to ending his day with two periods of auto mechanics at the satellite campus. We were stuck here.

"Cheer up, Bucko. I'll be thinking of you in chemistry while I'm playing with cars!" Adrian laughed and punched me in the shoulder. He flashed me his signature grin and then whispered, "I'm glad I'm not you today. You look like you haven't slept in weeks."

"Feels like it too," I grumbled. Then I brightened a little. At least I wouldn't have PE in the rain like Alex but the constant strain of watching for Evilia, dealing with Bob and training was wearing me down to nothing.

"See you at practice, Buddy. Be awake by then. Our last game is tomorrow."

"Sure Aid, I'll get right on it."

I took my seat and prepared to endure my day. I kept getting a weird vibe – that strange sense that I was being watched again, yet I couldn't sense a *dark watcher*. The feeling persisted through practice making me even edgier.

I exited the locker room from our final practice of the year. I was just about the last one out. I was tired and frustrated. Many thoughts churned through my mind like fall leaves flying around in a strong wind. The lights on the field went out, throwing the area behind the stands into darkness and someone stepped in front of me. I dropped my gear and lunged to the side. Another body appeared at the end of the stands by the parking lot. I sprinted toward him but altered direction at the last second and headed for the ramp to the upper gym, grabbed the railing and flung myself over. I hit the top of the ramp and ran up the wall at the end and flipped over the top. He would have to go around unless he knew parkour like me.

I could hear the pounding feet of the men behind me. One spoke so softly I couldn't hear but the other I could make out. "I hate these kids!"

Someone else loomed in front of me. I had to get them away from the high school and other students. I stepped forward, grabbed his shirt and dropped to my back with my foot at his lower belly. I tossed him on over the top of me with a crash. I was on him again in an instant before he could recover. I pounded my fist into the side of his face with a crack and then I was choked from behind.

A garrote yanked me backwards and I couldn't gain my footing. A black bag was thrust over my head. My last thought before I passed out was Lucie and the prayer that she would find my dropped gear by the locker room.

I woke up to the steady thrum of wheels on asphalt and rough carpet under my arm. The black bag was still over my head, my arms bound behind me and my ankles tied. My cell phone was gone but I had GPS in my shoe. It was costly but Bob had funded it for all of us and Marlo diligently tracked Mitchell, Lucie, Alex, himself and me. I tried to sense the van. Were these *dark watchers*, hunters, stalkers, or reapers? Were they taking me to Evilia? Would this finally be over? I couldn't tell what I was feeling.

The van came to a halt. The doors opened and I was dragged out by my armpits. Since I could see nothing I focused on what I could hear. My hands weren't asleep so I hadn't been out long. The time lapse told me we couldn't have gone far and the distinctive buzz of a far-off plane confirmed it. I could hear the steady swish of cars but it was very faint under three more distinct sounds: Water rushing over rocks – a lot of it, occasional cars at a closer distance than the freeway sounds and the slap of metal sheeting.

"Are you sure you've got the right kid?"

"Yeah, the picture matches the one we got, his cell phone is locked up tight and he can fight."

"Both of you shut up."

"Lots of kids lock their cell phones. That doesn't prove anything."

"What do you care? He'll make use of him either way."

"I'm just afraid of what he'll do to us."

"Shut up you idiots. He can hear you – you know."

I was shoved from behind. They stopped talking but I listened to their boots and felt gravel under my own feet. There was also some patchy asphalt and then the breeze ended as my feet touched concrete. The sounds of banging, loose metal sheeting increased and I could hear faint whistles and howls as the wind blew around what had to be a large structure. Where was I? A truck nearby used his Jake brake giving me another hint.

"Tie him up. He'll be here soon. I gotta get some ice for my face. Damn kid cracked my cheekbone."

One set of feet walked away and I was pushed into an old metal folding chair. The moment they cut my feet apart, I tried to kick but they were ready. The garrote was back around my neck and pulled tight until I held still. One held me by the garrote and the other zip tied my ankles to the chair. I hated being hampered by the hood. I would have to wait. My stomach growled, reminding me of the time. After San Diego these guys didn't scare me much and Lucie wasn't here to worry about. Sooner or later Marlo would have me tracked down.

A train whistle blew in the distance. The sound of the wheels hitting each new section of track grew in intensity until I wondered if I was sitting on the tracks. The vibration increased until I could feel it through my bones and the whistle about deafened me. We had to be right at a crossing. Train, freeway, road, falling water but no boat sounds... THINK! Train, freeway, waterfall... old Oregon City? Could we be by the falls at the abandoned paper mill?

"When's he coming?" one of them asked as soon as the train noise died down.

"Soon. Why do you care? You're being paid well."

"Should we give him some water or something?"

"Are you kidding? What's wrong with you? You're a bad guy."

"Well, I just thought..."

"Don't do that."

"Do what?"

"Think!"

"But he's just sitting there, not moving. Maybe he's sick."

"He's not sick, dumb ass, he's waiting."

"I'm just saying, maybe we got the wrong kid, maybe he's scared, maybe we hurt him, maybe he's crying, maybe…"

"Will you shut up?" the other guy interrupted.

These guys had to be the most retarded douchebags ever to exist. Now was as good a moment as any - their attention was off me, on each other and I was down to two foes. I had pinpointed their locations from their voices. I tightened all my muscles, whapped my wrists against my back, breaking the ties and cutting my wrists. I grabbed the chair back, stood up and slammed the chair against the floor, using all of my body weight to break it. I caught myself in a squat and flipped the remains through my legs, smacking the nearest captor and knocking him to the ground. What was left of the chair crumpled on impact. I swung the piece of chair-back left in my hand at the other guy as I yanked off the hood with the other. He tried to slap it away but I came in under his guard and sunk the broken piece of tubing into his thigh.

"You're pretty good, but it's done like this, kid," the captor with the damaged cheek snarled. I turned and saw an old Colt revolver in his hand. I dove toward him and rolled, his bullet pinging off the floor where I'd just been moments before. His eyes went wide as I tackled him to the floor making the Colt spin free.

The guy I hit with the chair picked up the Colt and fired in our general direction. I quickly rolled, putting the guy with the damaged cheek between us. He fired again but the bullet hit his buddy in the back. I pushed him off, flipped to my feet and charged the last man standing. He fired again and pain seared through the side of my head. I kept coming. He was so startled, he dropped the gun. I kicked it away. When he reached for it I kicked him. He bent at the waist but used the movement to throw me over his shoulder. We went down in a heap to fight from our knees. He came in for a jab. I used that arm to spin to my feet, continuing the spin to kick him to the ground. I dropped to his side, took his neck in my hands and squeezed.

"I know who you are – I've seen you fight before. You are the one and only… Owen Ryer."

I looked up startled. I'd not heard anyone else enter but then I couldn't hear very well out of my left ear right now anyway.

"Now, stand up slowly or I will put a bullet in you myself." I slowly released my hands and the man I'd held rolled into the fetal position and covered his neck. I stood. I could smell blood and feel the hot stickiness of it oozing down the side of my face and into my shirt.

"You've been changed in ways that only someone like me could understand."

"Who are you?" I grated past my damaged throat.

"It doesn't matter. It is the job, not the name that counts. I've been a prisoner. I know what that looks like. I've also been a captor. Being a prisoner has made me *very* good at my job."

I tilted my head to the side to better evaluate the opposition. He was dressed all in black, with dark hair, skin and eyes. His eyes crinkled at the corners making him look old, yet the scraggly mustache and goatee made him look youthful. He had dangerous written all over him from his long hair to his beat-up boots. His long black coat made me think of the Matrix films. He had beads, woven bands and leather bracelets around both wrists. The scariest was black leather with a metal medallion sporting a multitude of skulls. I swallowed hard even though I didn't mean to and I wanted even less to give something away to this man who I felt… already knew almost everything. He smiled slowly making me think he could read my mind.

"What about them?" I asked, indicating his buddies in an attempt to distract him.

He continued to smile. "Oh, them? They aren't important. They did their job. Now I don't have to pay them." And then he shot each kidnapper in the head and quickly retrained the weapon on me.

This man was no *dark watcher*. He was… something else, but no less terrifying. At the moment he reminded me of Evilia. "What do you want?"

"I want to be paid." Apparently he liked to play games because he kept smiling that smile that said he knew something I didn't.

I would play the game but only because I needed information and the longer I delayed the more likely Marlo was to find me. "Who do you work for?"

"Ah, now we're getting somewhere." He was good. His semiautomatic had not wavered at all. "I work for Stephan Kraeghton."

My eyebrows shot straight to my hairline. I didn't mean to give anything away but this news was... unexpected. "What is he paying you to do? Kidnap me? Kill me?"

"You disappoint. The plan is much more intricate than that. If I wanted you dead you would be. We shall be allies."

"I don't think so."

"That is very nearsighted of you. You haven't even heard the offer yet."

Clearly he was waiting for a response from me. "Fine, what's the offer?"

"You are going to help me assassinate Madame Evilia Alejandra Malvada."

"Freeze!" A disembodied voice shouted.

He didn't flinch. "Oh good, your friends have arrived to take you home. Think hard on my offer. I'll see you soon, *watcher* boy."

"Put down your weapon." He squatted to lay down the semiautomatic but then flicked his wrist, a cable burst out and he zipped into the rafters. Shots were fired but he was in the shadows and then simply gone.

I stayed staring at the spot he had disappeared from, as chaos erupted around me. Lucie broke through the crowd of agents to lunge at me and squeeze me in a fierce hug.

"Are you okay?"

"Yeah."

"You're bleeding again."

"Yep." I noticed some people in the group I did not recognize so I held my tongue.

"What happened to your ear?"

"Failed piercing," I quipped.

"What's wrong with you?"

"Feed me and I'll tell you." I put my arm around Lucie's shoulders and led her over to Sarah. "I'm not talking until I know it's safe."

Sarah got us out of there as fast as she could. "Thank goodness they didn't do anything to your phone," she said sounding relieved.

"He wanted me to be found. He didn't care about the guys who grabbed me."

"Who?" Sarah and Lucie asked together.

"I don't know his name. I'll work up a picture with Joy and then we'll put Marlo on the hunt for his identity. For now, the mystery man just wanted to talk. He told me that he works for Stephan Kraeghton and Kraeghton wants me to help this mystery man to assassinate Madame Evilia Alejandra Malvada. He wanted me to think about it. I said no, but it does hold a certain appeal."

"Owen, No!" both of them spoke again.

"I told you, I said no."

At least they fed me as promised by picking up take-out before we returned home. Lucie fixed up my ear and wrists as best she could. This time I'd have to confide in Mom. I had the feeling she had a new threat to look out for. I trudged home from Sarah's dreading the confrontation each step of the way. I got lucky and found them in the kitchen and was able to pull her and Alex into the garage to tell them what had happened to me. I had to let them know that I was afraid if Kraeghton and his assassin couldn't get to me that

Alex might be the next target. I hated seeing even more worry and fear in their eyes. It was just how I'd felt looking at Sarah and Lucie earlier.

FIFTEEN

We decided my latest wounds would be from a riding accident. I'd gone off-road and drove into a wire, seeing it only at the last minute. I'd thrown up my wrists. I'd saved my neck but not my ear. At least I'd look scary for Halloween without a costume.

For once my day was going okay but not Marlo's. Caitlyn broke up with him at the football game. It left him feeling half sad and half relieved. It left me wondering if we were receiving some evil juju or something. At least football was done and I vowed I would not return no matter what Adrian or my dad wanted. It just wasn't worth it anymore.

I spent the weekend at the shop - partly to get away from my dad and partly to get back in touch with my *watcher* side – the side I'd neglected for football. I had said no, but the offer to get help killing Evilia… lingered. Marlo spent the weekend with his dad dickering over a used, ten-year-old Chrysler Cirrus. He was putting some of his hard earned money into something other than electronics. Lucie admitted that she was a little jealous. A car, gas and insurance were too much for her to swing right now.

Adrian hung with us some at school but mostly it was just Lucie, Marlo and me. The funny part was that it was that way all the time because of Marlo's computer magic. His latest endeavor had been to figure out how many classes we could miss and not come under too much notice. We would just have to be sure that one of us was always there to pick up our assignments. We did them together but we were on our own for tests. I never studied for those and it showed. I'd have been getting D's in almost everything if it weren't for Marlo and Lucie.

I again felt eyes watching me wherever I went and I would have thought it was my imagination except Lucie felt it too. I tried to find the source but I couldn't pinpoint it. Had Evilia learned something about us, or at least me? Maybe it was the assassin. Whoever it was, if they could keep themselves hidden, I had lost my advantage. The letters and photos in the mail became more frequent. Sarah's team had yet to prove anything but we knew it had to be Evilia's work. There were never any prints and the ink, paper and photos were not uncommon. The envelopes you could get at any OfficeMax. The postmarks showed that they came from all over the state and occasionally from other parts of the US in a seemingly random pattern - just to be sure we never forgot her - but it got to where they didn't even scare us anymore.

Three weeks went by and I had no more contact from the strange man who'd me kidnapped and Evilia stayed frustratingly out of reach but clearly visible to Bob who seemed to delight in letting us know, under the guise that we were safe from her. We all knew it was a big steaming pile of… you know. We knew she could send an envoy at any time. I could sense that she enjoyed taunting us but maybe she was in my head again.

I took in the clouds – they were some of the darkest, blackest, heaviest looking I'd seen in quite a while. I would have expected a torrential rainfall but a consistent mist fell instead, fitting my mood perfectly. If I was a normal kid, I would have been happy. It was almost Christmas break but Mitchell's increasingly frequent nightmares were keeping me awake too. It wasn't his fault but it damn sure made me cranky.

Over and over Mitchell revisited the same nightmare. He would see Lucie tied to an old wooden chair in a tired old, barren room where the window was covered by plywood and a single bare bulb hung. The room was familiar to him but he couldn't place it and his description didn't mean anything to me. "No!" she would scream trying to come out of the chair. Rage would tear through her voice, her face would flush, and she'd nearly topple to the dusty wood floor as she fought her ropes trying to escape. Someone was with her but he could never see who it was. He just knew it was a presence he recognized.

If Mitchell's nightmares had been about me or Evilia, I would have been fine but they were all about Lucie. Somehow he struggled through his finals and didn't drop below B's. Tess worried over him and worked hard to do everything she could to help. I understood exactly how she felt. She had finally found someone who mattered more to her than anything else.

We decided as a group to never leave Lucie alone. Tess offered to take a turn and Lucie surprised me when she accepted her help. I guess so much had happened to her lately that jealousy felt like a waste of energy. Maybe she'd finally figured out she didn't have to worry any more about Tess liking me or envying our brief romance in the past.

A sound I hadn't heard in a while scared me awake. It wasn't my alarm, but the ringing of our landline. I fell out of bed and stumbled into my parents' room. The ringing began again, jangling my nerves. I tried to focus my eyes on the bedside clock. I felt confused, like I'd been dropped into someone else's life. I checked the readout on the phone. Tess. Tess? Why hadn't my alarm gone off?

"Tess?" I asked.

"Owen, help me! No one's phone is working. I had to call your mom at school for this number. I'm in a ditch. They took Lucie!" Her voice sounded shrill and panicky, breaking through the fog in my mind.

"Where are you?"

"You didn't show for our run so we went without you. We made it to 42nd before a car came out of nowhere and ran us off the road. They were waiting for us."

"On my way." I tossed the phone onto the bed and sprinted to my room where Mitchel was thrashing from a nightmare.

I reached for his shoulder but he sat bolt upright smacking my forehead with his, screaming, "Run!"

Our eyes met.

"Get dressed. There's trouble."

"I know," he said, sounding devastated.

We both dove for our clothes, yanked them on and about tripped over each other on our way down the stairs.

"Cell phone?" I barked at Mitchell.

"Dead. You?"

"Same. Go start your car. I'll call Mars." I took a moment to grab the kitchen phone. Marlo's cell was also unresponsive so I tried their landline. Once he was going on the problem, I dialed White Eagle. His phone was down too.

Alex stumbled in rubbing his eyes and yawning. "Evilia warned you. Taking us in a group didn't work so she's picking us off one at a time." He sounded just like a miniature adult. That old voice coming from his young body freaked me out.

"You need to go to Sarah's or come with us."

"Are you kidding? I'm coming with you. That's where the action is!"

"Then get some pants and running shoes. We gotta go. Oh, and your cell if it's working."

Alex was back in a flash. We rushed out the door, locked it and then jumped into Mitchell's waiting car. Without our cell phones it took us longer than I would have liked to locate Tess. We found her sitting by the road, bloody and bruised. Her leg didn't look good to me. Mitchell administered first-aid while Alex and I sensed the area. We got the best hits off of Tess since she had been struck by the SUV.

Lucie was smart. She knew I got my best messages off of objects and she had left me her house key since it was on her when they grabbed her. Alex and I held it together so that a burst of images played out for us.

We helped Tess into the back seat with Mitchell. I drove them to the hospital where Tess would report being hit. She could give the make, model, color and a partial plate thanks to Lucie and a little coaching. Alex and I left them in ER and headed back to Marlo's.

A surprised Marla let us in. "What are you doing here? It's almost time for school."

Exuding as much trust as I could, I looked her right in the eye and did the thing I hate most… I lied. "Alex is having an assignment problem and we could really use Marlo's help."

"Well…"

"Oh hey, guys," Marlo interrupted sounding overly cheerful. His hair was stuck up at odd angles and his old glasses were perched crookedly on his nose. "Come on up to the man cave and I'll give you a hand."

We edged past Marla. Her forehead was wrinkled like she was thinking way too hard. "If you need his help, where are your books and papers?"

"It's on Google docs," Alex promptly answered, moving in to give her a hug. "Boy does it ever smell super good in here! Did you make extra, Mrs. Saggio? I skipped breakfast."

Marla immediately shifted gears. Food is her whole life. While Alex kept her distracted, Marlo and I headed upstairs. Marlo plopped himself in front of his monitor and began to mumble to it.

"Your alarm didn't go off either, did it?" I asked, unnecessarily by the look of him.

"I've been out-teched! No one out-techs me! I'm going to find this… this person and send them a Trojan virus!"

"You can do that?"

"I can do all kinds of stuff and some of it I shouldn't. Do you know how much money I'd make if… Never mind. I can tell you where we last had a location on Lucie and I have new cells for all of us. Give me the intel on the vehicle that took her down and I'll have that to you as soon as I can."

"Thanks, Mars. You rock tech. Don't let them make you think otherwise."

"I try."

"Hey. If your mom asks, tell her you helped us with a Google docs problem Alex was having."

"I hate lying to her."

"Believe me, I know," I said sadly and then I gave him everything I had on the SUV and the guys who grabbed Lucie.

Marlo handed me a piece of paper with all the phone numbers for our new secure network and Lucie's last known location. "I'd memorize that as fast as you can and get rid of it permanently. They are not going to succeed with that trick twice."

We headed downstairs where Marla tried to stuff me with an omelet and hash browns. I made it out of the house with barely enough time to get ready for school, except I wasn't going. I sent Alex up to his room to get ready and did a little research of my own. I logged onto Marlo's server and entered everything from Mitchell's nightmare room that I could remember. It had to be familiar to him because he'd seen it and if he'd seen it doing *watcher* business then Marlo had a record of it and could match it up.

Sarah came in the door just as I should have been leaving for school so that she could get Alex safely to the middle school as part of our buddy system that wasn't working. At least it hadn't worked for Lucie.

"What are you still doing here?" she asked, looking at her watch. "You're going to be late and where's Lucie? I thought I'd find her up here. She's not at home."

"She went running with Tess." No lie there.

Sarah gave me an odd look. "You know anything about Earl's phone? It was dead this morning."

"Weird. Maybe he forgot to charge it." I gave her my best smile, gathered up my books and headed for my bike. I had murder on my mind. I was done playing around. I didn't know how she'd missed me before, but I was taking her out or I'd die trying. No more games. It would end now and I would do it alone!

As my Kawasaki ate up the road, my mind began to wander, coming at the problem from many angles. Conflicting ideas fought for domination. Just as I was pulling off the highway my new cell buzzed and I hit my Bluetooth. "Ryer."

"What in the world do you think you are doing?" Shit, it was Sarah.

"Ending this and saving Lucie."

"You lied. Why would you do that?"

"Sarah, at the end it's got to be me. Evilia can't keep doing this to us. She can't keep ruining our lives and making us feel watched and scared all the time."

"Come back. We'll do this together like we always have."

"No."

"Please!"

"I'll make her think I'm on her side and corrupt everything from within. She still wants me. She'll let me get close. I'll trade for Lucie. Take care of my family. Tell them I love them and I'll see you again… someday." I disconnected before she could say anything else and shut off my phone. Marlo and Alex had tipped her off. I knew they cared and had my best interests at heart but they had to know I had to do this.

I rode on knowing I didn't have much time before they'd be after me. I went to where Lucie's GPS trail ended. I recognized this road and now I understood why Mitchell knew the room where she was being held. *Watcher* business had led us here. That guy we'd helped when he thought he'd killed his uncle... Pierce... Keith Pierce was his name. This property was still in foreclosure. It must have too much bad karma or at least too many bad vibes to sell.

Bad vibes... that's why Evilia had brought her here - all the horribleness would scream at Lucie... or would it? We'd helped Keith so would the ghosts be at rest?

I approached on foot, walking my bike, looking for a place to hide it. A copse of trees would provide a nice screen. From there I watched the house. I still couldn't feel Evilia but I was afraid to let myself be discovered by completely opening myself to sense the area.

It was strangely dark and quiet. I was glad. It provided me with better cover. I could feel the temperature dropping as the wind picked up. Heavy clouds loomed on the horizon, threatening rain. It would be good cover.

I closed my eyes and felt for a moment, quickly shutting my gift off and then changing my position. There was no sign of activity at the house. There was no Evilia here or she was hiding but something was here – something both familiar and strange.

A twig snapped. I turned and pain exploded through my head. Starbursts of light stole my vision and then it was consumed by blackness.

I came to with a pounding headache. I tried to touch the side of my face only to find my wrists secured to the sides of a chair, wood this time. Guess they didn't realize that for someone like me, they'd just tied me to a weapon. My ankles were secured to the chair's legs by some old telephone line and it felt like they'd used the same stuff on my wrists... and they were just healed up from the last time! It was quiet and the room bare. It had been emptied but not cleaned. Plywood covered the window and a bare bulb was exposed in an overhead fixture where the glass had been removed. I was in Mitchell's nightmare. Last time I'd been in this room it still had a bit of furniture in it. The only visions I got were of Lucie sitting here. The memories of Keith's uncle were gone.

I heard a sound behind me – the complaint of a floor joist, like you hear in a house that's settled and the weight of a foot is pressed on an end of a floor board as it pivots on a beam. My back was to the door but I could hear the squeak of it as it opened. There was a brief moment of silence and then I could hear a weighted chair being dragged across the floor.

A man dressed in boots, military-grade camo pants and a t-shirt entered my peripheral vision. He was tall, well over six feet and dark-haired. The hair was shaved close to his scalp. He turned to look at me with dead, dark eyes. I couldn't even make out the color. A scar ran across one side of his face like he'd been on the losing end of a knife fight. The muscles under the short sleeves of his t-shirt bunched as he pulled his load forward.

Another man came up on the other side of me, snagging my attention. He was smaller, wiry and mean looking. Neither of them sent the warning prickles over my skin like *dark watchers* usually do. These guys were just guns for hire.

I turned my head back the other way. Lucie was tied to another old wooden straight back chair. I recognized them from the dining room from our last visit. We'd changed this house – changed it for good but now it would have more bad vibes. It just wasn't going to have the effect on us like Evilia probably hoped it would.

Figuring I had nothing to lose at this point, I sensed the area. Carmichael walked in. He felt a little different. There was still no Evilia and that weird otherness that I couldn't lay a finger on lingered.

Carmichael smiled at me and it wasn't friendly. I hadn't seen this side of him since he'd had Lucie back at the warehouse - back before he made deals with Kraeghton.

Lucie looked right at me from where she had been placed, directly in front of me but out of reach. She appeared to be unharmed except for a few surface scratches and bruising. There was minimal damage to her jacket, running tights and shoes. I didn't feel drained and I was certain she hadn't been, so what was Evilia's game this time?

"I am incredibly surprised and disappointed to find you alive, Owen. We had it on good authority that you did not survive your adventures in the south."

My mind raced. Had the *dark watcher* lied to Evilia? Did he tell her I was dead? That was good news, right? Knowing we could lie to her was helpful but how had he done it?

"We suspected she had lived. I was sent to confirm. Imagine my dismay when I saw a boy who looked like you with a girl who looked like her. Madame thought she'd lost out on you. She doesn't care about her so I thought I'd have another taste of Lucie. Now that you are here, I think I'll try a different approach. Death. You'll be easier to manage without the girl and I will secure my place as her number two. She was angry about what happened last summer. She almost killed me. I must re-earn her trust and this is such a lovely first step."

The two men pressed down on my shoulders as Carmichael took ahold of each end of Lucie's scarf, twisting them around his hands and began to pull. She was helpless to ward him off, her hands held firmly behind her back and I was helpless to help her. I raged, I struggled and I fought harder than I ever had in my life. Lucie would not look at anyone but me. Her eyes said, *I'm sorry*. Tears pooled and trickled down her beautiful face as she began to gasp, her face turning red. I could feel tears building in my eyes too. Break loose! Two of us - three of them. You can do it. You have to!

I continued to struggle but a rough hand yanked at my hair to hold my head in position. "You're going to watch!" He shouldn't have brought his head so close. I jerked my head to the side, smashing him in the nose with the side of my head. He released me to grab his face. The moment his hands left me I raised myself as high as I could and slammed myself back down, smashing the chair. I swung my leg over Lucie, kicking Carmichael in the head. They should have tied my feet together instead of to the chair. He fell to the side knocking Lucie over. I swung around and smashed the heel of my palm into the chin of the smaller man in an openhanded uppercut and then kicked the guy with the broken nose. When they're down, keep them down. I lost track of what I was doing. I just kept hitting and kicking until they ceased to move. A hand touched me. I spun and almost struck Lucie.

"Stop," she whispered hoarsely past her damaged throat. I stared at her for a moment trying to come back to myself. I had become a wild animal. Where was the goodness in me now? Carmichael groaned and something inside me seemed to snap back into place. I took Lucie by the hand and we rushed from the room. I closed my eyes and felt our surroundings. No one was close, but there were other *dark watchers* here. How had I not sensed them before? Did they know my tricks? Had Evilia taught them to hide from us?

The storm had accelerated so that the wind and rain tore at the house relentlessly in a continuous pounding howl. I began to wonder if the siding and roofing would hold on and could imagine it clutching the wooden framing for dear life. It had all been a trick, a trap and a ruse. I hated Evilia and all her minions. I evaded the remaining *dark watchers* and hired guns. I could sense them but they didn't seem to be able to sense me.

I led Lucie into a room and shut the door. She wheezed a bit and clutched at her throat but her eyes told me she would be okay. I slowly opened the window and felt outside. I crawled out the window and reached for her. She fell into my arms. I set her down and closed the window. We crouched low and hurried to the next building, pressing our backs against it. Lightning flashed, illuminating us for a brief moment; we froze until the sky darkened again and then we hustled on to the trees beyond.

I pulled her behind the nearest tree and took a moment to look at her neck to see if I could heal her some. "No," she croaked. "Save it."

"No," I replied back firmly. I moved her hands away and studied her for a moment. She didn't look the same. She had aged. She was no longer the girl I had fallen over the recycling bin for in eighth grade. I knew I was different too, but I felt like I had been different ever since I touched the watch in the pawn shop. Who were we now? What had we become? I led Lucie back to where I'd left my bike, but it wasn't there.

"Hello, Owen."

"What did you do with my Kawasaki?" I growled.

"Manners! I was hoping for a warmer greeting. Does this mean you won't take me up on my offer even after I helped you."

"You helped me?"

"Certainly." We stared at each other for what felt like several long minutes. Lucie stood ready for anything at my side.

"How did you help me?" I finally asked, feeling completely frustrated.

"You are here and free to go… Oh wait, did you think that you got out of there all by yourself? You had my help and now I want yours."

"Who is this?" Lucie asked in her still scratchy voice, sounding worried.

"Let me introduce myself, I'm…" He reached out his hand. Lucie reluctantly took it and time froze. I could feel the energy burst through me but was helpless to do anything about it. The raindrops moved so slowly that I could count them. Who was this man? What was this man? He held power but what kind? He was neither dark nor light.

He released Lucie, but she stood still as a statue. He turned to me. "She will be fine. Carmichael will be fine. Sorry about that but he is not the objective. Balance is the objective. Neither good nor evil can get too strong. I cannot allow you to give yourself over to Evilia Malvada. I will not let you turn to darkness. I do however need for you to be smarter. You will not beat her alone. Caleb Carmichael made a mistake today. He is worried about his standing with her and wanted to prove himself. He is a climber. Given half a chance he'd kill her himself and she knows it but for now they need each other. He should have left his allegiance with Stephan. Had he done that, our conversation today would have been very different. We'll let Caleb and Evilia fight out some extra energy. Now take her home and get her well," he ended flicking a hand toward Lucie. "You need her."

He turned and disappeared into the tress. A tingling spread out over my skin and I was free.

"Who is that?" Lucie asked again and then seemed to realize we were alone.

"Someone who doesn't want evil to win. Except I think he works for Kraeghton. So I'm confused."

"That was the guy who had you kidnapped and then let you go?"

"Yes."

"Wow. Next question. How do we get out of here?"

"Walk?"

Lucie's face crumpled into a frown as she looked toward the sky. When she turned back to me I could feel her pain.

"Is Tess okay?"

"She'll be fine."

"Really? 'Cause I won't. I keep telling myself I will but I'm nowhere near okay. I hate it – this life. I was running to stay in shape so I could fight *dark watchers* but what happens? They get the drop on me and my bodyguard. They took my phone. I can't afford another. Carmichael tried to strangle me with my own scarf. A strange man who works for Kraeghton claims he helped us and now wants something from you in return and now we get to walk home? Freaking fabulous!" Her voice rose in pitch with each sentence, screaming her distress.

Her eyes had pooled with tears but this time she didn't let them go. She took an unsteady breath, turned and trudged off toward the road. I decided it was better to keep my mouth shut so I walked behind her and planned my next move.

"Where's your cell?" Lucie finally grumbled about a mile down the road.

"I haven't had it since I came to in the chair."

"Super," she replied sarcastically.

"Look, Luce, I'm sorry for whatever I did to make you so mad."

She stopped walking. "I'm not mad at you. I hate them. *Dark watchers* are ruining my life. I'm scared. I can feel the end coming. I'm afraid we're going to die but there is still a part of me that wants to take Evilia on and spit in her face."

I smiled. "That's my girl."

She smiled back but it slipped off the moment a car slowed near us. We were about knocked over by Alex. Sarah popped open an umbrella in a dignified manner, gave me a ferocious scowl, burst into tears and then hugged us all. White Eagle slowly got out of the car with an unreadable expression on his face. His eyes slid away and he spoke into his phone.

A burst of feeling shot through me. White Eagle had been terrified and grief-stricken when he'd found out I was gone. He'd done everything he could to get here and had even gotten pulled over for speeding. He was shaking inside. He was so very relieved that we were okay but he was so disappointed in me that the only way he could express it was to let me just feel the raw emotions. My throat closed up and I hung my head. Saying I was sorry would never be enough. He could see me turning into Miles and he was helpless to stop it. I would have to re-earn his trust.

His attention left me and went back to his call. He punched his phone with an angry finger and tossed it in the car. "Rick just arrived. The house is empty. It looks like no one has been there in years. Except your cellphones were waiting in the middle of the room and there isn't a print on either of them – not even yours. Oh, and they're clean – no bugs."

SIXTEEN

The feeling of being watched temporarily vanished and then reappeared with a vengeance. I could feel the creep of watchful eyes skitter over my skin almost everywhere I went, especially at school. Either the mystery man was watching or Evilia had turned a student or a staff member to her side. I was pretty sure it was the latter. Lucie, Marlo and I knew that if it was a staff member it sure wasn't any of the staff that we interacted with. It was time to put Adrian's social network to a new use. Who was acting odd and suspicious? We all began to intensely observe the students and staff. The people we trusted the most were asked to keep their eyes open but for all they knew it was another Skimmer trying to dope the students. We couldn't afford to raise suspicions with Evilia's feints becoming more frequent and pronounced but we had to protect our school. I was amazed by the number of people Adrian could touch… all the people I'd ever helped were anxious to return the favor. Katie and Jesus were the first ones to sign up, followed shortly by Rose who I'd helped in my first year as a *watcher*. It was weird. I had more friends than I thought. Had I imagined that everyone was afraid of me?

Ironically, despite our *super powers*, it was Adrian who finally got the hit we needed. None of the rest of us could peg any obvious *dark watchers*. The end of the semester was coming and I felt strongly that they would try another attack soon if they were stalking us here. At school we had a set routine which would change at the start of the new semester and they'd have to figure out our schedules all over again.

Adrian chose not to eat with us and hung out with his sports buddies instead so that whoever was monitoring us would think we were no longer friends. Lucie, Marlo and I made it a habit to sit with two of us with our backs to a wall and one sitting across when we were in public places. It allowed us to observe and focus our attention. Today we sat in the commons at a table by the wall under the windows so that no one could see us from outside and we could see all the doors and entrances. It was Marlo's turn to have his back to the rest of the students. Adrian and his crowd sat at tables on the upper level where he had the best view.

Adrian had gotten really good at scanning classes, hallways and the commons at lunch time. He had been doing it since eighth grade in the cafeteria when I used to have to watch out for Calvin. He would have been an amazing *watcher* but that wasn't the cards he was dealt. Now he lived two lives - one with us and one with his sports buddies. My cell vibrated in my pocket. I casually pulled it out and held it under the table to see the readout - a text from Adrian with a photo. I slid my cell to Lucie and pulled her in close at the same time. I pretended to nibble her ear while I ran my own scan of the room.

"Stop," Lucie giggled and pretended to push me away as she passed the phone to Marlo. "Got him?" she asked me in a soft low mumble.

"I think so. He reminds me of Devin," I whispered as I pointed surreptitiously in his direction.

"Let Mars have a look. Marlo, pull out a textbook and pretend to ask me a question. Then come around and sneak a look at him."

Marlo did as he was asked and Lucie scooted over to let him sit between us. She mumbled at Marlo as she pointed at the textbook. Her eyes moved to me like she was involving me in the conversation and then quickly skittered past me to our foe. "Got him," she hissed under her breath. "He makes me think of a hipster. He's tall and skinny with long reddish hair partially hidden beneath a beany. He's wearing mirrored aviators which is a little off for indoors. I'd say the gages in his ears must be about three quarters of an inch. Man, I thought I had white skin but that kid has mayonnaise skin. He's in skinny jeans like they made you wear in San Diego and he's got on Doc Martins with an unzipped gray sweatshirt over a fitted t-shirt. He's nervous and jumpy as all get out. I'm sure he hasn't been a *dark watcher* long. We hardly ever see this level of ineptitude any more. They haven't trained him well if at all. He's meant to be temporary. They either don't give a crap or they expect to lose him. I wonder what they promised him. It had to be something big."

"He has got to be our guy. Weirdly, I can barely feel him but I can feel him watching. Here's the real question – what is better… the devil we know or the one we don't. Do we quietly take him out or do we watch him watching us and see what happens?"

"I vote for the latter," Marlo supplied. "I can hack the school data base and get as much info as I can. I can have his schedule in about five minutes. The rest of his school records are probably fake but maybe we could feed him some false information to muddy the waters."

Lucie leaned behind Marlo and whispered, "He's still watching. Can't he feel us *looking* at him?"

"He's raw, Luce. He doesn't know what he's feeling. I saw him shiver, so I know he's sensing what we're doing. He'll learn if he lives long enough," I ended with a scowl.

"Owen, you're scary. I'm glad you're on my side," Lucie whispered.

"You're tougher than you think. You've proved that over and over."

"I know you're both braver than me," Marlo added, patting Lucie on the shoulder.

She flipped her head to look at him. "Why would you say that?"

Marlo snorted. "You're kidding, right? I love fantasy in computer games and literature, but now it invades my real life. The *dark watchers* practically paralyze me. I hate it. That's why I work so hard with the computer behind the scenes. It's something I feel like I can control."

"Mars, you are amazing with the computer, but you're brave too!" Lucie argued in a harsh whisper. "I'll never forget how you helped save me from Carmichael that night in the rain or what you did for us at the warehouse."

Marlo blushed and smiled as his computer let out a soft beep. "Gotcha," he said his smile turning triumphant. The computer pinged again before he even began to speak. "Ah," he added as he looked at a few different screen shots. Marlo turned his eyes to us. "He's a transfer student from Vancouver. He's old enough to be a junior but barely has sophomore standing. Guess he should have turned in a few more assignments."

The corners of my mouth quirked up at the comment. Leave it to Marlo, our Valedictorian, to overanalyze the opposition. "What else have you got? I know there's more," I said quietly. Kids were starting to clean up and filter out of the commons.

Marlo gave me a hard look and powered down his laptop. "Come on."

Lucie and I got up and followed him outside where he quickly pulled us behind the corner of the building. "He knows our schedules. I'm sure of it. I'm pretty sure he's targeting Adrian too but he's watching all of us as best he can – a big project for one guy, so he must have help. I just don't know who it is… yet." Marlo squinted at me as he spoke. I could see the fire in his eyes. He was thinking someone had out-teched him again. "His name is Peter Doyle and right now he is my number one priority."

"Fine, you trace him down and we'll pursue his… friend."

Lucie and I tracked down Adrian. We thanked him and set him loose on his new task. He'd pegged the last guy, but who was Peter Doyle working with? There was no doubt in my mind who he was working for. Now the trick was to watch them without letting on. If Evilia knew we were on to them they'd be gone in a blink and new ones would be on the job.

Lucie went to find Marlo and I headed for our last class, deep in thought, and ran into another student. "Sorry," I mumbled. He jumped away from me almost shaking, his green eyes wide. His reaction struck me as a little odd. I'm not that scary. I shrugged as he took a step away and the wind shifted. The smell of stale cigar seized my senses and locked up my ability to breathe for a moment.

Thank goodness the guy around whom the aura hung, kept moving away taking the stink with him. I was struck again by the shear oddity of it – how often did young guys smoke cigars so much that it clung to them like that? How could they afford it? Cigars are a very unusual choice for a young person and secondhand they smell different. Miles had taught me to notice things that were out of place and this fit that category. Had I stumbled upon our missing link to Peter?

I decided to turn the tables and began to follow him at a distance to observe casually. I was thankful that I wasn't trapped next to him in a classroom because all my senses had accentuated. Maybe I had just learned to really use them but his odor would give me a tremendous headache. White Eagle also had many tricks and I was continually amazed that he could seem to dole out another one when needed. I knew we were all getting better and that some of White Eagle's teachings took time to soak in; some things we weren't even aware he was teaching until… boom… we used them. I followed ode de cigar. Strangely, it looked like he couldn't tell. Was I really good, really lucky or did he know I was there? If he'd actually been following me, wouldn't he be better than that? I hid among the students in the hall and managed to snap his picture just in case. I twisted out of sight and around the corner before I sent it to Marlo and Adrian.

I ran to class and made it in the door just as the bell was ringing. I slid into my seat and handed Lucie my phone, under the table we sat at together. She looked at the picture and had my phone closed out and back to me before the teacher even began to lecture.

I glanced over at her and Marlo. Both gave the illusion of putting their full attention on the instruction. I knew better. I saw their eyes flash to the door and back every minute or so. I knew they were both working on the problem and checking to see if we were being spied on. I guess it's nice not to be alone.

The teacher turned us loose to work on our packet. We quickly divided the thing up and did a couple of problems each before sharing answers and turning to our real problem. We were a good team, each of us was talented in a different area. Lucie picked up White

Eagle's tricks or brand of magic even faster than I did. Our presence alone made *dark watchers* uncomfortable, just like theirs did to us but White Eagle had taught Lucie how to amplify that sense of unease and make it really uncomfortable for them. I wondered aloud to her as I watched her work on the packet, "Why didn't E ward her house in Florida? Why did she allow us to break in?"

"She did ward and booby trap it. I know that now. Remember the door you touched that incapacitated you? Remember how we felt when we first entered?"

"I thought it was just all that dark energy trapped in one place."

"Save it for the shop," Marlo murmured, drawing our attention to a student who was leaning too close. He added for them to hear, "Game talk is best done while we're gaming."

I made eye contact with Marlo to let him know that I appreciated his quick thinking.

We changed the subject and finished our work but I'd never seen the hands on the clock move so slowly. The second the bell rang we all popped up and hurried to the door. We walked out boldly, hopped in Marlo's Cirrus and headed for the shop. Today we were paying attention and we definitely had a tail. As we pulled into the pawnshop lot they drove past. They must have thought we'd be here for hours or they planned to come back and spy from across the street.

Marlo got hung up with Max on a bookkeeping problem, but Lucie and I went straight into the back. "Talk to me, Sunshine."

She held up a finger and did a system check on Marlo's many machines in the back. I said nothing but the look on my face clearly asked what she was doing.

"We're clear," she replied. I raised an eyebrow at her. Lucie sighed and then answered, "Marlo runs continuous scans checking for bugs and surveillance both inside and outside the shop. We're doing all we can to keep it safe here."

"Wow, good for you. I didn't realize…"

"You have plenty of other things to worry about," she replied and then she moved in close to hug me. "We'll handle this end and you do what you do best."

"Please unload what you're thinking about Evilia. I know there's something going on in that beautiful head of yours."

"You asked about dark energy at Evilia's. There was plenty of that and you're right, there's more. You know how Willie used to hide things?"

"Yeah."

"Well, Marlo and I believe that Evilia can force you to feel; she gets in your mind and your body reacts. I believe she can put her power into an object almost like Willie could. I also believe the force of her mind is so strong that she can do more than just make you feel things. I think she can make your mind believe so strongly that there are real physical outcomes. She makes things come true just using her mind. It's how she broke Claudia's bones. She steals energy from her victims, channels it and uses it. We knew she wanted Kraeghton for his gifts and I believe Carmichael is now her front man. He only wants to please but Kraeghton is a wild card. She needs him and he owes her but it's not the same kind of blind allegiance that Carmichael seems to have. Kraeghton can hold her mind off, but maybe Carmichael can't. She doesn't own Kraeghton and that makes him dangerous to her."

"You know this or it's speculation."

"I've read all of Marlo's research on them. He's shown me reports that have come from Bob for Sarah. I've talked to Mica. I feel like I… know, but it really is all educated guessing. As I'm learning this new skill from White Eagle it is putting a different spin on what I have come to understand about us, our abilities and… magic."

"Don't say the 'M' word in from of my dad. He already has trouble with us."

Lucie smiled at me. "He's getting better, I think."

"Mmmm."

She quickly changed the subject. "I've also been working with Alex. I was wrong before. I should never have suggested that you shut off his gift. He is so talented. Evilia was horrid to use him. When she did she inadvertently made him what he is. You boys both have your mom's reading ability - it has just come out in different ways. Alex worries about turning evil but it isn't your nature. The dark will never snuff your light. I believe you now – any of us can do bad things but that won't turn us. We do too much good. We are a scale that will never get that far out of balance.

Marlo burst through the back curtain. "It's happening again."

"What is, Mars?"

"A high school student overdosed on 2C-I, otherwise known as Smiles, last night. It's a new designer psychedelic drug."

"A what?" I asked to clarify.

"It's a hallucinogenic that's reported to be more intense than LSD."

"Was the student from here?" Lucie asked.

"Not this time. I think they thought they could fool us by going after another high school but I can feel it. There's something wrong here. It was no accident. Who does Smiles the same day they sign a scholarship offer to play major college basketball? I smell Evilia. Her reach is wide and deep. We keep our campus clean but what about everywhere else?" Marlo was the one looking dangerous today.

"I'm not surprised she reactivated her drug network here. I'm sure she's opened and shut down many of them over the years to cover her tracks. I bet my next test score she's pulled in students to operate it. To her they are expendable and with what she can offer… it would be hard for many kids to turn down. It all fits with her human trafficking and other activities. She's even tried sending teenaged spies after us. She's hideous." Lucie looked as ferocious as Marlo.

"Now we're being followed again. I wonder… since the direct strikes at us haven't worked, do you think she's going back to her old ways?" I queried my friends.

Lucie and Marlo both nodded. Then Lucie moved over to one of the computers and got to work though I knew she was still listening and thinking.

"Mars, what have you found on Carmichael and his goons?"

"I've kept up on all the logs. There's a whole lot of nothing, which means somebody covered it up. You know that Rick and his crew were there about the time Sarah and White Eagle picked you up. A neighbor did report noises around the time you were escaping, but by the time the police arrived, the house was undisturbed, just like Rick said, and the whole incident was considered to be a misunderstanding."

"You're kidding." Marlo just gave me a look. "You're not kidding. How about Carmichael himself? Any sightings?" Marlo shook his head. "And no unexplained bodies have shown up, other than the overdose?"

"Come on, this is Evilia. She wouldn't leave anything worthwhile for us to find if she could help it."

I knew he was right. I was pretty sure Carmichael was being punished right now and if she was spying on us, she had plans. Whatever they were, it would not end well for any of us. I walked up behind Lucie who looked to be deep in thought and wrapped my arms around her. I knew my hold had an almost desperate feel. I buried my face in her hair, deeply breathed in the scent and fought the instinct I felt rising in me to take her and just run. Together we could hide from Evilia, Bob and the stranger who moved silently, gracefully and powerfully, like a jungle cat on the prowl and just as scary. Maybe I was lying to myself? But what about the rest of the people I loved? I felt like a spider trapped in a web of barbed wire. Could I save us all?

I closed my eyes as my chest and throat grew tight. A sob was caught inside but I wouldn't let it out. The strain of it made me shake.

"Are you okay?" Lucie asked softly.

"No."

Lucie turned on the stool so that she could wrap her arms and legs around me. "I've got you." It was all she said. She shouldn't have been nice. She shouldn't have asked if I was okay. The dam broke and hot tears spilled. I was angry, frustrated and desperate. How could I possibly do this? The sob turned into an almost hysterical laugh when Marlo came and put his arms around both of us.

"It's going to be okay," he said softly.

"I hope so Mars, I just don't feel very confident right now."

"We are going to do this together! She doesn't understand how to work as a team but we do," he added vehemently.

SEVENTEEN

Marlo was focused and relentless in his tracking of Evilia and all her known associates. Adrian was just as dangerous when it came to Peter Doyle and Martin Sheering, his cigar smoking fellow *dark watcher*, who was no student but a twenty-three-year-old plant. Those two idiots were so busy watching Lucie, Marlo and me that they seemed to have forgotten Adrian, Brenda and our other friends. It appeared that the triplets especially confused them. I had been afraid that they were on to Adrian but they showed no further signs. I would not assume that they were safe however.

I had to stop grinding my teeth before I had none left. We were all on edge and it manifested in each of us in different ways. In addition to the grinding of my teeth, I became a workout maniac. Lucie would only run on a treadmill or spar with me at the shop. She and Marlo studied like crazy. Mitchell's nightmares changed and amped up but then so did Alex's. Doom was coming and why I wasn't receiving any nighttime visions had me concerned.

Every bit of training I had ever received snapped into sharp focus. It looked like maybe I was up to the task after all and that I wouldn't have a nervous breakdown. School didn't hold my interest but I knew I had to graduate or I couldn't keep doing what I was doing. Part of me felt like school was a waste and that I should just focus on Evilia but if I survived I had to have something. There was also the piece of me that wondered if I really wanted to keep being a *watcher*. Could I choose not to? Then I'd think of the good that we had done and I could feel my resolve return. I had to save the kids Evilia was taking the life from through drugs or trafficking.

Lucie was the best distraction when I'd get so spun up I couldn't think. She could take my mind off anything and today was no exception. She set cheddar cheese, butter, bread, milk and cans of tomato soup on the counter and then began assembling the sandwiches. Once the buttered bread was in the pan with cheese slices resting on top, she opened the cans and stirred them together with milk at the stove. This was my kind of Sunday. My parents were with my grandfather and although I was watching over my brothers, they were happily gaming upstairs. I tried to work on our history assignment but my eyes were continually drawn to her. She was humming a song softly and sort of dancing as she worked. The sparkles on her jeans pockets seemed to wink at me as she gracefully moved. I couldn't stand it anymore so I slowly walked up behind her and placed my hands on her gently swaying hips. As I started to dance with her, I slid my fingers to her hipbones and my thumbs to her back. I had hardly touched her since the pool in San Diego because I had the vibe that she didn't want me to, but I missed her. It was not nearly enough so I bent my head down and kissed the skin of her shoulder next to the edge of her shirt. I was drawn to her like the need to breathe. I nibbled my way up the side of her neck. She shivered and leaned into me. I nipped at her ear causing her to suck in a breath and snap off the burners almost angrily. "I can't cook when you do that. You should stop and go back to work."

"Mmmm."

Lucie gave up the fight. She turned and kissed me. Her hands slid to my face. She tasted delicious. I slid my hands from her hips to her butt, pulling her toward me. She sucked in a surprised breath and hesitated as her hips met mine. I moved her away from the hot stove, lunch forgotten. I lifted her up onto the counter next to it. She wrapped her legs around my waist. I could feel my heart pound and tightness in my chest like my heart had grown too big for the cavity. Lucie. I sucked in a deep breath which was a big mistake because all I could smell was her. She rested her forehead against mine, her breathing heavy. She was my personal drug. I moved in to kiss her some more. Her breath was warm against mine, her lips soft. She filled all my senses. She made me weak and strong. I wrapped my arms tight around her, pulling her close. I moved from her lips to her neck. I could kiss her forever. I heard a low moan escape her and then I heard feet pounding down the stairs. I moved back a bit still holding Lucie, feeling both frustrated and thankful. She uncrossed her legs from behind my lower back quickly and sat up straighter on the counter.

Alex slid around the corner and into the kitchen. "Do I smell lunch? I mean..." and he cleared his throat comically, "something burning?" Amid peels of laughter he ran away. "Call me when lunch is ready," he yelled from the stairs, still on the move.

"I'd kill him, but he's family," I said as I lifted Lucie off the counter and then stepped over to the stove to restart it and to stir the soup. Lucie went and sat at the table and then started giggling.

"What?" I asked, sliding her a glance that caused her to laugh even harder.

"Oh... was it good for you too? Your concentration on lunch is now so... complete," she said with a huge grin.

How could I be mad at anyone but myself, especially when she laughed all happy and lighthearted like that? We were doing what we shouldn't be doing. I was going too far. Lucie was like an accelerant to the fire that burned in me. It was so difficult to be seventeen with powerful hormones and remember being a thirty-four year old man at the same time. I remembered doing things I had never actually done. I had to get myself under control. What I wanted to do with Lucie went against everything I had always been taught and believed in. My parents had been very clear. Lucas was the youngest child that would live in their house. All others were welcome to visit. I loved Lucie more than life itself, but then I had the odd mix of seventeen and Miles' memories of college girlfriends and a married life all mixed up.

Lucie had gone back to homework seemingly obliviously. I stirred the soup some more, put the top piece of bread on the sandwiches and flipped them trying to calm my mind and body. And to peel the present away from a past that wasn't mine. I called my brothers to lunch and started more sandwiches. I ladled up some soup for everyone, set it on the table and flipped the next batch of sandwiches. Lucie stacked up our homework and laughed and joked with my brothers. She fit in here like she belonged. She was around more and more and my family just absorbed her. I could imagine being married to her and having our own place but then in my mind I had been married before. The older man that lived in me needed to go away so I could be a kid. Lucie needed a chance to be a kid. My feelings for her made me feel happy and light but they also scared me to death.

After lunch, my parents returned and Lucie and I headed to the pawnshop. I could almost feel the stress seeping from my body. I didn't have to be anybody but me in the back room. There were no expectations and no one waiting to pick a fight. Having an argument stinks but waiting for one to happen is almost worse. The older I get the more I understand my mom's hatred and dread of confrontation. They rarely end without a price and the confrontation with Evilia would have a big one.

Marlo's eyes lit up when we entered the back room, "Finally you're here. I know you had to brother-sit and all, but… I didn't want to call, but… Bob called me."

"What? Why?" we asked.

"He wanted to talk to me about some information I'd dug up, but first the good news. Julie is as close to fully recovered as anyone can get and is back to work."

"Why do I smell a big 'but' coming," I inquired when Marlo paused for breath.

"Well, you won't like it, and it bothers me too… she will now be housed under Bob since she lost her mentor a year ago. She needs someone to watch over her and he was very clear that it would NOT be us. I think he still worries about our little group." *I was glad that he had started with the good news because from my perspective that wasn't good news. That Julie was nearly well – great. That she was under Bob's thumb – not great.*

Marlo took in the angry look on my face and waited a beat before he continued, "There's more."

"Of course there is," Lucie added sourly.

"The real reason he called is because a second high school student has overdosed in our area. Apparently, we weren't the only ones who found that suspicious. He was giving us a heads-up that Evilia is, and I quote, 'Ninety-seven percent likely to be involved.'"

Marlo let that sink in. White Eagle came through the curtain as if on cue. "I see you're taking it as well as I did. Sarah is on the phone now with Bob to get all the pieces in place. Owen, you are going undercover again."

I felt my gut clench and then I sensed Lucie's rigidity beside me.

"Then I'm going with him," Lucie growled.

"No, you're not."

"But…"

"No, buts – we need you here, to cover for Owen. We also need him to get close to a girl."

My eyebrows came together in a frown. White Eagle wouldn't ask this of me, but Bob would. I wanted to get Evilia personally. I didn't want to keep shutting down the edges of her operations. It was time to go for her directly – I needed to cut off the head of the snake.

"I think I should consider the mystery man's offer."

"No," White Eagle replied firmly.

"You don't like Bob either, so why are you going for his plan?"

"I'm not *in* with Bob. I believe in Sarah and I believe in you. We need a high school student to pose as a high school student. I guess you could say we got the idea right from Evilia and those kids she has spying on you. It has to be believable and *you* can pull that off. The girl I mentioned has information. We're sure of it, but she's afraid to talk now that her friend is dead. We need you to earn her trust."

"There has got to be a better way to do this. Maybe we could kidnap her and bring her here."

"Not with Evilia watching."

"You think you're going to sneak me in under *her* nose?"

"No way!" Lucie exclaimed. "It's too dangerous."

"We don't have a choice. It's our job."

"After our last undercover job, how can you say that, Owen?"

"This is different."

Lucie shook her head. I could see that her eyes were extra damp and that she was biting the inside of her cheek. "It's not different, it's Bob playing games."

"What is it, Luce? What's really bothering you?" I asked as I put an arm around her.

She tore her eyes away from White Eagle and looked at me, "I just have all these feelings – all this emotion in me. I have fear and anger that I barely keep in check. The traffickers were almost too much for us. Now maybe I'm weak but at the same time I'm tired of being scared all the time. I want to run away but I can't. Everything is all a jumbled up mess. I feel almost hyper, my chest hurts and I can't decide if I want to fight or run. Things that don't usually bother me are making me twitch. I can't find my center and I feel like screaming right now. Most of all I don't want you to leave me behind. I don't want you to do this alone and I really don't want you to… befriend a poor lost soul of a girl… and…"

"Luce, I won't leave you. If I do this it will all be an act."

"It won't be an act for her. You'll be using her and I know what that feels like."

"I'm sorry, Luce." I hugged her to me and looked over her head to White Eagle. He really didn't look happy and neither did Marlo.

Sarah rushed in the back door. She took in the scene as she slowed to approach us. "You told them," she said sadly to White Eagle.

"I didn't have a choice. Marlo was inadvertently letting the cat out of the bag."

"I didn't know…"

"It's okay, Marlo. You're right, you didn't know," Sarah said soothingly. "As soon as Bob was done with you, he called me. Earl got the gist of the story, saw that Lucie and Owen had already left and came on over. I know this sucks but it's a good plan. Please listen with an open mind."

Lucie held me tightly but looked at Sarah and nodded.

"I'll listen but from where I'm standing at the moment, I believe that it's time to think about our other offer," I said, anger showing in my voice.

"No! Marlo hasn't been able to find out anything about the mystery man and there is nothing in Bob's database. The man has no record, no driver's license and no apparent past. We can't trust him," Sarah replied firmly.

"Can't or won't? He's not evil. Trust me on that."

"We don't know what he is," White Eagle insisted calmly.

"Fine, I'm listening."

"The tentative plan is for you to miss school here. Your mom will say you have mononucleosis and we will forge a doctor's note. We will disguise you and Earl will enroll you as his son in Lake Oswego. Bob is setting up a small apartment for the two of you. You will wear a small wireless earpiece and special glasses that will be continually monitored. The earpiece will be disguised to look like a hearing aide. We'll put it in the ear with the scar. The story is that your speech is fine because the loss is recent from a car accident. You two moved to get away from bad feelings associated with the loss of your mother from that same accident. You are now Jesse Montgomery from Iowa and your job is to become friends with a girl named Piper Downing. She was friends with the first student who died and Bob's team believes she knows more than she's letting on."

Mica and Joy came in the back door, their arms full of bags. We didn't have the fancy facilities they had in San Diego but the atmosphere was much more comfortable here. The women set to work bleaching my hair and eyebrows. Then they had me sit down and gave me a trim. I keep my hair pretty short, so they couldn't do much. They even tweezed my eyebrows a bit to reshape them a little. Lucie looked on with an unreadable expression but her crossed arms and fisted hands told another story.

I looked in the mirror and admired their work. This transformation was more drastic than my last one in some ways. My hair was now light reddish brown; my eyebrows were different and also had been bleached. I looked taller thanks to the lifts inside the Doc Martens they'd given me to wear. I also had on jeans, a plain tee and a flannel shirt. At least this time I got to keep my watch; it was retro and fit the image. Then White Eagle sat in the chair and they went to work on him. I watched in amazement as he let them cut his hair without a word. They dyed the top and back but left the sideburns gray. He had not shaved today and they trimmed what was there into a goatee so he would have a pattern to follow.

White Eagle traded in his favorite denim jacket for more flannel. He already wore jeans and cowboy boots so they let him keep those. I wasn't sure what Iowa looked like but not many kids dressed like this around here though a few did. White Eagle would fit in anywhere.

Mica handed us our new, Bob approved, IDs. Then she gave us two new cell phones. We handed our old ones over to Marlo as Mica was warning us not to call anyone we knew, except each other. Finally she fitted me with a beige wireless unit that looked like a hearing aid and we ran a test of it to be sure that it was sending and receiving. Then they gave me a pair of glasses that would snag video and transmit the images back to them.

Lucie held her body stiffly, like she was afraid if she gave into it she'd fall apart. Sarah said goodbye to White Eagle and I gave Marlo a quick bro hug. "It's gonna be okay."

"I hope so. It didn't work out so well last time when Bob split us up," Marlo replied solemnly.

I turned to Lucie. She gave me a fierce hug and whispered, "Come back to me." Then she kissed me. She was mad, but not at me. "I guess you're still you. You taste like grilled cheese and tomato soup."

I gave her a half smile. "I'll be back."

"Good, 'cause I'll be right here."

Marlo checked his computers and then poked his head out the back door before giving the all clear. White Eagle and I jumped into the back of Mica's car. She headed downtown, taking a circuitous route and watching for tails. We pulled into Bob's down-town offices and parked in the underground garage.

Mica turned and looked at us. "Good luck guys and off the record, I'm sorry. What he's doing is wrong. He should send another, older *watcher*. It doesn't always have to be you. It's almost as if he's trying to get you killed." Mica beat the steering wheel twice with her fist. She took a breath and continued, "Down two levels you'll find and old Ford truck that's packed full of your household goods." She handed over the keys and added, "Directions to your new apartment are in the glove box. If you see any of us around your school or anywhere… pretend you don't know us."

"Thank you, Mica." White Eagle's voice was calm and steady. At least he sounded better than I felt at the moment.

We slid out of her car and hoofed it to the truck. I was impressed that they had been able to put it together so fast. The truck was outfitted with Iowa plates and a bug spattered grill. "Don't be too impressed, kid. I have the feeling that Bob has been planning this for a while and just now decided to let us in on it." *Dang him, he was reading my mind again.*

White Eagle hopped behind the wheel and I went for the directions. They were detailed out from a medium sized town in Iowa all the way to Lake Oswego. I buckled up and we were off on our big adventure.

White Eagle drove around for a bit and then headed to Lake Oswego and to our new apartment. We buzzed for the manager. I didn't like him. I couldn't put my finger on why. He was shorter than me with a pink scalp peeking through greasy strands of hair. Dandruff flaked his shoulders and nicotine yellowed his crooked teeth. When we shook, his hands were soft and damp, leaving me with the urge to wash mine as soon as possible.

"I see your hearing aid," he shouted. "Are ya deaf?"

"Only in my good ear," I quipped.

"How's that?" he asked, confused.

"I said, I understand you fine," I replied.

"You speak pretty good for a deaf kid."

"Thanks," I replied sarcastically.

"You have some papers for me to sign, I believe," White Eagle interrupted the rude little man. I didn't scan him because I didn't want him to feel anything but something was off. I looked around his makeshift office that he'd set up in what would have been his dining room. The piles of dirty dishes in the kitchen made it look like he lived alone.

He photocopied our fake IDs and swiped White Eagle's fake credit card for our deposit. The transaction went through without a hitch and White Eagle signed his new name, John Montgomery. Then he handed over a check with both our names printed on it for our first and last month's rent. I hoped Bob could get his money back because I sure didn't plan to be here that long.

He led us across the drive to a townhouse with a carport. He'd be able to see us coming and going from his kitchen window. The vinyl flooring was okay but the carpet was a hideous early eighties burnt orange. The woodwork was dark and the walls were white. I was enormously relieved that nothing spoke to me here. I had time to take a super quick tour and grab a load out of the pickup before a delivery truck showed up with two familiar smiling faces. The manager seemed reluctant to leave but White Eagle told him firmly that we had it covered as the truck pulled perpendicular to the driveway but about half way across its width so that we could get past with its contents.

The manager raised his voice over the noise of the truck, "No really, you've come a long way. The least I can do is help you unload."

"No thank you, Mr. Jones. As you say, my son and I have had a long trip and we would just like to unload and settle in by ourselves. Have a good evening now," White Eagle said with quiet calm as he bravely patted his dandruff covered shoulder.

The landlord or manager or whatever he was grumbled something I didn't catch and wandered off.

Saul and Rick hopped down and came over to where I stood in the carport. "Mister Montgomery?"

"Yes."

"Good, we're in the right place." Rick pulled out a clipboard and pointed at me. "If you'll check off the boxes, we'll unload?" He was doing a great job of acting for Mr. Jones.

"Sure I replied but my eyes followed the manager. He went back into his townhouse. His windows were dark but I saw the kitchen curtain twitch as Rick engaged White Eagle in a brief conversation and handed him another clipboard. Saul opened the back end of the truck and pulled out the ramp. I could see a lot of old gently used furniture. *Let the fun begin.*

In the first load that Saul brought in with the dolly was an amazing array of electronics. He checked the whole apartment for bugs and surveillance while the rest of us unloaded. He whispered to each of us that it was all clear in the townhouse and that Bob had scheduled Neil to do a phony cable install tomorrow. Mica would be on the grounds crew the next day and would check the outside as she was pruning the shrubbery.

After about an hour, White Eagle took the fully unloaded pickup to find some pizza while Saul, Rick and I finished unloading the moving van and began assembling the furniture. We wrestled a used washer and dryer into the hall closet by the galley kitchen. The kitchen was tiny but functional and had a pass-through to the equally small dining area where we set up a table with four chairs.

Into the narrow living room we arranged the couch, recliner, end table, entertainment center and TV. We assembled one twin bed in the upstairs bedroom and one in the downstairs. We didn't get dressers but fabric covered bins and shelving units to store them on. White Eagle and I each got two boxes of our own clothes that looked like they'd been hastily packed. We also got one more box with clothes that better matched our new style.

White Eagle had chosen the downstairs bedroom with the sliding glass door. I opened it and confirmed that we had a semiprivate patio. We secured the door with two bars, one at mid-level and one at the bottom and then covered it with a big blanket the guys had brought with them in lieu of curtains. "You knew this door wasn't protected or covered," I accused.

"Yep," replied Saul. "We were given complete schematics with the loaded moving truck.

"I'm amazed that Bob got us such a nice place."

"You had to fit in," Rick answered. "He wants *her* badly and is willing to fund her downfall."

"I guess he could loan us furniture and pay for a decent place. He sure isn't paying us."

"Let's go unpack the kitchen, kid. You look like you're thinking way too hard."

"I'm sorry, Rick. I know you've had different experiences with the man but I just don't trust him."

"I never saw much of him until I was promoted to Sarah's job when she took her leave of absence. I've now worked directly for him for over three years and I still don't really know him. I did learn this… his real name is Robert Bowman and he is not to be messed with."

"Why all the secrecy? Why doesn't he even want us to know his name?"

"If we are captured we could revel it, I guess. That's what they say anyway."

"You should have Marlo help you dig around."

"I love that kid, Owen. There's no way I'm putting him in that kind of danger."

"But you let him research Evilia."

"What does that tell you?" I opened my mouth to speak but he laid a hand on my shoulder. "If I have to choose, I choose you, but I don't want to have to draw that line. "We're done talking about this for now."

We went back to putting things away in the kitchen. We'd be living sparse but we had enough. Bob had even provided groceries in the old beater pickup we'd driven. Dry goods were boxed or bagged and there was a cooler for the milk, cheese, eggs and lunchmeat. The more I unpacked the more suspicious I grew. Bob had not arranged for this… Sarah had. It was all the brands they had at their house and only food White Eagle and I liked. There were no mistakes and no random guessing. She even threw in a bag of my favorite junk food – Jalapeño Kettle Chips. I smiled.

Since White Eagle wasn't back yet I went up to my room to unpack my clothes. Lucie had been at work here. In one box was an old shirt that she'd had since eighth grade. It smelled like her. She even packed a small plush song sparrow that sang when I squeezed it. I held them until I heard White Eagle arrive and then I left them on my bed.

We had a quick meeting at our dining table over pizza and R.C. cola, a favorite of White Eagle's. We ate off of paper plates. Rick showed me pictures of the girl I was to locate and befriend. She had a great smile and nice dimples to go with her long straight black hair and big brown eyes that gave away part of her heritage. I read over her profile… medium build and a little shorter than average at only five foot three. Her bio was brief… she was a student who was above average but was quiet and didn't have a lot of close friends. The only things she really seemed to care about were music and theater. She'd had a boyfriend but that romance had ended with the musical that they were both in. She was an only child with junior standing but hoped to graduate early. She had plans to go to community college and she was being watched by Evilia because of her friendship with a dead future basketball scholar. I would have to be very careful.

"Be cautious with your gift," Rick advised. "We don't know who she has tailing the girl."

"Are you reading my mind?"

"Nah, I've just known you long enough to get a handle on how you think," he replied with a smile. "We've included her schedule and our best guess as to what they'll give you. There's also a map of the school so you'll know your way around. Just act natural and try to bump into her."

"What's happening with my classwork at home?"

"It's being done for you."

"How?"

"You won't like the answer."

"So not Marlo?" I said giving him a look.

"Okay but you'd be happier not knowing. Bob made Marlo turn in every bit of school related material you had at home and at the shop. He had it analyzed and the computer will spit out the most likely answer that you would have given if you'd done it yourself."

"On the surface that doesn't sound so bad. What else is he doing with it?"

Rick twitched in his seat and averted his eyes before looking back at me. "I'm sure he'll do a personality profile on you while he's at it."

"Poor Marlo."

Rick did a double take. "That's not the reaction I was expecting."

"It's no secret that I hate Bob and I don't trust him. What he's doing is wrong and therefore not unexpected. He should be hunting bad guys and leave us alone. I bet Marlo is beating himself up right now because he thinks he betrayed me and I bet Bob threatened to wreck his GPA if he didn't hand it over. It was either that or cut him off from us or… return Lucie to her father."

"How'd you know?"

"There is very little that Bob could take away without people finding out. Marlo's a good asset; he'd be a fool to push him too hard. I also believe that Marlo is way smarter than Bob gives him credit for."

After Rick and Saul left, I went back to the file loaded onto my computer. I opened the police report on the first victim, Piper's friend. The police aren't dumb but they were made to believe it was an accident. They still had questions and so did I. Why would someone who just signed a scholarship, who'd never used drugs before celebrate with a drug like Smiles? The family needed closure and we needed answers. This had the mark of Madame Malvada all over it. Marlo had done some intensive research on the school and the girl. While I was pursuing this end, Marlo, Mitchell, Lucie and Tess would go to the funeral of the second victim and watch. They would figure out who did not belong and see if they could get some leads. These kids were not random attacks. I felt it in my gut – they were killed because they knew something and I'd be damned if I'd let a nice kid like Piper be next.

EIGHTEEN

White Eagle and I were up at six to test my communications devices and go over the plan for the day. I was almost too nervous to eat so I took a Cliff bar and an apple with me for later.

We were at the school right when building hours began. We walked straight in to the main office and the filling out of paperwork began. White Eagle handed over my phony transcript and proof of identification. Once we had caused all the trouble we could they sent us on to the bookkeeper to pay my fees and then we headed for the counseling office to set up my schedule. White Eagle told the same sad story about the passing of my mom. He discussed my hearing loss from the same accident but insisted I needed no special accommodations. I was pretty quiet and shrugged a lot because I truly didn't care what classes they put me in but I remembered that Piper liked music so I added choir to my choices of electives.

We found out what bus I would ride and gee what a surprise - it was the same one that Piper rode. Bob had done a lot more research than I'd guessed. The counselor handed me my schedule. White Eagle signed the final form and turned to me. "You ready?"

"Yes, Dad, I'll be fine."

"Have a good day and I'll see you after school. Love you, son."

"Love you too, Dad."

"Welcome to our school. If you have any questions or need help, come see me," the counselor said with the requisite smile.

"Thank you," I replied without one. *Yeah, I get it lady. You hope I don't come bother you because you're overloaded.*

I gave White Eagle a nod and preceded him out the door and to my first class that I already knew I had with Piper. I still had a little time so I wandered by where the busses were letting kids off.

I spotted my mark, Piper Downing. I made it my first job to follow her and to see who else was watching her. She was avoiding people, speaking only when spoken to and wary. She watched the people around her like she suspected they would bite yet I had the sense that this same crowd also made her feel safe – that she was more afraid of being alone than of swimming with the sharks. There was no clear sign of surveillance and I was afraid to use my gift so I kept it sealed up tight and used all my other senses.

The halls were filled with jostling student bodies. The noise level was just as I expected. Maybe all public schools were the same. It sure had the same aroma of sweaty gym socks, tater tots, body odor, Axe body spray and flowery perfume. I would bet a week's lunch money the walls were painted with the same paint and probably by the same contractor.

I beat most of my new classmates into the room. I looked around to get a feel for it. It was ringed with lab tables all jutting towards the center. The teacher was behind a long counter with a built-in sink. Along the entire wall behind his table was whiteboard covered in multi-colored chemistry notes. I paused to check my schedule. I had two classes with Piper so I would know where she was part of every school day. I knew that sadness hung around me like a cloud. I missed Lucie and my family but anyone who heard my phony story would think it was my mother's tragic death that had me down.

I handed the teacher my note. He said nothing and barely looked at me so I moved to an empty stool in the back corner of the room where I could see the whole space. Just as the warning bell was ringing, he dumped a thick chemistry textbook on the lab table and had me fill out a borrow slip. Under the slip was the class syllabus with today highlighted in pink. I wondered if he was trying to bait me but I kept my expression neutral and said nothing. I cracked the book open to today's pages. He was still standing there so I slid my eyes from the book to him. He just stared at me for a moment and I could feel the hostility in his gaze.

Finally he spoke, "We have assigned seats." It was said with no emotion. What was this guy's deal and why hadn't he bothered to tell me when I first handed him my entry slip? Maybe this was a test of some kind. And I thought I was here for chemistry, not psychology.

"Where would you like me to sit?" I asked, using my most nonconfrontational manner.

"Here's fine. You're in group F." With that cryptic statement he left. The students were sitting and opening books and reading or getting note taking equipment from their bags and backpacks. Piper finally entered the room. The teacher watched her more closely than anyone else I had observed yet. She made note of me and headed warily in my direction. Today was my lucky day after all – It looked like I was part of her lab group.

Her eyes moved from me to her books and then slowly slid back. I gave her a half smile and looked back at my own book. A kid with black hair and surprisingly blue eyes snagged the stool next to me with a foot, spun it away from the table and plopped down on it as he threw his backpack on the floor. He laid his arm on the lab table, exposing a skull and crossbones tattoo and several bead and twine bracelets. Was *Captain Jack Sparrow* his hero? My eyes moved from his arm to his face which was covered with the beginnings of a scraggly beard.

"I'm Quentin. You know like Quentin Tarantino, the director. You must be new."

"Yeah. I'm Jesse."

"Jessie. Ain't that a girl's name?"

"It can be," I said bristling slightly.

"Hey. No worries. I'm just pullin' your chain. Where you from, Jesse?"

"Iowa."

"Iowa, I like that. That's what I'll call you. Iowa. Iowa, this here's Piper. She don't talk much anymore on account of her friend Becca OD'ed."

Piper sent me a pained look and turned away.

"Hey, Pipes, at least were not in a lab group of two anymore." He sounded so jolly. I wondered if he was caffeinated, high or naturally hyper. She ignored him.

I noticed the teacher watching so I ignored him too. Class began and my new best friend chattered on incessantly. I think I had his whole life story about half way through class. I missed working with Marlo and Lucie. It was nearly impossible to concentrate with all that talking. No wonder no one else wanted to sit here.

Once the teacher had assigned an activity he moved around the room to check on the class' progress. He visited our group last. He nodded at Piper and scowled at Quentin. He started to use the same facial expression on me but changed at the last minute to a brief smile. He didn't think I was getting my work done.

The bell finally rang. I wanted to follow Piper but Quentin was on me and all eager to help me find my next class. I'd memorized the map – I knew where it was but I played along. He dropped me off at English, sad to see we didn't have lunch together. He punched me in the arm in a friendly goodbye before he ran off to his own class.

I approached the teacher who was more welcoming. She'd had a little more warning so she was more prepared. She handed me a novel I'd already read. Yes! I got another syllabus and I was excused from today's essay but I was to spend class reading to get caught up.

I pulled out my schedule and gave it a look. They had purposely gone easy on me. I was now in regular instead of advanced placement classes and some were repeats. I had already finished my language requirement for graduation and they moved me back one level in math. I just hoped I could get caught up on all my real work when I returned home. I know Bob wanted me to focus on the job but maybe I could sneak in some real work during study hall. Not that I cared deeply about school or grades, I just didn't want my dad on my ass.

I went to Spanish 2 which I'd had last year and finished out my day in beginning choir, where the teacher was at a total loss as to what to do with me. No one else in this class could sight read correctly on the first try or for some, hold a pitch. She ended up asking if I could stay after to try out for another choir. Lucky for me they nearly always need more male voices. I told her not today, but could make arrangements to come before school, after school or during my study hall - which matched up with her prep time so we settled on that. I was glad because it meant riding the bus with Piper and the chance to better align my schedule with hers.

I ran for the bus and was happy to see the seat next to her was open. "May I sit here?" I asked, sending her loads of good vibes.

"I guess," she mumbled.

The bus driver shut the door and the engine rumbled to life.

"So… how was your day?" I asked, taking a stab at conversation.

"Look. You seem like a nice guy, but I really don't want to talk."

"Okay, I understand." I closed my eyes for a moment and ran through the information Bob had been able to dig up on her. The girl who had died had been her best friend since third grade. She didn't have a lot of other friends. There were kids she hung out with but now my bet was – it wasn't the same.

I'd kept my gift shut off all day. Now I thought I'd try to open up just a little bit and focus on her. I reached out and touched her elbow. Random images flashed through my mind. I didn't even try to make sense of them right now.

"I'm sorry about your friend. I know it's hard. I just…" I paused and swallowed. "I just lost my mom." I let all the hurt and anger I was feeling show for a moment before I cleared my throat, released her elbow and looked straight ahead. Neither of us said anything else.

I let her up at her stop. She turned and looked at me before she walked down the stairs to leave. I had made progress. In that moment, I was closer to her than anyone had been in a long time.

I was shocked to find White Eagle having coffee with our landlord, manager or whatever he was. White Eagle and I shared a look but it was Mr. Creepy who spoke, "How was school, kid?" He used that overly loud voice that he adopted around me.

"Okay," I replied neutrally with a hint of disrespect.

"Make any new friends?"

"Sort of. I've got homework. I'll see you later," I answered, headed for the stairs. In the loft that we'd turned into an office I found the blinds slanted steeply downward. I took a peek to see why. Out of our office window, I could see over to the townhouse that belonged to Mr. Jones, my new favorite manager. His unit sat at a right angle to ours and across the road. From his upstairs window, he could look right into our unit and he'd have had a fantastic but partial view of the office. He'd even left his binoculars on the windowsill. I turned to put my back to the window and reevaluate our office. White Eagle had moved all of our equipment to the side overlooking the balcony and as far from the window as he could get it. I looked down to the living room and realized that window was now blocked by a mini-blind as well. I peeked in my room to find the blind closed completely.

I walked over to the desk and dropped my stuff next to me. We each had a computer and an iPad. The iPad was giving White Eagle fits since its operation system was so different from what he was used to. I had to give the guy credit though, he was giving it hell. He had YouTube paused on an iPad tutorial on his computer.

I took off the glasses and pulled out the fake hearing aid and put them on their chargers before I set to work typing up the notes on my impressions of the day. I heard the front door open and close and then White Eagle's step coming up the stairs.

"Why'd you let him in?" I asked as soon as his head cleared the railing.

White Eagle smiled and held up a plastic bag with one mug inside.

"Prints," I said, answering my own question.

"Yeah, I don't like him either. He's not our job right now, but worth watching regardless."

"His townhouse didn't say much to me but I've clamped down pretty tight on my gift. I can't have any *dark watchers* getting a whiff of me right now. It's weird. I've relied so heavily on it for so long, I've almost forgotten what it feels like not to have it. I feel like I'm walking around in the dark. I can still do it but I've got to be really careful."

"What's your impression of the girl?"

"She's a tough nut to crack but I think I connected to her today. I just hope I can get her to trust me enough to tell me what we need to know. I touched her arm and got some hits off her jacket. She's scared and she's hiding something. That's all I've got. I see the choir director during study hall tomorrow to audition my way into Piper's choir."

"You don't see feelings. What did you literally see?"

"Flashes of her with Becca – they were smiling. I saw no sign of drug use in any of those images. Then I got a burst of them spying on people. I feel like I need to touch more of her stuff to get a fuller view. I could really use Lucie for sound. I didn't realize how much… how much I'd come to rely on her. I do feel handicapped right now."

White Eagle patted me on the back. "I miss everybody too. It was hard to be alone today. Before you came along I'd been living like this all the time. Now it's too quiet. Good thing I start work tomorrow."

"What? No way. I thought you were going to hang out around here and pretend to look for work."

"New plan. You keep following the girl and I get to tend bar with the other victim's older brother. When Neil was here to set up our surveillance he passed me my new orders."

"Bob must really have confidence in our disguises if he's leaving us on our own so much." I didn't feel confident that was his reason however. "How can Sarah trust that snake?"

"She doesn't and neither does Rick – not anymore."

"What do you mean?"

"Sarah uses him for information, funding and backup. That is a whole lot different than trust. After what happened in San Diego – how he put you into a damaging situation with no remorse – she can't..." He trailed off. I'd rarely seen him so upset. He swallowed hard and looked at me. "We can see what it's done to the both of you. Lucie lost her confidence. She wakes up several times every night from nightmares. She refuses help and you... I can see the guilt, anger and remorse that cling to you like burrs from a dry field. You both try to hide it but I know..." I could actually see tears in his eyes. He swallowed hard again.

I hugged him tight – this man who had come to mean so much to me. He was a teacher, coach and favorite uncle all rolled into one.

"How'd we get ourselves into this?" I asked softly as I released him.

"At the end of the day, we are who we are and despite Bob and all his machinations we have a driving need to do what's right – at all costs."

He started to walk away and turned back. "Be sure to wear something of your own every day. Marlo's tracking you with our special tags. If you go anywhere except here or school let him know." White Eagle opened his phone and showed me a number. "He swears it's untraceable. It's an extra cell account he created for emergencies."

I smiled. I felt closer to home already.

The next morning I stood waiting for the bus. It was cool and misty but not horrible, other than the hour. It sucked to get up for school that started a half hour earlier than what I was used to. Maybe it was the gray of low hanging grumpy clouds that I was sick of. It's that time of year when you start praying for a sunbreak. I'd thrown on a wool plaid shirt that Bob's crew had provided and the required boots but the rest was all me. I even had my glasses and earpiece on and had kept my hair in my new style.

The hair on the back of my neck prickled and I turned to find Mr. Jones watching me. He was up early and boy did he look industrious as he pulled haphazardly at a few stray weeds. Mica and the grounds crew must be coming today. What was he really up to? I sent him a tentative wave. He neither waved nor smiled and headed back into his house.

I shivered. I so wanted to sense him but I couldn't trust that he didn't work for Evilia and that he wouldn't notice so I focused on not scanning the area. It was almost as hard as not breathing.

The bus appeared and I felt relieved. Three stops later Piper got on. She looked at me so I smiled a little but her eyes skittered away and she took a seat five rows ahead of me. I would see her second period anyway so I purposely did not look her way again.

I handed my rumpled entry slip to my math teacher, collected my materials and found a seat. I tried to convince myself that listening to a math lesson again would be good for my brain but I just couldn't fake it. The second the bell rang I was out the door and looking for Piper. I plastered a surprised look on my face when I saw her and then repeated my new kid drill. Since we had walked in together, the teacher assigned Piper to help me get acquainted with the ropes. My history teacher was my new favorite at this school. Piper didn't look nearly so happy. I guess I needed to be a little more charming.

She barely spoke to me but I was able to touch both her messenger bag and her books, netting me a few more images. We did not have lunch together but maybe that would change with my new schedule that I hoped to get right after I impressed the socks off of the choir director. *Please let me be up to the task!*

I went to the choir room and waited quietly by the door as she talked to another student. She looked up when she heard my backpack hit the floor with a soft thud. "Well, hello, Jesse. I'm glad you could make it. This is Manny. He's going to run you through some drills."

He was nice. I liked him right off. Turned out that he was here because he could not only play the piano but he was the President of the choir, a senior and in both the show choir and the top choir. His opinion was clearly valued. I could sense the mutual respect and friendship these two shared as he ran me through several scales, had me sight read and then sing a piece I knew fairly well. For a brief moment I was almost sad I wouldn't really be a part of this choir but this was not my path.

"You sounded too good to be true in beginning choir. Is your hearing loss new?"

"I can still hear normally in one ear and yes, I lost it in the accident when… when my mother died," I ended, looking at my feet.

"I'm so very sorry for your loss," she replied with true feeling.

"I would really like to put you in both advanced and show choir."

I paused for a moment in thought. Both choirs would give me more time with Piper but it would also put me in the spotlight and worse I would let those kids down when it was time for me to move on. "Thank you so much for the kind offer but I'm really not ready for show choir. Maybe I could try out again for next year."

"You think seriously about it," she added with a kind smile. "Now go take this note to counseling and they will adjust your schedule for you. Thanks, Jesse and I'll see you for choir first period day after tomorrow."

I went to counseling like she said and waited in line to see the overworked counselor that was hoping not to see me again. At least I wasn't here because I was in trouble. She only looked relieved until she realized she had to redo my schedule. We discussed back and forth, she put in a call to White Eagle and finally she gave me what

I wanted. I would now have four classes with Piper. Today might have felt like my lucky day but I was pretty sure the feeling wouldn't be mutual.

I took my note to my study hall coach and then headed for my last class. I still had the Cliff bar in my bag from yesterday which was awesome because I'd missed lunch today. I was the first one in the room. I quickly swallowed the last of my bar and talked to the teacher and let him know I would be in a different section starting tomorrow. He seemed pretty cool about it.

I was one of the first ones to the bus. As I watched it fill, I kept glancing at my watch and worrying about Piper. I hadn't seen her since second period. The bus doors closed and the engine rumbled to life. My stomach clenched. Should I get off, stay on, or what? A pounding on the door stopped the bus. Piper hopped on, looking a little frantic. I had one of the few open seats so she plopped down next to me.

"Are you okay?" I had to ask even though she'd warned me about not talking to her.

She turned haunted brown eyes to mine. "No," she whispered.

"How can I help?"

"You can't." She looked straight ahead but I saw a lone tear glitter on her cheek before she swiped it away.

"I know you don't know me and I'm new but believe that I am more than meets the eye." I spoke soft and low, sounding more like the real me and not like Jesse.

"I don't want to get you into trouble." She was talking so softly I could barely hear her over the engine's rumble.

"Yet you sat by me. Your gut must be telling you, you can trust me." I turned my head and upper body so that she could look into my eyes if she wanted to. I didn't touch her. I needed to have her come to me. I thought of all the things my mother did to make sick and hurting children feel better. I thought of how Lucas was with animals.

"What are you thinking right now? I just saw your eyes change. It was like ice melting off a lake."

"I was thinking of my mom. She was a… nurse and I was thinking of my younger cousins that I left behind. Tell me about frozen lakes."

"I'm not from around here. When I was really little we lived in Michigan. I can still remember what it's like when the water stops moving." She looked out the window and for a moment she was somewhere else.

I didn't disturb her; I just waited. Today I got her to talk to me. Maybe that was enough. She turned quickly, almost urgently, like she'd just make a decision. "You're only a couple of stops away from mine, right? Would you walk me home?" I could hear the uncertainty in her voice.

"I would be happy to," I replied simply, hoping for more conversation. I pulled out my cell and texted Marlo at his new number. I called him 'dad' and told him I was walking a girl home and that I'd be back soon. "He worries," I explained.

She just smiled shyly and turned away again almost like she regretted her decision but I could feel her relief too. When had I last been around someone with emotions this conflicted? Lucie, almost two years ago, when she discovered her gift but this girl was no *watcher*. It didn't make her any less confused.

We got off at her stop and walked side by side to a small neat house. It reminded me of White Eagle's place but it had less yard. Judging by the size of the trees and the style of the houses the neighborhood was old. It had a comfortable lived-in feel – like it was broken in – not broken down.

"You like architecture or something?" she asked when I paused out front.

"Yeah, I guess. Maybe I like big trees more."

"Big trees have a lot of leaves to rake in the fall."

I smiled. "Yeah, I guess they would. I don't suppose you want to tell me what you meant when you said you didn't want to get me into trouble."

Her look turned wary. "I… for a moment I just wanted… you don't want to be my friend."

"Why?"

"Because bad things happen to them."

"Nothing's going to happen to me, Piper."

"Yes, it will. You should forget about me. Thanks for walking me home and I'll see you in class." She turned and fled up to her front porch and in the door. I let her go; it was too soon to do anything else. As I walked away I felt a wash of malevolence almost as strong as I had in San Diego. I let it pass me by and didn't even try to find it. I couldn't let anyone know who I was but turning my back on it scared the crap out of me.

I paid close attention to everything around me but in a normal way. I'd almost made it home when rain began to fall. I sprinted the rest of the way to our front door as the drops grew in size and their numbers increased. A thunderous pounding began on the roof as I closed the front door. I joined White Eagle at the window to watch hail the size of peas beat down heavily, mixed with a soaking rain, only to jump back up to knee height and then roll to a stop. I looked through glass marred by a sheet of water and an occasional melting bit of hail to the growing piles of hailstones. Soon they were deep enough that the bouncing stopped but the rattle on the roof, vents and windows continued on. Then just as suddenly as it had begun it all stopped leaving my small corner of the world in eerie silence.

"She's being watched, that's for sure. We should see if any houses on her street recently rented or sold."

"I wrote down her house number while you were looking at it and you were smart to focus on the street signs. I'm starting to like those glasses. Because of them, I've already started researching."

"Who's going to monitor me while you're at work? You also need sleep if you're gone until the bars close."

"I'm new; I won't be closing for a while. You be careful while I'm gone though."

"I'll try. Who's going to monitor you?"

"I'm not in the same kind of situation as you. I just need to be someone he can talk to. No one actually thinks the brother knows anything and there is no sign that he's being watched."

I plopped down on the sofa. "I've got a new schedule starting tomorrow and she let me walk her home today."

"You're doing great."

"I just hope we're fast enough. I don't like her being watched like that."

I suddenly realized the blind was pulled wide open. I hadn't paid attention during the hail. "Why's the blind…" Just then Mica, dressed as a groundskeeper walked by. A moment later a soft knock sounded on the back door. White Eagle opened it and Mica quickly stepped inside. That door was blocked from the manager's view by some fencing. Each portion was L shaped providing minimal privacy to the sliding glass door to the downstairs bedroom. Too bad he could see everything we did at the front of our townhouse.

"You're clean for now, out there. Don't count on it staying that way. Use the secure line to contact us and we'll follow the feed. Good luck, guys." Mica pulled two envelopes from her pocket and handed them to White Eagle with a warm smile. She looked out the window and quickly snuck out the back door.

I recognized Lucie's and Sarah's writing immediately. No new orders today but at least some contact from home.

White Eagle and I each read our letters and went about our own business. I resisted the urge to text either her or Marlo. I did the little homework I had and reread the novel I'd been assigned for English. I pulled out my new schedule, compared it to Piper's and then figured out where all my new classes were. I had the same teachers in the same rooms, just at different times. I didn't want to flash my schedule around too much, it was one sure way to get bullied and I had enough to focus on.

Piper ignored me on the bus the next morning. The dark circles under her eyes told me she hadn't slept. If anyone needed a friend, it was Piper. She might have been trying to ignore me but I could feel her watching me. She tracked my movements as I left the bus, went to my locker and on into class. Finally she spoke, "I want to be your friend but I don't want to lose another one... and... and it's not safe to be around me because.... because... I feel like people are watching me."

"Why do you think that?"

"You don't think I'm crazy? You believe me?"

"It happens and something is clearly bothering you," I replied carefully.

"My mother doesn't believe me. She thinks it's just as well Becca's gone. She thinks she was a bad influence. Mom thinks she would have gotten me hooked on drugs but Becca wasn't a user. She was trying to sto..."

"Hey team! What's up?" Quentin sounded even more hyper than last time. His eyes were dilated and a fine sheen of sweat covered his forehead.

"Not much. You?" I asked quietly. Piper suddenly found her backpack extremely interesting.

"All's well with the Quentster."

"You're full of energy this morning." Piper jerked her eyes up and gave me a look before adding a subtle shake of her head.

Quentin ignored her. "I know, isn't it awesome?"

"Uhh."

"Let me know. I'll hook you up."

I gave him a hard look. "My drug of choice is caffeine."

"Another goodie two shoes. Whateves. Your loss."

The teacher called for attention. Quentin vibrated through classes. He was here physically but no help for the lab. In fact, he was more of a hindrance. Piper was pleased with my answer to his offer. She and I did our best with Quentin but he'd had just a little too much happy juice.

He kept flicking mothballs at Piper and the surrounding lab groups while he giggled. That he didn't get caught was a small miracle. They won't hurt you but the smell is pungent. I could tell that Piper was about ready to crawl over the lab table and strangle him. His arm flashed out again and I grabbed it without even looking in his direction. Quentin's eyes went round.

"Stop," I said firmly, using my most authoritative voice and every trick I knew about intimidation. He had frozen the moment I touched him and looked from my face to my hand. Right next to where I gripped his arm was a mark... *her* mark.

"You like?" he asked following my gaze to his ink and totally misunderstanding.

"Not into ink," I said, releasing his arm and looking back at the lab sheet.

"I got it for free. It's awesome. I have a job. They did it for me."

And if they knew you were talking about it, they'd kill you. "Well, you're a lucky guy then." I don't think he caught the sarcasm. I had to be really careful here. "Right now we need to finish our lab." I hoped to redirect him. I felt tingles travel my spine and looked up to find our teacher watching our exchange. I turned my attention once more to our lab. "What's his deal?" I asked under my breath.

"Don't know. He has his favorites. Acts like he hates being here. Dude's gotta be close to retirement. I mean some of the stuff he hands out is date stamped 1983." Maybe Quentin was smarter than he'd led me to believe.

We cleaned up when we were asked and shot from the room like racehorses at the gate when the bell rang. Each of us went our separate ways but I would see Piper again third period for English. My new information was killing me. I hated to wake White Eagle when he'd be at work so late tonight, but someone needed to get hot. Marlo would be at school and so would Lucie. Rick? I turned a corner and stepped into an alcove. I tried the door and finding it unlocked, eased inside. I gave the room a fast scan. Nothing dark or particularly ugly lived here, so I dialed with my back to the wall.

"What's wrong?"

"Are you watching the feed?"

"Among fifty other things."

"Watch it closely at about 8:30."

"For?"

"I found some interesting ink."

"Got it."

We disconnected and I turned my head to look out the small window in the door. I saw nothing so I reached for the doorknob only to have it pushed into me.

"What are you doing?" asked an outraged teacher.

"I'm new. I just moved here. I… I was homesick and I called my uncle."

He gave me an odd look. "Let me see your phone."

I handed it over and waited. He activated the phone and searched my recent calls. He looked from the screen to me. I knew what it showed – a call to Uncle Rick that lasted less than two minutes. "I should take this."

"I know," I said looking at my feet and hunching my shoulders.

"Okay, kid. This once I'll let it go but stay out of my room unless you're invited," he said, handing me my cell.

"Yes, sir. Thank you."

I slunk out of his room and off to class. What I really wanted was to go home. Instead I headed to my computer class and handed the teacher my change slip. He took it with a big sigh and assigned me a new seat.

NINETEEN

A big kid stared at me instead of his assigned computer screen. When I couldn't stand it anymore I spoke, "Can I help you?"

"You're new." *Yes, Einstein, I'm new.* "I don't like you," he continued.

I just looked at him. He couldn't be serious. "You don't know me," I replied calmly and then looked back at my screen.

"I'm talking to you," he said raising his voice.

"I have work to do."

The teacher appeared by my chair. "Is there a problem here?"

The guy across from me morphed before my eyes. He gave a sweet, innocent look to our teacher. "No, Mr. Vandyce. I was just welcoming the new guy and offering to meet him later – maybe walk him where he needs to go."

Mr. Vandyce smiled warmly. "Well, isn't that nice, Dillon." He moseyed on over to another student to check their work.

"Yes, isn't that nice," Dillon mimicked in an unflattering high, sing-song voice. "I want to be sure you know your place."

"I know mine. I hope you know yours." I could take this guy. He was taller than me and probably outweighed me by seventy pounds or more, but I was fast and knew what I was doing. I hoped I wasn't making a big mistake because I would be in a lot of trouble if I got suspended. At the very least I would lose Piper's trust – at worst it could cost her her life. I gave him my most vicious scowl. He looked a little taken aback.

"I hate bullies," I said soft and low so that only he could hear but with enough venom to push him back like a loud voice would. We stared each other down until the teacher circled back around. I snapped my eyes back to my screen. The teacher praised my work on his way past and the minute his back was turned I sent a secure message to Dillon. I heard it ping and watched his eyes grow larger and then shrink as an angry flush moved up his neck. He turned to call the teacher over and my message vanished like fog in the sun the moment his eyes were off the screen.

Mr. Vandyce came over and looked at Dillon's monitor and then at the guy himself. "Are you showing me that you're not working?"

"What? No. The message."

"What message, Dillon?"

"He threatened me," he insisted, jabbing a finger in my direction. While he was distracted I had eased down in my seat, hunched my shoulders and turned slightly so that my hearing aid was prominent. *That's right Mr. V, I'm small, weak and innocent.*

"Jesse, did you say something to Dillon?"

I looked up from my monitor, a look of surprise on my face. "No sir."

"No, no, he sent me a message."

The teacher hit a few keys on Dillon's computer and then looked at me. "May I see your computer?"

"Sure," I said, moving away. He came around the table and I watched his key strokes carefully. He found nothing. I haven't been friends with Marlo all these years for nothing.

"I don't see any evidence of a message. Maybe you should have Jesse help you with your work." A waving student hand caught his attention. "Get your assignment done, Dillon," he said and then walked over to the fluttering hand. I pressed a series of keys on my computer.

"You're dead," Dillon hissed.

I hit more keys. "Like I said, you don't know who you're messing with."

I finished my work and sent an embedded file to Marlo. I forwarded what I'd learned so far – not much, and included a video file of Dillon – taken right from Dillon's computer. I didn't have time to deal with him but I sure could get him suspended for threatening me. By the time administration worked it out – I'd be gone. If there was dirt on this guy – Marlo would find it and bring it to the light of day. I also added a message for Lucie. *Tell her I love her and I think about her every day.*

"You gonna cry, baby? Do you miss your mommy?"

"I miss her every day. What would your life be like if someone took your family away? Or are your parents the kind that causes the drunk-driving accidents that take away good people like my mom?"

Dillon just stared at me. The bell rang and he gathered his stuff but left his computer on. I quickly cleaned mine but left his video rolling, hoping the teacher would catch it. I collected my own belongings and headed out. Dillon's angry face, inches from my own flashed through my mind. Trouble was coming. I pulled my backpack strap over my other shoulder so that my hands would be free. I had barely cleared the door and I knew… I was gonna miss the bus.

Dillon was waiting for me and he had friends. He must have sent a text during our class – they were here too fast for any other form of communication to have occurred. I glanced at his friends who stood with their arms crossed while students brushed by hurrying for the buses. Then I looked back at Dillon and stared him down. He'd been leaning against the lockers with his chest puffed out, his arms crossed and a big scowl. A kid looked longingly at his locker behind Dillon's bulky form, shrugged and hurried on. No one here would help me and the hall was quickly emptying. They were either afraid of Dillon and his goons or on their side. Even our teacher locked his door and hurried away. Must be a staff meeting day, I thought, but I kept most of my attention on Dillon.

My attitude seemed to almost throw him. His eyes flickered. He could tell that I stood there knowing I was outnumbered and didn't scream for help or try to run away. I looked unafraid and I could see the uncertainty in his eyes.

He shoved himself off the locker and blocked my path. "I don't like you."

"You don't have to like me, but you should leave me alone," I answered calmly.

"Says who?" he snarled.

"Seriously? Don't be dumb. We fight – we get caught. We get caught – we get suspended. It's not worth it."

"Maybe it's worth it to me."

"If you want to get suspended there are lots of alternatives that don't involve me."

"But I want to involve you."

"No thanks," I said, turning to head down the hall and out the side exit.

He lunged to block my way but I darted past. I wasn't quite quick enough. He snagged me by my backpack and yanked my back so hard I hit the ground. I sprung back to my feet not wanting him to jump on me.

"Ooh, new kid has some moves," one of his buddies threw out.

I tried to get past again but now his friends blocked my way the other direction. I would not hit first and I couldn't show all my skills or I'd risk giving myself away. One of Dillon's large friends pushed me backwards and I hit Dillion's chest. He threw an arm over me pinning my right arm to my side. I heard the click and swish of a knife blade. Dillon pressed it to my neck. Now I was mad.

"Give me your money."

"No."

"I said, give me your money."

"No," I repeated, snapping up my left arm to hit his wrist as I turned my head to the side. The blade flashed past my face. With my now free right arm, I smashed the heel of my palm into his elbow. The knife flew free as I spun to my left and used my momentum to smash my fist into his cheekbone. Then I punched him in the gut for good measure. I heard his breath explode from his body and he staggered back a couple of steps. I turned and faced his buddies hoping they would run.

"Leave me alone," I stated firmly.

"It's still two against one, numb nuts."

"No it isn't," Quentin's voice said calmly behind me but I didn't turn to look.

"Quentin, you don't want to get involved in this," I said not taking my eyes off of Dillon's friends.

"Sure I do. I love a good turf war."

The guys actually looked a little afraid. Quentin was smaller than me and he didn't strike me as a very threatening guy. What was going on here?

Dillon had recovered and tried to get back behind me again as his buddies converged but Quentin was faster. My adversaries' eyes went wide and they froze. I turned to see Quentin riding Dillon in a crazy cross between bucking bronco and a piggyback ride gone horribly wrong before Dillon lost his balance and they both crashed to the ground, pinning Quentin. I lunged in that direction but Quentin freed himself without my help. He surged to his feet, grabbed my arm, and ran, dragging me with him out the side door.

"He's gonna have a horrible headache. Come on," Quentin yelped, panting. We were off the school grounds and out of sight when he finally stumbled to a halt and bent at the waist, hands on knees to gasp for breath. No one followed us.

"Man… you can… run. You… hardly broke… a sweat," he wheezed.

"I've found being a good runner can be useful," I replied watching him closely.

"Geez, you're weird. You sound so old sometimes."

"Yeah, I've been told. I wish you wouldn't have gotten involved. I don't want to bring trouble down on you."

"Relax, will ya? They're afraid of me."

"So I sensed, but why? You've been nice to me."

"You're new. Things are probably different where you come from, but here… there are factions. There's a hierarchy. I've made my place. Stick with me and yours will be guaranteed."

"You're right. I don't understand. I just want to get done here, graduate and move on. My dad and I have been through enough." *All true and all believable.* Who was Quentin Stowe?

"I just saved your skin. Give me a chance."

"I think…"

"Yes, do give him a chance," Bob's voice came over my earpiece. The first voice I'd heard since we tested the equipment.

I looked heavenward and blinked several times. Quentin would probably think I was upset about my mom but I was really recovering from Bob's close involvement here. How long had he been watching. I should never have put him out of my mind.

I looked at Quentin. "Okay, Q, but I really don't think you know what you're in for," I said as I grabbed his hand to give it a shake and at the same time rolled it so that I could get another look at his tattoo – the one that marked him as property of Evilia Malvada.

He laughed. "Yeah, you either," he answered cryptically.

I took off my glasses to rub my eyes and then pulled out my cell and texted Marlo, *I'm okay, Dad. Going to a friend's. I'll be home for dinner.* I didn't want Bob seeing what I was doing.

"Ah, isn't that sweet. You still check in." I cringed but Bob remained silent if he was even still watching.

"Come on, Quentin. Give me a break. We're both a little… we only have each other now."

"Yeah, sorry, Dude. It sucks. Come on. And do call me Q. I like that. Very James Bondy." He laughed and bro-punched my shoulder. I slid my glasses back on and indicated for him to lead the way.

My gut said I could trust him, but the mark told me another story. He led me through the neighborhood. I looked purposefully at every street sign and visible address along the way. It was clear people around here had a little more money on this side of the river.

I was surprised by the house we stopped in front of. "Is this your house?"

"Nah, my buddy lives here. You wanted to know why those guys were afraid of me… I have some unusual friends."

We walked through a thickly treed, overgrown yard to what could have easily passed for a haunted house. It looked old enough to be on the historic register if it wasn't so worn down. As we walked up the front porch stairs, I could smell the distinctive aroma of pot overlaying other smoky scents and a familiar sickly sweet odor I couldn't put my finger on. This house was far from its neighbors and could be virtually ignored. Darkness pressed in on me – that I couldn't ignore.

"Hey Quentin, I told you. I only do caffeine," I said sounding a little alarmed.

"Don't be such a pussy. No one's making you do anything. Just stick with me and don't talk. You'll be fine."

My gut clenched and my chest grew tight. I am an observer. I am an observer. I repeated the phrase over and over.

The noxious cloud swooped over us and pulled us inside. Weed, cigarettes of all types and many brands of cigar smoke all swirled together to steal what few senses I had left. The strange sickly sweet odor was stronger inside. The smoke barely masked… death. That was it.

The creep of *dark watcher* power oozed over me in a lazy manner. I fought every instinct screaming in me to react.

"Who's your friend, Quentin?"

"This here's Iowa. He's just a kid from school. You got my schedule?"

I tracked the voice down to an oversized armchair. The room was dark, the curtains drawn over all but a slice of dirty window that hadn't let in good light since the house was built. The only real illumination came from the entryway behind us, throwing the living room into even deeper shadow.

"Your quota goes up this week. Maybe you can get the new guy to help you."

"Yeah, maybe I'll do that," he replied offhandedly.

I said nothing, letting my eyes travel over as much of the entry and living room I could see without moving. The figure in the chair rose slowly, but I still couldn't see his features. He moved like an old person. People who suffer from pain and stiffness have an odd stilted gait - almost as if they are limping on both sides of their body at the same time.

"Did you bring what I asked for?" His voice was deep and low. It made me think he'd been a smoker for a long time.

"Of course," Quentin replied. He swung his back pack off his shoulder and to the floor. He dug around for a bit and pulled out what looked like a packet of student information. He handed it over without a word.

The old man reached forward and took it. "Wonderful. I knew having you T.A. in the counseling office would be valuable." Clearly Quentin was a whole lot smarter than I gave him credit for.

"Hey boy," I snapped my eyes to the frail *dark watcher*. He stepped closer and my eyes were adjusting to the dim. His raggedy hair and unshaved, gaunt face were graying and looked neglected. His clothes were holey and stained. The clothes matched the weathered face and faded gray eyes. Did he not care or was it all an act? He studied me as I studied him. With my boots on, I could look right over the top of his head but there was no denying his power. It would be a mistake to prod him. The image of a sleeping rattler flashed in my mind. "There – now I see it. The fear. Let's keep it that way. Now go in the kitchen and get some Cokes. They're in the fridge."

I turned to see which way to go. Then I turned back to ask but he was already pointing back toward the entrance with a gnarled finger. I glanced at Quentin but he looked calm enough, like this was no big deal.

I walked back to the kitchen, listening as hard as I could. The kitchen was brighter but only because the window was covered with a fabric of less weight. The appliances looked like they matched the vintage of the house and like the windows, I wondered if they had ever been cleaned.

I opened the fridge and saw cans of Coke, beer, moldy cheese, a shriveled apple and some mushy carrots. Didn't this guy eat? Movement caught my attention. A mouse scampered behind a cupboard. I suppressed a shiver. I wouldn't eat here either. Pet mice are fine, I guess, but as pests they carry diseases – too much Biology maybe. Whatever the reason, I didn't want to share living space with them. As my eyes moved back to the fridge a door registered… It had a brand new shiny latch and padlock. The sickly sweet odor was stronger here.

I realized that the front room had grown quiet – too quiet. I prayed Quentin was okay but was too afraid to use my gift and blow everything. I wondered if I should call for help. Would that ruin my ability to help Piper?

Quentin appeared in the doorway. "Never mind the Cokes. Let's go."

"Okay," I said as calmly as I could while I put them back. What had happened? Quentin's demeanor had changed. He was no longer happy-go-lucky. He looked… worried. I wasted no time heading for the door. I spared a glance toward the living room but I saw no sign of life there. Where had the *dark watcher* gone? I had the creepy sense he'd turned into a bat and flown away, but that was crazy.

The further we got from the house the more relaxed I felt. I didn't say a word for several blocks, thinking about what I would tell White Eagle and wondering about my new friend, Quentin.

"Why do you work for that guy?" I finally asked.

He sighed and that worried frown slid back over his face. "Come on. I'll show you."

He stayed quiet, not a state I'd yet to see him in. "Q, buddy, where are we going now?"

"I'm taking you to meet my family."

I could feel strange mixed feelings hovering around him. We walked on and on. He held tightly to his backpack which he had slung over one shoulder. His shoulders drooped and his head hung down. He had to know the route by heart because he rarely looked up. He was taking me somewhere he didn't want to go but he didn't think he had a choice. This was not the Quentin that I knew – this Quentin was desperate and afraid. He stopped walking and looked at me for a long time. I could see the change in his eyes and knew he'd reached a decision.

We stood in front of a tiny house, much smaller than its neighbors and also old. This one did not feel like the one we'd left. This one was sad… no heartbroken, but it held love too. The yard was in dire need of some work and the house needed painting. A well-worn bike and tricycle hung out with the lumpy grass and crooked flower beds.

"I can trust you to be nice and not say anything about where we were, right?"

"Yes." I was formulating what more I should add but I didn't get the chance. The front door banged open and a young teen ran down the steps and over to Quentin.

"You're late."

"I'm sorry."

"Don't do it again. I've got to go nanny. It's your turn here. I'm late."

"Yes, Angelina." The teen was a girl? She was small and thin but on closer inspection, she was older than I first thought. Still she could only be fourteen at the most. She looked like her brother and with her hair pulled back under a ball cap and no makeup I could see why I'd been fooled. In fact she was wearing the shirt Quentin had worn on Monday.

She slid her eyes to me causing a real smile to tug at Quentin's lips like he knew what she was thinking.

"This here's Iowa. Iowa - my sister, Angelina. You know like Angelina Jolie the actress."

"Hi, Angelina. So, I guess your parents are real movie fans, huh."

She didn't answer but asked a question of her own, "So you go to school with Quentin?"

"Yeah."

"He never brings anyone here. You must be different."

"He helped me out today."

"My brother has his moments," she added with a half-smile and then turned and ran up the street.

"Never mind her - she's late." Quentin's voice hinted at false cheerfulness.

"Yeah, I got that."

"Come on." Quentin led me into the cramped little house. It was spotlessly clean – the polar opposite of the house we'd just been in.

"Never mind my great-grandma. She's had a stroke," he mumbled under his breath.

I heard a baby squeal and the thunder of small feet, followed by their owner who flung himself at Quentin. Suddenly we were bombarded with kids of all ages, coming from all directions. An old mutt with a gray muzzle and a constantly wagging tail followed behind the herd. I hadn't even sorted out all the kids when a woman older than Bettylou McMurtry appeared with a cane in one hand and a baby on her hip. The side with the cane looked different from the other half of her body and it wasn't just that the side of her face looked like it was beginning to melt like softening wax.

"Hey, Quentin. Who's your friend?" she slurred.

"Iowa, this is my great-grandma." He moved over to her and took the baby. "This is my brother, George."

"Let me guess," I said with a smile not being able to resist. "Like George Clooney the actor?"

A girl of about eleven laughed. "Yeah, we're all famous. I'm Jennifer Aniston and this is my sister, Sandra Bullock," she said indicating a girl of about eight.

"I'm Brad," interrupted a six year old boy.

"Brad Pitt that is and that leaves, Steve Carell," Quentin informed me as he swung around his leg where his preschooler brother was clamped like a limpet.

"Jenn, did everyone get homework done?"

"Yeah, and dinner is started. You're late."

"Yeah, I know."

"Is your friend staying?" their great-grandma asked with the slur.

"Uh. Thanks so much but I really shouldn't. We just moved here and it's just me and my dad. I hate to let him eat alone… after… my, uh, mom isn't with us anymore."

"Only two of you? How weird," Sandra exclaimed.

"Yeah, it must be real quiet." Brad added.

Quentin smiled the happiest and most realistic smile I'd seen on him yet. He led the way into the tiny kitchen. His great-grandma took a seat at the kitchen table and he handed her baby George. He set the rest of the kids to work on various projects from setting the table, to ripping up head lettuce, to measuring rice and water. I was impressed. This Quentin was not like any of the other versions I'd seen. He was happy here yet I could feel his worry and pain.

The front door banged open and shouts of "Nana," lured us to the kitchen door-way. Kids were retasked to go unload the car. She was… beautiful for someone who had to be close to seventy. I could feel her warmth and vitality. She loved these kids deeply. Her suit was worn but she wore it with quiet dignity. I noticed that a split on her thumb was held together by plain first aid tape, not even a real band-aide. Her graying brown hair was pulled into a low ponytail. I had the feeling Angelina cut her hair. Her car was a 1980s vintage station wagon and like the house it was worn down but clean.

Quentin's soft voice pulled me back from my thoughts as I gazed out the kitchen window. "I lost my mom too. Cancer. They found it when she was pregnant with George. She wouldn't give up on him. She left us alone instead. They started chemo the minute he was born but it was too late. She only lasted a month. We brought her home to her mom to die. My dad… tried but he couldn't handle it. He started drinking and stopped paying the bills. He lost his job and then our house… well he tries to help out but losing Mom about killed him. Now I have to work to help take care of everyone."

"I'm sorry, Q."

"I just… I wanted you to know I'm not a bad person. No matter what anyone says about me, you'll know why. I tell myself I'm like Robin Hood and it doesn't hurt so much, you know?"

"Okay, Q. Okay." Inside I wanted to cry as I watched him look away from me and scrub at his face before the others returned with their plunder. I decided I'd go help and give him a minute. I held open the door and watched the younger kids stream by. Even the preschooler helped, but none of them held shopping bags. Nana hadn't been to the grocery store. She'd worked all day and then she'd been to Gleaners. It was generous of her to help others and get some cheap food for her family. I knew a little bit about them. I knew that Urban Gleaners was a small, Portland-based organization that picked up edible, surplus food from all kinds of local places and then helped to redistribute it to those living below the poverty line. It looked like they more than qualified. I'd seen the cupboards as they worked in the kitchen. They were about bare.

I went out to the car to bring in a load. "Hello, Quentin's grandma," I said quietly. "Sorry, I don't know your real name. I'm Jesse Montgomery. Quentin and I have classes together."

"I'm pleased to meet you. I'm Marion Browne."

"Mrs. Browne. How can I help?"

She smiled at me and handed me a box. She picked up one herself and then bumped the door shut with her hip.

"Are you their maternal grandmother?" I asked nodding toward the house.

"Yes, my daughter…"

I waited a beat but the rest seemed to have gotten locked up in her throat. "I'm sorry for your loss. I just… my mom's… she's gone too. A drunk driver… and now it's just me and my dad."

"I'm sorry for yours. It's nice to have you here. Quentin doesn't have many friends anymore and I worry. Maybe he finally found someone who understands him."

I smiled at her. "Thank you for letting me come over today. I should be going though. I need to eat with my dad. Meals are hard right now for him."

"I'm sure they are. I hope I see you again soon," she said softly as she set her box down and picked up George. "How's my little man?" He giggled and spoke nonsense to her in response.

"Thanks, everyone," I said to the group and then I turned to Quentin. "I'll see you tomorrow, Q?"

"Yeah," he answered, not looking at me.

I stepped right next to him where he worked at the sink. "I understand. You do it for them," I whispered.

I saw myself out and closed the front door with a soft click. I picked up my backpack from where I'd left it on the front porch and began the long walk home. No, not home – to our fake house in my fake life where there was plenty of food and I wouldn't have to share a room or take a shower on a schedule. I would do something for Quentin. I didn't know what, but he deserved… better.

TWENTY

I spent a sleepless night worrying about Q and his family. I had tried to enlist Bob but he was adamant. Quentin was NOT our problem and not our mission. He told me to focus on Piper Downing. He didn't even really want to hear about the weird drug house and the *dark watcher* who lived there. He didn't care about the locked door in the kitchen and what I was afraid of most… that the owner was dead in the basement.

I had talked to White Eagle when he came home from the bar. He couldn't believe I was still up. He at least listened to my whole story with his full attention even though I could tell he was tired. He reminded me to be careful and told me that we didn't need Bob's approval to help anybody. We would find a way to do something but he'd have to think.

I was in a grouchy mood the next morning as I stood waiting for the bus. Of course it was raining. I'd opted for a hoodie today even though it made me look more like me. I had to keep the earwig and glasses dry. I took a seat toward the middle and tried to decide what I would say to both Q and Piper when I saw them.

When Piper climbed on the bus she looked right at me and at first looked relieved and then angry. She walked right up to me, started to walk past and then plopped herself onto the seat next to me.

"Where were you yesterday? I was worried."

"I hung with Quentin."

"You're kidding."

"I'm not. He's an okay guy once you get past his crap."

Piper looked genuinely worried now. "Stay away from him. He's not who you think he is."

"Is anyone?" I sighed.

"What do you mean?" Piper turned to look at me, but I didn't answer her. I finally had a good look at her face. She had a swollen cheek and her eye was discolored. Holy hell. I'd been hanging with Q instead of watching her. I reached out and touched her face.

"What happened?"

"Nothing," she said, trying to turn away.

"Tell me."

"It's nothing. I just made my mom mad. Forget it."

"Your mom did this to you?"

"Sort of."

"Piper, what happened?"

"She was drinking with her new boyfriend. She caught him looking at me. She got all pissed off and started yelling at me. She said it was my fault he was looking, that I'd led him on or something. Whatever. It's fine now."

"It's not."

"Let it go, Jesse."

"Come hang out with me after school."

"No."

"Please. I want to know you're okay."

"Look, that's sweet, but I don't really know you. I'll be fine." She turned and looked straight ahead. Then she gave in a little and smiled shyly at me. "Maybe I'll let you walk me home again."

"You've got a deal."

We went to our classes. Today was a day that we didn't have lunch together. I hadn't seen Q yet and I was more than a little worried about him. I didn't really know anyone else here and the way things had been going I wasn't sure I wanted to. What I would give to have Lucie here.

I looked up from my lunch. The hair on the back of my neck was at it again. I scanned the lunch room and then I saw him - the man who had kidnapped me only to talk. He was dressed as the janitor so kids were moving around him completely oblivious. I'd lost my appetite so I walked over to the garbage can by where he stood.

"How did you find me?"

"I don't look at the world the way others do."

"What does that mean?"

"Join me and find out."

"I play for team White Eagle and I'm not looking to sign a new contract right now."

"Why are you so stubborn?"

"Because I know who hired you."

"Haven't you heard the phrase, 'the enemy of my enemy is my friend'?"

"And I heard the guy who said that was stabbed in the back by the very people who were his new 'friends'. I believe trust is earned."

"Well then. Have it your way for now, but I'll be watching and we'll talk again."

"I'm sure."

I hated to give him my back but I walked away and off to my next class. This had to qualify as a Marlo-worthy event and worse, if he found me, could Evilia be far behind? I looked back to where he'd been, but he was gone.

I stepped into a bathroom stall, texted Marlo and asked him to check the feed @ 12:30 for our mystery man. Then I closed out the phone and headed to class. At least I had math with Piper so I could convince her to let me walk her home in case she'd changed her mind from this morning. She was quiet but then so was I. I had a lot to think about. I hadn't seen Dillon or his friends all day either and I really wasn't looking forward to it tomorrow.

I tentatively picked up Piper's hand on the bus. I just worried that it meant something entirely different to her than it did to me and then I began to worry whether or not Lucie was watching. I would have to beg her forgiveness later. I felt like I was close to having Piper talk to me. She just had to trust me and I couldn't stay here forever. I'd missed almost a week of school back home already.

We got off the bus and I felt that feeling again that someone was watching Piper. It grew and grew as we approached her house. I felt the distinctive pull of *dark watcher* power and shut off my gift as tightly as I could.

"Are you nervous?"

"Yeah, I don't want to get you into trouble with your mom."

"I think if she meets you, she won't worry about me liking her creepy boyfriend."

I didn't get to reply. The boyfriend opened the door. Piper blanked her face and turned sideways so that she could enter without touching him.

"Who's this?"

"My friend, Jesse. We have math homework to do."

"Your friend, huh?" he asked, wiggling his bushy black eyebrows. His slick voice matched his manner. There was nothing spectacular about him except that he was fit. He wore his darkness like a cloak and that reminded me of Kraeghton. Few *dark watchers* were smooth like Kraeghton. This guy was good and if I wasn't very careful, we were dead.

"Hello," I said trying to give nothing away. *Dark watchers* were everywhere in this town. I could understand the Quentin connection but why here unless it was everything that Piper had hinted at.

"Your mom's at the grocery store. Do your math at the table, not in your bedroom."

Piper looked like she wanted to say something but pressed her lips together instead. She took my hand and pulled me into the dining room and started pulling out math stuff. Her mom's boyfriend went in the living room and turned the volume up on the TV.

Piper leaned toward me and fiercely whispered, "Look, Quentin is not who you think he is. I've seen…"

"Now is not a good time to talk about Q."

"Now's as good as any."

"Look, would it make a difference if there was a good reason?"

"No reason is good enough."

"What if you were protecting someone you love?"

She shook her head and I swung my gaze over to her mom's boyfriend and then back to her.

"Let's grab a snack," she said and pulled me into the kitchen.

"I don't think we should discuss this in front of him," I whispered.

"He doesn't know what we're talking about."

"I don't know. Seemed like he was listening pretty hard." She pushed me against the fridge with her hands on my arms and left them there while she peeked around the corner at the man in question. She seemed to realize what she was doing and yanked her hands back off of me. She turned her back to me and rustled around in a cupboard. She pulled out a bag of chips and then gave me a pointed look. I moved and she pulled soda from the fridge.

Finally she looked at me. "I like you. I don't want to see you get hurt."

"All right, I give up, what do you know about Q?" I asked softly as she clinked ice into glasses.

"I'm afraid for you. Don't be his friend. I don't care why he... did what he did. No reason is good enough. Stay away from him. He may not be a bad person yet, but one day he'll lose himself to darkness."

I stared at her. Did she know? Did she sense... was he here because? No! I had sensed her at school. She was no *watcher*.

"Let's go over to my house where we can talk."

"No. Another day."

I tried to focus on math but I kept wondering what she had seen. When her mom came home she all but threw me out even though she could see we really had gotten most of our math done. It had started to rain again. Piper's mom neither offered me a ride nor asked if I had one. White Eagle was probably still at the bar trying to worm information out of the brother of the other dead kid, so I put up my hood and prepared to jog to our townhouse. I turned back at the corner to look. Piper was still on her porch. She looked sad even from this distance. She waved and then turned and went inside.

I felt completely frustrated. I hated to push her too hard but I was worried about her. I couldn't just come out and tell her she had a *dark watcher* in her house. I'd have to come back and spy but I didn't have the resources here that I had at home.

White Eagle wasn't home when I got there. I left him a message and he called me back when he went on his break. Tonight he was off at midnight. I told him my plan to go spy on Piper which of course worried him deeply. I swore I'd wear the glasses and earwig and I also promised I'd call Rick so that someone from the team could at least monitor me while I was out.

I dressed all in black after talking to Rick who promised they'd take turns watching over me. I went out the back door and locked it behind me. I walked down three units away from the manager's townhouse before I hopped the fence and began the hike to Piper's. It wasn't even dark yet so I left my hood down and just kept walking like I was out for an evening of fresh air. I walked the long way around her block to scope it out. Who had dogs on the block and who didn't? Who had lush foliage and whose yards were sparse?

I found a good spot. Three houses in a row had no dogs and lots of big trees and bushes. One neighbor had even thoughtfully planted a hedge between himself and the property next door. I was going to get wet from the plants but I could deal with it. One minute I was walking down the street and the next I was hiding in the shrubbery. I waited for some kind of alarm to sound or a helpful neighbor to come check but nothing happened. I made myself wait for seven minutes before I eased further in and then to the back of the property. A six foot cedar fence was hidden behind a huge rhododendron and some other shrubs. I found a broken slat that I could look through. I really wanted to climb the tree to watch but without its leaves it would leave me too exposed.

I found a comfortable position and settled in to wait. I sent Piper a text asking if she was okay. She said she was fine. A few minutes later, I saw it was true for myself as she began to wash dishes. Her mom came in and had words with her. I could see a glass of amber liquid in her hand. I wanted to reach out and choke her. The boyfriend came in and said something to her mom. While Piper's back was turned I saw him slip his hand inside her shirt and give her goods a squeeze. Poor Piper. He didn't even stop when Piper turned. I could see her go rigid, throw down the towel and stomp from the room. Piper's mom turned into his arms, kissed him and then he was pushing her away. Piper's light came on upstairs and then the tryst in the kitchen ended and the light went out down there. Piper sat staring out her window and swiping at her cheeks. A door slammed and an engine roared to life. A moment later Piper's mom was in her room yelling at her again. I saw Piper put her hands over her ears. Piper's mom turned and left, slamming the door so hard, the bedroom window shook.

My phone vibrated. *I should have come over. I hate my mom right now but at least he's gone for the night. Call me if you want.*

I did. "Are you okay?" I asked when she answered.

"Not really."

"Tell me what happened."

"I'm so sorry. I shouldn't bother you with this... I just. What is it about you? You make me feel better."

"Thanks, Piper. I want to help you."

"Do you... do you like me?"

"Yeah, Piper. I like you." *Oh man, I was going to roast in hell. I did like her, but not like she meant and she wasn't Lucie.*

"Can I... um... can I come over tomorrow? If it's okay with your dad?"

"Sure Piper that would be great. Hey, is your mom's boyfriend really gone for the night?"

"Yeah, I think so. Why?"

"He just made me uncomfortable. I want you to be safe."

"Thanks, Jesse. I better go. I'll see you tomorrow."

"Okay Piper. Good night."

"Bye."

I closed my phone, wishing badly that I could call Lucie. I looked into the distance between the houses. It was light enough to see but everything was losing its defining edges as the night crept in soft and slow. A breeze pushed around the fat buds of spring and daffodils slouched with the weight of many fine rain drops. The wet asphalt became a shiny smooth charcoal gray as the sky turned an indeterminate shade of deep blue gray. A hazy mist had turned the

Douglas firs on the distant hill to smudgy, bristly darkness almost like the nap of wet fur.

I stayed in my spot until it was good and dark and I was so cold I was starting to shiver. I kept watch over Piper as she worked on her laptop, left to brush her teeth and get ready for bed and then take her laptop and sit with it in her lap propped up in her bed. She never closed her blind but at least the bottom half of the bathroom window was obscured so that I never became a real voyeur. Her mom never came back and it was just after eleven. White Eagle was off at midnight. I would try to hold on.

All I could think about was how cold, wet and tired I was. I was just about to call it quits when my phone vibrated again. I was pretty sure it was Piper and I was pretty sure I really didn't know what to say.

It wasn't. "Q? What's up? Where were you today?"

"Jesse. I'm... I've made a mistake. Please help me."

"Where are you?"

"I'm at Lake Grove Park. Can you come?"

"Well yeah, but it will take me awhile. My dad's at work." I pulled up the GPS on my phone. "Geez, Q. It's gonna take me like half an hour to get there by foot. Can you start walking toward me?"

"No. I've got to go. Just... hurry. Okay?"

"Sure, Q, but..." and I was talking to dead air. Well hell! I called Rick as I worked my way back to the street.

"Hey, we've got trouble and I don't know what kind."

"Piper?" he asked, sounding concerned.

"Nah, Quentin. He's at Lake Grove Park and he just asked for help."

"Crap," Rick hissed.

"Yeah, I know, right? I'm on my way but I don't know what's waiting for me. White... um... he doesn't get off until midnight."

"Correct. I'll have Neil take over here and Melody and I will be on our way. I'll call the man and have him head straight over when he gets off work."

"Thanks, Uncle Rick."

"Yeah, kid. The boss will hate it but he can't deny you've got good instincts."

"Tonight I hope they're wrong."

I closed out my phone and pocketed it. I stretched a little and then broke into a jog. Soon it was a run. I was a little over two miles away. I wished I had my bike. My phone remained quiet except for the cues from the GPS and I grew more and more worried about Quentin.

I hadn't noticed how far apart the street lights were until I needed them. What kind of an idiot runs in the dark dressed in black... oh yeah, me. Dumb, dumb, dumb. *What did you get yourself into, Quentin?* At least there weren't many cars. So maybe I wouldn't die getting to him. Maybe I was going to die when I got there. I pressed on, fear clawing at me.

I approached the park. I didn't see any cars in the lot so I stopped to turn off my GPS. I was afraid to leave it on vibrate and afraid to turn it off. I took a couple of deep breaths so that I would have a chance of hearing over my ragged breathing and pounding heart. I wondered if anyone was even here. The gates were closed and the barbed wire was daunting but I had to find Quentin.

I walked the length of the entrance area. One end looked like I could get past and the house next door either didn't have a dog or it was inside. I made it about half way down when I heard it beginning to bark. I froze, checking my options. It was late, the owners were probably sleeping. So I hurried as fast as I could to the end, falling and whacking my knee pretty good.

I listened for all I was worth and could hear the sound of distant, muffled arguing coming over the water. I crept closer, moving from tree to tree and using any other camouflage I could find. It was hard to make them out but it looked like Carmichael and the old *dark watcher* that Quentin knew. I saw movement and trained my eyes in that direction. Piper's *dark watcher* was here too. I ground my teeth together. I couldn't take on three. It would be suicide.

I couldn't hear more than a word or two but their gestures and postures made me nervous. I was almost worried for the old *dark watcher*. Where was Quentin? Piper's *dark watcher* took the old one roughly by the shoulder and pushed him toward the water. I could just make out a boat. The three of them climbed in and the motor started. This was a huge lake. They could be going anywhere. I watched the direction the boat headed. There was no good reason to be tricky tonight, right?"

As soon as the engine's roar became soft, I began to call. "Quentin? Q? Q, where are you?" There was no answer but the distant bark of a dog. "Come on Q. I'm here. Where are you?" I could hear a soft repetitive thud that matched the lap of the water. I scanned the shore and moved closer. Part of the water was not reflecting back.

I reached out a hand and touched fabric. A number of images flashed through my mind but I pushed them aside. I felt my way until I had ahold of an arm and pulled for all I was worth. Quentin. His eyes stared at nothing, his mouth still open in a final scream. No pulse, no heartbeat, no breath. He was cold already from being in the water. Quentin. I let go and sat down hard on my butt, right on the edge of the walkway. Quentin. Q. My friend and Evilia's toy.

I pulled out my cell and dialed.

"Thomlinson."

"Rick it's me. We're too late. Carmichael and the other two left by boat and Quentin… Quentin is…" my throat closed up.

"Are you secure?"

"I… I think so."

"Sit tight. The cops will get there first. Tell them the truth… that your friend called and you went to see if he was okay. I'm almost there. I'll call it in. Give me five minutes and then you call it in. You can do this."

I clicked off and noted the time. As soon as five minutes was up. I dialed and began talking to the operator but I could already hear sirens in the distance. I was still talking to her when the first car pulled up and then the second. She was so calm. I tried to be calm but my nose was running, I was getting stuffed up and my face was wet with tears.

TWENTY-ONE

I looked down to the body in the water. Lights flashed, reflected and wavered as the crews worked. I didn't think even Bob would be able to save me this time. I was in a closed park at one in the morning. A tear slid down my cheek and here I thought they were all gone. "Tell me again. How did you know that boy?"

"Quentin. His name was Quentin. Like Quentin Tarantino, the director, but his last name was Stowe. I want to wait for my father to get here. You're not supposed to question me without him here, right?"

The man shook his head and walked away with purpose to go and bother someone else. I half fell, half sat on a bench. I stared at the water. "How'd you get mixed up in this, Quentin?"

"Jesse!" I turned to the sound of my new name. Piper ran along the waterline like I had and darted in my direction, avoiding the police. She threw her arms around me.

"What are you doing here?" I asked in confusion.

"I saw the news. They said they found someone… a boy… and I thought…"

"What? Why?"

"You started hanging out with Quentin. I didn't want…" The tears welling in her eyes spilled over. "I don't know you that well but I feel like you're my friend. I was afraid it was you. I heard the news and I was afraid…"

"Slow down. What are you talking about?"

"Don't you see? Quentin was killed just like Becca - killed because he knew something."

"I thought Becca OD'ed."

"That's what they want you to think. They'll find drugs on Quentin too. You'll see. Trust me, he didn't commit suicide and it's no accident *you* found him. They wanted you to find him. They wanted you to know that if you talk, they'll kill you too."

"Piper, what are you saying? I know he didn't commit suicide but what does his death have to do with me?"

"Promise me you won't talk. It's the only way to save yourself. Promise."

"I promise, but what do you know?"

Piper's eyes skittered all over the area and her voice dropped to a whisper, "The last time I went with Becca to spy on Quentin and the other kids, her phone died. She had me use mine to record their meeting. Jesse, there's a video on my phone. I'm afraid to share it and too afraid to delete it. Becca's phone is missing. The police don't have it. They asked if I had it. I was one of the last people to see her alive. See what I'm saying, Jesse? If I don't have it, her family doesn't and the police don't have it… then *they* must - the people on the video - and they have all the videos she took - all except the last one. I know she didn't tell them about me or I'd be dead by now too, but they suspect. My mom's new boyfriend showed up right after Becca died - Right after. Why didn't I see that before?"

"I swear I'll take care of you. Let me see your phone." The sky had turned a deep denim blue and the mist continued. Piper looked at me, but it was so dark that all I could see in her eyes was black, white and the reflected lights. "Trust me," I added, throwing every bit of persuasion I could her way.

I fiddled with her phone for a moment and sent the videos to Marlo's special cell without even looking at them. I wiped her phone before I gave it back. "Stay with me. I'll keep you safe. I swear."

"Okay," she whispered, looking lost.

"How did you get here?"

"I took my mom's car. She drank herself to sleep. She won't know I'm gone."

I put my arm around her and we sat in silence, watching the river. She cried softly and hung onto my waist. A disturbance in the line let me know that White Eagle had arrived. The officer went to meet him and then they turned to me. He waved to White Eagle to wait and he rushed ahead but White Eagle followed him anyway.

"Young lady. What are you doing here?" the officer who had spoken to me earlier asked, sounding frustrated. "How did you get by?"

"Trust me," I whispered quickly to her and then I turned my attention to him. "This is my girlfriend, Piper. She was worried about me."

"She's got to go."

"No, please. Can't she wait with an officer until you're done with me? No one is home and she doesn't want to go to an empty house."

"No."

"Please. It's the middle of the night and she's scared," I begged.

"Okay. Wait here." He walked over to another officer. I did a quick scan; just enough to be sure the officer was okay and there were no *dark watchers* nearby. There were so many people here now that they couldn't pin it on me. It felt as okay as it could considering what had happened here tonight.

"Piper, when my dad gets here - you can trust him too. I swear on my mother."

White Eagle was almost to me so I said loudly enough for the officer to hear, "Dad, you remember my girlfriend, Piper."

"I most certainly do. It's good to see you again," he said smoothly, buying right in. He gave me a look and then turned his gaze back to Piper. "You're still coming over, right?"

"I sure hope so," she replied weakly.

The new officer took her gently by the arm. "Come on, Miss. Let's get you some cocoa."

"Now, your father is here and I have his permission to speak to you. Tell me what happened."

I started with the call from Quentin and worked my way forward to now. Then I talked about meeting Quentin's family and about how he'd been sucked into something but I wasn't sure what. I told him about the house where we went to get Quentin's job and how I didn't like the smell. I told him I thought it was pot but I really wasn't sure and I left out the *dark watchery* bits. I did include that the guy made me uncomfortable and at the very least he deserved a welfare check because of the state of his kitchen.

White Eagle admitted that I had mentioned the house but he didn't know much and he was more worried about Quentin's family than the house and its strange occupant. The officer let us know that they were already talking to Quentin's family and they would check out the house I'd mentioned. He was impressed that I knew the address. We told him I was good with numbers and he bought it.

I kept glancing toward Piper. She looked scared but otherwise okay. I saw Rick pull up and wondered how White Eagle had beaten him until I saw him flash a badge and realized he'd come on official business. The person who came after him made my heart freeze in my chest. Bob walked in with Melody. I must not have done a good job keeping my face blank because White Eagle and the detective turned to look.

The three of them went right over to the officer who was talking to Piper and I began to shake. Something wasn't right. Melody came and pulled the detective talking to us aside. There was much hand waving and gesturing in both groups. Soon Bob had Piper by the arm and was leading her away. Melody followed and I started to rise but Rick strode quickly in our direction and pushed me back down. Piper gave me one last scared look and then Bob was pushing her into a black sedan and Melody hopped in the front. They were pulling out and there was nothing I could do.

"You two come with me now," Rick hissed under his breath. I stood and we followed him up to the parking lot. A driver was waiting in another black sedan. We got in the back and Rick got in the front. We pulled out. Rick said nothing so neither did we. White Eagle looked nervously over his shoulder to the truck.

"What?" I asked as I took off my glasses and pulled out my silent covert listening device. I tossed them on the back seat, not really caring what became of them.

"The truck."

"Don't worry about it," Rick replied. We'll have it picked up before they can check it out.

We sat in silence all the way to Bob's Portland office. Rick marched us from the underground garage and up in the elevator to Bob's floor. All the lights were on and it looked like a beehive of activity. We were brought into the conference room. Rick tossed me a backpack and took a seat. "Go take a shower. Come right back and just so you know... *he*'s having you watched. Don't try anything. I've only got so much clout around here right now."

I nodded and exchanged a look with White Eagle before I left the room. I did exactly what Rick said. Right now I wanted information more than I wanted to cause trouble.

It felt wonderful to have the hot water beat over me but I wanted to know what was going on so I dried and dressed quickly and hurried back to the conference room. White Eagle and Rick were watching the screen with intensity. A team was taking the house where the old *dark watcher* had been dealing.

I could hear Neil speaking into a mic and sounding like a commentator. Maybe today he was wearing a pair of the glasses. The old *dark watcher* was found dead at the scene. They had gotten there just in time. A fire had just started to cover the murder but it wasn't smoke inhalation that killed him. *No, it wouldn't be.* I caught a glimpse of the body back in the chair in the living room. He looked like he had been scared to death and I was sure that was exactly what happened. They had probably drained him until his heart quit beating. The fire department and the police were there so there was only so much Neil could do to cover things up and maybe he shouldn't. Maybe Evilia needed to be exposed and not have any idea that we were involved.

The feed was live and although we had no windows I could see that dawn had turned the sky almost green as an orange sun kissed the horizon. The fog had vanished like the last drops of water from a skillet on high heat. There was a shout and Neil returned to the house. A woman was found in the basement. She'd been dead for weeks.

I turned to Rick. "I'd put money on her being the owner and that *dark watcher* was posing as a relative. Poor lady."

"Looks like he got his."

"Yeah, it's what happens when her underlings fail. You know that. So, how did you remove me from the clutches of the local authorities?"

"Bob had paperwork showing that you were in witness protection and that it was very important to a federal case that you disappear."

"Of course he did. What about Piper?"

"You'll never see her again."

"You know that's not what I'm asking," I grated. White Eagle put a hand over the one I had resting on the table.

Rick leaned forward. "You know that I can only do so much. It's out of my hands. He's already got her on a plane."

"What?"

"She is the one in witness protection." He waited for it to sink in. "He had her mother deemed unfit and has whisked her away. We got the video you sent. It's all crumbling down and she's the only witness who's still alive."

"I promised her I'd keep her safe."

"And you have, Owen."

"It doesn't feel like it."

"What was on the video?"

"You didn't watch it?"

"I didn't have time."

Rick hit a few keys on the control panel by his chair. "Agents have finished packing your townhouse and will deliver it all here. Your manager has been arrested. He's been stealing from his renters and the evidence is mounting. He even tried using John Montgomery's credit card. That's how we got the warrant to check his townhouse. The fingerprints that White Eagle collected were in IAFIS. Mr. Jones has been hauled in for theft and fraud before. All evidence of your existence will be gone by morning."

"Not all. I tried to get a kid suspended."

"Quentin tried to tie that loose end up for you, it looks like. That may be how he got himself in trouble. That and he never should have taken you to that house. They were on to him then."

"So it's all my fault," I said, my voice breaking.

"I've been with you every step of the way. I've seen files you weren't allowed to see. You did Quentin a favor."

"Sure I did. He's dead, Rick."

"Evilia can't hurt him anymore and now we can get his family the help they need. He's a hero and so are you."

"Being a hero feels like shit."

"Owen, you were a friend to a young man who hadn't had any since his mom died. This situation wasn't caused by you. You meant so much to Q that he…"

"Don't call him that."

"Ok, Owen. I want you to know that Dillon wasn't at school because he did get suspended. He worked for Evilia too and Quentin turned him in for bullying and drugs. The police offered him a deal. They were supposed to protect him. He did it for you. He was trying to take care of you, the only way he knew how."

I couldn't take it anymore. I tried to hold it in but all the hurt, anger, pain and frustration burst out. I put my head down on my arms and sobbed. White Eagle patted my back and Rick moved into the chair on the other side of me and did the same.

"I'm sorry, Owen," Rick said softly. White Eagle didn't say anything. He didn't need too. He knew me better than anybody. I just needed him to be here. I pulled myself together and wiped at my eyes and nose.

Rick played Piper's video. It was slightly blurred and wavery but I could clearly see Quentin, three boys I did not know, Dillon and his two goon friends all having a meeting with the old man *dark watcher*. The boys were looking a little restless and the old *dark watcher* was clearly telling them to wait. The camera panned as a car door slammed and then Caleb Carmichael entered the screen. Most of what was said could not be heard but the passing of money and pills was plain.

"The video corroborates Quentin's story. You saved him," Rick said gently.

"Can we go home now?"

"Not yet. We have to make you look as much like you as we can and get all your paperwork in order for Monday."

I sighed and sat back. "How'd it go with the other kid's brother, White Eagle?"

"I didn't have as much… luck as you did. He just didn't know anything."

"Was it worth it?"

"When we bring the *dark watchers* down - it's worth it."

"Owen?" I looked at Rick. He looked distracted and worried. "I know you don't need any more bad news right now but I thought you should know…" he paused. "Your dad is not at all happy with any of us or your mom. I'm sure he has your best interests at heart but I'm worried about… Bob. He always gets his way and… Lucie's dad is in town."

I slumped in my chair. I suddenly felt exhausted. Maybe being undercover wasn't so bad.

I had about dozed off when Joy showed up looking like she was up way earlier than she'd like to be. She spent twenty minutes returning our looks to nearly our former selves. While she worked Rick kept us up to date with the little forward progress that was made. We were finally released and Rick drove us home. Bob only spoke to us on the phone from wherever he was managing Piper. It was probably best that I didn't see him face to face. It might not have been healthy for him.

When we got to our street, the sky was still a pale blue and shadows were long. Sarah's car was at the curb which was unusual but it all made sense when Rick pulled into the garage. He closed the door before he would let us out.

Sarah was dressed and waiting not so calmly at the kitchen table. Both hands were wrapped tightly around a cup of tea that looked like she hadn't even tasted. Her laptop sat open and I could see reports streaming by. The look on her face told me that she'd had it much worse than us. All she could do was watch and there was nothing she could do to help either of us.

"Ma'am," Rick said respectfully and then he closed the door and returned to the garage. Sarah hugged us both tightly like she was afraid Bob would take us away again if she loosened her grip. I heard engines rumble and knew Rick was returning Sarah's car to the garage.

"Where's Lucie?" I asked softly.

"She doesn't know. I didn't wake her. Last she knew, you were leaning against a tree watching Piper."

"Oh hell. Did she see everything?"

"Yes."

"It didn't mean anything."

"Yes, it did. You cared about her. Bob used you, she knows that. She also knows that girl loved you. I bet she even knows you could have loved her back if you would have let yourself."

I didn't know what to say. I felt... sick. I felt like I'd cheated but I hadn't. All I'd done was be nice and held her hand... on the surface, but Sarah was right. I could have loved Piper and Bob knew it too. That's why he picked me for the job instead of Mitchell. Bob knew me much better than I knew him... and that was frightening.

"Go wake her up. She'll be relieved that you're okay." I tried to smile at Sarah but I just didn't have it in me.

I walked down the hall feeling totally conflicted and heartsick. I rested my forehead against her door and splayed my hand out over the surface. There had never been a time that I didn't want to see her until now. Now I was afraid.

I opened the door. It was still dim with the shades closed tight but morning was working its way in. Any minute her alarm would be going off for school. I watched her sleep. She was so beautiful. She reminded me of Quentin's Nana - the one who would never see him again.

I forced myself forwards far enough to close the door. I pulled off my boots and knelt by her bed. She turned in her sleep and a soft smile touched her lips. "Owen," she breathed.

I brushed her hair back and she opened her amazing blue eyes. "Is it you?" her voice caressed my mind but no sound crossed her lips. I leaned in to kiss her. She pulled herself up and slid gracefully onto my lap. "You're not okay," she said gently, aloud this time.

"Nope. Not even a little bit," I said raggedly. I could feel the tears again just below the surface. "I'm so sorry. I hurt you. I would never intentionally do that."

"I know that but I won't deny that you did."

"I'm sorry, Lucie. I'd take it all back if I could but I can't – not any of it."

"What happened?"

"As I was leaving Piper's… I knew her mom's boyfriend who was a *dark watcher* wouldn't be back…"

"I know about him," she said, trying to get me to move on.

"I got a call from Quentin."

"Do you know what he did for you?"

"Yes." Her hand was on my chest over my heart. Her hip was on my thighs and my feet were going to sleep. I picked her up and set her on the edge of her bed next to me. "Lucie, he's dead. Quentin is… the *dark watchers* got to him before I could…"

"It's not your fault."

"It is at least partly my fault."

"I won't let you blame yourself. I blame Bob… and that girl."

"Don't be mad at Piper. That is on me too. I just wanted to help her…"

"You liked her."

"As a friend."

"You liked her more, I could see it. Do you know how hard that was to watch?"

"I didn't know you were watching."

"Does that make it all better?" she asked with acid in her tone.

"No," I answered. "I just wanted to be her friend. She needed a friend."

"She wanted more."

"I can't control that!"

"I think you could but you didn't want to. You thought she'd talk to you faster if…" She clamped her lips together like she wanted to say more but was afraid to.

"I didn't mean for any of this to happen. Besides how is my being friends with Piper any different than you being friends with Marlo? How do you feel about Marlo?"

"How did Marlo get into this?"

"Don't worry about Piper. I'll never see her again. Bob put her in witness protection. She saw Quentin and some other kids exchanging pills and money with Carmichael and another *dark watcher*."

"You'll still think of her."

"Yeah, I will. Her and Quentin. I won't lie. They touched my heart."

"I'm sorry he's gone. I think you could have turned him."

"I did. That's what got him killed and now I get to live with that too."

Lucie's alarm buzzed and I started to get up. "No."

I looked at her. "I'm sorry. Please don't go. It's been a rough week. My dad's in town."

"I heard."

"Please… stay."

Suddenly I was so tired. Lucie threw on a robe and left the room. I sat with my head resting on my palm, my elbow on my knee and tried to stay awake. I closed my burning eyes and tried to remember if I'd had dinner yesterday. Lucie's bed was still warm and was looking really inviting.

She came back in with a pair of White Eagle's pajama bottoms and handed them to me. "No one at your house knows you're back. You can sleep here until you're ready to face them."

"Thanks, Luce." I pulled off my sweat shirt and took off my jeans and socks with her standing there. I threw on the pajamas and fell into bed. She crawled in with me. It was not my most romantic moment but right now I was just happy to hold her. I wouldn't even pretend that she had forgiven me but at least she didn't hate me enough to kick me out.

I came to a little when she got up about an hour later but I just couldn't seem to wake myself up enough to worry about it.

TWENTY-TWO

Lucie was gone when I finally got up. She had decided to make it to at least part of the school day. White Eagle was still sleeping but Sarah fed me breakfast. She had alerted my mom that I was safely with her and would be up when I once again rejoined the living. Since she was home from her half day kindergarten job I figured I might as well go face her.

My mom was watching Netflix and grading papers when I walked in. She turned and smiled at me but the voice on the screen had snagged my attention. Emily Thorne from the series Revenge said in a closing voiceover, "Power can be hoarded by the mighty, or stolen from the innocent. Power provides the ability to choose... but has a proclivity for corruption. The use of power is not to be taken lightly... for it is never without consequence." I continued to stare as the closing credits rolled. What was Evilia's nature – was she in my head – had she gotten into the heads of the dead students? What would she do now? One thing was certain, she didn't care about how she used power or the consequences of it, but I knew that eventually it would consume her. Too bad it couldn't be today.

"You don't have to talk if you don't want to, but I'm here when you're ready," Mom said as she hit pause.

"I know. It just hurts… all of it."

"I talked to Sarah. We're not at all happy with Bob on many levels."

"No one is right now, but that doesn't matter. There's nothing we can do about it at the moment," I said, hearing both resentment and resignation in my tone.

"What had your attention captured on the TV? You don't usually go for the drama stuff."

"What the actress was saying made me think of Evilia. One day all this power she has taken and corrupted is going to bite her in the backside."

"I sure hope so, honey."

"Right now there is nothing we can do about her either but there is someone we can do something about. How are we going to handle Dad?"

"He loves you," she replied softly.

"He has a funny way of showing it sometimes."

"He has been manipulated by everyone from Evilia to Bob and his own father to us. That's tough for a guy who needs to be in control."

"None of us controls anything," I growled in frustration.

"Not with people like Evilia and Bob around, no, but maybe we can get smarter about how they use us."

"I'd say you've been watching too much TV but I'm open to suggestions." I sat next to her on the couch and pulled over a stack of her papers and picked up a green pen. She never used red to correct papers. "How's kindergarten?"

She laughed. "Are you changing the subject?"

"For now."

"Then kindergarten is the same as always... busy. I really am more interested in hearing about you. You look... battle worn."

"You said that Dad feels manipulated... well, I feel completely used. Did Sarah tell you about Piper and Lucie?"

"Yes."

"I see it as one of my many failings. I love Lucie but Sarah was right. I could have loved Piper if I had let myself. Bob chose me because he knew that was true. He could have just as easily used Mitchell. In many ways Mitchell would have been better for this job with his skill set. Bob purposely drove a wedge between me and Lucie. I feel guilty because I let him do it."

"I think you're looking at this the wrong way. What you said about Bob is very likely true but not what you said about yourself. I've seen some of the clips too, Owen. You were kind to Piper. You were a friend when she needed one. You never even kissed her and you could have. You showed strength, loyalty and integrity."

"It still feels like I cheated on Lucie."

"Only if you pursue Piper."

"I don't even know where she is. I do care about her being safe. I promised her."

"I know. I believe in you."

"Is that why you made me talk? You knew you could make me feel a little better?"

"I can't bring back Quentin but I can help with Lucie. She loves you. She is feeling a little hurt and jealous right now. Don't feed that beast. Show her you care and let Piper go. Bob may be a huge frustration for us but he does get the job done."

"Does he? I wonder. I think we need to take control and stop waiting for his go ahead. We need to stop being pieces on his board. I need to contact our mystery man."

"I think that's desperation talking and I don't think we're there yet."

Mom returned to her papers but I knew she was watching me. She would be able to feel the turmoil boiling inside of me. She wouldn't be able to help herself. She would believe she had to fix me. Her role in this universe was to smooth out all the rough and ugly spots for her boys, but she couldn't fix me anymore nor could she stand in front of me when danger came. It was time I stood in front of her.

We finished grading her papers and I wandered around doing every chore I possibly could so that I wouldn't have to look at my pile of homework. The hands of the clock acted like they were weighted down. I needed to talk to Marlo and Lucie but I dreaded when my father would come home. Lucas was a nice distraction when he came home at 2:10. I helped him with his homework, which I hardly ever did anymore and then I got him to fire up the PlayStation so we could game for a while.

"I missed you," he said quietly when the round ended.

"I missed you too."

"Even when you're busy around here, at least I know you're around here. You know? Now you have to leave to fix stuff and I don't know if you're coming back."

"I'm sorry, Lucas. It's not fair. You shouldn't have to worry." Quentin flashed in my mind. "No matter what, I'll always love you. Sometimes it doesn't seem like it but I do what I do for you. I don't want people like Evilia or Bob to interfere with your life."

"That should be mom and dad's job."

"Yeah, but sometimes big brothers get the privilege of watching out for their favorite younger brothers."

"Sometimes if feels like Alex is your favorite."

"I'm sorry if I ever made you feel that way. I love you just as much as Alex but sometimes it looks different. Don't mistake different for less." *Maybe that was what I needed to understand about my dad.*

Lucas hugged me tight without putting down his remote. It dug painfully into my ribs but I wouldn't have complained for anything.

At 3:28 I heard a car door slam and knew it was them. I raced down the stairs and jumped the last six or so like I used to. It seemed to startle them and made me smile a little. "Catch me up. You guys know everything I've been doing but I know next to nothing about what's going on around here."

Lucie looked a little tentative but Marlo recovered quickly. "I'm glad you're okay."

"I'm not, but I will be. Come on up. Let's rehash."

They followed me up the stairs but Lucie still hung back. "Give me a minute, Mars, would you?"

"Sure," he said, moving on into my room and slinging his messenger bag onto my bed.

I held Lucie back in the hall. "Are you okay?"

She looked at me and gave her head a slight shake. I brushed her hair off her face and pulled her to me. I opened my connection to her and just let her feel for a moment all the things that were swirling through me in a kaleidoscope of colors and sound. I thought of the people whose lives I'd touched and who had touched me in return and I thought about Bob and Evilia and then my family and friends and last of all her. How I'd always felt about her - my light in the darkness.

Lucie touched my face and then kissed me, but our connection was still open. What I saw and felt about knocked me to my knees. I wasn't the only one who was conflicted about a number of things. Every time I'd kissed her or touched her flashed through my mind and a strong reaction moved through my body. I felt it move through her and reflect back to me. A small piece of my brain kicked me and reminded me that Marlo was only ten feet away and Lucas only about fifteen, though neither could see us through the walls. I came up for air and the moment was broken.

"Wow," Lucie breathed softly.

"Sorry… I"

"That was my fault. I knew what I was doing."

"I looked at her in surprise."

"I don't want to lose you. It hurt watching you with Piper but it reminded me that… you are the most important thing in my life."

I started to speak but she put her finger on my lips. "And I have some… interesting news." I raised my eyebrows to let her know I was listening. "You heard my… father is in town. He wants us to join him for lunch tomorrow before he leaves."

"Okay," I said slowly waiting for the other shoe to drop.

"I had told him you were sick and I wasn't sure you could make it, but I really don't want to go alone. He has some paperwork for me to sign and… he still has power over me. I'm scared."

"Of course I'll go."

"There's more."

"Oh?"

"He's bringing his new girlfriend. She's an attorney."

"I will definitely be there."

Marlo had everything spread out over my bed when we got back in my room. He proceeded to walk me through subject by subject. He covered what I had missed, what had been forged in my absence and what was left to do. Marlo had even created a prioritized schedule for me for handing in every bit of remaining work I had before midterms and then a detailed list of what needed to be done by the end of the year based on the syllabus we had been given. He even included a plan for how we could work together most efficiently to save us all as much time as possible. There is no better friend than Marlo.

"Dude, I see you as a CEO or CFO in the future. How many high school kids are this organized?"

"I figure, none. I think I have a corner on the market."

We all laughed and then we set to work on the items Marlo had outlined. My dad was home at six and merely checked in on us. Since we were hard at work on actual school work he left us alone to go do whatever he did these days to keep himself busy. I hated to see Luce and Mars go because I was afraid it would mean a talk but

I was mistaken. He had other things on his plate this evening that didn't include me. He had a meeting with my grandfather and their tax guy, so I was off the hook. All that meant was that I could stew about my meeting with Lucie's dad tomorrow.

I dressed in slacks and nice shoes and added a dress shirt with the sleeves rolled up to my elbows but no tie. I parted my hair and combed it back in an attempt to look older. I was nervous but I had to find a way not to let it show.

My dad about ran into me in the hall. "We need to talk."

I glanced at my watch. "Okay."

"You have someplace you need to be?"

"Lucie and I are meeting her dad for lunch."

"Is that how I get to see you? Make an appointment?"

"No. She just asked me yesterday and I've been gone so…"

"So you're too busy for this family?"

"No. I just happen to have plans today. What did you want to talk about?"

"I don't want you working for Bob anymore."

"I don't really want to work for him either but sometimes it's not a choice."

"There is always a choice."

"Dad, there's not always a choice with Bob that I can live with."

"You better learn. Bob is no different from any other corporate beast. You just have to learn how to tame them."

"I suppose that's true."

"So you're done then."

"For now."

"No, Owen. You are done with him. Your priorities are school, family and then other obligations."

"Dad, I think that…"

"You are not eighteen. Until September 26th you will do as I say." Anger bloomed inside me. I started to speak but closed my mouth. He didn't give me a chance. He turned and walked away. He had spoken his piece but I hadn't gotten the chance to speak mine. He probably wouldn't have listened anyway. It seemed like he never did.

Alex poked his head out of his bedroom and looked both ways. "Is the coast clear?" he whispered.

I pushed my anger down and gave him a half smile. "At the moment."

Alex gave me a huge grin and then went back in his room. I listened for a moment and heard him strategizing with his World of Warcraft team. All was well in his universe for now.

I went to find my mom, but dad had her cornered in the kitchen. I could tell that their conversation wasn't going much better than mine had. I took the chicken way out and sent her a text. I decided to walk down to Lucie's early. I didn't care if she wasn't ready. I would just sit with White Eagle and work on my well of peace.

He and I sat on the covered back patio with cups of caffeine free tea. It was Sarah's idea. We looked at the yard and decided after all our hard work last summer it was still looking pretty good. Another round of work this summer would keep it in nice shape. I liked focusing on things I could actually fix. Lucie came out with her own tea. She was dressed down by her father's standards. I was surprised to see her in dress pants, a nice blue top and a jacket. She could be headed downtown for corporate work. She'd twisted her hair up on her head in her own bid to look older.

"I think I'd rather have a root canal or a pap smear today," she said as she flopped into one of the lounge chairs. "Though I may throw up before I even get in his car."

"Lucie, sweetheart, it's going to be okay," White Eagle said as he laid a hand over the one she had resting on the arm of her chair. They were quiet for a moment so I figured he was letting peace wash over her. "Breathe," he added softly.

She took a long slow breath. "I can hardly wait until this is over."

We all looked at the yard. Green is a calming color, right?

Too soon his car pulled up and Sarah alerted us. She hugged Lucie and wished her good luck. Then she hugged me but not like she usually did. One arm went around me but the other pressed into my neck by my collar. I met her eyes. With her back to Lucie, she put a finger to her lips and then brushed at my shirt and pointed to her ear. I let a half smile touch my lips for a moment. Sarah wouldn't be advising today but she'd be ready to clean up afterwards if needed. She just didn't want to worry Lucie any further at the moment. One more thing I would probably have to apologize for.

Lucie opened the door for her father. "Well, don't you look… nice." The pause made me think he meant the opposite. "Owen."

He smiled at White Eagle and Sarah and then turned back to Lucie. "Shall we?"

"Yes, let's," she said, but her voice sounded brittle.

Her father was driving a BMW either rented or on loan from his company. To me it appeared to be a dig at Lucie and a reminder of what she could have had, except that I knew that money meant a whole lot less to her than happiness did.

He opened the front passenger door and drew out a lovely tall slender woman. She was clearly younger than him. This didn't look like the bonds of love but more like a power play. Her four inch heels made her nearly as tall as him. Her tailored dress screamed money. It was her make-up that threw me. She looked like she'd been made up for a photo shoot or a live interview. Every hair was in place like it wouldn't dare do anything but behave exactly as she commanded. Our eyes met and I felt a stare-down commencing.

"Chloe, this is my daughter, Lucie and her… friend, Owen."

"Lucie, Owen, this is Ms. Tate."

Oh, so we were to address her formally. Move one in the power struggle then.

"It's lovely to meet you," she said insincerely.

"You too," Lucie replied sweetly. I said nothing and just opted for a thin smile. He helped her back into the car but didn't open Lucie's door. He was in the way for me to do it, so I waited. Lucie and her father had a stare-down for a full minute. I noted that Ms. Tate was making use of her side mirror.

"Would you like us to take our own car and follow you over, Mr. Ness?" I asked to break the building tension.

"That won't be necessary." *More like – you have a captive audience this way.*

I reached for Lucie's handle and opened her door which forced her father to step out of the way. He gave me a dark look before turning and walking around the front of the car. I got Lucie's door and hurried around the back before he could pull out without me. He did succumb to the door lock game and then a fake apology.

I took Lucie's hand and tried to let her feel that this was no worse than our work down south last summer. She turned and a look passed between us. This was hitting closer to home. I watched her breath and knew she was practicing White Eagle's relaxation techniques. Ms. Tate attempted stilted conversation by asking us about school. I tried to hold up my end by asking about her work. I pulled out all the stops and let my power wash over them. It is difficult to read normal people but after not using my gift it felt good to be able to again.

He gave no explanation of where we were going so I watched closely in case we had to get home by bus or foot. We were headed for the Pearl district. He went for valet parking and it looked like we were eating Italian.

It seemed that we had a reservation because we were seated immediately. The awkward small talk continued. I could feel the power play as it rolled out and I hated it. It was tricky playing nice but not giving too much ground. I could best liken it to running on slippery rocks as the tide is rushing in. I searched the menu for something I could eat that would be inexpensive. My plan was to listen carefully and order last.

Lucie's father ordered a bottle of wine. To me, noon was a little early to be partaking in that but maybe he thought he needed it to get through lunch. Maybe today was a fine day to start drinking, except we weren't offered a drop.

As the plates were cleared and desert ordered, her father got to the heart of the matter and pulled out the papers he wanted her to sign. Lucie's first move was to pick them up and reach for her bag.

"No, no, read them now. Time is not on your side and we can wait while you look them over."

"I would like to read them later and not ruin lunch."

"Who said anything about ruining lunch? I just need your signature, it's no big deal."

"Then you won't mind if I read them."

"Yes, please do read them now." Lucie pulled them down toward her lap. Her father stared at her for a long beat and then turned and shared a look with Ms. Tate that made me uncomfortable. I reached over as if to take Lucie's hand and touched the papers instead.

The image of a loop of rope was quickly followed by it morphing into a noose and Lucie hanging. I squeezed her hand hard in response. I saw her father laughing and Sam looking sad and lost. Next I saw Lucie bleeding dollar signs and her father sitting on a pile of gold coins as he changed into a dragon. *What was in my lunch? This was not the kind of images I usually got.* I glanced at her father as Lucie turned the page. He was already reaching for a pen. I got another flash from the papers of Lucie's mother looking at herself in the mirror, her husband in the background. Her gaze shifted to a family portrait and then back to the mirror where she held a finger to her lips.

"Mr. Ness, I'm curious. What are these papers all about?"

"Not that it's any of your business but it's some charity work of Lucie's mother's. It got missed in the move and now it seems that I need Lucie's signature to continue Rebecca's good work so that Lucie doesn't have to bother with it."

"It seems to me that Lucie should decide what she wants to do with her life and that charity work would be something that would be close to her heart."

"I'm family. You're not. I think I know what's best for Lucie."

"Fortunately, Lucie can decided that for herself," Lucie said firmly. "Don't talk about me like I'm not even here, Dad. I've decided to have a friend go over these with me. I'll get back to you soon."

"But I really need those signed for Monday."

"Fine I'll go over them tomorrow."

"We leave tomorrow and I want to take them with me."

"Fine, how about I give you an answer by eight tonight."

"You will give me an answer now."

"Theo, darling, really, let's give her a chance to look those over. We have plenty to do today while she reads them. You did promise me that you'd take me to the Pittock Mansion for a tour."

He stood. "Well then, my dear, let us go. I trust you can find your way home?"

Lucie's mouth hung agape for a moment before she closed it with a snap. "Yes, we can find our way home."

Mr. Ness turned and took two steps before Ms. Tate laid a hand on his arm and gave him a look. "If you want her to sign, pay for lunch." She didn't want me to hear but I could. Lucie looked like she was having a mini anxiety attack by the way she was clutching the papers to her chest.

Mr. Ness threw a hundred dollar bill on the table. I'm sure you can cover the tip if that isn't enough and then he stomped out without a backward glance. Our surprised waiter had to have caught the end of the exchange. He looked a little worried as he approached with the tray of desserts.

I looked up at him calmly. "Would you mind boxing those to go please and we're ready for the check."

"Yes, sir. Shall I um, have the hostess call you a cab, sir?"

"No thank you, we've got it covered." Lucie gave me a startled look and reached for her bag. "It's fine," I said to her.

The waiter left with the plates. I was pretty sure his fingers were itching to snatch the hundred before we did and tried a dine and dash.

"Why are you so calm after the weird images you got?" Lucie asked under her breath.

"Because I know that White Eagle and Sarah are on their way. I would also bet money that she's already on the phone seeking out some legal advice and that she has Marlo digging around to see what he can find. Heck, she may have been going on that the moment you told her your dad wanted to meet and had some papers for you to look at."

"And what makes you think all that?" she asked.

In answer I flipped up the collar on my shirt. She looked irritated for a brief moment and then she smiled. "She's smarter than I am. It was the hug wasn't it?"

"Yes, and she's not smarter, she wiser because she's been doing this longer. She's looking in from the outside and she loves you. You are right in the middle of it."

The waiter returned with the check and the box of desserts. He looked half relieved that we were still there but I could tell that he felt bad for us too. I would bet he observed all kinds of interesting things in his line of work. He walked a discreet distance away to give us a moment.

I opened the bill. The food and wine alone were well over a hundred dollars without the tip. I didn't carry that kind of cash. I could either drain my debit card or put it on my mom's credit card and hit my college fund. I actually sighed aloud.

Lucie looked over my shoulder. "Bastard," she whispered under her breath. "A forty seven dollar bottle of wine? I want to get him where it hurts."

"Don't sign that paper. I have a feeling that's a good place to start."

Lucie smiled. "I do believe I need to use Sarah's attorney friend again and I'll put lunch on my debit card."

"Luce, I don't want you running your account too low."

"You usually pay, even when I argue. Today it's my turn. Your job is to help me get him where it hurts."

Lucie handed the waiter her card and the cash. We waited in grim silence for his return. I was right about Sarah, though. She walked through the door as Lucie was signing the receipt.

"Are you ready to go?" she asked as if the plan all along was for her to pick us up.

"How'd you get here so fast?"

Sarah brushed some invisible lint from her suit before she answered, "We followed you."

Lucie laughed out loud. "Of course you did. And are they really off to the Pittock Mansion?"

"As far as I can tell."

"Good. We have a lot of work to do." Sarah sent me a slightly worried look as we headed out the door. I could see White Eagle driving toward us. He must have been circling the block. "I think it's time for me to add revenge to my repertoire."

Now Sarah gave me a distinctly alarmed look. "Um, Lucie, dear, I think that…"

"We need to hit him where it hurts. I couldn't agree more. And after today I feel confident that you of all people are in my corner."

"Um, yes dear."

"With every resource."

Sarah sighed. "I think I see your soul darkening."

"Let's just call that a necessary evil."

Lucie handed Sarah the document she was supposed to sign. We loaded up in Sarah's sedan for a much more comfortable ride home. As promised, Sarah got right on her phone and began assigning the team to look into not only the document but Theodore Huntley Ness' life, business, assets and everything they could find on Ms. Tate. Lucie and Sarah had turned to blackmail.

"Please tell me you are only using this information to protect yourself and that you are not turning into him?"

Lucie thought seriously for a moment. "You're right. I'm angry. He can be his own problem. What I really want is for him to leave me alone. We have enough problems without him. He doesn't even realize what we do to keep him safe from Madame Malvada. He should be more appreciative."

"He should be, but he isn't. We appreciate you."

"Yes, we do," White Eagle added.

"The hunt has begun, Lucie. Let's just be sure that what we do with what we find is for good not evil and be warned – you may not like what you uncover."

"Point taken."

TWENTY-THREE

I wondered where the time had gone as a breeze stirred the newly minted leaves. There were more shades of brilliant green than I could give name to. The sky was pale blue in the distance but straight overhead it was an amazing shade of deep endless blue without a cloud in the sky. Yeah, it happens around here – a day without clouds.

Lucie never signed the papers and her father was furious. What held him at bay was the fact that Lucie could tell him exactly what the papers really were – an undisclosed trust from Rebecca Ness' side of the family that was to go directly to her children and not to her husband. It wasn't a lot of money but it would pay for Lucie's college and Sam's. The document had been worded with deep legalese that we had no hope of untangling without help. Lucie also hinted at other things she knew about him that would be a shame if they came out and perhaps he should consider leaving her alone so that she wouldn't be tempted to spill about his affair while married to her mother, the business money that leaked through his fingers and into his personal accounts and the insider information that had come to his attention and allowed Ms. Tate to make a killing in a less than friendly market. Lucie ended with the wish that he marry Ms. Tate because she believed they truly deserved one another. After the call she had a migraine so I hoped to brighten her day.

I bought our prom tickets just like I'd promised Lucie last summer. I wasn't sure that going was a good idea but there was no way I was letting her down and I had fond memories of that dress. I also felt like I needed to prove to her that Piper was gone and out of reach, so she had nothing to worry about.

The one thing I couldn't seem to fix no matter how hard I tried was my rocky relationship with my dad. He understood what we were doing but his priorities weren't on the same page. He knew that Marlo was on track for valedictorian and he couldn't understand why I wasn't. He thought I didn't care. A part of me did, a part of me was a little jealous of Marlo and Lucie for their grades but mostly I just didn't have the time to devote to school. I wondered what my grade would be if I were to receive one as a *watcher*.

I parked my bike and came in through the garage. I noticed that dad was home early and I hoped that it was a good thing. Lately, who knew? His body looked stiff and tense, his shoulders hunched and his jaw tight. Oh boy. He was checking the temperature on a roast he'd pulled from the oven. I wondered if I could get by him but thought I better just face whatever was on his mind.

"There you are. Where have you been?" He seemed almost startled that I had snuck up on him.

"I had to wait in line to buy our prom tickets and then I got hung up at the shop. Why?"

"We need to talk." *Oh boy, here it comes*, I thought.

"What is going on with you, Owen?"

"What do you mean?"

"I get that you're not like other kids. I don't like it that you have to work during high school. If you don't want to play football next year, I understand, but I cannot accept these grades that are creeping toward D's. You missed a whole week of school on *watcher* business and you haven't been the same since. I already said that you could just play one sport. Now I'm willing to cut all sports but I will not accept the grades or any more moping or missed school! Clearly you don't care but I do!"

"I do care, Dad. I'm doing my best. I just don't…"

He interrupted, "Don't you dare tell me you don't have time. No more sports and I'm cutting your shop time!"

"You can't do that. I have to be there."

"I can and I will. It's what needs to be done. You will bring up your grades. You will cut one half hour a day at the shop and you may only see Lucie on Friday and Saturday. Your mother won't do it, but I will."

I could feel my anger rising. Heat built up and I needed to go running or punch something. I pushed my tongue hard against the roof of my mouth so I wouldn't get into any more trouble.

"I would like an end date or objective," I finally forced out between tight lips.

My dad sighed, "I can see you're growing up. I appreciate that you didn't yell or throw a fit." In my mind I was yelling alright, but I didn't want to make things worse. He still didn't understand me. He still didn't accept who I was.

He looked at me thoughtfully. "Let's do this, if you have at least a B in every class, I'll leave you alone. I will check the website every Thursday. If you have B's you're clear for the week. If you don't, you're grounded until the next Thursday. If your grades slip further then you will have no Lucie time outside of school and your work time will be cut further."

"Understood," I snarled and ground my teeth. I didn't like it but I did understand him. Now the question was, how to jam all that data into my brain in the limited time I had. Miles was never a good student, so he wouldn't be much help. Marlo and Lucie would be my best bets as far as help went and my Lucie time had just been cut.

I turned to go but looked back. I felt like he wanted to say something else. He stared at me for a moment and then opened a drawer. He pulled out a box and flipped it to me. "You've been different since you came back from California. A trip I did not want you to go on I might add. These are for you. Your grades are already tragic. We don't want any accidents." I looked down at the box in my hand – condoms. I looked back up at him. He still looked like he wanted to say something or maybe he was just waiting for me to say something. Instead he just ended with, "Well okay then. Go do homework or something."

Awesome. Just awesome. I thought sarcastically. I headed for the stairs, still looking at the box. I ran into Alex. "You too? Does he know I'm in seventh grade? It's kinda inappropriate for me, right? They'll expire before I can even use them."

"Uhh." He had me there. Why Alex?

He seemed to read my mind as he said, "Maybe he's given up on us. I know he thinks we're weird."

"He's just showing that he cares in his own way. I think this was an opportunity for him with mom at school for whatever was going on there tonight."

"She took Lucas and they're setting up for art night."

"Yeah, that's it. She's at art night with Lucas so it was his chance to talk to us individually."

"At least my grades are okay. He couldn't ream me about that. He did want to know why I'm introverted and have no friends."

My eyebrows shot up in surprise. "He asked *you* that?"

"Yeah. I know I'm not like I used to be but I do have friends. I just don't let many of them close anymore. When they're here we have to be careful and when I go somewhere I have to take a guard with me. Not that my friends ever see them but I know they're there. It's just weird. It's like being a celebrity without the cool part."

"I'm sorry, Alex."

"Well, I'm not. This is our job and when we fix things for people or stop *dark watchers*… it feels really good. I think it's worth it."

"You are absolutely right." I gave him a hug. When had Alex gotten so smart? It was nearly always worth it. Quentin flashed before my eyes. They hadn't even let me go to his service, but an anonymous donor had set up a trust in his name to help his family so his Nana could retire and his sister could focus on school instead of nannying. I knew that Sarah was involved and I figured she'd pressured Bob, but that wasn't the case. Sarah's mother, Bettylou McMurty, adjusted her non-profit organization, got some donors and grants and started the Quentin Stowe Endowment for Underserved Children in Oregon. I'm beginning to think that Sarah can move a mountain if she wants to and I think that Bob should be very afraid.

Marlo worked out things with Caitlyn and we secretly marveled at the fact that Brenda still put up with Adrian. At school we continued to watch the spies Evilia had planted to watch us and pretended that we were normal. Every school day we were mentally exhausted by the time we got to the shop from holding it all together. In no time prom was upon us and Marlo worked up a whole new security system just for the event. We were dangerous for Caitlyn and Brenda to be around so it was up to us to protect them.

The prom pictures at Sarah's with Adrian and Brenda, Marlo and Caitlyn felt like a déjà vu of Sarah and White Eagle's wedding. Lucie looked fantastic in her dress from that day but that only added to the feeling - that and the fact that I was back in the same shiny gray suit with the light green shirt. This time I switched it up and added a dark green tie. Mom helped me choose a spectacular corsage for Lucie with white orchids and some little blue and lime green flower things. They even put it on a beaded bracelet that Lucie could keep. After my cheeks began to hurt from so much smiling for the camera we finally left for dinner.

We met up at The Old Spaghetti Factory with the triplets and their dates and Jesus and his date. The ladies looked lovely but none compared to Lucie. I was a little sad to find that we would be seated at a long table where all the men ended up on one side with our dates across from us. The ladies barely ate. I let very little stand between me and food but Lucie's foot sliding up my leg was pretty distracting. At least I hoped it was her foot. I finally grabbed it and checked the toenail polish. Yep. It was green. I was good. I looked up to see Lucie smile at me and mouth, "Were you worried?" At my nod she burst out laughing and had to cover her slip so she wouldn't give herself away.

We drove to the prom venue but decided to walk around downtown a bit. The line at Tiffany Center was outrageous. We burned about half an hour admiring the evening lights as we walked down Yamhill toward the Yamhill Market Place. By the time we strolled back the line had shrunk but we still had quite a wait. Strangely we didn't need our tickets; they only wanted our school ID and checked us against a list. Sarah should have chaperoned. She would have been much more efficient.

The noise was loud outside but nearly deafening as we entered the ballroom. I wondered who had chosen this particular DJ because he sure wasn't to my liking. It was incredibly dark with flashes of bright light. Colors bloomed and bled out in random succession. The roar of the crowd and the music was making my ears throb but I was here for Lucie and she did look amazing. She held my hand and stayed glued to my side.

She sensed my eyes on her and turned to smile at me. "Let's get our picture taken."

"What?" I asked over the din and tried to focus on her lips so that I could read them.

"Let's go get our picture taken," she said again, this time putting her hand on my face so I could hear it in my head too. Lucie continued to smile as she pulled me toward Brenda. We collected Adrian, Marlo and Caitlyn. We wandered down to the photo booth. There was another long line but at least it was quieter here and we could talk. We had a group shot taken and then each of us with just our date. The price made me grouchy. Again I reminded myself this was for Lucie. For our picture, Lucie and I chose to look at each other.

We wandered back upstairs and reentered the dance. The music was still earsplitting and mind-numbing. I like loud music, don't get me wrong, but this was... too much and I felt completely distracted by everything around me. Hold on... oh geez... really? I turned Lucie toward the nearest darkened corner and then pulled her in the other direction. "Where are the chaperones?" she hissed.

I shrugged and pulled her onto the dance floor. "It does bring new meaning to 'get a room.'"

"Maybe the rush of getting caught adds something to the hand job," Lucie giggled. "After what we saw when we saved Julie from the traffickers, this is nothing."

"Still, it's wrong to do that here and yeah, it could be a whole lot worse."

"I don't get it, why get all dressed up and then…" Lucie just stopped talking as something going on past my shoulder caught her eye.

I bent in close to whisper in her ear. "You thought it'd be okay if I wrinkled your dress a little at Sarah and White Eagle's wedding and then there was that time in San Diego."

"That was different. We were alone – not on display," Lucie griped as she slapped at my shoulder.

"See what the internet and social media have done to today's youth?"

Lucie rolled her eyes and laughed. "Yeah, blame that. It's not about people making bad choices."

"Maybe they have nowhere else to go, Luce."

"I disagree. Teenagers are smart generally and underestimated frequently. I don't think they care if people see. It's like reverse voyeurism – they can be a star for fifteen seconds."

"But they'll pay with their reputation forever," I finished her thought for her.

"I don't want someone at our thirty year high school reunion to remember me as the girl who screwed Owen Ryer at the prom."

"No but it looks like you could learn how here."

"Awesome," Lucie quipped sarcastically. "I should say, 'shame on you.'" She looked into my eyes and I saw many feelings flit through their depths. The lights glinted in her hair and her eyes reflected the lights. I could see how someone could get lost. I thought about the feel of her and how her body moved beneath the fabric of her dress and then I caught sight of the dance floor grind going on behind her and my mind snapped back into place. Not here, not now.

"You know what?"

"Let's just get out of here. It isn't what I thought and…"

"It's loud?" I laughed.

"Yeah, among other things."

I texted Marlo and Lucie texted Brenda to let them know that we were leaving to go for a walk. We had come in separate cars so Lucie and I figured it was no big deal. We were warned that if we left we would not be allowed to reenter. "Whatever," Lucie murmured under her breath but I heard her and tried not to crack a smile. We strolled around until Lucie had goosebumps and was hugging herself even with my arm around her. I put my jacket over her shoulders and we headed for the car.

Mom looked up startled from her book when we walked in. "How was the prom?" she asked sounding like she might already know the answer.

"Educational?" I quipped with a smile.

"That doesn't sound good," she answered looking both sad and serious.

"I guess it was fine; it really wasn't our thing. Maybe next year we could just have a party. I mean all that money for too-loud music that we didn't like that much and … I can watch cable if I want to see… never mind. You're a good photographer and we could use the money to have Marla cater or something and just have our friends over."

"If that's what you want, that's what we'll do."

"It sounds so easy when you say it."

"It can be easy."

"Mom, nothing for us is easy. Look at all the prep we had to do just to go to the prom. There is always a price. I'm tired. I want to be a kid but I can't. I want to plan a party but I shouldn't." Lucie put her arms around me in sympathy.

"Owen, honey, it's going to be okay. Have faith and keep hope alive. Just the way you look at things can make such a difference," Mom said.

Lucie and I gave her sad smiles. We knew she was right; it was just so hard to look at our gloomy world that way. We negotiated for Lucie to stay. Mom loaned her some jammies for after her de-makeup-ing routine. I had other things on my mind than Netflix but Alex joined us so I kept it clean and just played with Lucie's hair. Running my fingers over her scalp put her in the zone pretty quickly making me think she was asleep with her eyes open. Two weeks until her birthday and about a month until our junior year was over. At times it had crept by but now it seemed like it had gone too fast.

I hadn't noticed Peter or Martin, our local spies, for a couple of days. I found it odd but blew it off. Baseball was almost over and I thought I'd watch Adrian practice. I wasn't alone in the stands. They were on to him. Crap. I'd been selfish. I'd used Adrian and now he was the target. That's why I hadn't seen them. I never looked right at them but kept them in my peripheral vision.

When practice ended they followed Adrian off the field and into the locker room and so did I. They had lost all interest in me and didn't even acknowledge my existence. Most of the other guys had cleared out.

I froze. It had grown quiet… too quiet. I closed my eyes to feel around me. Something… something bad was near. My eyes and ears strained. A shift in the air was my only warning. I dove to the side in a feeble attempt to escape the blow. The blade sliced into my shoulder as it swerved past. Damn it. That would slow me down. I rolled under a bench and flipped to my feet.

The space between the lockers was narrow and the benches would be a blessing and a curse I'd have to keep track of. Peter, Martin and a boy I'd never seen before had surrounded me. I lunged at Peter and a hand landed on my bleeding shoulder. I spun toward that side and punched Martin in the gut. Without pause I followed up with a palm to his chin. I grabbed his head and shoved it into the nearest bench. I popped up and took ahold of Peter's hand as he tried another swipe with the knife. I pivoted on his knife arm and kicked the guy behind him, twisted his arm across his face and the knife popped free. I spun Peter around, bent him backwards and put my other elbow into his sternum taking him to the ground. The last guy stood up in time for me to deliver a front kick to the chest sending him into the lockers.

A man pushed the baseball coach around the corner with a gun to his head. He took in the bodies all over the floor and narrowed his eyes at me. I slowly raised my hands into the air and a half dressed, sweaty Adrian swung a bat like he was going for a homerun. The gunman and coach crumpled to the floor.

Adrian gave me a hard look. "I just covered your six. That's my job, remember, Bro? You and Marlo are the brains – I'm the backup plan. You still need me."

"Darn right I do. Never doubt it."

"Sometimes it just feels like you really don't. Sometimes I feel jealous but days like today remind me why I shouldn't be. Sometimes your life just plain sucks."

"I couldn't have put it better myself, except today it was you they were after."

"Yeah, thanks for reminding me. What do we do with the bodies?"

"This is a job for Sarah because I don't do clean up. They'll fix you up with a story… I was never here. Today you are the hero!"

"Yeah, well, awesome. Maybe being a sidekick has its moments, huh?"

"Yeah, it does," I said and gave him a hug. I felt good in that moment. I felt happy and like we had a chance of beating Madame Malvada. But I felt angry too. How dare she come after Adrian! She wanted to separate us and knock us off one by one. Two could play at that game. I just had to figure out how to do it.

Sarah and her team were in the locker room in less than fifteen minutes. White Eagle met with his police contact, Evelyn. She had her own crew on site the second Sarah's team and I were gone. Adrian had been coached by Rick and Evelyn and I hear gave a flawless report. The coach was confused after being pistol whipped by the guy who took him. The other players and coaching staff who were still left in the room at the time of the incident never saw me. They all bought the story that it was gang related.

At least I thought it had been all swept under the rug. Adrian was the local hero alright but someone must have seen me because rumors were crawling over the school like unwanted cockroaches in a humid, food-filled environment. I guess it was mainly the girls who watched me because Lucie was tense. She made a point of holding my hand as much as possible and was in my space way more than usual.

We took our lunches outside today since it was pretending to be summer. Marlo sat down a couple of benches away talking to Caitlyn and Adrian was in the middle of a big crowd of hero worshipers. I set my lunch on the bench, closed my eyes and tilted my head back to enjoy the sunshine.

"I love you," Lucie said softly.

I turned to look at her. She wasn't eating. "I love you too, Luce." I waited a beat, wondering what she wanted. She smiled at me. It was the kind of smile that made me go gooey inside like chocolate on a hot day. "What?" I asked, returning the smile and wondering how I was going to be able to think about anything but her for the last hour and a half of school.

"You look…" She stood and took hold of either side of my belt to draw me toward her, "…amazing. I'm glad you're mine." She leaned into me to kiss me but she didn't let go of the belt. I slid my hands around her and she pressed in closer. She moved her hands around my hips to pull me so that no empty space existed between us.

"What are you doing?" I mumbled against her lips. "You don't usually act like this and you're risking getting into trouble for PDA."

"I'm staking a claim."

"Why? I'm not going anywhere."

"You may not think so, but I don't like the way you're being looked at by other girls these days. They think I'm the stuck-up crazy chick. They think they can steal you away, but I won't go down without a fight."

"Luce, what are you talking about?" Maybe she wasn't making sense or maybe it was her body pressed against me that had shut off my brain.

"I hear the rumors even if you don't. You think people avoid you but they want to be near you. You are the flame and they are moths. You are beautiful and mysterious. You don't let other people get this close to you. I'm making a point. I want them to know that I'll fight for you and that as of this moment you are interested in only me."

"Sometimes I wish we were back in California and that I'd made a different choice. They'd feel that… somehow they would sense that there was nothing that could drive us apart."

"It's not too late…"

"Hey! You two." Awesome, here it came. We would get a talking to. I also got another one at home from my father about Lucie and my grades. My mom opened her mouth to speak a couple of times but I just gave her a subtle shake of my head. I figured it was better to just let him talk and get it off his chest than it was to argue. He had come a long way in his acceptance of me but it was so much easier to do my *watcher* job when he was away. At least he didn't ground me but I was frustrated with him and I was glad that he was going to be gone the next couple of weeks so that I had plenty of time to cool off before I said something I shouldn't.

My grades were not improving but at least I wasn't failing, though I was almost out of time. I had missing assignments because of *watcher* business that interfered with school. I don't think I had ever missed so much. Marlo tried to keep up on it for me but he was having his own struggles to maintain his four point. Lucie had slipped some too but still had nothing below a B. It was bad enough that *watcher* business interfered with school but it was even worse when it came to our lives in general. Evilia was really putting the pressure on us. I felt like I just couldn't win. I guessed the worst part about my grades was that I just didn't care. I hadn't been this bad since seventh grade but my reasons today were completely different. It made my mom sad and my dad frustrated. They were afraid that I was closing doors to good colleges. I knew where my path lay – I was meant to be here. Even after all our work in San Diego… Portland's trafficking problems had grown to be one of the worst in the nation and I knew Evilia had her hand in it. I just couldn't prove it… yet, so here is where I had to stay.

Today I was paying Marlo and Lucie back by getting them a hard to get copy of the last book we needed for AP English. Why is it, when you're in a hurry, the only bookstore in town that carries what you need is the one furthest away. Well, not furthest. It's not like I had to drive to Florida or Maine. I was only going downtown. Good old Powell's Books. They always have what you need when you can't wait for shipping. I hopped on my bike and headed out. A shiver ran down my back. Maybe I should have worn a heavier jacket. Nope. Not cold… something didn't feel right. Strangely, nothing felt particularly wrong either. What the heck? I took a route I don't usually use and tried to take as many corners as I could and yet the feeling persisted.

I parked in the underground garage and made my way to street level. The feeling briefly intensified and then went away. I walked to Powell's, my senses on full alert. The feeling surged and receded like the tide. I quickly found the book I needed and moved among the aisles trying to locate the source but I couldn't pinpoint it. I bought the books and decided to hurry home where I had more backup. As I turned the corner to the garage I was about knocked over by a blast of malice. I moved into the nearest shop and watched the street from behind a display. Nothing caught my eye.

"May I help you sir?" A clerk had appeared at my elbow. I swept my eyes over her and quickly around the shop.

"Yes. I need a birthday gift for my girlfriend - something in blue. She looks really good in blue." The clerk gave me her best smile, took hold of my sleeve and pulled me to another display. The mannequin before me was wearing a fantastic top made of dark blue lace-like material. The mannequin had a black tank top thing under it and wore flame red pants. I caught sight of the price tag and cringed.

The clerk watched my reaction. "It's thirty percent off."

I saw movement outside. Was that Kraeghton, Evilia, Carmichael or someone else? "I'll take one of the blue tops in a small if you have it. Do you gift wrap?"

"Yes, sir." I handed her my credit card and watched impatiently as she selected a top and began to wrap it.

"May I come back later and pick it up? I don't want her to catch me. It's a surprise." It would be a huge surprise to Mom too, when she saw the bill. So much for the latest version of the Max Payne game I'd been saving for. Oh well. I would probably have to put in some extra hours at the shop to cover it.

She ran my card. I glanced out the window. It was definitely a male loitering across the street. He leaned against the building casually. He was tall and wearing a ball cap low over his eyes. I fidgeted from foot to foot. "Are you okay, sir?"

"I thought I saw her. May I leave the books with you too, please. I promise I'll be back."

"I suppose," she said grudgingly. "I'm not supposed to do that." She handed me my slip and looked in my Powell's bag and nodded.

"Just this time," she added, giving me a smile that begged me to ask for her number. She would have to be disappointed.

"Thanks." I signed and fled the shop, hot on the trail of a man who looked like Kraeghton. I saw a flash of him up ahead and threw my awareness at him to see if I was right. He froze, hunched his shoulders and ducked into a doorway. It was most certainly a *dark watcher*; I just wasn't sure if it was Kraeghton. No normal person would have felt that. Whoever this guy was, he wasn't trying to sense me. I had to wonder why.

TWENTY-FOUR

I crossed the street and ducked into another shop. I watched him ease out the doorway and continue down the street. What was he doing here and what was he up to? Was he following me? Had he lost me and now I was following him? Was he a lead to Evilia and the trouble she was causing in town or was it a trick? White Eagle would have a coronary if he knew I was off on my own again.

I moved up the street using every skill I had ever learned about urban camouflage to blend myself into the surroundings, yet I was sure he knew I was there. I could feel it. The hair stood up along my arms and it prickled at the back of my neck. Stephan Kraeghton isn't dumb. He's had years more training and practice than I've had. *Years, who am I kidding?* I thought sarcastically. *The man has had decades.* If what we'd learned was true, he had to be close to sixty but he looked to be in his mid-thirties. Not even Marlo had been able to fully track him or find any data on his past. He would vanish and reappear. It was eerie. He turned a corner and disappeared. He had to know I was following him. He was leading me somewhere. I sent Lucie a text and then I sent Marlo the coordinates of the building and a camera shot of the alley. Crap. Not good, so very not good. It would take them about twenty-five minutes to get here once they got the information. I sighed, slid my phone into my pocket and took a breath before I peered around the corner.

Kraeghton's coat flapped once as it disappeared through the rapidly shutting door. I slid my back against the wall of the building he had disappeared into so as not to be seen, which was probably just an exercise in futility. The windows were too high to look through which made me grind my teeth. I quickly scanned the alley for weapons. There wasn't much here. My phone vibrated. Lucie was on her way. I hoped she was bringing a posse. This building looked like a factory or warehouse. It was odd to be so close to civilization and yet this was clearly not retail. I saw a window above the dumpster just down the alley past the door. I ran at it and leapt lightly onto the surface. I pressed myself flat to the building and peered through the dirty glass. Kraeghton had paused in the open area, pulled off the ball cap, looked around and then walked over to a door on the far wall. Piles of junk and crates littered the floor, but no other living creatures seemed to be about. I took a look around, jumped down and made for the door. It was unlocked. How careless of him or was it intentional? I edged it open and listened carefully. I heard nothing but the street traffic and normal downtown type sounds. The inside of the building was silent. I slipped in. Moving crate to crate, I approached the door I had seen Kraeghton enter.

I listened at the door. I was just reaching for the handle when my phone vibrated. I thought about ignoring it but decided to check it anyway. Marlo had texted. "Building ownership looks dodgy. Looks like one of her holdings. Get out!"

"But SK is here. It's a great opportunity."

"GET OUT! Wait for backup!" Marlo texted back.

"NO. I'll lose him and we haven't seen him in months," I jabbed out, hit send and closed my phone. My phone vibrated again but I ignored it and put my hand back on the doorknob. It was yanked open pulling me forward into the room. I was hit hard across my shoulder blades driving me to my knees. I spun on a knee and rose to my feet. Kraeghton was looking at me and smiling. He pulled a hand from his pocket, twisting it away from him and put it up to his mouth like he was going to blow me a kiss.

It was no kiss; the dust Kraeghton blew hit me full in the face. I shook it off and moved in for a strong hook. Kraeghton nimbly jumped back with a laugh as he hit me with another puff of dust. My vision blurred and the bitter tang of chemicals burst over my tongue. Shit. I didn't want to wipe my eyes and make it worse. I spat at his feet and tried to blow out my nose, but I could feel the chemicals entering my body quickly through my pores. I scraped my tongue with my teeth and spat again what I could, right in Kraeghton's face. He slowly wiped a hand over his cheek and scowled at me with all his hatred showing through.

"You haven't gotten back to my envoy," Kraeghton growled.

"I don't believe for a moment that the enemy of my enemy is my friend. We've made compromises but that's all. We're not friends."

"No one said we were. We just have to work together."

"No."

"You want Evilia dead as much as I do."

"Yes, but I don't trust you."

"That's not an answer. You don't have to trust me."

"Every time I see you, you want something different from me."

"My objectives have changed."

"Where is your friend, your envoy, today?"

"Working."

"You don't know where he is or what he's doing."

"I do know that you haven't found out anything about him. Marlo is letting you down."

"Maybe there is nothing to be found. Why are you following me?"

"I needed to talk to you."

"Try a phone." I started to step away and stumbled.

He went to make a grab for me but I lunged past and caught him in the temple with my elbow, dizzying him. I quickly spun and kicked. It felt as if the ground was beginning to undulate beneath me. I could hardly keep my footing. Kraeghton snarled and spit blood.

What had he gotten me with? It had to be a hallucinogenic drug. I felt dizzy and cold but I could feel sweat forming. He swung, I blocked. I threw an upper cut that I thought slowed him but he was beginning to warp and shift before my eyes. He struck at my sternum with the heel of his hand, sending me flying through the air to hit the concrete hard, whapping my head. Kraeghton dove on top of me before I could move.

He had me flat on my back with nowhere to go. He laid a hand on my chest and tried to drain me. I didn't really feel much so I figured I was either, sadly, more used to it by now or battle-hardened. I could feel my energy seeping away, but it wasn't excruciatingly painful or perhaps it was the drugs that had me muddled. This should hurt worse. I should be screaming.

Something clicked in my woozy, scattered, dizzy brain as I struggled to get him off me. I wrapped my legs around him and tried to squeeze. An image of Evilia and the skill she accidentally taught me crawled through my brain. I found Kraeghton's connection to me and followed it back. Then slowly, tediously I began to reverse the flow. I knew his black energy would feel awful from my experience in Nevada when we went to save Mitchell, but it was a necessary evil. What a horrible phrase to come to mind now, but what choice did I have? He sucked in a breath and tried to fight the reverse flow.

His dark energy burned in my veins. I could feel the fire move from where my hands connected with his body, up my arms to settle in my heart. I swear I felt it slow to a stop and then change rhythm as it sped back up. I began to wonder if it could take the strain. In response to my thought or the drain, I began to sweat profusely as an uncomfortable heat flashed through my body. I could feel Kraeghton growing weaker. I began to see snippets of his life. *A butterfly cut up with scissions and a little girl's tears. Pushing a small girl down who skinned her knee, the blood making him smile. The day he discovered he could manipulate people. The day his mentor found him. Draining his first watcher. The day he decided he wanted to be in charge of his own destiny and took the life of his mentor. I watched the light slowly leave her eyes as he simultaneously squeezed off her air supply and drained what she had to give. He fooled people into believing he was her son and took everything she had. He started over and moved on - killing watchers and stealing their lives.* My stomach heaved, my throat grew tight and tears slipped silently from my eyes. They would never turn me to darkness. I felt their victims' pain and the pain of the friends and family they left behind.

I watched with detached horror as Kraeghton killed Miles' wife. *He looked up to see Miles but he was too far away to stop it.* I felt Kraeghton smile and tears slid down my cheeks. *I could feel Melissa's warm neck and the last few feeble beats of her heart as if it were my hands that were squeezing off her air.* He knew Miles had been hunting him and he thought that killing her would put an end to the chase. He thought he had caught her at home alone. He did not know that Miles would hound him until one of them was dead.

He wanted to leave Miles broken. When what we love is taken away, we are weakened. It would ruin Miles and ruining Miles would in turn ruin…White Eagle. In a former life he had approached White Eagle to be his mentor and White Eagle refused, sensing the darkness within him. Killing Miles was a way to get back at White Eagle. My mind reeled.

I saw Kraeghton's eyes widen but I couldn't seem to stop. *I could see a beautiful young woman with fiery red hair. The way she moved captivated… me…him. I knew I loved her at first sight but I didn't believe in that nonsense.* Several more images of her flitted past as I slipped in and out of Kraeghton's perspective. He loved her more than anything, but she saw him for what he really was. *Rage flashed through me. I could not control her. If I could not control her, then I would chase her relentlessly, break her and force her to stay. How dare she run from me. She belongs to me. She turned as she fled, tripping, her hand reaching for her abdomen.* He knew why she ran; it was his child that rounded her belly despite her thin form. He had fooled her too, at first. He was good at that when there was something he wanted. *When she tripped she turned to look back at me. The look on her face said that she knew I wouldn't stop, give up or back down. She sprinted onto the bridge, put her back to the railing and watched me approach. Before I could reach her, she climbed the support, teetered and then stepped off the edge to fall to the water below. There wasn't a sound, not even a scream, but maybe there was a faint splash. I rushed to the edge but there was not even a ripple.* He never saw her again… White Eagle had warned her… He would pay. In time he would pay the ultimate price. When the right one came along…

Kraeghton gasped and the scene changed. He was fighting back but still he seemed unable to stop the drain of dark energy or the images that assaulted me. *I saw Mica standing across an opening in a deserted building... Kraeghton had gotten the drop on her twin. He held her in front of him within Mica's clear view. A gun shook uncontrollably in her hand. "Go ahead. Kill your sister," he hissed at her. Mica shivered and brought her other hand up in an attempt to steady the weapon. Kraeghton finished his drain and snapped the neck of the young lady he held, dropping her body into the opening before him. "You missed your chance," he snarled as he leapt across the impossibly wide opening, hitting Mica so hard she flew through the air, the gun leaving her hand. She skidded to a stop when her head struck the wall...*

My head hit the wall. Something shifted. The images blurred and coalesced and the lighting had gone foggy and dark. The drain continued and now I could only clearly define the sounds coming at me except that they didn't fit with the images I was getting.

"I will not give you what you want," a vaguely familiar voice said softly.

"Then I shall take it," Kraeghton said.

"You cannot take what isn't freely given. I'm not a *watcher* for you to drain and steal secrets from." A mysterious form swirled away into the darkness before I could get a good look and then everything became black.

Kraeghton was weakening and out of it, but not unconscious - yet the images had stopped. I sensed someone else had entered the mix and the balance shifted again. Suddenly Kraeghton seemed to be replenished. He gave his head a shake and went for my throat. I wrapped my legs around him and squeezed while I threw a series of punches into his side. He went slack for a moment so I tried to crawl away but he must have regained consciousness quickly because he grabbed my ankle. I kicked him hard, gaining some ground for myself and a moan out of him. I stumbled to my feet and turned.

Blood and sweat ran down my face and into my eyes. My vision was crazy weird. Things moved within the room that shouldn't and the shadows danced across the dirty floor and cobwebby walls. Images wavered and Kraeghton transformed into a huge black-cloaked figure with red eyes. Or was it blood running into my own? He rose up before me, smooth and fluid as if pulled from above. I swung at him but hit nothing and he laughed when my miss caused me to overbalance and stumble.

I shook my head to clear it but it only made things worse. He roared and pulled something from his pocket. Not again. I spun and kicked. Whatever it was flew out of his hand and landed with a shattering crash. Sparks and smoke burst forth as his eyes went wide. I kicked again right at the center of the three chins he seemed to have developed. I felt my foot connect and he windmilled backwards for a moment but righted himself quickly.

Violence filled his voice. "What have you done? You have broken my talisman and ruined everything. She can find me now. I am no longer protected and neither are you. You may have become one of us now but I don't count you as an ally. Welcome to the dark side, foolish boy."

"I am not one of you," I rasped back.

"I have twisted you. You hold my dark energy. You have become a *dark watcher*."

"Power is power and energy is energy. It's what you do with it that matters."

"Is that so? Then I want it back. Give it to me." His frightening form wavered and flew at me. He took me again by the throat. I twisted and slammed my elbow down on his forearms breaking his grip. Before he could recover I put an elbow to his temple, recovered and elbowed his jaw. His head snapped to the side, a scowl marring his features for a moment before he crumpled to the side.

While he was down I kicked him several times. He tried to belly crawl toward whatever I had kicked out of his hand but I stomped on his fingers. "You don't know what you've done," he whispered again, cradling his smashed fingers.

"I don't care about what you think I've done. I must put an end to you and Evilia for the safety of my family."

"You don't understand."

"What is there to understand? You're trying to kill me again. When it isn't me it's someone I love. This has to end."

"There are shades of darkness and light. You are her pawn. Everyone is. Kill me and your transformation will be complete. It's what she wants. She almost owns you now; you just haven't realized it yet. There is no escape this time. Evilia is practically immortal. Not even The Gypsy has been able to beat her and I have run out of time, so now my only option is to trade you for me."

A shaft of pain shot through my skull. "What did you drug me with?" I gasped, grabbing my head as I fell to my knees.

"A little something to make you… smile."

"Smile? Smiles? You hit me with the street drug Smiles?" I screamed and lunged at him. Somehow he was standing again.

He sidestepped me and laughed. "I tried to make things different between us but you wouldn't accept. My alternative was to do what she asked but I have done that for the last time. Now I shall be free. I win either way. She told you, you wouldn't know what was real and what wasn't anymore. The drug will unlock the door to your mind."

"This is real," I snapped.

"Is it?" he asked.

My visions blurred as the drugs that had entered my system continued to take effect.

"What is real and what is fantasy? Who am I and who are you?"

"I know who I am!" I shouted.

"Do you?" The voice remained the same but the image warped and shifted. I was looking at *her* - the person I most hated and feared in this world. "Owen, my love. How can you hurt me like this?" Evilia simpered at me.

I snarled and lunged at her. Just as my hands closed around her neck she became Lucie. I landed hard to keep my weight off her as we fell to the ground. Pain shot through my elbow bringing me some relief from my delusions but not enough.

"I want you," Lucie's lips said but it wasn't her voice. It was Evilia's. I closed my eyes. They were failing me. I had to count on another sense. It felt like my hands were wrapped around a chunk of ice cold gelatin. "I should have known that this version wouldn't move you like this one can." I blinked and I was squeezing Tess' neck. "You know what they say about suffocation." I rolled and wrapped a leg around her as we twisted on the floor. I meant to flip her away from me but my body wasn't behaving. She ended up on top. "Ah, I see how it is… this is better. Are you submissive?" Tess smiled seductively at me but I knew it wasn't Tess. A whiff of citrus brushed over me, clearing my head for a moment.

"No, Lucie," I croaked. She had to get away from me before Evilia got her too. *Get out of my head - save yourself!*

Evilia misunderstood my intent and thought I was speaking to her. The image wavered and Tess was once again Lucie. "I knew you loved me. Show me, Owen." She leaned in and licked along the side of my face like Evilia had and Lucie would never do. Lucie was light and Evilia was blackness.

I hit her shoulder hard as I shouted, "No!" She fell to the side with the blow but instead of hitting the ground she swooped upward like a bat and then lightly landed on her feet. I crawled unsteadily to mine.

"You disappoint," she snarled as she flew at me, hitting me so hard that I was swept into the air like I was nothing. I landed hard enough to make my teeth rattle and the air rush from my lungs. My vision stretched and shrunk like it was rubberized as I gasped for breath. Time was doing weird things. She was far away one moment and on top of me the next. I held up my arms to ward off the blow but a deceptively light touch brushed over me instead. The room went black and I was held immobile.

Voices and strange sounds were everywhere all tumbled together and twisted up making them hard to distinguish in the blackness, but Evilia's voice rang above the rest, almost as if it was coming from my own head. "*It's not working – you'll get your payment in full – No – you shall not disappoint me again. Did you really think you could beat me? I know who you are. I know your tricks. You thought you'd have the boy kill me? You turned the boy over to the Gypsy. I know you're in league with him – You would have had them team up but it didn't work – In some ways Owen is smarter than you - You are so naive – I know what you've been doing – No one gets the drop on me – no one! I don't like your answers, Kraeghton. You are dead to me.*"

"*NO!*"

A blast of pure energy burst through me, deafening my ears and turning my eyelids bright red, followed by pain so intense I was sure my nerves were on fire. My muscles cramped and then sweet relief washed over me. The sounds faded and I blinked several times. The room had gone still and at first I thought empty. Light returned but time still moved at a rate that defied physics. Dust danced and swirled slowly in a shaft of sunlight that had finally broken through the clouds of the overcast sky. I slowly rolled onto my side. A lump lay not far from me. I took stock of myself and my surroundings. I had the expected aches and pains. My sinuses, throat and eyes burned. Other than the dust motes, nothing moved. I pulled myself to my hands and knees and cautiously approached the lump.

Kraeghton lay in a crumpled heap but he'd tricked me before. I could not see the rise and fall of his chest. His dark energy and the faint taint of Evilia still surged and burned within me, so it was difficult to tell what was coming from me and what was coming from them. What was within and what was around me? Was this real? Fear gripped me tightly, making my heart flutter raggedly like a wild bird trapped in a cage.

I crept closer. He remained silent and still. I rolled him onto his back, ready to jump away if he so much as blinked but he just stared open-eyed at the ceiling. I stared at him, waiting. I didn't look away even when my own eyes began to water. Finally I moved in to feel for a pulse. Shouldn't he dissolve into ash or go up in green flames or… something? Could you really have that much evil within you and then just leave your human remains behind? I could hardly believe there had been this much human left in Stephan Kraeghton.

Maybe a better question was… if this was real… what had happened? And did I kill him? I scuttled backwards until I bumped into a crate and then I sat watching. I felt cold and sweaty. My heart raced and I could feel its pounding in my head. My whole head burned and ached. I put my hands to my head and closed my eyes to hold the throbbing in.

The room went dark behind my closed lids. I jerked them back open to see if the sun had gone behind a cloud or if this was another delusion. I began to shake. I didn't know if it was the drugs or nerves. I wasn't even sure what the drugs would do to me. I'd heard of them in passing at school but I was no expert.

The outer door creaked open. I was not in control of myself or the situation. I rolled behind my crate and squinted at the overly bright light. A silhouette filled the door and I shrank back. I tried to feel the presence but I still held Kraeghton's dark energy. My shaking intensified and the crate rattled. A soft step sounded nearby and I threw up an arm. The figure evaded me and cool hands touched my sweaty overheated face.

"Owen, are you okay? Can you hear me?"

"Luce?"

"What happened?"

"I… I don't know… Kraeghton…"

"He's dead."

"Did I? Where's Evilia?"

"She's not here, Owen. I can't feel her. It's just you and what's left of him."

"He drugged me and I…"

"Help is coming. Hold on…"

She had a device in her hand. Before she could use it, I grabbed her arm. "Luce, was she here or in my head? I've been working on blocking her… but… Alex and I have tried… Luce, my head hurts and I'm so confused. I bought you something earlier. Help me remember… remember to pick it up," I ended on a whimper as the worst migraine of my life consumed me.

"What? You're not making any sense."

"Just help me remember," I mumbled as I closed my eyes and started to drift.

"Owen, stay with me!" Lucie said, shaking my shoulder.

"Ahhgh. Don't do that. It hurts. Where would I go anyway? There's no one like you," I rambled.

"White Eagle will be here in less than five minutes and Saul is coming."

"I don't need them. Just you. Is it you?"

"What?" Her voice sounded worried, confused and frustrated.

"Pinch me."

"I will not!"

"It is you. Only the real Lucie would say that. I reached up and took a handful of her shirt.

"What are you doing?" she gasped in surprise.

I had already seen what I was looking for – the pearly white fingerprints over her heart. I didn't answer her; instead I kept ahold of her shirt and used it to pull her towards me. I needed to kiss her. When her lips touched mine the pain in my head eased and tears began to burn behind my eyes. Anguish enveloped me and a sob wracked my body. I visualized my soul flash from white to black and shoved Lucie away. "Don't touch me… I'm dark… poisoned. I'll hurt you."

"You won't. I'm going to help you," she said softly as she wrapped her arms around me. I fought her for a moment and then collapsed against her, shaking like a tiny, fragile newborn kitten. I was the cause of another death – I could not hide it or push it away. I could not displace the blame. I would have to live with this forever – knowing what I had done.

When I was calmer she spoke, "You didn't have a choice."

"There is always a choice. Kraeghton was right. I'm moving toward darkness. I may have been tricked into it but I've done it nevertheless," I raged in a cracked voice.

"Owen, No! You are who you are. This does not change who you are in here!" Lucie said firmly as she thumped my chest over my heart with her fingers.

All the anger. All the resentment. It rolled together in my gut, churning like a volcano. I reached for Lucie and pulled her toward me. My arms surrounded her – the only good in my life today. I crushed her body to my chest and kissed my way down the side of her face finally reaching her lips. It wasn't enough. Not nearly enough. I could not taste or touch her enough. Many times she had wished she could crawl inside of my skin – today it was my turn. She was my anchor. My sanity. My soul. I wanted to live within the warmth of her smile and nowhere else. She was like summer lightening, the heat of it travelled over my skin as my hands travelled over her.

She pulled back and sucked in some air. "Owen, stop."

It took a moment for my brain to catch up. "What?"

"Not here. Not now. This isn't right. I don't know what's going on in your head but this won't fix it."

"I... I'm sorry. I don't know what I was thinking. I didn't... hurt you did I?"

"There are things I want to do with you but not right now. You're hurting, angry and not... you. You'll hate yourself later. I know you will, so take a breath. White Eagle will be here soon anyway."

Lucie held me like I was a small confused child. I jerked when I heard the door open again. I tried to shove her behind me but she pushed me back. "It's okay, Owen. Help is here."

"What's wrong with him?" Was that White Eagle's voice? I focused on Lucie's hand holding mine. Remember the shirt. Remember the shirt – became a litany in my confused mind. Everything else was random but that thought stuck. That and Kraeghton. Did I kill him? Did Evilia? Did he do it to himself or was he even really gone?

"Several things are wrong at the moment," Lucie stated, sounding concerned. When will Saul be here?"

"Maybe five minutes or so. We should get out of here as fast as we can. Do you think he's mobile? Did you try to heal him?"

"Stop. Don't touch him yet. He's infused with Kraeghton's dark energy. I already tried. We've got to let that burn out first before we can do any good and I think he's been drugged."

"What about you?"

"I've got this, White Eagle. Trust me."

"Don't touch... not safe... don't forget... the shirt," I mumbled and passed out, unable to hold on any longer.

A fingernail clicking against glass brought me around. I cracked an eye and focused on Saul who had a dark red fluid in a vial. He tilted the vial back and forth several times and watched it change color. "Looks like Kraeghton doped him good. I can't tell you for sure what all's in there yet. I need better equipment than my field kit."

"Will he be okay?" White Eagle asked, sounding worried.

"Nothing we can't handle," Saul replied with confidence.

"What about Kraeghton? What happened? There's plenty of dark energy speaking to me here but it's all jumbled and weird. It feels like Evilia was here but she wasn't. I'm confused and Owen can't help me," Lucie commented.

"I haven't taken a good look at him. I was focused on our boy here. White Eagle, what do you think?" Saul asked.

"Owen was my priority too. I could tell that Kraeghton was gone, so I didn't really look." I knew he was sensing the room with his gift. "I see what you mean, Lucie. Kraeghton's gift is in Owen. How did that happen?" White Eagle got up and cautiously approached the body. He flipped out his cell. "Where's our cleaning crew? Be sure they preserve the evidence… If I knew anything I'd tell you!"

"Ouch!" I yelped. They were the first words out of my mouth in who knew how long. Saul had stuck a needle in my arm and was starting an IV drip that he had Lucie hold. "Damn it, why didn't you warn me," I grumbled groggily.

White Eagle still had his cell to his ear but his eyes were on me. He was now kneeling by Kraeghton and his eyes turned back in that direction. "Yeah, he'll be okay… eventually." White Eagle used a pen he pulled from his pocket to move Kraeghton's shirt aside to look at his chest over his heart. "There isn't a mark on him that I can see," he said into his phone.

"Lucie, keep holding the bag, just like that and I'll go help White Eagle." She nodded and looked at me with a soft smile on her lips. Periodically tremors shook my frame but I fought to hold onto both reality and consciousness. Looking into Lucie's eyes helped. When I felt stronger I looked around.

White Eagle and Saul carefully looked over Kraeghton and murmured to each other. Lucie whispered to me, "It's going to be okay. Just hang on."

"Well?" I asked when they returned to us.

"It may have been an aneurism. I can't tell without an autopsy," Saul answered.

"Is it my fault? Did I drain him?" I asked, looking at my hands.

"We don't know," White Eagle answered gently. "Everything is confusing and warped. As soon as it's safe, maybe Lucie and I can get in your head and sort it out."

"Kraeghton drugged him to let Evilia in. I don't think we can wait. We need to go in now while we're still here," Lucie said with conviction.

"We should wait until we're safely back with Alex," White Eagle insisted.

"There isn't time. You're right that we've got to get out of here but I will get information from here. I don't have a choice! Alex would be helpful but I can do this."

"Luce, no!" White Eagle and I spoke as one.

"Trust me. Please. After what he did to my mom, Kraeghton freaks me out beyond all reason, but my need to help you is stronger than my fear of him. I have to do this here so that the location can speak to me, too. It will be my way of telling what the truth is. I'm strong enough. I can do this."

I gave her a pained look, but didn't resist as she entered my mind. I could feel White Eagle in the background helping her but letting her lead the way. I watched everything happen all over again but slightly different as two more perspectives blended with mine. I could see Lucie standing in front of Kraeghton, her ghostly image shouting, "I'm not afraid of you". She began to wrestle with him much as I had. White Eagle and I flickered in and out but Lucie stayed consistent.

I lost track of everything but Lucie. I focused on her. My body felt both hot and cold, my skin prickled and my mind raced. Breathe - relax - picture a glass to hold your problems - pour it out like water - breathe. From head to toe, I focused on relaxing my muscles but still the fiery burn persisted over my skin. Maybe it was Kraeghton's dark energy eating away at my goodness like acid. I could feel it crawling over my upper back and shoulders and then seeping down my arms and legs. I realized I was clenching my jaw… You can't fix it now. Tomorrow. We'll fix it tomorrow, I argued with myself. Think about something else… Time whirled and I was once again clutching Kraeghton's neck. He morphed into Evilia, Tess and Lucie. Pain ricocheted through my body, sound screamed in my ears, starbursts of color exploded before my eyes and then there was nothing.

I drifted. My eyes popped open to darkness and I automatically looked to my alarm clock. Wait… what? I was in Lucie's room. Was it all a dream? I began to shake again and then there were hands on me – holding me. "It's okay," Lucie breathed. "I've got you. It's going to be okay."

"Something did happen. It wasn't a dream or am I still dreaming?"

"It wasn't a dream, Owen. You still have drugs in you and… Owen, we couldn't pull all the darkness out without hurting you. We don't know what all Evilia did to you but…"

"I can see it," I whispered, terrified. "She still has a hold on me."

"I can't break it this time. I'm… I'm sorry. I'm doing my best but Kraeghton is still in you and she still has a hold on you both."

I began to cry and I didn't even care that Lucie was there to see it. I floated in and out of sleep as the numbers on the clock clawed their way toward the dawn. Every time I fell asleep I awoke from nightmares but Lucie was always there. I didn't know if they were real, my imagination or Kraeghton's memories. With the latest one, I cracked a scratchy, burning eye and looked at the hated alarm clock one last time. It would go off soon anyway. I eased out of bed so that I wouldn't wake Lucie and made my way to the bathroom. I looked at myself in the mirror and wondered when I had grown so old. Maybe I'd leave the stubble today. It went well with the bruising, stitches and bloodshot eyes. It made me look rough and mean. I guess I was feeling pretty mean this morning. Mean enough to… what? I still felt nauseous when I thought about killing Kraeghton. Up until now I'd only rendered folks unconscious. Could I kill *her*? Was I motivated enough? I thought maybe I could, but what did it say about me if I did… so what if she was the greatest evil ever known.

I trudged back to Lucie's room as quietly as I could and hoped I had some clean clothes to put on - which raised the question, what had happened to the ones I was wearing and more importantly, where was my bike?

"Come back to bed," Lucie called softly.

"The alarm's about to go off," I sighed, feeling weary.

"No it isn't. It's Sunday."

"It is?"

"Owen, come here. Let me help you."

"Do you know where my bike is? And my clothes… and how did I get here? Did you go to the shop for the shirt and the books?"

"Come here, please." I took a breath and then walked over to sit on the edge of the bed.

Lucie put her hands on me and I immediately felt peace wash over me. She began the massage she was so good at as she spoke, "Your packages are on the kitchen table and your bike is in the garage. White Eagle rode it home. Saul did all he could for you. Alex and your mom helped me carry you in here. We cleaned you up and put you to bed. When White Eagle arrived, Alex helped us work on you some more. What you said last night was true. She still has a hold on you but we're working on it. It's going to be okay. Trust me."

"How did I stay out that long and how could I miss… everything?"

"White Eagle put you out when… when you started screaming," Lucie paused and then her look turned mischievous. "Don't worry. I've seen your boxer briefs before."

"And now my mom and brother know it too. Awesome. I'm surprised they let you stay."

"They didn't have a choice. You were worse than that time in Florida and once you pulled me back from the edge so I'm going to help you now."

"You… you didn't overdo it like in Florida?"

"I've learned a lot since then. I have a good teacher."

"I don't feel so good now. I can't even lead by example."

"You are wonderful." Lucie slid her knees past my hips to hug me from behind. "And you're going to be okay. It's just going to take some time."

"What happened to me?" I asked to distract myself from her warm body pressing into mine.

"We're still not sure if she was there or just in your mind. It's a jumbled mess and we may never know. One thing is for sure – she still wants you. It's like you've become a strange obsession."

"Oh geez. It's *her* that's manipulating me, isn't it. When I feel anger, fear or sadness, it's her? She's good at that and if I feel guilty I might act differently and do something stupid or worse, she might convince me to come find her because I'm ready to embrace the darkness."

"We will fight her off together. She wants you… but then so do I."

"Now I understand why you told me to run after your mother's funeral."

"I was wrong and you're wrong if you think I'm going anywhere."

I turned suddenly to face Lucie. I took ahold of the back of her neck and kissed her. Then I touched my forehead to hers and brought her hand to my heart. "Help me. I don't want to be a *dark watcher*."

"I won't let that happen."